Learning to Dance Again

FRANKIE VALENTE

Copyright © 2013 Frankie Valente

All rights reserved.

ISBN-13: 978-1493542314
ISBN-10: 1493542311

For Becky Sherry
and my sisters
Christine, Stephanie and Helen

ACKNOWLEDGMENTS

As time goes by I become increasingly grateful for the support from friends, family and random strangers who have told me how much they enjoy my work. If I had not received so much encouragement from people I would have taken up another hobby by now. I love writing; I love entertaining people; and I hope I continue to do this in future. Thank you to everyone who has taken the trouble to email me, send messages via twitter and Facebook, or stopped me in the street to say how much they enjoyed one of my novels. I really appreciate it.

Particular thanks go to Melanie Hudson, (author of the Wedding Cake Tree) for hours of long distance phone calls as we discussed plots and heroes and who we would pick as our leading man if our books ever made it into films. It is good to have someone else to talk to who is as mad as me.

This book would still be in draft on my laptop if it had not been for the online whip-cracking from Becky Sherry. She is an amazing woman and although we have never met, I am delighted to call her a friend – and even more delighted that she managed to kick cancer in the butt!

This novel was written during a period of upheaval and sadness in my own life, and it is thanks to my friends – Jenny, Kim, Melanie, Ruby, Diane, Anne-Lise and many others, who rallied with their support and kept a smile on my face.

Thank you!

1

Julia Robertson sat up in bed and watched her husband of twenty eight years get dressed. In all the ups and downs of their very ordinary marriage, today was most definitely an up. It was a day they had hardly dared to dream of just a few months ago, and the pleasure she took in seeing her husband getting ready for work was enough to make her overlook the fact that he had abandoned his wet towel on the floor in his usual absent minded way.

Duncan was just doing up his tie when the phone rang. Julia reached over to the bedside table and answered it.

'Hello,' she said, instinctively turning to look at the clock. 'Oh hi darling, how are you?'

Julia grinned at Duncan and handed him the phone.

'It's Jamie.'

Julia got up and left Duncan to talk to their eldest son. She decided to take a quick shower. When she entered the bathroom she laughed at the chaos Duncan had left behind. Another wet towel was strewn across the floor, as was the cap from the toothpaste and two cotton buds. The toilet seat was up and the sink still contained shaving foam and fragments of hair.

'Oh for heaven's sake,' Julia muttered to herself, as she picked up the debris and cleaned the sink.

When she had finished in the bathroom she got dressed quickly, putting on a pair of dark blue jeans and a white linen shirt. She glanced in the mirror and ran her fingers through her blonde hair, trying to minimise the dark roots and grey strands that were becoming far too noticeable around her temples. Somebody had once told her she looked like a young Lulu. Frowning at her reflection today, she didn't think Lulu would be flattered by the comparison. She opened the wardrobe and pulled out a floral silk scarf and draped it around her neck, with the long ends of the scarf disguising her rather less than toned abdomen.

In the kitchen she found Duncan dropping bread into the toaster, having somehow managed to leave a trail of crumbs all over the worktop.

'You sit down; I'll make your breakfast.'

'You mean, stop making a mess.'

'I never said that,' she replied brightly.

'It was implied.'

Nevertheless he took a seat at the kitchen table and sipped at his coffee for a moment then put it down, wrinkling his nose and staring into the mug as if he was surprised at the taste. Julia was busy buttering toast and didn't notice his discomfort. She carried the toast and a jar of homemade marmalade over to the table and set it in front of him.

'Thanks love,' he said quietly. He didn't make a move to start his breakfast and Julia finally tuned in to his anxiety.

'Don't worry; it will be great. I bet everyone's missed you.'

'Humph! Not many kids miss their maths teacher, I can assure you.'

'But I bet you've missed them.'

Duncan looked up and grinned, his sea green eyes crinkling with delight.

'I suppose I have. After moaning about work for years on end, I can't believe I've missed the little devils so much.'

He picked up a slice of toast without bothering to put any marmalade on it, and took a bite. He chewed slowly for a moment then pulled a face.

'I feel a bit queasy. I never thought I'd be so nervous about going back to school.'

He disappeared upstairs to brush his teeth so Julia helped herself to the uneaten toast from his plate, as it was clearly going to waste. She wandered over to the kitchen window and looked out, trying to judge what the weather had in store for the day. For the time being at least it was a day of fine sunshine, and the sea was sparkling joyfully in the distance. She decided she would go for a walk once Duncan had left for work.

'Nice of Jamie to call,' Duncan said, as he wandered back to the kitchen, 'poor lad's been up all night at the hospital. He's only got eight hours to get some sleep before he has to be back on the ward.'

'It'll be worth it. And he's young; he'll cope.'

'I know; but sometimes I wish we weren't so far away from them.'

'Well that's the downside of Shetland; when the bairns go off to University, sometimes they stay away. But we came back didn't we? And I bet you anything they'll both move back here once they have families of their own; if only for the free babysitting.'

'Promise? Anyway, what have you got planned today?'

'You mean apart from cooking, cleaning, washing, ironing? I thought I might do something to escape all the domestic drudgery and apply for that job.'

Duncan sighed, not wanting to rehash an earlier discussion about Julia's wish to go back to work now he was finally in remission.

'Well it's up to you, but I'm only going to be at work for twelve weeks before the summer holidays start. It would be nice to have a really long holiday together this year; and you're probably more in need of it than me.'

Duncan opened the fridge and took out the packed lunch Julia had made for him the night before. As he put it in his briefcase he looked at her and smiled.

'I've been thinking about that programme we watched about Sicily last night. We should go there this summer; just you and me. If there's one thing cancer has taught me, you should make every moment count, and I think a second honeymoon is long overdue.'

'We'll see; although I can't imagine Jamie and Bryden wanting to tag along with us this year. Anyway, you'd better get going; you don't want to be late for your first day.'

Duncan glanced at his watch and frowned. Julia hugged him, almost pushing him over in her rush of affection.

'Hey steady!'

'Sorry! Have a great day; and let me know how you're getting on.'

Duncan kissed her quickly, but held her for a moment longer, then turned to go. Julia followed him out to the front door, feeling a peculiar groundswell of emotion, akin to when she had sent her sons off to their first day of primary school. As Duncan walked over to his car it seemed as if the years had melted away. He was now as skinny as he had been when they first started dating, when he was nineteen and she was eighteen. His hair was much shorter now, and almost completely grey, and as she watched him ease into the driving seat, she realised he was rather less agile than he used to be. But she found it hard to believe over thirty years had passed since their first date; and they were still together. It was nothing short of a miracle.

She waited at the door a little longer until Duncan turned his car around on the drive and then she waved him off, and blew him a kiss when he waved back.

Julia went in search of her iPad which she found charging in the lounge. During the last few months, when she had given up her job to look after Duncan, she had become addicted to Facebook. Duncan teased her about her obsession with what her friends were getting up to, so now she only logged on when he wasn't around. She knew it was ridiculous. Her friends were people she saw all the time and she could pick up the phone and speak to any one of them whenever she wanted. But sometimes, during the darkest moments of Duncan's illness, when they couldn't be sure of the outcome, Facebook had been a source of distraction, amusement and comfort.

She updated her status: *Duncan's first day back at school. There were times when we never thought this day would happen. We're so lucky! Thank you everyone for all your support. We will never forget your kindness. Definitely having a big party to celebrate in a few weeks. XXX*

She scrolled down to see if there were any snippets of news posted since she had last logged on. Unsurprisingly, since she had taken a sneaky peek just after midnight, not much had happened. However, within a few moments she saw her status had received a few "likes" and Marianne had written: *Yay – so excited for him! Did you take a picture?*

Julia replied instantly: *Bugger – should have done! I could have put it on the wall with the ones of Jamie and Bryden on their first days at school.*

She noticed Bryden had also commented: *I was going to ring Dad this morning. I'll maybe catch him on his mobile at lunch. Got to run. I'll be late for Uni. XX.*

Julia clicked "like" on Bryden's post, and then with an unusually strong burst of willpower she left Facebook to look at the local job vacancies website. She downloaded a job description and scrutinised it for the third time since Friday morning.

Damn; Duncan was right. The Deputy Manager's job at Nordheim would be a step back in her career and when she stopped to think about it, she wasn't even sure she wanted to work in a care home again, at any level. The job she had most enjoyed had been working as a theatre nurse at Aberdeen Royal Infirmary. But she didn't really want to go back to nursing either. The trouble was she didn't know what she wanted to do. This was the year she would turn fifty, and it felt like a huge turning point. However, she felt she had missed the boat in terms of changing career. Fifty felt too old to start again; and really, what else could she do?

She switched off the iPad and flung it down on the sofa beside her. She was definitely not going to apply for the job. She would do as Duncan suggested and take the rest of the summer off and then make a decision. In the meantime, she had promised herself a walk on the beach.

Julia set off across the field heading to the tiny stretch of sandy beach that began where their half-acre of garden ended. She climbed over the wooden stile and marched along the well-worn path that humans and sheep used to access the shore. She stopped when she got to their bench; the bench Duncan and Jamie had carried across the field and cemented into the ground, so they would have somewhere to sit and enjoy the view.

Naturally, other people used the bench too, and occasionally they would leave their mark, quite literally, in the form of carved initials or juvenile graffiti. Julia never minded much, although

Duncan used to grumble about it; until Julia suggested they carved their own initials into the bench.

Their initials were still visible and she touched them for luck as she sat down. DR loves JR. Julia smiled, and then turned her attention to the sea. A fishing boat was steaming along between the mainland and a tiny island that looked close enough to swim across to; although the year-round sea temperature had so far acted as a deterrent to Jamie and Bryden, who often tried to egg each other into doing so.

Julia sat for nearly an hour on the bench. Every time she thought about going back to the house to do something more useful, she reminded herself she should take advantage of the good weather while it was here. The balmy sunshine might not last the hour, let alone the whole day.

She was proved right, when a sea mist started to roll in from the south. First the island disappeared, and then the sea. She turned to look at her house and that had vanished too. The temperature plummeted without the sunshine, and she reluctantly gave up her place on the bench and hurried back home.

She spent the next half hour pottering about, doing a bit of cleaning, not that it had been very dirty in the first place. Both their sons were away in Edinburgh, with Jamie studying medicine and Bryden in the last few weeks of teacher training. The house was much easier to keep clean and tidy, even with Duncan doing his best to make up for their absence.

Before he was ill, when they had both been working full-time, they had shared the domestic tasks pretty equally. But lately, it seemed it was now her sole responsibility. Not that she minded - yet. Duncan still tired quickly, and his doctor had told him to take it easy for a little while longer. Duncan had taken this as permission to be a lazy bastard, as he would often joke.

While Julia swept the kitchen floor, she turned her attention to thoughts of her job situation, dithering again as to whether or not she should apply for the job. She concluded it didn't matter whether she was the manager or just the deputy; she had finally had her fill of caring, although she knew it would be hard to voice that aloud. She wouldn't want Duncan to feel guilty about his illness; he felt bad enough she had given up her job to spend time looking after him. It had been unspoken, but there had been an understanding this might be the final time they would spend together, so she had done it willingly.

But that was then. Duncan was in remission and it was time to start enjoying life again. But how? What would she do with her time now? Money wasn't exactly a problem; they owned their house outright, and the only significant drain on their money was supporting their sons at University, and since Bryden was in his final year their outgoings would reduce soon. Julia wondered whether she should make an appointment with a careers advisor, but at her age she felt too embarrassed.

The sun reappeared and she went out into the garden. She often fancied she would like to work outside; but that was only on days like today when the sun was warm on her face. She bent down and pulled up a patch of weeds from the flowerbed and then stretched out on the grass which had dried up from the morning dew. It was peaceful in the garden. The only sound was the incessant warble of a skylark, and the distant hum of an outboard engine on a passing boat. On fine days like this Julia loved Shetland, and couldn't imagine living anywhere else in the world.

A few minutes later she scrambled to her feet. The sun had slipped behind ominously dark clouds that in true Shetland style had materialised from nowhere, signally the imminent arrival of rain.

She hurried indoors and made herself a sandwich for lunch, which she ate standing up watching the rain trickling down the kitchen window, silently cursing the fickle weather. She decided to go and visit Duncan's mother after lunch, knowing she would get a few minutes to catch up with Marianne at the same time.

2

When Duncan arrived at the school he sat in his car for a moment, gearing himself up to go inside. What he most wanted was to breeze through reception, pick up a coffee in the cafeteria then sit down with a newspaper for five minutes in the staff room. That had always been his routine before he had taken time off to do battle with bowel cancer.

He sighed and picked up his battered briefcase; it was time to face the music. He prayed people would ignore him and pretend it was just an ordinary day. Duncan plodded up the concrete steps to the entrance, slightly breathless. He paused at the top, surprised by his lack of fitness. He turned and looked down at the steps as if they had mysteriously become steeper during his absence. It's just nerves, he told himself; don't be such a baby.

As he pushed open the door, his worst fears were realised. Sandra, one of the administration assistants, was crossing the lobby on her way back to the office.

'Duncan! You're back! It's so good to see you again.'

She flung her arms around him, while he stood awkwardly, watching over her shoulder as he noticed some of the cafeteria staff approaching, as excited to see him as if he'd been returning home from war.

There were hugs and kisses, and gushing comments on how great it was to see him again. There were tears from Beth, who had recently lost her mother to cancer. Duncan had got to know Sheila at the hospital as they had sat through some of their chemotherapy treatments together. He was sorry to see Sheila's daughter so upset, even though Beth said they were tears of happiness. He felt a strange sense of guilt he had survived and not Sheila.

He spotted one of his pupils, Gordon, looking markedly older and taller.

'Alright Mr Robertson!' Gordon said, and high-fived him as he passed by.

Duncan grinned; now that was the kind of welcome he could cope with.

He decided to skip his visit to the staff room and excused himself from his impromptu welcome party and made his way up to the relative privacy of his classroom.

He switched on his laptop to allow the ancient beast enough time to warm up before the first lesson, and then turned on the electronic white-board. He took out his timetable and checked, for the hundredth time, which class he had first. Fourth year advanced; one of his favourites.

When the bell sounded to signal the start of the class, a gaggle of twenty teenagers, casually dressed in the de-facto uniform of jeans and casual tops wandered into the room. Duncan was one of the few teachers that favoured the lack of formal uniform. He loved the individuality it inspired, although sometimes it seemed to produce its own peculiar sense of conformity. The boys all wore jeans and football shirts. The girls however, were a little more interesting in their appearance, although he could never voice his opinion on this without sounding like a pervert.

'Hey Mr Robertson! You're back – that's so cool!' Shona said, as she floated into the classroom in a waft of expensive perfume. She was one of the fashion icons in her year, and today she was wearing the skinniest of jeans, a pair of glittery ballet pumps and what appeared to be a mini-dress over the top. It was a strange combination in Duncan's opinion, but Shona seemed to carry it off, and as he watched the other girls take their seats he noticed that wearing dresses over the top of jeans had somehow become the norm.

'Can we celebrate you being back at school with a homework-free week?' Shona said, giggling as she took her seat at the back of the class.

'No chance! In fact, I might even set you a bit of a test later this week; just so I can catch up with how you're all doing. Don't forget you have your exams soon.'

There was a collective groan, amid the clattering of books and bags being dumped on desks, and pencil cases being unzipped.

He gave them a moment to settle down.

'OK guys. As you can see, I'm back. Thanks for all your cards and good wishes while I was away. I really appreciated it. And there's no doubt all the support I received helped me to knock the cancer on the head.'

There was a spontaneous round of applause, and when two girls stood up in the front row, the rest of the class quickly followed.

'Well,' Duncan said, as the applause died away and everyone sat down again, 'that's the first time I've ever had a standing ovation in a maths class. In fact that's probably the first time in history any maths teacher has had a standing ovation. Thanks!'

He felt touched by their welcome, and took a deep breath before speaking again, noticing a slight discomfort in his chest as he did so. He ignored it and continued to speak.

'OK then, shall we talk about what you've all being doing in my absence – and let's just keep this to what you've learned in maths, I don't need all the gossip thanks!'

Within fifteen minutes he felt like he'd never been away.

When it was time for lunch Duncan opened the door to the staffroom and discovered to his surprise it was almost empty, and the only person in the room was someone he didn't know.

He said hello and walked over to the kitchen area and made himself a coffee and opened up his lunchbox. Inside was a healthy salad, some fruit and a yoghurt. He missed the good old days of sandwiches, crisps and a bar of chocolate. He frowned as he picked at the chicken salad. He was hungry, but the food seemed unappetising, although he wasn't really sure what he fancied.

He drank the coffee whilst flicking through a newspaper he found abandoned on a table. He ate half his banana but threw the rest away. He had a fierce craving for chocolate so he wandered off to the cafeteria, safe in the knowledge Julia wouldn't get to hear about it; she had become such a nag about his diet.

'Hey Duncan; how's it going?'

He turned to see Helen and Maria, fellow teachers, walking through the cafeteria carrying trays.

'Great! First day back and already it seems as if I've never been away.'

'Well nothing much has changed here. You haven't missed anything at all,' Maria said, as she put her tray down and gave him a quick hug. 'It's great to see you back. How's Julia? We must have you both over for a drink sometime.'

'That would be nice. I think Julia's glad to have me off her hands again. I don't make a good patient; far too grumpy.'

'Jesus, I'd have been a grumpy bitch if I had to have chemo and all that shit. It's barbaric what they do to cure you isn't it?'

'Yeah, but it works.'

'True; thank God!'

Duncan excused himself and went off in search of chocolate, but by the time he had bought a bag of chocolate buttons he had gone off the idea. He was feeling weary. He looked at his watch; he wouldn't be home for another three hours and he couldn't wait to have a lie down.

The bell rang for the start of the afternoon session. A group of gangly sixth-form pupils shuffled in to the classroom; all chatting loudly to each other and scarcely seeming to notice Duncan. As he waited for them to sit down, he felt a wave of nausea wash over him, and he regretted not eating properly. He opened his desk drawer and reached for a bottle of water and took a sip, and glanced out of the window, momentarily distracted by the sight of rain. There was silence in the room as he replaced the cap on the bottle.

He realised everyone was staring at him, but he lost his train of thought for a moment and couldn't think what to say.

'Mr Robertson, are you back for good now?'

'Er, yes I am.'

'That's great; only we've had some bonkers supply teachers while you've been away.'

'Bonkers?'

'Yeah, for one week we had Miss Duffy yeah, she's the new drama teacher. She couldn't even spell trigonometry, let alone teach it.'

'Sorry about that. Let's see what catching up we have to do for your Highers then?' And with that they got down to the business of the maths lesson.

The class had their heads down working on an example exam question. It was quiet in the room. Duncan glanced up at the clock; just over an hour to go until he could go home. He still felt sick and couldn't wait to shut his eyes and go to sleep. He was beginning to wonder whether it had been too soon to return to work after all.

The rain had stopped and the sun had come out again. It had quickly warmed up the classroom and now it was unbearably hot; although as Duncan looked around the room he realised none of the pupils seemed to be unduly bothered. He retrieved a tissue from his pocket to wipe away a trickle of sweat running down his face, noticing as he did, that he had pins and needles in his hands. He took a deep breath. His chest felt as if someone had sat on him, and just when it occurred to him this was something new to worry about, he was overcome with an insistent urge to vomit. Without time to run to the bathroom he reached for the wastepaper bin and threw up.

He was aware of the sudden uproar in the classroom; cries of disgust and chairs scraping across the floor, as pupils stood up in horror.

'Mr Robertson, are you alright?'

'Oh my God, that's disgusting.'

'Ewww! That stinks.'

'Shut up, you moron!'

'Mr Robertson! Mr Robertson, are you OK?'

Duncan staggered to his feet and then fell heavily to the floor. He heard a scream and then nothing. His eyes were open, but he did not see a girl from the front row rush towards him, or the boy sitting next to her run out into the corridor, yelling for help. He did not feel the girl rolling him on to his back and tugging at his tie to undo it, her hands trembling at the shock of having to put her newly acquired first-aid skills to use. He did not feel her start to do chest compressions, nor hear the sound of her urgent whispered plea to God.

3

Duncan's mother, Alice, was a resident of St Ninian's, the care home Julia used to manage. Julia had seen her mother-in-law almost every day for the last few years at work, and had continued to visit her frequently after she had resigned. Not that Alice ever noticed. She was suffering from the advanced stages of dementia and did not recognise anyone. But Julia remembered Alice as the kind-hearted energetic woman she had been years ago, and was determined to make sure her last days were comfortable.

Julia opened the front door to the care home, setting off the automated alarm as she did so. Marianne stuck her head out from her office to see who had arrived. When she saw it was Julia she grinned and came out to meet her.

'I was going to ring you this very minute. How's Duncan getting on today?'

'I haven't really heard from him apart from one quick text this morning to say it's been great so far, but he's knackered and can't wait for home time.'

'Poor love; he will find it tiring at first. Still, at least it's not long to go until the summer holidays. My lasses are already counting down the weeks.'

Julia sat in one of the armchairs in the office and glanced around quickly, noticing the many changes Marianne had made since she had taken over as manager. The office seemed more colourful, with the addition of some plants, pictures and a collection of porcelain sheep that had somehow migrated from Marianne's home to her office. Julia picked up a black sheep and smiled, before putting it back.

'How's Alice today?'

'Hmm, that's the other thing I was going to ring you about. She had a very poor night. She was crying a lot and calling out for her mother. She seems to be in a bit of discomfort, so we gave her some meds and it settled her a little; but we haven't been able to take her to the day-room for a few days now.'

'That's not good; I'll get Duncan to come along and see her tonight. I don't think it will be long now, do you?'

Marianne shook her head sadly.

'I'll go in see her. Are you busy just now?'

'No; I'll come too.'

They walked along the corridor to Alice's room. The bedroom curtains were partially drawn and Alice was curled up in her bed like a baby. The cot sides were up and one frail hand gripped the bar. She was muttering to herself.

'Hello Alice,' Julia said, 'how are you? Duncan's back at work. I think he's enjoying it so far. Isn't that super?'

Julia smiled at Marianne as she spoke. They knew Alice was oblivious to what was being said, but it had always been their policy to be cheerful and chatty with their residents, regardless of their ability to communicate. Who really knew what it was like to suffer from dementia after all?

Marianne went over to the window and opened the curtains a little to let in some light. Julia sat down on the chair next to the bed and reached out to put her hand over Alice's. It was cool to the touch, so she took Alice's hand in both of hers to warm it. Alice opened her eyes and stared vacantly at Julia. Julia smiled, wishing her mother-in-law could hear the good news about Duncan, although thankfully she had never even known her son was ill. Alice had lost her eldest son Martin in a car accident when he was fifteen, and her husband had died four years after that. She had had more than her fair share of heartbreak already.

'So, are you going to apply for that job then?' Marianne said.

'I don't think so. Duncan thinks I should wait until after the summer before looking for another job. He wants us to have a long holiday together. He's decided he wants to take me to Sicily this summer, for a second honeymoon.'

'Nice! Did you watch that programme last night?'

'That's what inspired him. He wants to see what life is like on a hot sunny island.'

'Don't we all? I'm sick of this sodding cold and rain. It's the middle of April already and we've barely seen the sun this year.'

'This morning was nice. I had a lovely walk to the beach; well not much of a walk really, more sitting around wondering what to do with my life, than actually walking.'

'I'm glad you're not applying for the job actually. I think you should have your old job back.'

'How's that going to happen? You're in it now, you cow.'

Marianne laughed and pulled a face at her.

'OK; can you keep a secret?'

Julia turned away from Alice and directed her full attention at Marianne.

'I'm going to be a grandmother!'

Julia stood up quickly, her hands covering her mouth in surprise. Then she threw her arms around Marianne and hugged her.

'Oh my God; that's amazing. I take it you mean Rachel's pregnant, not Sophie or Isobel.'

'Thankfully yes; although, between you and me, even Rachel's a bit young. I wish they'd waited a little bit longer; Ivan's only just started his new job, so money's going to be so tight for them.'

'You were younger – so was I.'

'I know, I know. Anyway, it's early days, so nobody knows except the grandparents – and now you.'

'I won't tell a soul.'

Julia sat down and reached for Alice's hand again.

'Anyway, what has becoming a grandmother got to do with your job? You're not going to give it up are you?' Julia said.

'Well, I was thinking about it. Rachel wants to go back to work afterwards; well needs to really. They can't manage on one salary. And the cost of childcare…'

'But they'd be entitled to tax credits or whatever they're called now, and there's a couple of really good nurseries in town.'

'That's true – but actually I offered. I can't wait to be a granny – a full time professional one.'

'I know, but this is your career you're talking about. You worked so hard to get this job.'

'It's just a job though, and as much as I love working here, I'd rather be at home with a peerie bairn again.'

'Yes, I suppose I would too,' Julia conceded.

'So there you go; this time next year the job will be free again.'

'That's a long way off. I'll have to find something useful to do before then.'

'Lose weight, get fit, re-decorate the house; all those things you keep saying you're going to do, if only you had the time.' Marianne counted out the tasks on her fingers as if it was a well-oiled routine.

'Very funny!'

'But true though. Don't hurry back to work. Remember, you've been through a really stressful time too. It wasn't just Duncan who suffered. Take your time to get over it. Then come and get your old job back next year.'

'Maybe you're right…' Julia said, and was about to add something else when Alice snatched her hand away from Julia, and screamed in fear of something unseen to anyone other than herself.

Alice threw her blanket aside and struggled to sit up. Julia instinctively reached out to help her. Marianne hurried to the other side of the bed and gripped Alice's elbow. But Alice started to flap her arms around and both Julia and Marianne stepped back a little, to give her some space.

'What's up my love?' Julia said, soothingly, 'everything's going to be alright; there's nothing to be afraid of.'

'Duncan? Martin?' Alice called, clearly becoming more agitated as she tried to get up. She started to weep and covered her face with her hands, her chest heaving with distress, and continued to cry out for her sons.

Julia watched in horror. Although she had witnessed similar scenes before it was all the more distressing now it was Alice that was so upset, and it was hard to know what was causing it, other than perhaps some awful memory she had dredged up. It had been at least five years since she had stopped recognising Duncan when he visited.

Marianne looked at Julia and smiled sympathetically.

'Do you think a sedative might help?' Marianne glanced up at the clock on the wall, 'it's 2.30 now, if we let her sleep it off this afternoon, maybe she'll feel a bit better when you come along with Duncan this evening.'

Julia nodded; but almost immediately Alice calmed down on her own. She slumped back against the pillows and stared intently at something in the corner of the room. She smiled and lifted her hand as if she was greeting someone who had just appeared.

Julia turned to see what Alice was looking at. There was nothing but a chest of drawers with a group of family photos on it. Julia picked up a photo of Duncan and Martin that had been taken when they were teenagers. She put it on the bedside cabinet so Alice could see it more easily; but Alice wasn't interested in the photo. Her face had lit up in a picture of pure joy, and it was possible to glimpse the warm and friendly woman she used to be.

Julia drove home, saddened by the burden of telling Duncan about his mother's decline in health. She parked the car on the driveway and sat for a moment, after she had taken the key out of the ignition. She stared at the white silk daises in the little vase on the dashboard; the flowers Duncan had laughed at when she first bought her beloved Volkswagen Beetle. She brushed away a tiny cobweb that had appeared on one of the daisies, and then noticed she had left her mobile phone on the passenger seat while she had been visiting Alice. She checked it for messages and saw she had missed five calls from the school. She looked at the time; Duncan would have left by now, so she didn't bother to ring back. He hadn't left a message, so it couldn't have been urgent.

She went indoors and headed straight for the kettle to make some tea, wondering at the same time what she should make for dinner. She opened the fridge and took out some chicken and vegetables and decided to make chicken in red wine, one of Duncan's favourite dishes.

She set about preparing the meal, drinking her tea as she did so, and then put the casserole dish into the oven and washed her hands. She made a fresh mug of tea and carried it over to the kitchen window where she had a view of the road leading down to their house. She couldn't wait to hear how Duncan's first day back at work had gone. She rested her arms on the deep window sill and stared up the hill.

Their house was at the end of a long narrow track that branched off the main road half a mile away, with the result there was never any passing traffic. Sometimes the house could feel isolated, but since they were only a fifteen minute drive away from Lerwick, they didn't normally feel lonely. Their house was a place of tranquillity and peace. They had chosen the plot deliberately, as the perfect haven from the demands of their busy and sometimes stressful jobs - but it was also close enough to civilisation and their friends.

Julia was taking a sip of tea when she noticed a police van meandering down the road towards her. She guessed it would be Jamie's best friend Liam, who had joined the police force at the same time as Jamie had gone off to University. The boys had been friends since they started primary school together, and Liam had stopped by a few times while Duncan had been ill, just to see how he was getting on. Julia often used to joke he was their third son.

The van pulled up behind her car and Julia grinned and waved as Liam got out. He looked world-weary and she wondered whether he had come round to let off steam about his day.

She went out to the front porch to welcome him and opened the door as he approached.

'Oh dear, you look like the world's just ended. Come in and tell me all about it.'

Julia grinned at Liam, marvelling at how the quiet little mouse of a boy she had known for so long had grown up to be such a capable young man. He had become so much more confident since he had joined the police; able to talk to anyone. However, he didn't seem very confident at this particular moment in time; in fact he seemed barely able to look her in the face.

Liam followed Julia into the kitchen. He still hadn't spoken, although the silence had been broken by the crackle of the radio he wore on his jacket. He fiddled with it instantly, turning it off as he took a seat at the kitchen table. Julia picked up the kettle to fill it while she waited for him to speak. The poor boy had clearly had a bad day and she had to fight the maternal urge to give him a hug.

'Duncan will be home soon,' she said, as she switched the kettle on, 'it was his first day back at work today.'

Liam leapt up as if he had been scalded. Julia hurried over and touched his arm.

'What's wrong Liam? Has something happened at work?'

'Oh God! I don't know how to say this. I came to find you, because you weren't answering your phone. Duncan has…Duncan… he collapsed at school. They called an ambulance and rushed him to hospital. But…'

Julia shrank away from him, covering her ears with her hands and stared down at the floor, trying to block out what she knew he would say next. She slumped against the kitchen unit and slid down until she was crouched on the floor.

'I'm sorry. They think he had a heart attack. They tried to resuscitate him but…'

Liam sat down heavily on the chair. He looked at Julia and then looked away again. He caught sight of a family portrait on the wall, taken before Duncan was ill, and before Jamie and Bryden had gone off to University. He stared at the face of his best friend, who would also need to be told soon. Liam was aware many people had witnessed Duncan's collapse, so the news would spread quickly around the community. He had volunteered to go and find Julia as he didn't want a stranger to be the one to tell her; except he hadn't counted on how hard it would be to tell her himself. Nothing he had learned at the police training college in Inverness had prepared him for this situation.

'Julia? Shall I drive you to the hospital?'

Julia looked up but did not reply. She looked as if someone had just slapped her.

'We need to tell Jamie and Bryden soon; before they find out from someone else.'

Julia nodded, but did not move.

'Do you want me to call them?'

She shook her head.

Liam walked over to her. He bent down and offered her his hand. She took it and he helped her to stand up.

'Can I get you a drink? Water? Tea?'

'No, it's OK,' she whispered.

He stood in front of her and put his hands on her shoulders.

'I'm so sorry. I can't believe it myself yet.'

'Can you take me to him?'

'Of course I can. Do you want to do that now, or call Jamie and Bryden first?'

'I'd better call them.'

Julia picked up her mobile phone from the kitchen worktop and stared at it blankly.

'So, he's really dead? You're sure.'

'Yes, I'm so sorry. I was at the hospital, dealing with a drunk and I saw him come in with the paramedics.'

Julia scrolled through the numbers on her phone until she found Jamie's mobile. She pressed dial, but as soon as it started ringing she realised she couldn't speak. She handed the phone to Liam, shaking her head in frustration.

Julia paced up and down the kitchen, her arms wrapped tightly around her body, trying to contain the grief. She listened as Liam spoke to Jamie, desperate to speak to him herself, but unable to voice the words she needed to say. Her throat had constricted so much she could barely breathe.

'No, it's Liam. Your mum asked me to call you. I have some bad news...Your dad suffered a heart attack at school today...I'm sorry mate...They couldn't bring him back... He died about an hour ago...No he doesn't know yet... I'll pick you up from the airport. Yeah, I'll make sure she's OK.'

Liam handed the phone back to Julia.

'Jamie's going to ring Bryden right now and then sort out flights to come home. It's probably too late to get back tonight, but hopefully tomorrow morning. I'm not on duty then, so I can pick them up if you want.'

'I should have told him,' Julia whispered.

'Don't worry; he understood. And you know Jamie he was more concerned about you and Bryden than himself. Anyway, shall we go to the hospital now? Or can I call anyone else? What about one of your friends?'

'No; I'll ring them later.'

Julia took one last look around the kitchen and noticed the oven was on. She switched it off and followed Liam out to his van.

4

Julia had seen many dead bodies in her life, one of the perils of her profession. Over the years she had learned to view them coolly and professionally, sparing her main thoughts and efforts on looking after the relatives of the deceased. Now she was the relative she didn't know how to react. It was so unreal and she wanted to shake Duncan awake. She put her hand on his arm; it was already cool.

She had steeled herself for his death so many times over the last year, but each time he had rallied and recovered, and now, like the boy who cried wolf, she couldn't believe he wasn't faking it.

Liam stood sentry by the door, his arms folded, his head bowed as if he was praying. There was a knock on the door and he opened it a touch to see who was there, and then opened it fully to let in a young doctor who wanted to see Julia.

'Hello Mrs Robertson, I'm Nathalie Parker, I tended to your husband when he came in. I'm really sorry we couldn't resuscitate him. I understand one of the pupils made a brave attempt at doing chest compressions as soon as he collapsed, and the paramedics got there very quickly and used a defibrillator on him. We worked on him for quite a while, but we couldn't get a heartbeat again. We won't find out exactly what happened until we do a post-mortem, but we think he suffered a heart attack.'

'Post-mortem?'

'When someone dies unexpectedly like this... it's the standard procedure.'

'He'd just recovered from cancer; he's never had any heart problems.'

'I know. But there's a small risk with chemotherapy and radiation therapy the heart can be damaged. We won't know for sure until…'

Julia nodded. She couldn't take her eyes away from Duncan. His clothes had been replaced by one of the ugly hospital gowns. She spotted a white polythene bag in the corner of the room and recognised the blue shirt he had been wearing earlier on top of the clothes in the bag. The brand new shirt had clearly been cut from Duncan's body for speed of access. Julia had a flashback from that morning when he had put on, with its tell-tale creases from the packaging still visible. She wanted to turn back the clock to that moment when he was getting dressed. She should have made him stay at home.

She was aware the doctor was still in the room waiting for a response.

'Thank you; thank you for trying. I just need a few moments more, if that's OK?'

'Of course.' Nathalie nodded at Liam and hurried out of the room.

'It doesn't really look like him now, does it?' Julia said, as she stroked Duncan's cheek.

Liam moved closer to the bed and sat down on the chair next to Julia.

'No; Duncan was always smiling, or talking, or something.'

'He doesn't even look like this when he's asleep,' Julia replied softly, realising she had spoken about him in the present tense; wondering when she would have the strength to acknowledge him in the past tense. 'I just can't believe this, I really can't. Just this morning we felt so happy; so lucky.'

Liam drove Julia home and stayed with her for a while, making cups of tea and keeping her company while she plucked up the courage to ring Jamie and Bryden herself. He went in search of tissues for her while she cried on the phone with them, and failing that returned with a toilet roll from the downstairs cloakroom. She smiled her gratitude at him as she wiped the tears away.

When he was sure she was alright he got ready to go.

'I'm sorry I kept you so long. I hope you won't get in trouble for this,' Julia said.

'Don't be silly. It's part of the job, and in any case, my shift finished ages ago.'

'Well in that case you'd better get home for your tea then. I'm sorry you had such a horrible day. I know it must have been hard for you too. You did a good job; I'm so proud of you.'

After Liam had driven away Julia picked up the phone and called Marianne and within half an hour Marianne was walking through the front door, carrying a shopping bag.

'I bought some wine – probably not the most appropriate thing to do. But Lord knows I could do with a drink.' Marianne stowed one bottle of wine in the fridge and handed the other to Julia. On autopilot, Julia reached up and took out two wine glasses from the cupboard.

'I've got a chicken casserole half-cooked in the oven already. Shall I switch it on again?'

'Yeah, why not – you should eat something. Isn't that what people say?'

Julia had put the bottle of wine next to the glasses but she hadn't opened it. She seemed uncertain what to do next, so Marianne opened the bottle of Chablis and poured two generous glasses.

'Duncan's favourite.' Julia said, noticing the label.

'I know. He'd be pissed off not being able to have some wouldn't he? But it seemed appropriate to drink a toast to him with a bottle of the good stuff.'

They carried their glasses into the lounge. Marianne sat down in her usual chair, adjacent to the sofa. She had kicked off her shoes already and looked almost comfortable. However, as Julia sat down on the sofa she looked over and saw Marianne was struggling. Her eyes were unnaturally bright with unshed tears, and her bottom lip quivered; the bravado she had kept up since she arrived had drained away.

'To Duncan – God bless you my darling.' Julia said, lifting her glass to Marianne.

'Oh Christ; I can't do this. For fuck's sake! I thought it was all over now.' Marianne put her glass down on the table and covered her face with her hands.

'I know. So did I.' Julia took a sip of the wine as she stared at Marianne. She was feeling extraordinarily numb. It didn't feel real.

'All those times when we thought he wouldn't make it, I used to wonder how I could be a good friend to you when it happened. That time when he was in hospital in Aberdeen and it seemed so touch and go, I hardly slept at all. I was waiting for you to ring. I was ready for it then.'

'So was I; I think.'

'Why is life such a bastard?'

'I don't know. It just is.' Julia gulped back some more wine, praying for oblivion. 'Are you staying over tonight?'

'Of course; I rang to tell them I'd be late for work tomorrow. I told the staff; I hope you don't mind. They were gutted for you. Thank God poor Alice won't know what happened. Morag went to sit with her this evening. She's been sleeping soundly since her little upset this afternoon.'

'That's some relief at least.'

'To Duncan!' Marianne said, sitting up straight in an attempt to regain her composure. She took a sip of wine then pulled a face. 'Why didn't you have the decency to like red wine? This stuff gives me a headache.'

Julia laughed nervously and drained her glass. She pondered the merits of drinking wine on an empty stomach. She didn't want to be lying in bed with a hangover when her boys came home. She went out to the kitchen and returned with a large bowl of crisps.

'I always thought people were supposed to lose their appetites in these circumstances,' Julia said, as she helped herself to a handful of crisps.

'I think they do, normally.'

'But we're not normal are we?'

Marianne shook her head in agreement.

They talked all evening. They finished two bottles of wine, the bowl of crisps, and then had some of the chicken casserole, after which they started on whisky and chocolate.

They shared memories of Duncan; happy, sad and funny. They had both known him for most of their lives. It was Marianne that had goaded Duncan into asking Julia out. He had been too shy, but Marianne had known he had harboured a crush on Julia for years. It was Marianne that persuaded Julia she should give him a chance, as Julia had never considered Duncan to be anything more than just a friend. He had asked her out to a dance during one long summer holiday when he was home from University. Julia had just applied to do nurse training and wasn't really interested in getting serious with anyone. But Duncan wasn't just anyone.

'I keep waiting for him to come home.' Julia said, yawning with exhaustion. It was long after midnight and the alcohol was making her sleepy.

'Maybe he's already here. Do you believe in ghosts?'

'Yes, no, maybe; I don't know…I've been thinking about that thing with Alice. Do you realise she was calling for him at the same time he was dying.'

'Really? Oh God, that's spooky.'

They sat for a moment in silence.

'I really need to go to bed; but I don't want to go upstairs. I can't bear to get in that bed on my own.'

'Don't then. Sleep here on the sofa. I'll go upstairs and fetch the duvet for you.'

Marianne hurried up to Julia's room and pulled the duvet off the bed and picked up a pillow and carried them downstairs. She put them down in a bundle on the floor beside Julia, who reached over and picked up the pillow. Julia sat and cuddled it for a moment, deep in thought and then held the pillow to her face.

'This is Duncan's pillow. I can smell his aftershave.'

Marianne sat down beside Julia and pulled the pillow towards her and inhaled. Then she wrapped her arms around Julia as they both wept.

5

Marianne woke first; her head thumping. She felt hot, sticky and disgusting, after sleeping in her clothes on the sofa. She looked across at the other sofa and saw Julia was still fast asleep, buried under the duvet.

Marianne was desperate to use the bathroom, but didn't want to wake Julia. She didn't want to see the look on her face when she woke up and remembered what had happened. She sat up carefully and tiptoed across the wooden floor to the downstairs bathroom. With a sigh of relief she discovered a fully stocked medicine cupboard, so she helped herself to painkillers.

When she returned to the lounge she was relieved to see Julia was still asleep. She glanced at the clock; it was seven thirty. Julia was bound to wake up soon.

Marianne rubbed her face with her hands. She was exhausted and could do with going back to sleep for a while longer. She lay down on the sofa again, facing Julia, keeping watch for when she woke up. She didn't have long to wait, as a few minutes later the phone rang. Marianne jumped up quickly to answer it, as Julia opened her eyes and stared around her in surprise. Within a split second Marianne saw Julia's eyes widen with shock, and close again in grief.

'Hello? ...No, it's Marianne... I stayed over with your mam... OK, that's brilliant Jamie; see you in a little while.'

Marianne put the phone down, surveying the glasses, plates and dishes that still littered the coffee table.

'They've just landed. Liam's picked them up, so they'll be home in half an hour.'

'Jesus, look at the state of this place.'

'Don't worry about that. You run up and have a quick shower. I'll tidy up down here.'

'Thanks!'

Julia raced up the stairs to the bedroom dragging the duvet and pillow with her. She threw them in a heap on the bed and hurried to the bathroom. She glanced at the reflection of herself in the mirror. Her face was puffy and creased, and her hair was a disaster.

She washed her hair quickly, trying not to see the masculine shower gels and anti-dandruff shampoos cluttering the window sill. She took a deep breath.

'Duncan, where the hell are you? Why did this happen?' she whispered, as she rinsed the lather away. Her eyes stung in the water and she felt a little queasy. She was ashamed of herself for getting plastered the night her husband died. It was so undignified, and yet it had helped somehow.

She got dried and dressed quickly, putting on a pair of jeans and a pale green shirt. It occurred to her she ought to be wearing black; then she remembered something Duncan had said to her a few months ago.

'Don't mourn for me. I want you to live life and enjoy yourself. Wear your sexy red dress to my funeral.'

She had laughed at him and told him not to be so stupid. Of course she would mourn for him, but she had promised to wear a sexy *black* dress to his funeral. He had nodded his approval and told her he would be watching to make sure she did.

He had planned his own funeral, but since he had survived the cancer they hadn't talked about it in ages. Julia realised she would now have to implement his plans. She felt sick at the thought of it.

She sat down on the bed, breathless, her hands shaking. She turned and picked up the pillow she had dumped on the bed and pulled it to her face. She gritted her teeth and closed her eyes, resisting the temptation to scream. She wanted to get in her car and drive to the hospital and demand to see Duncan again. It could not be real.

She heard the crunch of a car stopping on the gravel drive, and she stood up and looked out of the window and saw Jamie, Bryden and Liam getting out of a blue car.

She hurried downstairs to meet them, taking deep breaths and trying to control her emotions.

Marianne was in the kitchen, loading up the dishwasher. She had cleared the lounge of all the debris and it was relatively tidy again. She pulled a face at Julia, an acknowledgement that seeing the boys would be a difficult moment. Julia nodded, still trying to compose herself. Marianne turned away and picked up the kettle to fill it.

The front door opened and Jamie marched in, ahead of Liam.

Julia looked past them both, waiting for Bryden to appear. He didn't.

'Bryden's spewing outside. He's a bit hung-over.' Jamie explained, as he crossed the room to greet his mother.

'Oh, right, I see… Well it's lovely to see you Jamie. I just wish…'

'I know.'

He held out his arms to her and she hugged him gratefully, reluctant to let go.

'Who would like some coffee? Liam?' Marianne said; keen to make Liam feel welcome in the middle of this awkward family reunion. 'Black coffee for Bryden? He's not the only one with a hangover. I'm feeling a bit fragile myself.'

'Yes please.' Liam replied. 'I'll just go and see if he's alright.'

He hurried outside, returning a moment later with Bryden, who looked pale and shaky.

'Sorry Mam. I didn't mean to get pissed last night. We went and stayed over at Graham's house in Aberdeen so we could get the early flight, and we stayed up all night drinking, and talking about dad.'

'That's OK, that's what me and Marianne did too.'

Bryden gave his mother a quick hug. Julia wrinkled her nose involuntarily.

'Do you mind if I run up and get changed, I probably stink a bit? I'm surprised we were allowed on the plane this morning.'

'I could do with a shower too. Shall I use your bathroom?' Jamie said.

'Yes of course, darling.'

Marianne handed mugs of coffee to Liam and Julia.

'I'd better head home soon and leave you all in peace; I expect you have lots to talk about,' Marianne said, as she poured herself a coffee.

'Really?' Liam said, 'are you sure you're fit to drive home, there's a powerful reek of whisky coming from your direction?' He smiled at her, but it was obvious he wasn't impressed.

'Well, maybe not. I'll stay here a little while longer then. I'll make us all some breakfast and wait until the coast is clear of policemen; then I'll get off.'

'I can give you a lift if you want,' Liam said, smiling at her, and acknowledging he knew she was teasing him.

'Stay, both of you. Stay for breakfast. You're both *family*,' Julia said. 'There's no need to rush off.'

'OK then. I'll ring St Ninian's and tell them I'm taking the morning off; actually I think I'll take the whole day off.'

'Well you're the boss now!' Julia said, nodding in approval.

When Jamie and Bryden came downstairs, wearing clean clothes and looking and smelling much fresher, Marianne slipped upstairs to take a shower. When she came down again she found Julia sitting on the sofa between her sons, holding hands. Liam was sat at the kitchen table looking a bit lost.

'Ah great Liam, you can help me make breakfast for everyone,' Marianne said.

He jumped up quickly, eager to have a useful role.

'You know the best breakfast I ever had was in a New York diner. It was mad; they eat pancakes with bacon and maple syrup. It sounds disgusting doesn't it? But it was brilliant.'

Marianne nodded thoughtfully.

'You know, I quite fancy the sound of that. Let's see what there is in the cupboards.'

In the end they settled for French toast, bacon, mushrooms, and tomatoes.

Liam set the table and made a large pot of tea and poured out glasses of orange juice.

'This is weird isn't it?' he whispered to Marianne, 'like anyone's got any appetite for food.'

'What else can we do to help? And they need looking after right now. They've been through such a lot this year. I can't *believe* this has happened.'

'Me neither. Duncan was so...' Liam paused, unable to find the right words. He shrugged in defeat.

'Yeah he was! He was a great man. We'll all miss him.' Marianne said, as she switched off the grill, and took out the pan of bacon and tomatoes.

'Shall I tell them it's ready?'

'Yeah, go on, thanks Liam.'

The conversation around the table was stilted as Marianne handed everyone plates of food. Julia looked dazed and she got up from the table and went in search of painkillers to take with her orange juice. Jamie asked for some too and then offered the packet to Bryden who shook his head as if the idea revolted him.

'Am I the only person who didn't get hammered last night?' Liam asked, as he watched Jamie almost choke as he swallowed the tablets.

'Seems that way,' Bryden said, looking at his mother and smiling grimly. 'What would Dad have thought about that?'

'We all spent most of the night talking about him. He'd have understood.'

'So what happens now?' Bryden asked, as he toyed with a mushroom on the end of his fork and then abandoned it. He put his cutlery down and pushed the plate away.

'We need to organise the funeral, but we won't be able to sort out a date for it until after the post-mortem.'

'Does everyone know already?' Bryden asked.

'Probably; you know how fast news travels here. I'm sure it's all over Facebook already,' Jamie said bitterly, 'so when you read about it, make sure you "like" this.'

Julia stood up suddenly and picked up her plate and carried it to the kitchen. She scraped the uneaten French toast into the bin and put the plate next to the sink.

'Thanks Marianne, but I'm just not very hungry right now.'

'That's OK; you managed a little bit.'

The phone rang and Julia froze. Nobody moved to answer it.

'And so it begins,' Jamie said, standing up at last and striding across the kitchen to get to the phone.

Julia watched him, marvelling at how quickly he had assumed the role of man of the house.

'Hello? It's Jamie... No she can't come to the phone right now. Can you call back, maybe tomorrow?... Yeah, thanks.'

He put the phone down.

'That was Mrs Leask, wanting to convey her condolences. So yeah, we can safely assume everybody knows now.'

'Don't be like that Jamie; it was nice of her to call. Why don't you boys go off to the garage and play snooker or something?'

'Because we're not twelve years old; and we don't need to be sent out to play.'

Julia recoiled, as if he had slapped her. She turned away from him and stared out of the window, blinking back tears.

'You might not be twelve, but you're still an idiot,' Bryden said, getting up from the table and going over to Julia. He put his arm around her shoulders. 'I'm sorry Mam, he didn't mean it. We're just pissed off.'

'I know. It's alright; I'm sure we're all going to say stupid things over the next few days.'

'Come on, we should go and play snooker. That's a good idea; we can catch up,' Liam said, standing up and signalling to Jamie to follow him.

'No whacky baccy!' Julia said, with an exaggerated stern voice. 'I know where you hide it.'

'What? I'm nearly a doctor, he's a policeman and the idiot over there is going to be a respectable maths teacher. We wouldn't dream of doing stuff like that.' Jamie grinned at his mother in an effort to smooth things over between them.

Julia snorted. 'Yeah right! I know you all far too well.'

'They don't really smoke do they?' Marianne asked, after they had gone.

'Not any more they don't. Duncan read them the riot act when he discovered their little stash. Silly little idiots; all three of them could have ruined their careers if they got caught.'

'Boys will be boys, eh? Well, they're all men now aren't they? Hard to believe isn't it; seems like only yesterday they were in primary school skinning their knees playing football in the playground. It's frightening how quick time passes. Right now my first grandchild is about the size of a walnut, but he or she will be an adult in the blink of an eye.'

'Yes indeed. We need to hold on to the good times.'

'We have had some good times, haven't we?'

Julia nodded, but before she could reply the phone rang.

'Shall I?' Marianne said.

'Please! I really don't want to speak to anyone else right now.'

Marianne picked up the phone while Julia walked to the front door and opened it. Julia stepped out onto the decking, and made her way to the bench in front of the house. It was sunny, but the early morning sun hadn't warmed the air yet, and she shivered as the cool breeze penetrated her thin shirt. She thought about the last conversation she had had with Duncan, and his desire to go to Sicily. She wished she could be there right now with him, sitting in the morning sun together, planning a day of exploration. She looked at her watch; this time yesterday Duncan had still been alive and had not long left for school.

She felt her chest tighten; the raw physical pain of grief made it difficult to breathe deeply. She gripped the wooden armrest of the bench and shut her eyes.

'Ah, there you are.' Marianne said, as she walked over and sat down next to her. 'You OK?'

Julia nodded. 'Just thinking.'

'That was Morag. Not good news... Alice has just passed away. She was still sleeping when they went into her first thing this morning, so they didn't wake her up for breakfast. Morag just went in to see her a few minutes ago and she had gone. I'm sorry Julia. Really, this is all too much for you.'

Julia shut her eyes and covered her face with her hands and remained silent for a moment before sighing and standing up.

'Do they want me to go in?'

'No, don't be silly. You've got enough on your plate at the moment. Plenty of time to sort things out later. '

'Poor Alice; she was all on her own.'

'She was asleep! Can't think of a better way to go myself.'

'I'm glad it was today and not yesterday anyway. At least Duncan never knew. Jesus – what else is going to happen?'

'Nothing! Nothing's going to happen. Come inside, you're freezing.' Marianne said, taking Julia's arm and leading her indoors.

6

A few weeks after the joint funeral took place for Duncan and Alice, Julia found herself alone in the house. Jamie had flown over to Barbados to do a course in diving medicine. He had rung her the previous evening from the beach, where he had been waiting for the induction to start. Julia had detected an undercurrent of excitement in his voice which he struggled to cover up. She had pleaded with him to stop feeling guilty about having a good time and made him promise to email lots of photographs.

Bryden was back in Edinburgh, having returned to finish his exams. He had taken Duncan's car with him, along with his father's golf clubs. Julia had been pleased to see the back of the car, as every time she had seen the silver Ford Focus out on the drive she had been reminded of the last time she watched Duncan driving it away.

However, this had caused something of an argument between the boys. Clearly Bryden needed a car more than Jamie did, as Bryden would be starting a new job in August, at a school seven miles away from where he currently lived. Jamie shared a large flat opposite the hospital and had no need of a car; but he was the oldest son, and that made him think he should have had the first refusal.

Julia knew her sons were acting out of character. With only eighteen months between them in age, they were normally very close, but Duncan's sudden death had knocked the stuffing out of them, and they had taken to bickering over silly things. They had also taken to ringing Julia every day, which was lovely; but it also made her feel as if they were doing it out of duty, rather than because they had anything they really wanted to talk about.

Despite Julia's misery, the summer raced by; the darkness of her mood punctuated by the light relief provided from time to time by her friends and her sons. In August Bryden started his probationary year as a maths teacher at a high school and he moved in with his new girlfriend, Anna. And although it seemed a little premature in their relationship, Julia understood his need to have someone close to him on a permanent basis.

Her financial situation had improved a little. Her meagre savings, which had been depleted by the cost of two funerals, had been bolstered by Duncan's life assurance and widow's pension. She was not wealthy by any means, but she did not need to rush back to work.

She managed to hold it together most of the time, while people were visiting, or when anyone rang her, but she was conscious she was sinking deeper and deeper into depression. Sometimes she tried to do something about it. She would cook something healthy and distract herself with a book or a film, or make a particular effort to go out for a walk. But some days she barely ate anything and didn't move from the sofa. She didn't always get dressed or take a shower. She couldn't remember the last time she had put on make-up or perfume or tried to look presentable. Her hair had grown longer, but it was greyer and what remained of her blonde highlights was parched and frizzy.

On a dreary day in mid-September Julia was lying on the sofa in the middle of the afternoon wearing pyjamas and one of Duncan's sweatshirts when the front door opened. Marianne walked in followed by a young woman Julia didn't recognise.

'This is Vaila Anderson, she's just finished her hairdressing training in Inverness, and she's come along to do your hair.' Marianne said brusquely to Julia, inviting no argument.

'I don't need my hair doing; it's fine as it is.' Julia said, not moving from the sofa. She didn't smile, or do anything to welcome her visitors.

'It looks like a bale of hay from where I'm standing.'

'So what; it's not like I'm going anywhere.'

'Maybe not. But it might make you feel a bit better.'

'How?' Julia replied sharply. 'How is getting my hair done going to make everything all tickety boo again?' She sat up sharply and hugged a cushion to her stomach, as if she was in pain.

'Well, maybe it will just make me feel better. Come on, please let Vaila do your hair. She's really good. She's just started her own mobile business.'

Julia frowned at Vaila, who stood behind Marianne looking as if she wished the ground would swallow her up. Julia remembered her manners at last.

'OK then. But can I at least go up and have a shower first.'

'Um, actually, your hair needs to be dry to do the colour. Maybe you could have a shower afterwards.' Vaila said, as she unzipped a large canvas holdall.

'I'll just take this sweatshirt off then. I don't want anything to spill on it. It was my husband's.'

'And I'll go and put the kettle on and make us some tea.' Marianne said, barely disguising the triumph in her voice.

Vaila invited Julia to sit at a chair in the kitchen. She took out a long black gown from her bag and fastened it around Julia's shoulders. She started to comb through Julia's hair which took some effort as it was tangled and uncooperative. All the while Marianne and Vaila kept up a bright commentary on local gossip, and cheerful banter. Julia listened, but did not make any attempt to join in.

'How do you normally style your hair?' Vaila asked Julia.

Julia squinted into the stand-up mirror Vaila had placed in front of her on the table.

'She normally has a lovely neat little bob; quite short.' Marianne replied, seeing as Julia seemed to have lost the use of her tongue.

'Oh, I was just thinking this long length was quite flattering. It really just needs the ends trimming and the colour doing, and perhaps some conditioning. It's a bit dry.'

'Yeah, you're right, it would look nice longer. What do you think Jules?'

Julia shrugged.

'I'll just keep it long then shall I?' Vaila said, looking to both Marianne and Julia for approval.

Julia nodded, although she really could not care less.

Two hours later, after Vaila had transformed her hair, Julia went upstairs to change, and came down a few minutes later wearing jeans and a pink tee shirt, looking self-conscious.

'You look lovely now,' Marianne said warmly, 'but my God you've lost some weight.'

'I always wanted to; but maybe not like this.' Julia lifted up the hem of her tee shirt and revealed the waistband of her jeans that were now two sizes too big.

'No; it's too much, you need to eat more; you're looking scrawny. We can't get away with it at our age, it's much too aging.'

Vaila had packed away her hairdressing equipment, but she had pulled out a plastic box full of nail polishes and set them down on the kitchen table.

'If you like, I can give you both a manicure.'

'Ooh super! My nails are a disgrace.' Marianne said enthusiastically, waggling her hands out to Vaila. 'Me first!'

Julia put the kettle on again and opened a packet of biscuits.

'No biscuits for me please,' Marianne said, 'I'm taking you out for something to eat after this.'

'Oh no; I couldn't. I don't feel up to going out.'

'I know you don't. But you must; it's my birthday and I insist.'

Julia dropped the packet of biscuits onto the worktop and spun round quickly.

'Oh shit; already? I didn't realise what day it was today. I'm so sorry.'

'So you should be. I'm fifty today; and I intend to celebrate.'

'But where are we going? You're not having a party are you?'

'Not tonight. But we might have a little party on Saturday night. I'm not going to insist you come to that, although you'd be very welcome. But you're coming out with us tonight missy. We have celebrated nearly every birthday together since we were six years old.'

Julia smiled for the first time in ages and sat down at the table next to Marianne, and hugged her.

'Yes we have.'

'So, we'll get our nails done and you can find something in your wardrobe that hangs a bit better on you than those jeans; and then we are going out. You can stay at our house, so you don't need to worry about drinking and driving. We'll get a taxi into town and go for an Indian shall we?'

'That is the tradition!'

'Since you were both six?' Vaila said, as she took Marianne's hand to start on her manicure.

'Well, we've only been going out for an Indian for the last fifteen years, but yeah, since we were six,' Julia replied, smiling at the memories.

Julia enjoyed her evening out at the Indian restaurant celebrating Marianne's birthday, and she enjoyed sitting up late with Marianne and Brian in their lounge after their teenage daughters had gone to bed. With her closest friends and a comforting dram of whisky she felt relaxed, and if not quite happy, then at least not desperately sad. Julia allowed herself to be talked into going to Marianne's birthday party on Saturday night.

7

Marianne's house was filled with lots of her friends and family. There was food, drink, music and laughter. Julia knew everyone at the party and quite a few of them were from their year at school, so they were swapping "war-stories" about turning fifty. Julia's own fiftieth birthday was just a few weeks away in October, and as the evening progressed she started to dread its arrival and knew she would not wish to celebrate it. She was happy for Marianne to be surrounded by all of her closest friends and family, but she had to fight hard to bury the bitterness she felt about her own life.

She was fast becoming someone she didn't want to be; and if she couldn't stand her own company, she wondered how soon it would be before her friends deserted her.

Julia helped herself to a nip of whisky and a couple of ice-cubes and pushed her way out of the crowded kitchen. Seeing the lounge was equally full of loud and joyful people she turned on her heel and walked towards the back porch. The door was open and there was someone standing outside smoking. He looked at Julia and smiled.

'You haven't taken up the evil weed have you?'

'No, it just a bit hot in the house; thought I could do with some fresh air.'

'Fresh? Aye, it's fresh alright. It's Baltic!' With that he dropped his cigarette on the ground and stamped on it and then hurried indoors.

Julia was only wearing a thin chiffon blouse and she soon shivered, but was reluctant to go back to the party. She stepped back into the porch and unhooked a jacket from the coat rack. She knew Marianne wouldn't mind if she borrowed it.

She zipped up the jacket, then picked up her whisky glass from the window ledge and leaned against the wall and stared up at the sky. It was only mid-September, but whilst the rest of the UK seemed to be enjoying a last minute resurgence of summer, it could easily have been mid-winter in Shetland. The strong northerly breeze made Julia's eyes water and she walked around the side of the house until she found shelter and a garden bench. She sat beneath the kitchen window and sipped her whisky.

The window was ajar and gossip mixed with music filtered out. Julia thought about going to sit somewhere quieter as she found the laughter and high spirits oppressive. When she heard someone say her name she leaned against the wall, with her head cocked to one side, listening.

'I think she went back to the lounge, why?' Marianne replied to someone, whose voice Julia couldn't recognise immediately.

'I'm surprised she came to your party. She's really miserable isn't she?'

'Wouldn't you be?'

'Yeah, but we all thought he was going to die from cancer anyway; surely she should be grateful they got another few months together.'

'Are you serious?' Marianne snapped.

'OK, but he really shouldn't have gone back to school when he did. I hear the lassie who tried to save his life has been traumatised by it.'

'How was anyone to know he was going to have a heart attack? It could happen to anyone, anytime. You can't not go back to work just because of that; Jesus, none of us would be working at all.'

Julia heard Marianne's voice fade away as if she had stormed out of the kitchen.

'You're a fucking idiot Paula, fancy saying that to Julia's best friend?'

'What? I'm just saying Duncan shouldn't have gone back to work so soon; maybe he'd still be here if he'd taken it easier.'

'Maybe so, but that's not Julia's fault; you could be a bit more sympathetic. How would you feel if something like that happened to you?'

'Pleased as punch; I'd be raking in the life insurance and jetting off somewhere hot.'

'Oi! I heard that,' a male voice joined in.

'Sorry dearest.'

The kitchen filled with laughter.

'It's getting a bit cold in here, anyone mind if I close this window now?'

Julia looked up and saw a female hand reaching up to the window, bracelets jangling merrily as she pulled it closed. The sounds coming from inside were instantly muffled. Julia stood up and headed towards the back door. She intended to go home. She lifted up the empty whisky glass and calculated how many units she had drunk. One small glass of Champagne and one whisky; she thought she would be alright to drive home.

She was about to go inside the house when Cameron appeared in the door frame; he stood back to let her in.

'Marianne was looking for you just now. Are you OK?'

Julia stepped back outside and stood with her back to the wind and looked up at Duncan's best friend.

'Not really. I was just about to go home. It wasn't a good idea coming out tonight.'

Julia looked down at her feet; she had her arms wrapped tightly around her body, with one hand clutching the empty glass.

'Early days eh? Tell me about it!'

Julia shrugged, but did not look up.

'I nearly didn't come either, to tell you the truth. I need a party like a hole in the head. But you can't turn Marianne down can you?'

Julia looked up and smiled.

'No, you really can't. You can tell her till your blue in the face you don't want to do something, but somehow she gets her way.'

'Ah well, it was nice to see you. I miss that idiot of a husband of yours,' Cameron said quietly. He leaned forward and put his hand on her shoulder.

'Me too!'

Julia turned away slightly and the cold wind slapped into her face, drawing tears to her eyes.

Cameron pulled her towards him and wrapped his arms around her and hugged her.

'It will get better. One day. It has to; you'll see.'

He let go of her and Julia moved away, not sure whether to feel comforted or embarrassed by his affection. She wanted to change the subject though.

'So, how are you getting on? I was sorry to hear about you and Laura.'

Cameron laughed caustically. He leaned against the wall of the house, as if he suddenly needed the support. He was a giant of a man, but now he reminded Julia of a small unhappy boy who was trying to put on a brave face.

'Well I could cheerfully kill my brother, but otherwise…'

'That bad eh?'

'I just can't believe it, can you? You'd think you could trust your own brother, even if you couldn't trust your wife? And now they're both living in my house – the house I built – and I'm back living in my mum's old house. And my poor old mum's not even there now; God bless her, so I rattle around on my own going nuts. It's not fair.'

'No, it's not fair. Why don't you just sell your house and move on, both of you?'

'Amy would be heartbroken if she had to move. It's bad enough her mum and dad have split up; and I don't know how she's getting on with her Uncle John as her new "dad". How does a five year old process that?' Cameron ran a hand through his hair and paused for a moment. 'I just think it would be better if we left it a while. Laura's not in a hurry to move, that's for sure.'

'I can't imagine she would be; it's a lovely house. What about John's wife? How's she getting on?'

'Well wouldn't you know it, but Fiona's started seeing someone else now. So everyone's all fine and dandy, except me. The great big fucking mug that I am.'

'No you're not. Don't be silly. These things happen; you know that yourself.'

Cameron stood up straight suddenly, casting a shadow over Julia as he blocked out the light from the porch.

'So you think this is divine retribution for my earlier mistakes?'

'I don't think the world works that way actually. But you did do your own share of breaking hearts years ago.'

'So I deserve it?'

'No, of course you don't.'

Julia watched as the anger receded a little from his face. She smiled at him, and put her hand on his arm.

'We'll both be fine. Give it time. But's it's cold outside; I'm going in to find Marianne to say goodbye.'

Julia took off Marianne's jacket and hung it on the rack and walked down the hall. She paused by the kitchen door and reached in and put her glass down on the counter and walked away without looking at anyone. She headed for the lounge and found Marianne dancing with her husband. Their two teenage daughters were sitting on the sofa, holding cushions over their faces and giggling with embarrassment.

The song finished and Brian kissed Marianne which made their daughters scream and hurl the cushions at them.

Julia laughed and picked up the cushions that had landed at her feet. She carried them over to the sofa and sat down between Sophie and Isobel.

Sophie leaned against Julia and put her arm around her.

'How's it going Auntie Jules?'

'Not so bad. How are you two enjoying the party?'

'It would be better if mam and dad would stop behaving like idiots. They're so gross.'

Julia looked up at Marianne who was still standing in the middle of the room cuddling her husband.

'Would you rather they didn't get on with each other?' Julia asked Sophie.

'No, of course not. Just wish they wouldn't do that in public.'

'Change the music then, put on something less smoochie.'

Isobel leapt up from the sofa and ran to the iPod docking station and a moment later the music changed to something young and funky. Marianne and Brian grinned at each other and proceeded to dance to the music in an exaggeration of how people might dance at a rave; which drew howls of protest from their daughters. Sophie and Isobel left the room in a hurry.

Learning to Dance Again

Marianne stopped her manic jigging around on the dance floor and turned down the music a little.

'That's better,' she said, as she sat next to Julia. 'We won't see those little minxes again for a while.'

'We would have been embarrassed by our parents if they'd been cavorting about, dancing and kissing.'

'Of course we would!' Marianne replied, giggling mischievously. 'Anyway, where have you been hiding? I thought you'd gone home.'

'I went outside for a bit of fresh air. I was talking to Cameron.'

'Ah, misery likes company eh?'

Julia laughed. 'Something like that yeah.'

'Poor love! I do feel sorry for him, although I expect his first wife is laughing fit to burst.'

'I don't doubt it. I'm surprised she hasn't come back to Shetland just for a gloat.'

'Well, she was a stuck up bitch anyhow. And he's definitely a changed man now, especially after Amy came along.'

'So he should be. You can't run around like a young man staying out drinking and clubbing at our age.'

'Bet George Clooney does,' Marianne said.

'Cameron isn't George Clooney.'

'He is kind of nice looking though, don't you think?'

At that moment Cameron walked into the room doing up his coat. His head was bent forward, revealing a slightly thinning patch of hair that was only just starting to grey. He normally wore his dark brown hair really short, but he had clearly neglected to visit the barber for a while. His face looked a little tired, but underneath the sadness remained the good bone structure, clear skin and deep blue eyes that had given him the edge over many men, back when they were all young.

Marianne jumped up suddenly and grabbed hold of Cameron.

'For God's sake man, it's not even ten. Where do you think you're going so early? Take that coat off and dance with me.'

Marianne wrestled with Cameron and undid his jacket again.

'I don't really feel up to partying at the moment.'

'Of course not; we're all too old to party aren't we? We should just put on our slippers and go and get some Horlicks.' Marianne said, as she tugged his jacket off.

Cameron grinned at her and then looked over at Julia and shrugged, as if to say, "see what I mean."

Julia smiled in response and made herself comfortable on the sofa. She could see her bolt for freedom would be similarly thwarted by Marianne.

After a few minutes Cameron managed to escape from Marianne and he flopped down next to Julia.

'I thought you were leaving,' he said.

'I thought you were too.'

'I did try.'

'We'll make a dash for it when her back's turned. It's Marianne remember; she'll be after a drink any time now.'

As if she had heard Julia, Marianne stopped dancing and started hunting around the coffee tables and sideboard for her glass. Then she left the room and headed for the kitchen.

'Told you!' Julia said, although she didn't make a move to get up and go.

'Would you like another drink before you go?' Cameron asked.

'I don't know; if I have another, then I really can't drive home.'

'We can share a taxi.'

'You live in the opposite direction.'

Cameron shrugged and stood up.

'Oh all right then, I'll have a whisky with ice.' Julia sighed, knowing she had just committed herself to staying for the duration of the party, which could go on all night if Marianne had her way. Julia could always disappear upstairs to the spare room of course, which Marianne had reserved for her in case she stayed over, but there would be little chance of getting any sleep until the party was over.

Julia stood up and decided to go in search of Cameron and change her drink from whisky to lemonade. She wanted to keep her options open. She found him standing by the fridge using the ice-dispenser.

'Oh good, you haven't poured me a whisky yet. I think I might go for a soft drink instead.'

Cameron turned and picked up a glass that contained whisky and ice.

'I already got yours. This is for Paula.'

He handed Julia her drink and then turned and passed the tumbler full of ice to Paula who sparkled at him flirtatiously. Paula caught sight of Julia and her smile vanished. She dropped her head to one side with elaborate sympathy.

'How are you Julia? This must be so difficult for you?'

Julia resisted the urge to slap her.

'It's not difficult at all. I'm just going to rake in the insurance money and jet off somewhere hot and sunny.'

Before Paula could reply Julia turned and rushed back to the lounge and sat down, her face flushed with anger. Cameron sat down next to her a moment later.

'What was all that about?'

'I heard her talking about me while I was outside. Two faced bitch!'

'Is that why you wanted to go home?'

Julia nodded and took a large sip of whisky.

'Well I'm glad you're still here. We can be miserable together; with alcohol. What's not to like?'

They sat and talked; about Duncan, their kids, marriages, careers and life in general. Occasionally someone else would come over and join in. Marianne cracked open some more Champagne and kept the drinks flowing. Before too long Julia started to feel a little woozy. She stood up to go to the bathroom, and swayed. Cameron took her arm and she giggled like a school girl.

'I think I'd better stop drinking,' she said.

'I must be getting old; all I can think of is having a nice cup of tea,' he replied.

Julia roared with laughter.

'Me too! Go and put the kettle on while I nip upstairs to the loo.'

When she came downstairs she went to the kitchen and found Cameron making tea. There was still a hard core of party animals in the kitchen. Brian was standing by the sink and he grinned at Julia.

'Are you moving on to the hard stuff now?'

'It was Cameron's idea to make tea, but I'm desperate for a cuppa now. All that whisky makes you thirsty.'

Cameron handed Julia a mug.

'White no sugar, right?'

'You know me well!'

Julia turned to leave the kitchen but not before she saw Paula nudging one of her friends and sneering in her direction. As the music paused she heard Paula say, '...she's moving on quickly...'

Julia carried her tea into the lounge and sat down again, this time next to Marianne's sister, Charlotte, and started chatting to her. Julia felt exhausted suddenly; the tea was not having the desired effect. When Charlotte got up to get another drink, Julia stood up and wandered out to the kitchen to put her mug into the dishwasher. She saw Paula and her husband were putting their coats on and saying goodbye to people. She turned and walked back into the hall and crashed into Cameron.

'There's a taxi outside. It's not for you is it?' Cameron said.

'No, but I really want to leave; I'm exhausted.'

'Let's go then shall we?'

Julia grinned. She grabbed her coat and handbag from the rack by the front door and ran outside. Cameron hurried after her.

Julia opened the rear door of the car and jumped in.

'Hi Julia, I thought I was picking Paula and Dave up,' the driver said.

'Oh they're not ready yet, if you call them another taxi it will be fine.'

Cameron climbed in beside Julia.

As the car pulled out of Marianne's drive Julia looked back and saw Paula open the front door and raise her hand to call back the taxi. Julia couldn't resist waving at her.

'Well that's blown it. Paula's going to be furious with me now,' Julia whispered.

'Serves her right,' Cameron replied.

Julia reached into her handbag and took out her phone and started writing a text to Marianne.

"Sorry I did a Cinderella on your party. Fit for nothing but my bed now. It was a great evening! Xx."

8

Julia went indoors, slipping off her high heels as soon as she closed the front door. She hurried upstairs to her bedroom and undressed quickly. Despite being exhausted, and it being long after midnight, she decided to take a bath. She poured a generous measure of Jo Malone's wild fig and cassis bath oil under the hot tap, lit the matching scented candle and then switched the light off. The candle flickered, and she stood watching the bath fill up, breathing in the scented oil; last year's Christmas present from Duncan.

The bathroom filled with the sweet perfume and warm steam. It should have been comforting, but Julia felt a renewed sense of grief, ably assisted by too much whisky and Champagne. She felt like her heart would break. She sank beneath the water and sulked, not caring the bath oil would make her hair greasy.

She surfaced again; breathless. She was wide awake now; having a bath never seemed to have the desired soporific effect on her.

She sat on the bed wrapped in a towel and switched on the television. As usual for a Saturday night/Sunday morning, there was nothing of interest to watch. She scrolled through the Sky+ menu looking for something she had recorded and not got around to watching. She came across the holiday programme she had watched with Duncan the night before he died. She pressed play as she rubbed her hair dry and then dropped the towel on the floor beside the bed, in the same way Duncan used to do. As she climbed under the duvet, Sicily came to life on the screen.

When she had watched the programme before, she had been too busy to concentrate. She had been fussing around in the kitchen, making Duncan's lunch for the following day. The television had been on in the lounge and Duncan had called her in a couple of times to watch it with him. She had seen the last twenty minutes, enough to agree Sicily looked lovely.

This time, with no interruptions, she watched the whole programme, gawping at the bright blue sea and sunshine. She understood why Duncan had been attracted to the place. It looked wild, exotic, and stuffed full of history; and the food looked amazing too. She watched as the presenter tucked into a dish of Parma ham and grilled figs. She pulled at a damp strand of her fig perfumed hair and inhaled.

The handsome Anglo-Italian presenter was talking about the weather and said one of the best times to visit was September, when the summer crowds had gone and the weather was more bearable. It was still in the mid-twenties Celsius and would stay reasonably warm through to December. It sounded like heaven.

Julia woke up with a headache, to the sound of rain battering the bedroom windows and the roof of the conservatory. She sat up stiffly, put her hand on her head and pulled at her hair, surprised to find it hanging in limp oily rats' tails. Her hair still reeked of figs; then she remembered taking the bath after the party. She picked up her mobile phone and checked for messages. There was one from Marianne, sent around 3.00am.

"Cheeky mare taking Paula's taxi! She was hopping mad with you. Why did I invite her anyway, she can be such a bitch? FYI she thinks you have your "hooks" into Cameron. Silly cow!"

Hooks? Into Cameron? Oh for fuck's sake, thought Julia. She felt like screaming. Wasn't it bad enough to be grieving for Duncan without people saying stupid things about her? She wished she hadn't gone to the party. She pulled the duvet over her head and prayed for sleep.

She woke up an hour later when the phone rang. It was Marianne.

'I'm so hung-over, what was I thinking at my age?'

'You don't sound hung-over? Go away and let me go back to sleep,' Julia said.

Marianne laughed before she replied, 'oh, are you still in bed? It's nearly eleven.'

'I didn't get much sleep last night.'

'You OK?'

'Yes, no, maybe.'

'Thanks for coming last night. I know it's hard work being at a party when you feel so terrible. I really appreciated it though. And I'm sure Cameron enjoyed your company too. He's not in a good place either.'

'I really hope people don't start thinking there's anything going on.'

'What does it matter what people think?'

'It matters to me; and I certainly wouldn't want Jamie and Bryden to hear anything.'

'But nothing happened last night, so why would they?'

'I don't know. Maybe I'm paranoid. I probably just drank too much.'

'Well you're entitled to let your hair down once in a while. I really missed Duncan last night. It's not a proper party without him.' Marianne sighed, and they were silent for a moment.

Julia got out of bed holding the cordless phone to her ear and looked out of the bedroom window. The rain had stopped but the sky was still gloomy.

'I don't know what we're going to do for your fiftieth in a few weeks. Maybe just a quiet dinner eh? Will the boys get back for it?'

'I don't think so. I hadn't really thought that far ahead,' Julia replied, without any enthusiasm in her voice.

'Well anyway, thanks for coming. I'll let you get back to sleep. See you later in the week, eh?'

Julia put the phone down and decided to get up. Her headache had subsided and she was hungry. She went downstairs thinking about her own forthcoming "big" birthday. She felt a sense of dread at the idea of turning fifty. She felt so old, which was not helped by having two grown up sons and being widowed. It was different for Marianne, whose younger daughters were still at school; or even for someone like Cameron who had married a much younger woman and now had a five year old daughter to keep him young.

As she waited for the kettle to boil she stared at the calendar and the little red heart drawn in felt-tip which Duncan had scribbled on her birthday. She doubted her sons would be able to get home in time. Bryden would be busy teaching and wouldn't be able to get away until a week later, for the school holidays, and Jamie would be in the middle of a surgical rotation.

Julia made herself a sandwich and some coffee and took her breakfast into the lounge. She moved her iPad along the sofa and put her feet up and thought about her birthday. She was certain Marianne would plan something for her. It would be lovely and thoughtful; but Julia didn't feel like being sociable, especially if it meant she might have to deal with Cameron again.

What she hadn't told Marianne was Cameron had tried to kiss her, in the back of the taxi. It was probably only intended to be a friendly kiss on the cheek, but somehow his lips had met hers, and she had pushed him away, jumped out of the taxi and hurried indoors without saying goodbye, or even offering to pay her share of the fare. She really didn't want to see him again for a while.

Julia finished her sandwich and switched on her iPad to check her emails. Her Facebook habit had diminished considerably; she only looked at it occasionally to check up on her sons.

Her only emails were spam and as she scrolled through the titles, checking them off to delete without reading, she spotted an email from a travel website announcing a sale on flights to Europe during October and November. She opened the email and clicked on the link to their website. One of the first offers to appear on the page was a return flight to Palermo in Sicily for £69. Despite the fact she knew this incredibly low price would not include anything such as luggage, booking fees and was probably for silly dates and times she clicked on the offer to see more details.

Without thinking very clearly about what she was doing she booked herself a return flight to Palermo from Gatwick for the entire month of October. She entered her credit card details and completed the purchase, and then leaned back on the sofa in triumph. Then she sat up again quickly. October was less than two weeks away and she hadn't booked any accommodation or flights down to London. She would be away for her birthday now and Marianne would not be pleased. Or maybe she would, but she wondered what the boys would say about her taking off on her own like that.

'I'm a grown-up!' Julia said aloud. 'Oh help. Where am I going to stay for a whole month?'

She got up and took her tray out to the kitchen then picked up the phone to call Marianne.

'I've just booked a holiday in Sicily.'

'Oh good for you. When are you going?'

'In a few days; for the whole of October!'

'A whole month? Are you serious? What are you going to do for so long on your own?'

'Four times what I would do if I just went for a week.'

'Very funny! Where are you staying?'

'I don't know yet. I just booked the flights and haven't even looked for somewhere to stay. I'll look for a nice hotel somewhere.'

'Why don't you rent a villa? We used that website, villas-direct or something, when we went to Spain last summer. It was far nicer than staying in a hotel.'

'Brilliant idea; I'll do that now. I don't know what Jamie and Bryden will say. They'll probably think I've lost my marbles.'

'So? You're a grown up now.'

Julia decided to book all her accommodation before telling her sons she was going away. She followed Marianne's advice and found a two bedroomed villa in a small village near Cefalu, close to the sea. The owner lived in the adjoining villa and there was shared access to a swimming pool and a lovely terraced garden with fig and olive trees. The rent she negotiated with the English owner for the whole of October was a bargain, as it was out of season.

There was so much to do before her holiday she really didn't have time to be miserable. She spent the next few days running around, buying clothes for her holiday and then taking them back to the shop when she realised they made her look like somebody's granny. She bought euros, travel insurance and medication. She made sure all her bills were paid, spring-cleaned the house, bought batteries for her camera and then packed and repacked her bags, unable to decide what to take. She took her houseplants around to Marianne's for her to water, and then raided Marianne's wardrobe for holiday clothes to borrow.

She rang Jamie to tell him her plans.

'Hello darling. I've got a surprise for you and Bryden. I'm going to be in Edinburgh for a couple of days?'

'Why?'

I'm travelling through, on my way down to Gatwick. I'm going on holiday.'

'Who are you going with?'

I'm going on my own – to Sicily.'

'On your own – to Sicily? Are you mad?'

'What's wrong with Sicily? It looks lovely.'

'I'm sure it is; if you stay out of the way of the mafia.'

'Don't be silly, I'm sure they're much too busy to bother with me. I bet that stuff's all exaggerated.'

'Really? Well I don't suppose you'll get in too much bother in a week. Might be good for you to have a break.'

'I'm going for a month actually; and Jamie, do try to be a little less patronising. I'm nearly fifty. I can look after myself.'

Clearly all Jamie heard was "a month."

'You can't go away for a whole month on your own, what if something happens to you?'

'There's Wi-Fi in the villa, I can email you or ring you every day if you want. Nothing's going to happen to me,' Julia replied, feeling less and less sure of herself as Jamie railed against her mad idea. Eventually Julia got annoyed with him and snapped she would see him in Edinburgh before she left, and put the phone down.

She rang Bryden and he was a lot more cheerful about the prospect, particularly when she told him she had booked a two bedroomed villa. He said he would think about coming out to see her during the school holidays. When Julia offered to pay for his flights he was even more enthusiastic about the idea.

Julia had finally packed everything for her trip. Her suitcase and handbag were in the porch and her raincoat was folded over the top; all ready to go the next day. She had gone through the "tickets, passport, money" routine until she thought she was in danger of developing OCD.

She was in the kitchen making something to eat when she heard a car. She went to the door and saw Cameron's Toyota Prius parked on the drive. He got out of the car and then opened the back passenger door and let his daughter out. Amy was struggling under the weight of a large bouquet of roses. Cameron took them off her and held his daughter's hand and led her to the house.

'Hello Amy,' Julia said, trying to sound welcoming, at least to the little girl. 'Come along inside. I've got some juice and chocolate biscuits.'

Amy let go of Cameron's hand and ran indoors and headed straight for the lounge. Julia heard the television channel change to a cartoon.

'Confident little thing isn't she?'

'She is. You don't mind me bringing her do you? It's my turn to have her tonight and we didn't know what to do this evening. I bought you these; to say sorry.'

Julia took the flowers from him and stood back to let him in.

'Sorry for what?'

'You know, for getting drunk and being silly.'

'You must buy a lot of flowers.'

Cameron grinned sheepishly, and shut the front door behind him. He followed her into the kitchen, pulled out a chair and sat down at the table.

'Would you like a tea or coffee? Would Amy like a drink?'

'Yeah sure, tea for me; Amy drinks milk or water usually.'

Julia took a glass of milk and a biscuit into the lounge for Amy and then came back and made a pot of tea. She handed Cameron a mug.

'Aren't you going to put the roses in water?' Cameron said, breaking the awkward silence.

'No, you'll have to take them home with you. I'm going on holiday tomorrow so I won't get the benefit from them. But thanks anyway.'

'Holiday? Where are you going?'

'Sicily. Duncan said he wanted to go there, just a few hours before he died. And I decided, if I'm going to sit around feeling sorry for myself, then I may as well do it where it's sunny and warm.'

'That's a brilliant idea. I've never been to Italy, although everyone who goes seems to like it. Good for you!'

'I'm going down to stay with Bryden to catch up with the boys for a couple of days, then I'm flying down to Gatwick and then off to Sicily for the whole of October.'

'Wow, you don't do things by halves.'

'It was a bit spur of the moment, but it was such a bargain for the flights and accommodation. And it gets me out of the country on my birthday. I shall have a memorial service for my youth on my own. A nice restaurant with a glass or two of Prosecco. Sounds perfect!'

'It does actually. God, I wish I could just take off for a few weeks.'

Cameron sipped his tea thoughtfully. Julia peered through to the lounge and saw Amy was curled up in an armchair watching a pop video. Her milk was untouched on the coffee table.

'So, we're still friends then?' Cameron said.

Julia snapped her attention back to him.

'Yes,' she replied cautiously. 'We've been friends since we were bairns, one stupid drunken kiss doesn't change anything. But two might!' She stood up abruptly and took her mug to the sink.

'We'd better get going, leave you to get ready for your holiday.'

'I'm already sorted, see!' Julia replied, pointing to her suitcase.

'Well anyway.'

Cameron stood up and went to get Amy. She got up from the chair without argument and switched off the television. She picked up her glass and drank most of the milk and handed it back to Julia.

'Thanks!'

'You're welcome.'

'Daddy's getting me a kitten tomorrow.'

'Is he now? That's very exciting. I'll have to come and see him.'

'It's a girl kitten; her name is Jessie J.'

'That's a bit like Postman Pat's cat. That's called Jess.'

Amy looked puzzled.

'She doesn't watch Postman Pat. Too old fashioned,' Cameron said, raising his eyes to heaven.

Julia laughed.

'Jessie J the kitten. That's going to be fun for you.'

Cameron shrugged. 'It will be company for me when she's not around.'

'I might have to get one too,' Julia replied, as she followed them out to the porch.

'You have a good holiday. Take care now!' Cameron smiled at her, and took Amy's hand.

'I'll put up some pictures of the sunshine on Facebook. Make you jealous!'

'Do that! See you when you come back.'

'Don't forget the roses.'

Julia hurried back and retrieved them from the kitchen worktop.

'Didn't you like the flowers? Daddy bought them in Tesco for you. They cost £9.99 and I put the money in the funny machine. I got a penny back,' Amy said, reaching into her pocket and producing her change.

Julia grinned at Cameron and handed the roses to Amy.

'You should have them in your room, Amy. Your daddy really bought them for you as a surprise.'

Amy's eyes widened with pleasure.

'Thanks Daddy. A kitten and flowers! Can't wait to tell Mummy and Uncle John.'

Amy stepped outside and didn't see Cameron put his fingers to his temple and pretend to shoot himself.

'The innocence of youth; thanks anyway. I'll see you when I get back home,' Julia said. She reached out and touched his arm and squeezed it. Cameron smiled and followed his daughter out to the car.

9

Julia emerged into the bright Sicilian sunshine from the starkly contrasting gloom of the airport arrivals hall in Palermo. Weary from an early morning start at Gatwick and a sleepless night in a noisy airport hotel, she made her way towards the adjoining train station.

The marble hall of the station was refreshingly cool and there was a train sitting expectantly on the platform. Julia hurried towards the ticket office, mentally rehearsing how she would ask for a ticket to Cefalu in Italian. The word for ticket seemed straightforward enough, if she remembered not to pronounce the g – un biglietto per Cefalu, per favore.

The young man behind the counter frowned at her as she stood, plucking up the courage to speak.

'Prego,' he snapped.

'Um, sorry? Oh I mean, un biglietto per Cefalu, si'vous plait, I mean, per favore.'

'Cefalu?'

'Si?'

He printed the ticket and tapped on the till so she could see the price. She handed over a fifty euro note and the man muttered under his breath in response, she could only guess it was because he was running out of change.

Julia took the ticket and turned towards the platform. The departures board indicated the train would leave in five minutes.

Julia dragged her suitcase along the platform and got onto the train and sat down gratefully.

She sighed with relief at having successfully negotiated her first Italian transaction. She put the ticket in her handbag and sat with her hands protectively over it, and looked around at the other passengers, listening to the sound of their voices; snippets of Italian gossip she had no hope of understanding, but it sounded so exciting.

The train doors slammed shut after a garbled announcement of the destinations. Julia realised she had not pronounced the name Cefalu properly when she had bought the ticket; it was Chefaloo, not Kefaloo. No wonder the poor man in the ticket office had been so impatient with her.

The train pulled out of the dark station and back into the bright sunshine that blinded Julia to the view. Her sunglasses were packed inside her suitcase, and she didn't want to open it up on the train. She picked up her suitcase and shuffled across the aisle to the seats on the other side.

Julia took out her guide book to Sicily and opened up the well-thumbed page containing the map. The train-line hugged the North coast and would cut through Palermo and other seaside towns until it reached Cefalu and would then continue on to Messina, where it was possible to cross the narrow stretch of sea to the Italian mainland. She looked up from the book and concentrated on the view. The landscape was browner than she had imagined it would be. For some reason she had envisaged green fields, full of lush lemon trees and olive plantations. There were a few trees dotted about in the gardens of the apartments and villas she passed, but there were vast patches of bare terracotta soil, bleached by the sun; rocky and barren in places. It was still exotically attractive, particularly with the deep blue sea in the background.

Despite the fact Julia had a sea view all year round from her house her attention was still drawn to the water. This was the kind of blue only available to Shetlanders on special days, when the skies were clear of clouds. Those were the days she loved best of all, and she smiled when she realised this would be her view of the sea for whole of October; or at least she hoped it would.

Julia turned her gaze to the young woman opposite her. She wore a cream linen skirt suit, with short sleeves that exposed lean bronzed arms and a jangle of bracelets on each wrist. She had a corporate looking briefcase beside her, which looked incongruous with her vertiginous strappy sandals, coiffed hair and oversized sunglasses. She flicked through her Italian *Vogue* magazine impatiently, and then flung it on the seat beside her and reached into her pocket for her phone. She appeared equally annoyed with the phone and after tapping at it with her perfectly manicured fingers, she set it down on top of her magazine, but did not let go of it. She looked up and met Julia's eyes and turned away to look out of the window, clearly disgruntled with something.

Julia wondered what it was like to be so young, glamorous and attractive; she had never looked as immaculate at this young woman. She turned her attention to some of the other passengers and noticed the women, even the ones who were clearly older than herself, all looked glossy and elegant. She looked down at her jeans and flat, comfy Clarks' sandals, her chain store tee shirt and felt very drab. She was like a dull brown Shetland wren by comparison to the pretty canaries that shared the carriage.

The door to the carriage slammed shut. She looked up and saw a man in uniform weaving his way towards her, pausing to check tickets. He grunted his thanks and passed the tickets back to people, without a smile on his face. However, when he noticed the woman opposite Julia, his whole demeanour changed instantly. He leaned proprietorially close to her and rested his hand on the back of her seat. The woman moved away from him and reached into her bag for her ticket. They exchanged words, none of which Julia could understand, but it was obvious the ticket inspector was trying, unsuccessfully, to flirt with her. Brushing off his rejection he turned to Julia and scowled.

Julia handed him her ticket, her hand waiting mid-air for him to give it back. However, the inspector did not seem very happy with it. He launched into what seemed to be a familiar speech. He poked the ticket and showed it to Julia.

'I'm sorry, I don't understand,' Julia said.

'You not validate ticket, fifty euro fine please.'

Julia stared at the man, who glared back.

'I bought the ticket just now, what's wrong with it? I don't understand.'

The inspector, having run out of the only English he knew to explain the situation, sighed in exaggerated bad temper.

'Fifty euro fine please.'

Julia had no idea what she had done wrong but she obviously had to pay some money or maybe risk being thrown off the train at the next stop. She started to unzip her handbag to get her purse out, but in her haste the zip caught on the silk lining of the bag and refused to budge. She tugged at it, making it worse, all the while the inspector stood beside her, muttering darkly. She didn't need to be bilingual to understand what he thought of her. When the zip refused to move in either direction, Julia's hands started to shake with frustration and nerves.

'I come back!'

The inspector handed Julia her ticket and walked away, checking other passengers tickets as he went. Julia took a deep breath and returned to the task of trying to open her handbag. The zip still refused to open though.

'Can I try?'

Julia looked up and saw the young woman lean forward and smile.

'It happens to me all the time. I'm good at this.'

Julia handed the bag to her. The woman slipped an elegant finger inside and eased at the fabric and then carefully released the fold of material that had jammed the zip. She unzipped the bag a couple of inches then passed it back to Julia.

'Thanks so much. I was getting really worried there; I wasn't expecting to pay a fine on my ticket. Do you know what's wrong with it?'

'Oh, it's simple; you did not validate the ticket before you got on the train. There are machines at the station that stamp the time and date so you can only use the ticket once. So many tourists get caught out. It's a silly system; but now you know.'

'Oh, right. How stupid of me; I didn't know you had to do that. I've never been on a train in another country before. In fact I have hardly ever been on a train, full stop.'

The woman smiled in sympathy. Julia took out her purse and withdrew a fifty euro note and held it in her hand in readiness for the inspector's return.

'You are on holiday on your own? You are visiting friends?'

'Yes, I'm on my own. My husband died recently. He really wanted to visit Sicily, so I decided to come here anyway.'

'Oh; I'm so sorry.'

Julia smiled her thanks, just as the inspector appeared at her side again. Once again he leered at the young woman, who turned away from him in disgust.

Before Julia had time to give him the money the young woman suddenly launched into a tirade of abuse at him. He stepped back in surprise, and although he was annoyed, his shoulders dropped a little of their swagger. He turned and looked at Julia, and she realised she was being talked about.

He waved away the money from Julia and stalked off in a huff.

'Thank you; but what just happened?'

'I told him off for being rude to a widow, and for harassing a young female lawyer.'

'That's very kind of you. And thank you for telling me how to use the ticket machines. I won't make that mistake again.'

'No problem. It's my stop now. Enjoy Sicily.'

The train pulled into *Palermo Centrale* station and the woman got off with a little wave to Julia.

The rest of the journey passed without any further drama and ninety minutes later Julia got off the train at Cefalu, into the scorching mid-day sun.

She wheeled her suitcase over to the café just outside the station and took a seat at a table outside. A waiter hurried over and handed her a menu.

She ordered a dish of strawberry gelato and a bottle of mineral water. While she waited for her order she watched people wandering in and out of the station. A young couple pulled up on a scooter close to her table. The girl climbed off the back of the scooter and kissed her boyfriend. Neither of them wore a crash helmet which made Julia feel anxious on behalf of their parents. The girl turned and walked towards the station, click-clacking along the pavement on high heeled sandals; she paused and blew her boyfriend another kiss and he revved the engine of his moped and sped off.

Julia took out her phone and sent the landlord of her holiday villa a text to say she had arrived in Cefalu and was at the café where they had agreed to meet. Almost immediately she got a text back saying he would be along to pick her up in twenty minutes. Her gelato arrived as she put the phone back in her bag.

Julia was pretty fond of ice cream, but this was strawberry flavoured heaven. She sighed with pleasure and put the spoon down. She did not want to rush this moment. It was so strange sitting in the sunshine eating gelato when just a few hours earlier she had been in chilly rainy London, and a few days before that in even colder, rainier Shetland. She took out her phone again and took a photograph of the gelato and sent it to Marianne.

She got a text a moment later.

"Lucky cow! It's not ice cream weather here. Enjoy! Any gorgeous Italian stallions in sight?"

Julia looked around and noticed an old man selling newspapers from a cart outside the station. He wore a dark blue cap pulled down over his eyes and a battered looking leather jacket, which made Julia feel hotter than she already was. She discreetly took a photograph of him and sent it to Marianne.

"You wouldn't think it was so hot here. He must be melting," Julia wrote.

She finished her dessert, savouring every intense mouthful, and drank her water and felt a little more refreshed after the tiring journey. She wanted nothing more than to get to her villa, unpack and then have a lazy afternoon by the pool, or even a siesta.

A bright red Fiat 500 convertible pulled up outside the station. An elegant middle-aged man got out of the car and leaned against the door. He wore a white linen shirt, cream trousers and brown leather loafers. He took off his sunglasses and looked over at Julia and waved.

Julia paid the waiter and hurried over towards him.

'Hello, you must be Julia. Lovely to meet you; I'm Tony Hugo. Welcome to Sicily!'

Julia shook hands with him.

'Nice to meet you too. Thanks for coming to pick me up.'

'No problem. Let me take your bag.'

'Lovely car! I don't think I've ever been in a car with the roof down before. This should be fun.'

'Oh that's right; you're from Shetland aren't you? Well this must be a pleasant change for you.'

Julia grinned at him as she got in the passenger seat.

'Just a bit.'

Tony started the engine and they set off along the busy street towards the town centre and then took a sharp turn towards the mountains that rose up almost immediately from the edge of the town.

A cooling breeze ruffled Julia's hair and she rested her arm on the edge of the door.

'How was your journey here?' Tony asked.

'Well apart from nearly getting a fifty euro fine for not validating my train ticket, it wasn't bad. And I'm a little bit tired now after getting up at five this morning.'

'Well you have a whole month to get over that. I've never had anyone staying that long before. Most people come for just a week or two. What prompted you to come over here for so long?'

Julia paused for a moment, wondering whether to tell him the truth or to find some more palatable explanation. She had no idea how much contact she would have with her landlord.

'It's my fiftieth birthday this month, and I really didn't feel much like celebrating it, so I decided to run away to Sicily and hide away from the world.'

'That's a bit drastic. You don't look that old; why are you so fed up about turning fifty?

'Well,' Julia sighed, 'the truth is, my husband died in April and I've been sitting around the house ever since, getting more and more fed up. I decided I might as well be miserable in the sun.'

'Ah, I see. I'm sorry to hear that. My wife died five years ago so I know how you feel. Well, I can certainly promise you some sunshine, and I hope it makes you feel a little less miserable.'

'Did it work for you?'

'Not really; no.'

Tony smiled conspiratorially at her as they stopped at a junction and waited for a gap in the traffic.

'What brought you to Sicily? You're English aren't you?'

'My wife was Italian. Eleonora taught English at the University in Palermo; but we met in London while she was still studying.'

'I see. So what do you do?'

'I'm a writer; so I can pretty much work where I like.'

'What kind of writing do you do?'

'Crime novels mostly.'

Julia turned to look at him; she was picturing the bookshelf in her bedroom. There were a number of novels sitting on the shelves that Duncan had enjoyed reading, and she had an image of one of them in her head.

'Don't tell me you're Anthony Hugo who wrote *In Too Deep*?'

'That's me,' he replied, looking faintly embarrassed.

'Duncan used to read your books. We have some at home. I haven't read any of them though, sorry. Wow, I can't believe it. Duncan would have been thrilled to have met you.'

'Thank you. I'm sorry I didn't get to meet him too. I don't meet many people who have read my books any more. I don't do book tours these days. My publisher gets pissed off with me, but since Eleonora died, I can't be arsed to leave Sicily much. I don't have many reasons to go back to the UK. My parents died years ago, and my son and daughter live in Italy. They're both at University in Rome.'

They were driving down a very narrow lane lined with trees and giant cactus plants. Tony slowed the car and turned into a driveway and stopped in front of a wrought iron gate. He picked up a remote control from a compartment on the dashboard and pointed it at a control on the gatepost. The gate swung open slowly and they carried on up the long shady driveway until the villa came into view.

An old and battered blue Fiat Panda was parked on the driveway next to a white scooter. Tony parked the car and got out and opened up the boot. He took out Julia's suitcase and led the way to the side of the main house.

Julia followed, feeling a quiver of excitement at seeing where she would be spending the next few weeks. At the back of the villa there was an open view of the sea. Julia hadn't appreciated how high up the side of the mountain they had driven; it hadn't seemed very far, and yet they seemed to be looking down at the sea from a great height.

'Wow, what a view. This is even better than it looked online.'

'Everybody says that. It's hard to get a photograph to do this justice.'

They crossed a paved terrace and stopped at a little iron gate in the middle of a low hedge. Tony opened it and Julia followed him to the little stone built villa. It shared the same view of the sea as the main house, but was actually quite private in its own little garden.

Tony opened the front door and stood back to let Julia in. It was disappointingly dark inside and Julia bit her lip anxiously, as she surveyed the open plan living room and kitchen. The windows were covered by dark wooden shutters that made it seem like late evening, rather than the middle of the day.

'I closed the shutters as it gets a bit hot in here when the sun comes up in the morning. It's up to you whether you open them or not.' Tony stood by the open door and indicated outside, 'it's quite private out here on the veranda; nobody can see you from my villa. You can get to the swimming pool from a gate at the bottom of your garden. The pool is heated by solar energy and I hardly ever use it so you will have it to yourself most of the time.'

'That's great thanks.'

'I was just wondering how you're going to get around, as you haven't hired a car yet? I can recommend a car hire company in the town if you like.'

'Actually, I have a confession to make; I've never driven a car on mainland Britain, let alone a foreign country. I was too scared to hire a car. But we're only a couple of miles out of the town aren't we. I thought I might just walk everywhere, and maybe get a taxi if I have groceries to carry.'

'It might only be two miles but it's not a road I would particularly recommend walking along. It's not very safe for pedestrians, not the way us locals drive along it; and taxis cost the earth in Sicily. Hiring a car might be your best option, if you can pluck up the courage; and it's probably not as bad driving over here as you might think.'

Julia pulled a face, as if she didn't believe him. He laughed.

'One of my sons is thinking of joining me for a few days, with his girlfriend. He'll definitely hire a car, so I think I'll manage alright. We'll see.'

Tony spent a few minutes explaining how the satellite television, the hot water and the air conditioning worked in the property. When he had finished Julia followed him out to the veranda and they stood for a moment looking down at the sea.

'I was just thinking; unless you go into town again this afternoon, you won't be able to cook anything for your dinner. I'm having some friends over later; you're more than welcome to join us. They all speak English.'

'Thanks, but I feel really tired now, I might just have a quiet first night here.'

'Well if you change your mind, we'll be eating around nine. Us Sicilians eat very late at night.'

'I think I'll be fast asleep by that time,' Julia said, yawning already.

'Just come to the house if you need anything. I work from home, so if my car's outside, then I'm in.'

Julia took a few minutes to explore the villa. It was even more luxurious than she had imagined it would be. There were two bedrooms which had large shuttered windows. One room faced the mountain and the other faced the sea. She couldn't make up her mind which one she wanted to sleep in. Both views were lovely.

The kitchen was equipped with everything she would need. There was a bottle of Prosecco chilling in the fridge, a large bottle of locally produced olive oil in the cupboard and a fruit bowl full of fresh lemons and limes, which she presumed had been picked from the trees outside. There was no other food though, and Julia realised she would have to find some way of getting to the supermarket fairly soon.

However, for the time being she was too tired to think about food. She took a quick shower and then changed into a floral maxi-dress Marianne had lent her. It was cool and elegant, and when she found her sunglasses at the bottom of her case she put them on and ventured outside.

Julia pulled a wooden sun-lounger into the shade of the veranda and lay down on it, not even bothering to find a book to read. She shut her eyes and was asleep within minutes.

She woke up three hours later, at the sound of someone speaking to her. The sun had almost set behind the mountain and it was noticeably cooler. She sat up and turned to see a woman standing by the gate to the property.

'Scusi, Signora. I'm Signor Hugo's housekeeper, Maria. I go shopping; you want a list?'

Julia stood up and smiled. She reached out to shake hands.

'I'm Julia; lovely to meet you. I would love to get some groceries; could I come with you?'

Maria took a moment to translate this then shook her head.

'I'm sorry, I go home now. I go shopping in morning when I come to work. I get what you need tomorrow.'

'Of course, Maria. Let me write a list; do come in won't you.'

Julia found a notebook and pen in her handbag and started to write a couple of things down.

Maria watched for a moment then frowned.

'I'm sorry, I not read English.'

'Ah, OK, how about if I tell you and you write it down.'

Maria smiled and took the pen from Julia.

'Bread, milk, coffee, butter .....' Julia paused for a moment. She couldn't really think what she needed and had no idea what was available in an Italian supermarket. Would she look stupid if she asked for dried pasta? And even more stupid if she asked for a jar of Dolmio pasta sauce? Of course she would.

'I buy you things for breakfast, and some meat and vegetables, and some rice and pasta?' Maria said helpfully.

'Yes, how about if I just give you some money and you buy what you think I need for a few days. That would be lovely. Then I will find my own way to the supermarket.'

Julia handed Maria two fifty euro notes, making a mental note to ask Tony how much she should pay Maria for doing the shopping.

'You are having dinner with Signor Hugo tonight? I make roast lamb for him; his favourite.'

Julia didn't want to have dinner with Tony and his friends, but she didn't want to tell Maria that, in case she thought she was snubbing her cooking.

'Oh yes, that would be very nice. Thank you.'

She followed Maria out to the veranda to say goodbye.

'I show you herb garden,' Maria said, taking Julia's arm and leading her to the side of the villa.

Tucked away out of sight was a fairly large vegetable plot, surrounded by fig and olive trees. Trained against the boundary wall was a grapevine and further along the wall was a wigwam structure weighed down by tomato plants. In a variety of pots and stone planters were a selection of herbs, garlic bulbs and onions.

Maria led the way towards the back of the garden to a wooden shed. As they got closer Julia realised it was a hen house. The hens had been put away for the night, but they started to cluck anxiously as Julia and Maria approached.

Maria lifted a lid of a box that jutted out from the side of the hen house. Inside was a bundle of straw and in the centre were two brown eggs. Maria took the eggs out and handed them to Julia. One of them was still warm. Maria lifted another lid and inside was a hen sitting there staring back at them. Maria pushed it gently out of the way and retrieved another egg and passed it to Julia.

'You take eggs every day and any vegetables you want.'

'Thank you. That's brilliant,' Julia replied, realising with relief she now had everything she needed to make herself something for dinner without having to go next door. She grinned at Maria and they turned back towards the house.

After Maria had gone, Julia went back to the garden and picked a handful of tomatoes, pulled up some garlic and then found some onions and potatoes which she helped herself to. She picked some oregano and carried her raided goodies back to the kitchen. She opened the fridge and took out the bottle of Prosecco.

She poured herself a glass of the sparkling wine and set about making frittata. She put the radio on and found a station playing Italian pop music interspersed with some British and American songs. She sang along as she chopped vegetables.

She felt inexplicably cheerful as she stirred the garlic and onions in the frying pan. She took a sip of wine and stared out of the window at the unfamiliar but beautiful view. She thought of Duncan and wished he was here to see how lovely Sicily really was. But for the first time in months she didn't feel as if she had been stabbed through the heart when she thought of him. She could only imagine it was because of the novel surroundings.

She served up her frittata and carried the plate outside with her wine and sat down and admired the view in the twilight. She could see the lights of Cefalu in the distance and in the dusk the sweet mixture of scents from the pots of lavender and climbing honeysuckle was intoxicating. The evening air was still and warm and she knew she would enjoy her month in Sicily. She raised her glass to the sky.

'Thank you Duncan. This was a great idea of yours.'

When Julia had finished her dinner and the best part of the bottle of wine, she decided to find her iPad and send a message back home to tell everyone how she was getting on. However, the Wi-Fi would not connect. She looked at her watch. It was only just after eight and she knew Tony wouldn't be eating for another hour, so she decided to go over and ask him how to switch on the Wi-Fi.

She went to the bathroom and brushed her hair and slicked on a tiny bit of lip gloss. She looked down at her dress; it was a little crumpled from where she had slept in it, but it was presentable enough for a five minute visit to her landlord. But to be on the safe side she slipped on a cropped cardigan to cover up her bare arms.

She put on her leather flip flops and strolled up to the house. Her path was illuminated by solar lights nestled in the fragrant lavender hedges. There were no signs of life in the garden as she made her way to Tony's villa, so Julia walked around the house to look for the front door. There were stone steps leading up to a large imposing double door, which had an old fashioned bell pull. Julia reached up to ring it, but stopped before it made a sound. She suddenly felt shy and didn't want to disturb Tony. She decided she would just send Bryden and Jamie a text instead of emails. She could wait until tomorrow.

She turned to leave, but as she did the front door opened and Tony appeared, holding a cat in his arms. He bent down to put the cat outside and looked up and saw Julia.

'Oh good, you changed your mind. Come in, do; I was just putting Gatto out for the night.'

The cat slunk off into the dark undergrowth of the garden as Julia watched.

She followed Tony into the house.

'I was trying to connect up to the Wi-Fi; I just came over to see if it was switched on. It doesn't seem to be working.'

'I'm so sorry; I did switch it off this morning. It's a habit of mine when I'm writing; otherwise I get distracted by the internet. I lose hours of my life looking at nonsense on Twitter. I'll put it on for you now, and try and remember not to switch it off while you're here.'

He disappeared into his office and came back seconds later.

'There, it's back on. Now, what can I offer you to drink? A gin and tonic or perhaps a glass of wine. I have some lovely Prosecco chilling in the fridge.'

He walked away into the kitchen as he spoke, which forced Julia to follow him.

'Um, well actually, I wasn't going to stay for dinner…'

'Nonsense, you're here now. Maria has made a lovely Sicilian roast lamb. You really must try it. Sebastian and Lydia will be here in a little while. I think Jürgen and Christine will be coming with them. Lovely people; you must meet them.'

Julia realised she was trapped, without any viable excuse not to stay. She really wasn't very hungry now, and was feeling a little tipsy already.

Tony stood beside a huge silver fridge holding an opened bottle of Prosecco in his hand.

'Will this do?'

'Lovely thanks!'

'You know I never normally socialise with my guests in the holiday villa, but then I've never had anyone stay here on their own. This is a lovely change for me.'

He handed Julia the glass of wine.

She took a sip and looked around the kitchen. It was the largest kitchen she had ever seen; with acres of spotless black marble worktops on top of hand-crafted cream wooden units. An eight burner range-cooker took pride of place along one wall, a large crystal vase of lilies stood in the centre of a farmhouse style table. It had not been set for dinner; although it was still early.

'Maria has done most of the cooking, it just needs serving up. I'm such a cheat aren't I?'

'Well it all smells delicious and I'm sure your friends come to see you rather than what you're serving for dinner.'

'Oh no; they definitely come for Maria's cooking. Although I think Eleonora was an even better cook; and a much better hostess too. I do my best though. And I'd be interested in your thoughts about how I manage later.'

Julia smiled, although she was rather puzzled by this remark. It seemed a little weird, but then again he was a best-selling author. He was the closest to a celebrity she had ever met; perhaps weird was the norm in these circles.

'Can I do anything to help? Lay the table perhaps?'

'It's all done thanks. We're eating in the conservatory. Maria set the table out there. Come and see.'

Julia followed him through the adjoining lounge and into a huge conservatory lit with fairy lights and candles. The French doors were open, and in the garden she could see a large pond with underwater lighting. It looked like something out of a Hollywood film.

'What do you think? Is it still too warm in here? I could put on the fan.'

'No, it's perfect; and very pretty.'

Suddenly Julia felt rather privileged to be invited for dinner. The food smelt gorgeous, the setting was beyond glamorous, and her only regret was she had eaten so much of her frittata earlier on. She did not have much of an appetite for dinner, although the wine was certainly helping her feel a little more peckish.

Julia noticed the table had only been set for five people, which made her realise Tony had not taken her presence for granted. He picked up some china and cutlery from a hostess trolley parked in the corner of the room.

'I'm glad you decided to come over, I hate odd numbers at the table. As you can see everything was here ready for you if you changed your mind.'

Julia helped him set the place at the other end of the oval table.

Just as they had finished they heard the doorbell.

'Ah that will be the rest of our guests; let's go and meet them.'

Julia followed him out to the hall. If his guests were surprised to find a stranger in their midst, they did not show it. They shook hands, kissed Julia, hugged and kissed Tony, handed him a huge box of handmade chocolates, exclaimed over the smell of food, and introduced themselves to Julia, as they made their way to the conservatory. Julia was left playing hostess while Tony went back to the kitchen to fetch wine for his guests.

'So Julia, where are you from; that's such an unusual accent? Are you Scottish?' Lydia said, as she stepped outside onto the terrace, followed by the others.

'I'm from Shetland actually, so yes I am Scottish, although my accent is probably a little different from most other Scots.'

'Ah yes, there's something almost Norwegian about your accent,' Jürgen said.

'Well, we did use to belong to Norway, and there are still lots of Old Norse words in our dialect, although I have to say, if I was speaking in dialect, you probably wouldn't understand me at all.'

'Oh really, oh do say something in your dialect for us,' Lydia said.

Before Julia could reply Tony came back holding a tray of Champagne flutes and another bottle of Prosecco which he opened with a flourish. He passed his new guests a glass each and then topped up Julia's glass.

'To old friends, new friends and friends who are no longer with us. Salut!'

'Salut!'

He winked at Julia and took a sip of his wine.

'Well, shall we all sit down? I'm sure you're all starving after your *long* drive.'

'Where have you come from?' Julia asked Lydia.

'Only from Palermo. Tony is just having a go at us because we haven't seen him for quite a while.'

'It's been six months. I feel betrayed by you all,' Tony said, as he took a seat at the head of the table.

'Some of us have real jobs you know. There's nothing stopping you coming over to Palermo to see us,' Sebastian said, as he sat down next to Lydia who had taken the seat on Tony's left. Christine quickly took a seat opposite Lydia and Jürgen sat next to his wife. Julia was left to take the seat opposite Tony. She suddenly felt exposed and inadequate amongst these glossy elegant people. She wished she had put on more make-up, or at least ironed her dress after sleeping in it.

'Julia, weren't you going to say something in your own language?' Christine said, in the moment of silence as they took their seats.

'Really? Did I miss something?' Tony said, looking down the table and smiling at her.

'I was just telling them Shetlanders speak a dialect most people wouldn't understand.'

'Well we must have a demonstration. We all speak English and Italian, Christine and Jürgen obviously speak German too, so we're all interested in languages.'

Julia looked out of the window for inspiration, she had no idea what to say and hated being put on the spot. She watched Gatto mooching along by the pond and remembered a poem she had written, many years ago. She took a deep breath.

'Da cat wheeches doon tae da loch and stauns peerie wyes
He watches sleekit for da peerie mootie deuk
Up in da skies a muckle bonxie skröls a warning
Tiger skelps back tae da hoose, greetin aa da way
Back tae neeb aside da roose
Nae more work fa dee, du bonny langsome cat.'

She took a sip of her wine and smiled shyly at Tony, 'so did you understand any of that?'

'Something about a cat, or a tiger?'

'It's about a cat called Tiger, so yes.'

'Fascinating!' Tony said, 'right, time for dinner I think.'

He stood up and left the room. Sebastian asked Jürgen a question about his work, from which Julia deduced Jürgen was an architect. The two men spoke across the table to each other, effectively cutting her off from starting a conversation with either of the women. She sat in silence and studied the two women. They did not look like they were particularly good friends with each other. Christine was a tall, athletic looking woman, probably in her late forties. Naturally blonde, she was dressed in a white silk sleeveless blouse and terracotta linen cropped trousers. She wore flat leather sandals and no jewellery at all. She didn't appear to be wearing make-up, which made Julia feel marginally better about her own casual appearance.

Lydia on the other hand, was wearing what looked like a very expensive silk jersey dress. Julia's addiction to women's magazines meant she was able to discern it was probably a Diane Von Furstenberg. Lydia was definitely wearing make-up, and possibly even false eyelashes, and she was probably on the wrong side of fifty, but making a brave attempt to hide it.

She turned her attention to the men. They were definitely in their fifties, but looking good on it. Jürgen wore a white shirt, with the sleeves rolled up, exposing a chunky Tag Heure watch. Sebastian was wearing a black Paul Smith polo shirt and the most ostentatious Rolex watch she had ever seen.

Tony returned to the room with a tray which he set down on the trolley. Then he handed out plates of antipasto; gleaming olives, grilled figs, prosciutto ham and artichokes. Julia smiled with relief it was something she recognised. Tony passed around a basket of fresh bread and Julia took a slice and put it on her side plate. The food looked delicious but she was still not desperately hungry; taking the bread was a mistake, she thought. Then the scent of rosemary wafted up to her nose and she decided she might enjoy it after all.

'What have I missed?' Tony said, as he sat down and picked up his glass.

'Jürgen was just telling me about that development he's working on in Agrigento. I think I might have to go and look at it sometime. Sounds fascinating,' Sebastian replied.

'Isn't that the project where the builders unearthed some Roman ruins?'

Jürgen shrugged, 'everywhere you turn on this island there is some kind of ancient ruin. Every one of my building projects has been built on something that was there before.'

'What kind of projects do you do?' Julia asked.

Jürgen turned towards her and half smiled, 'I build villas, like this one.'

'This is one of Jürgen's designs,' Tony said, waving his hand in the air to encompass his house. 'Italian styling with German efficiency; the perfect combination!'

'It's lovely. Is that how you know each other?'

'Eleonora was a good friend of mine,' Christine said, joining in with the conversation.

The mention of Tony's wife seemed to make everyone go quiet for a moment. Julia wanted to know how Sebastian and Lydia fitted into this group of friends. They seemed an odd bunch.

'What brought you over to Sicily on your own?' Lydia asked Julia. 'Tony tells me you booked the villa for a whole month. Are you a writer too?'

Julia laughed. 'No, whatever gave you that idea? I came over here to avoid my fiftieth birthday.'

Lydia smiled, as she stared at Julia; blatantly judging her age in relation to how she looked. 'That does sound a bit extreme. Turning fifty isn't so bad; you soon get used to it.'

Sebastian grinned. 'Yes indeed, Lydia has had lots of practice at turning fifty; she's been doing it for at least five years now.'

Lydia elbowed him in his ribs.

'Wow, you don't look it.' Julia said politely.

'Nor do you, my dear,' Tony said, raising his glass to her.

The conversation turned to local politics, which effectively excluded Julia from the conversation. She listened intently while she ate her food, which was delicious, and did much to overcome her lack of appetite.

She could not believe twenty four hours earlier she had been sat in a soulless airport hotel at Gatwick, sulking about her argument with Jamie the previous night, over her decision to go on holiday on her own. She wished she could take a photograph of this scene on her phone and send it to him, to show him how she hadn't been kidnapped by the mafia, or any other of the mad scenarios he had painted for her. It was nice of him to be concerned, but she resented the way he seemed to think she would not manage on her own. Bryden had also changed his tune a little, and chipped in with the warnings not to go out at night on her own, or to attempt to drive a car, or speak to strangers. She had felt more like she was turning five.

She marvelled at the fact she was sitting at the dining table of a famous author, two other English ex-pats and two rather wealthy looking Germans. So what if they weren't really including her in their conversation; the food was great and the wine was going down a treat. In fact, she really ought to slow down and change to water.

'So what do you do, Julia?' Lydia asked, after a brief lull in the conversation.

'I'm not working at the moment. I used to manage a care home.'

Lydia's face clouded over a little at her reply, as if this not a profession she cared to talk about.

'I'm thinking of changing my career though; that's another reason for my long holiday. I plan to spend some time considering all my options.'

'What kinds of options are available in Shetland? You're not going to take up fishing are you?' Lydia said, laughing as she looked around the table, inviting support for her joke.

'My father was a fisherman, but no, that's not something I'm considering. The job I most enjoyed was being a theatre nurse in a big hospital in Aberdeen. That was really busy, and I enjoyed the fact I was helping to save lives. But I don't want to go back to nursing now; after thirty years, it's time for a change.'

'What did your late husband do?' Tony asked.

'He was a maths teacher at the High School. My youngest son has just started teaching the same subject, at a school in Edinburgh. My other son is also in Edinburgh, but he's training to become a doctor.'

'Clever boys then,' Jürgen said, nodding in approval.

'So you don't have to stay in Shetland then, maybe you could move to Edinburgh too,' Sebastian said.

'Oh no, I couldn't imagine leaving Shetland. I love it there.'

'Really? It doesn't sound very appealing to me,' Lydia said, shivering as if the cold North wind had just breezed past her shoulders.

'No really, it's beautiful; especially in the summer, when it hardly gets dark at night. And the people; well it's a very different culture to anywhere else. So friendly!'

'A sense of community?' Christine said.

'Definitely!'

'But where do you go shopping?' Lydia asked, frowning indiscreetly at Julia's outfit.

'We have shops in Lerwick, and the internet of course. I tend to do my shopping when I go down to Edinburgh or Aberdeen. But we don't have much call to wear Diane Von Furstenberg very often. I would look overdressed if I wore that outfit around to visit my best friend; as lovely as it is.'

Lydia looked down at her dress and then narrowed her eyes at Julia, trying to work out whether that was truly a compliment.

'I was reading about a zero carbon-footprint house somebody built in Shetland; it looked really interesting. I would love to see it one day.' Jürgen said, deftly changing the subject.

'That was built by an architect friend of mine, Cameron Moncrieff. It really is a great house; even on a freezing cold day it's toasty warm inside. They don't pay any electricity bills; so it's cheap too. Well it was cheap, right up until his wife had an affair with his brother and he's now living back at his mother's house.'

Tony laughed. 'So you do get some scandal there from time to time.'

'Definitely! Sometimes it's like living in the middle of a soap opera,' Julia replied.

'So you could introduce me to your friend, the architect,' Jürgen asked.

'Yes of course. I'll give you his email address. He's working on another similar house. He's always really busy with work, especially since his house appeared on television.'

'I'm sure. We have much to learn in Sicily about carbon-neutral building. It costs so much to keep houses cool in the summer, so it is the same problem as Shetland, but in reverse I think.'

'I'm sure it is. I do love Tony's house though. It really makes the most of the views.'

'Thank you! What kind of house do you have in Shetland?'

'We built our home many years ago, so it was before all of the carbon-neutral ideas were around. But it overlooks the sea and we have a big conservatory like this, and it has five bedrooms, which is too many, now I live there on my own. But I would hate to sell the house. My husband designed it.'

'A maths teacher and an architect?' Jürgen said, raising his eyebrows.

'Well, he didn't produce all of the architectural drawings, but they didn't actually change much from his original design. Nearly every room has a view of the sea, which is only a hundred metres away. It's amazing to look out of the window during a storm. Very dramatic.'

'I would like to see that too. Sometimes this permanent good weather gets very boring.' Christine said, as she set her knife and fork down on the plate. She picked up her wine glass and leant back in her seat, and rested her arm along the back of her husband's chair.

'You should come and visit then. Whereabouts in Germany are you from?'

'We're both from Berlin. But we met in Rome. We chose to live in Sicily because it seemed like an adventure, and we loved the weather. In Berlin it rains a lot; but now I miss the rain sometimes,' Christine replied.

'I don't miss the rain at all. I love the hot weather. I wouldn't move back to England if you paid me,' Lydia said.

'You only love the hot weather because we have the air-con cranked up to the highest level. You would be on the first plane back home if it broke down. Let's face it, you'd be so desperate you'd even fly *Easy Jet*,' Sebastian said.

Julia had been about to ask Lydia and Sebastian about their reasons for living in Sicily, but after the comment about *Easy Jet*, she realised she didn't really care to find out more about them. There was something rather unpleasant about this couple.

When they finished dinner, Tony suggested they took their coffee into the lounge. Julia was about to make her excuses to leave as she was feeling tired after so much good food and wine. But Tony took her arm as she left the conservatory and whispered to her.

'Dreadful snob Lydia; well done for putting up with her. Come and try some Limoncello. I put a bottle in the freezer earlier.'

Julia followed him out to the kitchen, while the others sat down in the lounge.

'I was thinking of going off to bed; I'm pretty knackered now.'

'Oh, don't go yet; it's nice having someone new here. Otherwise the conversation just bounces around all the same old subjects. Between you and me, I could do without all this socialising. I find it hard work, but if I didn't see all our old friends, I really would become a recluse. And that wouldn't be good.'

'I know how you feel. Sometimes I just want to lock my front door and hide away from the world. But if I do, my friend Marianne comes along and drags me out. That's why I'm here. I need to mourn in peace and quiet, and sunshine. It feels very strange being in a new place, but it's helping already.'

'A change of scene is good. I hope it works for you, being here. But you must get out and about and see some of the sights. There's so much to do; you really ought to reconsider the idea of hiring a car.'

'Maybe; we'll see. I thought I might get the train across to Agrigento sometime. I would love to see the Greek temples.'

'Oh but you definitely need a car for that. The train station is about five miles away from the Valley of the Temples. It's much easier to drive.'

Julia pulled a face and shook her head.

'Let's face it my dear, if that airhead Lydia can drive around Sicily without any bother, then I'm pretty sure you could.'

Julia giggled. She looked at Tony who was rooting around in the freezer drawer; his shoulders were shaking with laughter.

'What are you two laughing about in here?'

Julia turned and saw Lydia standing behind her.

'I was trying to convince Julia she needed to hire a car to make the best of Sicily. But she's a little nervous,' Tony said, as he shut the freezer and stood up.

'Oh nonsense; if I can drive over here, then anyone can.'

'That's just what I told her.'

Julia's face froze, trying hard not to laugh. Unseen by Lydia, Tony winked at her as he passed her the bottle of ice cold Limoncello.

10

The following morning Julia was thoroughly surprised not to have any kind of hangover. She looked at her watch and saw it was after ten. The bedroom was roasting hot as she had opened the shutters in the middle of the night. Now the sun was streaming in completely unfettered.

She took a shower and then put on another of Marianne's "summer holiday" dresses. It was an orange sleeveless knee length dress; not the kind of bold colour she would normally wear, but Marianne had convinced her it would be appropriate for Sicily. As Julia looked out of the window at the bright blue sea, the dress did seem to fit the bill. She found her iPad and took it outside and sat in the shade of the veranda.

She had missed a number of emails and messages via Facebook, as well as texts from her sons, demanding to know whether she had arrived safely.

She held her iPad up to the view and took a few pictures and uploaded them to Facebook. She sent Bryden and Jamie a message each telling them a little bit about the dinner party she went to. She smirked to herself as she typed, knowing this would probably end up in some form of rebuke, from Jamie at least.

She had just finished catching up with the online gossip when Maria appeared at the gate loaded down with carrier bags. Julia jumped up to take the heavy bags from her, as Maria indicated she was going back to get more. Julia carried the bags into the kitchen, peaking in to see what pleasures awaited her. It smelt divine.

She opened one bag and took out some fresh bread, a box of cannoli pastries, a bag of dried pasta, a waxed paper package containing Parma ham, a large tub of olives, a packet of butter and various different cheeses. The other bag contained meat, rice, coffee, tea, milk, and flour.

Maria entered the kitchen with another heavy bag containing wine and juice.

'Thanks so much Maria, this is perfect. I won't need to hurry to the shops now.'

'It's good? You like?'

'Oh yes. It's making me feel very hungry now. Although I ate so much last night I can't believe it.'

'I am glad... I must get back to work now. Arriverderci.'

Julia made herself some coffee and stood in the kitchen as she drank it and tried a sweet, ricotta filled cannoli. It was so good she cut another one in half and ate that too. She put the shopping away and sighed with pleasure as she realised she didn't need to go anywhere. She could just sit by the pool all day, or stay in the shade and read. It was heaven.

She opened a carton of apple juice and poured herself a large glass and carried it outside and sat down. It was warm, even in the shade; warmer than it ever got in Shetland in the middle of summer. It was hard to believe it was October; even the garden appeared to be warding off autumn. Flowers were still blooming and insects and birds flitted about peacefully.

Julia had a quick look at Facebook to see if anyone had responded to her photographs. There was a message from Bryden.

"Looks lovely – and hot! Haven't booked our flights yet, but hope to get there on 16th for a few days at least. X"

Julia put the iPad down and settled back in the lounger, planning on sunbathing for a little bit, before the raw heat of the midday sun would send her scurrying for shelter.

She knew she ought to venture down into Cefalu and explore the town. It was a waste to fly all this way and just lounge around, but she decided one day of laziness was perfectly acceptable. She thought of Duncan and wondered what he would have planned for their first day in Sicily. He would not have wanted to sit around. On their family holidays he had been a demon for exploring museums, art galleries, historic buildings; anything to avoid sitting in the sun, or worse still, shopping. Julia blinked back the tears that erupted suddenly at the thought of him. She thought of the arguments they had sometimes had on holiday when she had tried to encourage him to chill out and do nothing. She would give anything to be sitting here with him nagging at her to do something other than soaking up the sun.

'Damn it!'

She stood up suddenly; all thoughts of rest and relaxation had vanished. She decided she would walk into Cefalu, have a wander around, maybe stop at a café for a drink and then walk back up the hill. It would take hours; but she had hours. She had days, weeks, an entire month. The month suddenly stretched out ahead of her, quiet, lonely and in all honesty, a little miserable.

She heard a rustle of plants, and heavy footsteps walking towards the property; she turned to see Tony standing at the gate.

'Hello there, just wanted to make sure you're alright after last night. Not too hung-over I hope.'

'No; although that was a pleasant surprise.'

'That's good, I'm glad you enjoyed yourself. It must be a bit odd having dinner with a bunch of complete strangers.'

'No, it was lovely; they were lovely - Christine and Jürgen especially. Did I really agree to go and meet them in Palermo some time?'

'Indeed you did. But don't worry; they won't hold you to it. But they're a nice couple.'

'I meant to ask how you knew the other two.'

Tony laughed.

'I met them at a party somewhere. Eleonora introduced us; I think she imagined I was homesick for some English company. Funny thing is they make me appreciate Sicily even more.'

'What does Lydia do?'

'Shop, I think. Oh yes, and she "writes" novels.'

'You don't sound convinced. Aren't they any good?'

'Good God no! Thankfully she's not found a publisher yet. And this tells you how bad they are, since she's a very well connected woman. Old money; never needed to work for a living. But actually, Sebastian's a good sort. I get on well with him, so I tolerate Lydia. And she was lovely after Eleonora …'

Tony stopped speaking and looked into the distance for a moment. He hadn't opened the gate and was still standing a polite distance away.

'I was just about to make some coffee, would you like some? Maria very kindly bought me lots of groceries this morning. What a lovely woman she is?'

'Ah yes, she has been with our family for about ten years now. Would you believe she's nearly seventy? She refuses to retire and works as hard as she ever did; maybe more so. She even comes to work on Sunday's after church. Her excuse is she needs to make sure I'm alright; but truthfully, she's lonely. Her husband died the same year Eleonora did. We've been keeping each other sane ever since.'

'That's just what I need. I was having a moment there. Funny how you can be sitting around quite happily, then WHAM, it hits you all over again.'

Tony still hadn't opened the gate, and he hadn't accepted or declined her offer of coffee. Julia stood awkwardly beside one of the pillars of the veranda not sure whether to repeat the invitation.

'Anyway, I'm not getting any writing done this morning, so I'm going to call it a day. I was thinking about going off for a drive somewhere. I would love some company if you're not doing anything. But please say no if you'd rather not. I won't be offended.'

Julia hesitated. What would Duncan have said? She knew he would have said yes to an opportunity to see more of the island, although she wasn't sure he would approve of her going off with a strange man. Jamie would definitely tell her not to, and Bryden would probably agree with his brother. Marianne, on the other hand, would have picked up her handbag and be half way out the door already.

'Actually, I was just thinking of going for a bit of a walk, but going out for a drive would be even better.'

'Brilliant. Meet me at the car when you're ready.'

'Five minutes!'

They set off down the hill towards Cefalu and then joined the motorway in the direction of Palermo. As he drove, Tony coached her on the art of driving in Sicily; and on the motorway it didn't seem complicated. The traffic was moving swiftly, but not as fast, or erratic as Julia had imagined. Tony pointed out places of interest and told her some of the history of the island, much of which Julia had been reading about in her guide book, but it was interesting to hear another version of it.

She could understand how he had become an author, his storytelling had a certain charm and humour to it. She imagined he had practised these stories over the years, maybe ferrying other guests around. He seemed to be enjoying himself.

Shortly after leaving the outskirts of Cefalu they turned left onto another major road that cut through the mountains. Suddenly the view of the sea vanished and it was now an entirely different landscape. The steep sloping valley supported vineyards, lemon groves and olive plantations; and occasionally they would glimpse a dark river running alongside the road. Small farmhouses were dotted around the hills, each seemingly miles from any neighbours. They looked much lonelier and more isolated than any Shetland croft house.

It took a while before she realised there were hardly any animals around. She had expected to see sheep, but had not seen a single one. There were just tiny herds of white cattle every few miles, often sheltering in the shade of the trees. It was an alien landscape, with its terracotta earth, prickly pear cacti and the deepest blue sky she had ever seen.

She had tied her hair back with a silk scarf and worn her sunglasses, as she guessed Tony would be driving with the top down on the car. She felt the tops of her arms starting to burn, despite the sun-cream she had applied earlier, so she pulled her white cardigan out of her bag and draped it over her shoulders to protect them.

'Not cold are you?'

'No, just afraid of turning into a lobster.'

'You wouldn't want that, not with your fair Nordic skin.'

'Not really. So, where are we going?'

'Hmm, well I wasn't entirely sure when we set off, but I've decided to drive to Agrigento. I haven't been to the Valley of the Temples in years. It gets far too busy in the summer, but it's quite a nice place to visit at this time of year. Most of the tourists have vanished, but it's still pleasant out; sunny without roasting.'

'Speak for yourself; it's roasting as far as I can tell. But then again, a Shetland summer day rarely gets above twenty degrees.'

'Really, it must be at least twenty five degrees today? Eleonora would have brought a jacket with her on a day like today.'

'Funny what you get used to; it takes a lot for me to feel the cold. I could happily sit outside in just ten degrees without a coat on.'

They continued the journey, and Julia took her turn at entertaining Tony, with stories about Shetland, and her life and family.

They came across a service station at the side of the road and Tony pulled in and filled up with fuel, refusing to accept any donation from Julia. She went inside the shop to use the bathroom and when she came out Tony was sitting in the passenger seat.

She shook her head at him.

'I can't. I'm not insured.'

'My insurance will cover you. Go on, get in. It's a really straightforward drive from here. If you find it too much we can swap again.'

Julia got into the driver's seat reluctantly.

She started the engine and then sat for a moment, fiddling with the gear stick with her right hand. Then she took a deep breath and engaged first gear and then pulled away slowly. There were no cars in sight in either direction so she pulled out onto the road and carried on. Tony immediately started talking about his son and daughter in Rome and she listened as she drove, and before long she realised she was doing fine. It wasn't hard at all. Other drivers overtook her from time to time and she sped up a little, and then started to relax and enjoy it.

Before long they approached the outskirts of Agrigento. Tony looked at his watch and then up at the sky as if he doubted his watch was telling him the right time.

'We should go for lunch first. Somewhere out of the sun for a bit. We'll head into the town and find somewhere to park. Don't worry, it won't be busy; most places are closed on Sunday.'

Julia followed the signs into the centre and when they drove past the grand Romanesque train station she pulled into a parking space in the shade of a high wall.

They strolled along an avenue, under a dark canopy of trees and found a restaurant next to a small shopping centre. Most of the shops were closed, whether it was for a siesta, or because it was Sunday, Julia couldn't tell, but it lent a peaceful atmosphere to the place.

The restaurant was fairly quiet and the waiter leapt up eagerly at the presence of customers. He seated them at a table overlooking the square and handed them menus. He returned moments later with a carafe of water, breadsticks and a dish of olives.

'What do you fancy?' Tony said.

'I'm not sure really. I don't usually eat a big meal in the middle of the day. This does look nice though.'

'I think I might just get some fish and salad. But you have whatever you like. Don't forget you're on holiday.'

'I would quite like to try some proper pasta. But I don't really understand the menu.'

'Do you like seafood?'

'Of course; I'm the daughter of a fisherman.'

Tony laughed. He turned to the waiter and gave him their order in fluent Italian, which seemed to catch the waiter by surprise.

'What did you order for me?'

'One of the chef's specialities, according to this menu anyway. Seafood pasta cooked in a creamy sauce, some salad and bread. Hope that's OK?'

'Sounds lovely. I don't think that waiter expected you to speak Italian.'

Tony laughed, momentarily looking like a naughty schoolboy.

'I know. Everyone sees me as this posh Englishman who couldn't possibly understand a word of their beautiful language. But I'm fluent in Italian and fairly proficient at the Sicilian dialect too; that's what really surprised the waiter.'

Julia looked up and saw the waiter talking to the chef behind the counter. They looked over at Tony as if they had been talking about him. Julia smiled at them. The chef lifted his hand in greeting.

Their lunch was perfect. Julia's seafood pasta was so delicious she asked Tony to get the recipe from the chef. She wanted to be able to cook it when she got back home. The chef came over to their table, perhaps to hear for himself how good the Englishman was at speaking Sicilian.

When they left the restaurant, Julia stepped out into the sunshine and shielded her eyes against the sun, which seemed brighter still after the cool dark restaurant. She reached into her handbag for her sunglasses.

'That was lovely, thank you so much.'

'My pleasure. Now let's go and see the Valley of the Temples. You'll love it.'

Tony drove down the hill towards the sea. It was a long and winding road, not particularly well kept, despite it being the road to a world famous tourist destination. Julia noticed a dead dog lying at the side of the kerb. There was something rather shocking about seeing the poor animal left to rot in full view of passing traffic. However, Julia forgot all about that when the first of the temple buildings came into sight.

After the long drive across the mountainous and rocky centre of the island they were now driving across a relatively flat stretch of land that hugged the west coast of Sicily. In the distance Julia could see a multi-columned reddish brown structure. The afternoon sun shone a spotlight on it, making it centre stage in the beautiful green landscape.

There were a couple of tour buses parked at the side of the road close to the monument, and within moments they had caught up with a group of American tourists, all speaking rather loudly, but good naturedly. Some of them were arguing about the origins of the temple.

'But it must be Roman, we're in Italy.'

'No, it's definitely Greek. They were invaded by the Greeks.'

'And the French,' said another.

'No; it was the Normans.'

'Same thing!'

Tony took Julia's arm and guided her past the crowd.

'We don't want to end up with that lot.'

Julia was more concerned about the way Tony had taken hold of her than with the crowd of elderly tourists. It was a peculiar paternalistic gesture but it made her a little uncomfortable, although she was too shy to shake him off. She walked faster, and soon there was just the two of them walking around the far side of the temple from the other tourists.

Tony let go of her arm and Julia moved away a little, as if she was in a hurry to inspect the building close up. Within moments she had forgotten her discomfort when they walked amongst the ruins of the Greek temple.

She tried to imagine it when it was first completed. She stood still and scanned the surrounding fields and hills and pictured the lives of the people who had lived here in this idyllic setting. The land appeared to be fertile and there would undoubtedly be plenty of fish in the Mediterranean Sea. It seemed like the perfect place to live.

They spent a couple of hours looking at the ancient monuments in the Valley of the Temples. By then it was late afternoon and clouds were rolling in off the sea. It was cooling a little, pleasantly so for Julia, but they decided it was time to drive back home. Tony insisted Julia should try driving back and since there didn't seem to be too many cars around, she agreed.

When they got back to the villa they were both tired from the drive. Julia thanked Tony profusely for the day out and went back to her little villa and took a shower before making herself something to eat for her supper.

It was still warm on the veranda so after she had finished eating Julia took her iPad outside and decided to send some messages home, along with some photos she had taken that day. She sat on the lounger feeling exhausted, but her head was buzzing after the conversation with Tony and the excitement of exploring a new land.

She uploaded some photos onto Facebook along with a status update: *My day trip to the Valley of the Temples. What a lovely drive it was across Sicily.*

She checked her emails and replied to a message from Bryden, and then she looked at car hire prices in Sicily. She felt more confident about renting a car now, especially as Bryden had just announced he was coming over for a week with his girlfriend. She decided she would ask Tony's advice on car hire companies before making the booking, and since that would have to wait until the next day she went back to Facebook to see what gossip she was missing out on.

Cameron had commented on the photographs.

"Looks amazing, great to see sunshine - a howling gale here."

Julia looked at the sidebar of the website and could see Cameron was still online. She clicked on his name and wrote a personal message to him.

"I actually drove two hours across Sicily. Can you believe that? Me, who's never even driven in Aberdeen."

"Well done you! Hope you're having fun," Cameron replied immediately.

"I am actually. The landlord is lovely; he invited me to dinner with his friends. He's a widower too, so he knows how I feel, which is nice."

"Ooh er, I hope he's not some Mafioso type."

"No, silly. He's English actually." Julia sighed at yet another stereotypical comment about the Mafia.

"Now I'm really worried!"

"Don't be daft. He's the perfect gentleman and he's a famous writer. Anthony Hugo. Duncan used to read some of his books."

"Impressive! You seem to have fallen on your feet".

"What's that supposed to mean?" Julia frowned at the screen as she typed.

"Nothing, just that he must be an interesting person to have running a holiday villa."

"Yeah, he is. He took me out for the day to see the Greek Temples. But it was a one off; he has a publishing deadline to meet, so now I have plucked up the courage to hire my own car. Bryden is coming over soon."

"Excellent, so you won't be lonely then."

"No, but it does feel very strange being here without Duncan. I keep looking round to see where he is. Is that mad?"

"Not really. I sometimes go to send Laura a text to tell her when I will be home from work, and then I remember – she doesn't give a fuck!"

"Sounds like you need a holiday too."

"Is that an invitation?"

"Behave! You will owe me another bunch of roses at this rate."

"LOL!"

"Anyway, it's been a long day - I'm off to bed now. Goodnight."

"Cheerio!"

Julia logged off the internet and put her iPad down on the little table beside her. She fancied a drink now so she poured herself a glass of red wine, which Maria had chosen for her. It was an excellent choice. She put on a cardigan and went back outside and sat watching the lights of the town below. It was so peaceful here; although it was far less peaceful inside her head.

11

The next morning Julia woke early, the warm sunshine once again beating its way through the un-shuttered bedroom window, and making sleep impossible. She got up and had a shower, feeling rather sluggish and tired, and the shower was insufficiently refreshing. She got dressed and made breakfast and took it outside to eat on the veranda.

There wasn't a breath of wind and the sun was already creating a heat haze over the town. The Tyrrhenian Sea merged seamlessly into the blue sky and it was all set to be another glorious day. Julia should have been happy; after all this was exactly what she had hoped for when she had decided to run away from the autumnal gales and dreich weather of Shetland. Instead she felt gloomy and miserable.

She struggled to remember the good times with Duncan. Sometimes she struggled to recall anything about him other than his funeral. As she held her cup of coffee up to her lips and inhaled the strong dark aroma, she tried to remember their wedding day, but her brain refused to call up any kind of comforting image. Instead, all she could see was Duncan lying lifeless on the hospital trolley. She could feel the awkward touch of Liam's hand on her shoulder as she sat beside Duncan. She heard the sound of the young doctor's voice explaining what they had done to try and save him. She heard people talking in the corridor outside. She could recall every minute detail of Duncan's death and the week leading up to the funeral. All she wanted was to see him smile at her; even if that was only a memory of a smile. And yet if she looked at a photograph of him, all she could still see was the photograph of a dead man. It seemed as if the light had gone out of his eyes in all the pictures of him she had once loved. It was impossible; a trick of the mind, but they gave her no comfort.

She had never felt more lost and lonely in her life, and yet there was nobody she wanted to share this burden with. All of her closest friends and family were struggling in their own ways to accept Duncan's death. If she rang one of her sons she felt she would only add to their distress if she told them how she truly felt.

She stood up abruptly and put down her coffee. She needed to do something, quickly. Anything; anything at all to stop thinking this way. The dark thoughts were moving in like black clouds on a stormy day and she was afraid for herself.

She hurried inside to the kitchen and poured herself a glass of juice. She drank it quickly, gasping as her temples succumbed to brain-freeze. She put the glass down and looked around the room searching for her iPad. When she found it she logged on to the internet with the intention of sending a message to Marianne, hoping she would have wise words to offer on how to get past this feeling of despair.

Instead she logged onto Facebook and, in a moment of madness, logged in as Duncan. She had never done this before, although she had always known his password. As his page loaded up she could see there were hundreds of posts that had gone unread, a new friend request and six private messages. She clicked on the friend request button, curious to know who had asked him to be their friend. She stared at the name, trying to place where she had heard of Alasdair Barton before. It took a while to remember he had been at University with Duncan, and now he was living in Dubai, which no doubt explained why he had sent a friend request two months after Duncan's death. Julia sent a quick message to explain and then turned her attention to the personal messages.

In reverse chronological order the first message was from Marianne, which really surprised Julia. She had sent it in the early hours of the morning after her birthday party.

"You missed a great party Duncan! I'm still so mad at you for not being here. We miss you so much. Love you! Marianne xxx"

It was typical of Marianne to rage at Duncan like that and Julia smiled sadly.

The second message she opened was from Bryden; sent at the end of August, on the first day of the new school year.

"Dear Dad, I feel stupid writing to you when you can't read this, but it's my first day teaching as a proper Maths teacher, and I wish you could be here so I could tell you how it went. I'm really nervous now. A new school, new kids, new everything. I miss you. Bryden."

Julia didn't even attempt to blink back the tears as she read her son's message. She wondered why he hadn't said anything like this to her. He had rung her that morning, sounding happy and excited. He had rung again after school and sounded exhausted but content.

The remaining messages were all sent in the first two days after Duncan's death. They were personal tributes from friends and colleagues.

It had never occurred to her to send Duncan a message like that. She almost felt guilty she hadn't attempted to contact him in any way, but whilst her beliefs about life after death were unfixed and changeable, she certainly didn't think Duncan was sitting up in heaven logging onto Facebook. He had hardly bothered with it when he was alive.

She looked at some of the new posts that had appeared in the newsfeed. There was nothing of interest. She stared at the message button and had half a mind to freak Marianne out by replying to her message on Duncan's behalf. But that would be mean. She did however, smile at the thought.

She switched off the iPad and decided to ring Marianne instead, risking an expensive international call. She looked at her watch and rang her at work.

'It's me, are you busy?'

'I'm never too busy to speak to you. How's Sicily?'

'Hot, well hot for me anyway. It's twenty seven degrees already.'

'Wow. Make the most of it; it's a day of utter shite here. I would give anything to come over and join you by the pool.'

'I wish you could…'

Julia paused, unable to release her vocal chords from the iron grip of sadness.

'Hey, are you alright? What's wrong?'

'Nothing; everything. I just logged onto Duncan's Facebook. I saw your message and one from Bryden…'

'I'm sorry; it was stupid of me … I was drunk.'

'No, I'm not mad at you; it was sweet. We did miss him at the party,' Julia said.

'We miss him every day.'

'I don't know what to do now?'

'In what way?'

'In every way. I feel like I'm being swallowed up by a black hole. I'm kind of scared actually.'

'It's not surprising. You've had so much to deal with. Not just with Duncan dying so suddenly, but with him being poorly for so long, and the boys leaving home. It's all taking its toll. Perhaps you should think about taking some medication to help you over the next few months.'

'Maybe,' Julia replied, doubtfully.

'I know you don't want to go down the route of taking anti-depressants, but they've changed since you took them after Bryden was born. It might help numb the pain a little.'

'I'll think about it when I get home. In the meantime, I just need to do something positive for the next few days. I need a project; something to focus on.'

'OK, I know what; you need to go shopping. Go and buy a new outfit. Something to wear to our Christmas party. I know it's ages away, but do it for me. New dress, new shoes, new handbag, the whole works. That's your mission for the day.'

Julia laughed. 'No, that would be your ideal mission. I have heaps of clothes already, and I can't imagine I'll be going to any Christmas parties this year.'

'But you don't have heaps of Italian clothes though. And most of your old clothes are too big for you now. Go on, I dare you to buy something totally different. Imagine you're going shopping with Gok Wan.'

'I would rather go shopping with you.'

'That would be fun. But really, you should do something nice for yourself. It might help you snap out of it, even if it's just for one day. Go to a beauty salon and get your nails done or something.'

'Oh yeah, like I can say that in Italian.'

'I doubt you need to say anything, just waggle your fingers. It's not rocket science.'

'I'll think about it.'

'You do that. And when you feel down, remember this, Duncan fell in love with you because you were always smiling and laughing. He told me that himself. So don't let him down. He'd want you to carry on and be happy, wouldn't he?'

'He would; but it's not that easy.'

'No darling, it really isn't.'

The phone call made Julia feel marginally more cheerful, or if not cheerful, she did feel a little more connected to the world. She wondered at the wisdom of taking herself off to somewhere so isolated from her friends and family. It had seemed such a good idea at the time, but now she felt lonely.

She thought about going home, but then she pictured the triumphant look on Jamie's face when she would have to tell him he was right, she shouldn't have gone. For some reason she didn't want to give him the satisfaction. She was still smarting from the argument they had just before she left Edinburgh.

She would just have to suffer in silence. She was already into day three of her holiday and it was now mid-morning. It was time to explore the town.

Julia put on some comfortable walking boots and stuffed a cotton cardigan into her handbag in case it cooled down; ever the Shetlander, she was never optimistic about the weather.

She strolled past Tony's villa noticing his car was not on the drive, although Maria's battered old Fiat Panda was. She marched down the narrow lane that led to the town. It was about two miles to Cefalu, but nearly all downhill.

It was Monday morning, and the houses she passed along the way looked unoccupied, no doubt because people were at work and school. The road widened and turned like a hairpin back on itself and she stopped to look down at the town, half a mile closer than she could see from her villa. Pale yellow buildings hugged the shore, and a huge promontory of a cliff overlooked the town, with a religious monument clinging precariously to the top.

However inviting the town looked, Julia could scarcely summon up the energy to continue with her walk. She didn't really feel like exploring today. She looked back up the steep road where she had come from and sighed. She could hardly be bothered to walk back either. She leaned over the low concrete crash barrier. There was a long drop down to the rocks below.

She wondered, fleetingly, what it would feel like to jump over the edge. It would hurt, she decided, after calculating it might be possible to survive the fall if she missed the rocks and landed on the grassy slope below them.

A car pulled up beside her and Julia turned to see Maria winding down the window to speak to her.

'Buongiorno! You are walking to Cefalu?'

'Si!' Julia said, smiling back at her.

'You like a drive in car?'

Julia frowned, not quite sure what Maria was suggesting. Then she saw Maria was moving her handbag from the passenger seat and making room for her.

'Si, grazie,'

'Prego,' Maria replied, as Julia climbed into the passenger seat.

As she did up her seatbelt Julia heard a strange sound and turned to see a toddler sitting in a baby seat. He gurgled and stared at Julia with huge brown eyes.

'Bambino!' Julia said, grinning at Maria.

'Si, my grandson, Luca.'

Julia turned back to the boy.

'Ciao Luca. Aren't you a gorgeous thing?'

'My daughter is working. I am babysitter today.'

'That's nice for you.'

'Si, molto bene.'

The journey down the hill in Maria's car did not take long and a few minutes later she stopped the car at the side of the road near the train station so Julia could get out. Julia turned and waggled Luca's foot and said goodbye to him, and thanked Maria for the lift.

Maria drove off with a wave as Julia stood at the side of the road and wondered where to go. She saw a sign for the Duomo, the Cathedral, and decided to head that way, as she remembered from the guide book it was surrounded by restaurants. She would have a drink and then decide what to do next.

She strode towards the Cathedral and soon found herself in a large square. The square was overshadowed by the towering rock that rose vertically out of the landscape. Julia sat down on a bench and stared up at the summit. She could see something colourful moving near the top and realised with a gasp, there were two climbers making their way up the side of the cliff face. She sighed with relief when she saw they had safety ropes tethering them to the rock, so she was not in danger of watching anyone fall to their death. Her own fear of heights made her feel slightly queasy watching them, so she turned her attention to the top of the rock where she could make out a small stone building topped by a crucifix. It could be reached via a footpath leading out of the town but Julia decided it was too hot to embark upon such a demanding climb, even if there were astounding views to be had.

She turned and looked around at the restaurants. They all looked quite busy and she suddenly felt a little reluctant to sit in one of them alone. She spied a shop that sold drinks and souvenirs and decided to just buy a bottle of water and walk down to the beach.

Julia emerged from one of the shady side streets into the full sun and was arrested by the glorious sight of a sandy beach; full of people sunbathing, swimming and strolling around. She sat down on a low wall that separated the beach from the road and looked out to sea.

The water looked inviting and she could tell it was still warm, as there were little children splashing around in the shallows, and some adults standing up to their waists in the sea. A strong but warm breeze propelled a windsurfer across the bay. Julia lifted her face to the sun and closed her eyes, revelling in the warmth. It's October, she thought to herself, and couldn't help but smile at the pleasure she took in being in a sunny warm climate, when it was windy and raining back home.

Her reverie was disturbed by the loud buzz of a moped that had stopped behind her. Julia opened her eyes and turned round to see a woman sitting astride a white Vespa. She wore pale pink jeans, a white shirt and a pink Chanel-inspired handbag with a long gilt strap across her body. Julia watched as the woman took off her helmet and shook her head and fluffed up her silver bobbed hair. Julia's eyes widened with surprise when she realised the woman was probably in her late fifties, or maybe even older. She was enviably chic and confident.

The woman lifted up the lid of the luggage box on the back of her scooter and popped her helmet inside. Then she strode across the road to a hairdresser's salon and disappeared inside.

Well I never, thought Julia, looking down at her own ill-fitting jeans, boots, and handbag which somehow did not convey anywhere near as glamorous an image. She felt frumpy by comparison. She remembered what Marianne had said about going shopping and decided it was time to treat herself. She was still only forty nine, for a few more days anyway. It was no age at all.

Julia stood up and headed back towards the town centre. She had passed a couple of interesting shops on the way down to the beach, but she had not stopped to look inside. This time she felt fired up with a little more enthusiasm. Maybe she would never look as stylish as the older woman on the scooter, but perhaps she could meet her half-way.

Julia stood outside a small boutique and stared through the window. She had lost her nerve already. The clothes inside the store were flamboyant, colourful and designed for women with a little more confidence than Julia. She caught a glimpse of her own reflection staring back at her. She looked old and tired and her hair hung limply around her shoulders, wilting under the heat.

Julia stood up straight and held her head up; a marginal improvement. Her navy shirt hung from her frame, shapeless, baggy and probably not the right colour for her skin tone, or indeed the climate. Her boot-cut faded blue jeans were too loose and although she had pulled them in with a belt, the overall effect was not flattering. Grief had aged her, creating dark hollows under her eyes, deepened the lines on her face and dulled her once sparkling eyes.

She turned away from the shop in disgust and wandered up the steep road towards the Cathedral and then crossed the square and stepped inside the cool building. She stared up at the light filtering in through the stained glass windows, or at least what remained of them. Some of the stained glass had been repaired by cheaper plain glass. The once-grand Cathedral looked shabby and worn out, but

Julia sat down in one of the pews, glad to be out of the hot sun. She watched an elderly woman shuffle past, genuflect in front of the altar and then kneel down to pray.

Julia stared at the altar, draped in a white cloth and buried under the weight of a variety of red flowers. The flowers reminded her of Duncan's funeral and she bowed her head in sorrow.

She considered praying, but what was there to pray for? If there was a God, then Duncan would be safe in heaven. If there wasn't, then what would be the point? What could she ask of God anyway? She wasn't going to ask for a miracle – to turn back the clock, to before Duncan died. All she wanted was to feel less pain, and to find a reason to smile again.

The dusty incense-scented air caught in her throat and Julia started to cough. She retrieved a bottle of water from her handbag and took a sip. As she tipped her head back, she noticed the sun's rays shining through the chancel window, highlighting a mural of the Virgin Mary weeping over the lifeless body of her son.

Julia stared at the mural for a moment. She thought of her own sons; two fine young men, who she had rather neglected for the last few months. They had lost their father, and in some ways they had lost their mother too. Julia sat up straight, took another sip of water and then stuffed the bottle back in her bag. This was madness, utter madness. She needed to get a grip and start thinking about other people besides herself.

She stood up and strode towards the door and then spotted a stand full of candles, some lit, some waiting to be lit. Julia fished in her pocket for some coins and put a donation in the honesty box beside the stand. She picked out a candle and lit it and stared into the flickering flame as it established itself; then set the candle down on the rack.

'This is for you my love,' she said quietly, 'I'm sorry we didn't get to come to Sicily together. You would have loved it here.'

Julia walked out of the Cathedral into the sunshine. She put on her sunglasses and marched across the square and over to one of the cafes. She took a seat under the shade of an umbrella and caught the eye of the waiter who weaved his way between the tables towards her, carrying a jug of iced water and a menu.

'Buongiorno Signora,'

Julia ordered a glass of Sicilian lemonade and a bowl of seafood pasta which she enjoyed as she watched the world go by. Then she ordered a cappuccino and a pistachio gelato and made plans for her future. When she had finished the ice-cream, she reached into her handbag and took out a notebook and pen and wrote a list of things she needed to do.

In no particular order of priority she needed to get a worthwhile job, spend more time with her boys, do something useful for them with the money she had inherited from Duncan and his mother, sort out her own health and appearance, get back out into the world and stop being so miserable. Marianne had been right; Duncan would be horrified to see her like this.

Julia left the restaurant and decided to go back to the shops, only to find they were closed for a long siesta. They were not due to reopen for another two hours so she wandered down to the beach and decided to do a spot of sunbathing, albeit, wearing jeans and a shirt.

When it was time for the shops to reopen Julia headed back towards the town centre and found a shop that had an attractive dress in its window. She went in for a browse, taking her time, looking for something Marianne would approve of. She found it tucked away in the back of the shop, a bold wraparound dress in pinks and purples. She tried it on and it fitted. It had a 1950's feel to it, with its fitted bodice, tight waist and flared skirt that ended at her knees. She was reluctant to take it off.

She bought the dress, and then found a pair of black skinny fit jeans in another shop, that fitted her more snugly than the ones she was wearing, and with a much more satisfying outline. She bought a red silk blouse to go with the jeans, a pair of stylish but comfortable gold sandals and a pair of red kitten heeled ankle boots. On a roll now, she turned her attention to handbags and found the perfect black and red leather bag in the same shop.

In another shop she found a skirt she liked, two more tops and a silk jersey shift dress in powder blue.

Weighed down by carrier bags, she discovered a branch of Sephora, and went inside hoping to find some make-up that might bring a more youthful bloom to her face. A young shop assistant, who spoke passable English, offered to try out some products on her and did a mini-makeover. The result was Julia looked rather more colourful than she normally would, but definitely an improvement. She bought most of the products the shop assistant had demonstrated on her, whilst forcing down the anxiety from spending over 100 euros on cosmetics.

She did a quick calculation in her head of how much she had spent so far and laughed nervously to herself. She carried her bags outside and made her way back to the square and sat down on a bench. She sent a text to Marianne.

"Just spent over 700 euros on clothes, shoes, makeup and a handbag I know you will try to steal from me!"

She held the phone in her hand expectantly, waiting for Marianne to reply, but Marianne must have been busy as the phone remained silent.

'Julia!'

She looked up and saw Tony striding towards her.

'Hi there, I've been shopping!'

'You don't say,' he replied, grinning at her. 'I'm just going back home if you want a lift, or have you rented a car yet?'

'I haven't got around to sorting that out yet, so I would love a lift thanks.'

Tony picked up some of the bags and cheekily peeked inside the carrier bag carrying the handbag and shoes.

'Nice! Glad to see you're putting some money into our ailing economy.'

'I spent a fortune!' Julia said cheerfully.

'Well, I'm sure you deserve it.'

'I think I do actually.'

12

When Julia returned to her villa she tried on all of her new clothes again, which looked even better on than they did in the shop. She posed in front of the mirror wearing the black jeans, red blouse and red boots. She held the new handbag in the crook of her arm in the manner favoured by supermodels on the cover of magazines. She smiled back at her reflection, unused to the sight of someone who looked shiny and glamorous staring back at her.

'What do you think, Duncan?'

She put the handbag down and walked over to the fridge and poured herself a glass of wine. She took it out onto the veranda and sat down to watch the evening sun sinking behind the mountains in the west.

She heard footsteps on the path and a moment later Tony appeared at the gate.

'Julia? Sorry to disturb you, but I was just thinking about what you said in the car, about wishing you could have a go on a moped, like that woman you saw.' Julia gestured for Tony to open the gate and come into the garden. 'I have a moped in the garage which I hardly ever use, but it works fine. Maybe you'd like to try it out. You could borrow it whenever you want,' he continued.

'Really, could I? I would love to give it try. I've only ever ridden a motorbike off-road before, when my sons had trail bikes, but I'm sure I could manage a moped. Is it an automatic?'

'Yes; it's really easy to ride; just a twist and go kind of thing.'

Julia gestured to her glass of wine.

'Well as you can see, it probably isn't the best time to try it out now. But I would love to tomorrow, if that's OK?'

Tony nodded.

'Of course; just come over any time after 10. I'm not a morning person.'

'Would you like a glass of wine?' Julia said, as she made a move to go inside.

'Well yes OK, that would be lovely thanks. Is that one of your new outfits? It looks jolly nice.'

'It is. I've been trying on all my new stuff; what a big kid, I just had to wear something right away.'

They sat down on Julia's veranda with their wine and some dishes of olives and nuts Julia had put out on the table between them.

'You seem really bright and cheerful today. It's lovely to see. It's funny because Maria told me she saw you this morning and said you looked really sad.'

'Hmm, not surprising, she caught me at a bad moment. I was in a very dark place this morning. But I've realised I should be thinking about others too, like my sons; and I should start to do something positive. What use am I to them if I fall apart?'

'That's true. My children are what helped me to hold on to my sanity – and my career for that matter.'

'I have to sort my job situation too. But that can wait until I get home. In the meantime I'm going to try and get my head together, rest and recuperate. Spend some time chilling out by the pool, read some books – maybe some of yours – and by the time Bryden and his girlfriend fly out, I will be a new woman.'

'Sounds like a good plan; although don't feel you have to read my books. But I do have a complete set in the house.'

'You mean you don't have any lying around this place,' Julia replied, looking inside towards a little bookcase she hadn't paid much attention to before.

'No, that would be a bit crass wouldn't it?'

'I don't think so. I had no idea when I booked this place it was owned by a famous writer. What a lovely surprise that turned out to be.'

Tony laughed.

'I'm hardly famous. I could walk down any busy street in London and nobody would know who I am.'

'Isn't that the best kind of famous? People know your name, but not necessarily what you look like. I would hate to be mobbed by crowds every time I went anywhere, and have people trying to take photographs of me looking awful – like this morning in fact.'

'That's very true. But you most certainly don't look awful.'

'I had some young lady give me a makeover. It's probably a more suitable look for someone in their twenties going out clubbing, but it did make me feel a bit better.'

'Ah yes. These young ones do tend to plaster on the makeup. My daughter is absolutely stunning, but she walks around looking like a hooker most of the time.'

Julia snorted with laughter. She stood up and went inside to get some more wine from the fridge and topped up their glasses before sitting down again.

'I've been thinking about what you said about Shetland the other evening. It sounds really inspiring, so I've been doing a little bit of research today. I might think about putting Shetland in my next novel. I know you don't get much crime there, but it sounds like an unusual and interesting place for a crime novel.'

'Hmm, I think you may find that's been done already. In fact there are a whole series of crime novels set in Shetland, which have even been serialised by the BBC.'

'Really? Who by?'

'Ann Cleeves.'

'Oh her! Damn that woman; she beat me to a crime writers' award once. It shows you how out of the loop I've been; I hadn't heard about that series.'

'Why don't you write a different kind of story then? Do you only ever write crime fiction?'

'Well so far that's all I've done. That's what my publishers demand from me. But I have been thinking of doing something different.'

'Well maybe you should take a trip to Shetland and see it for yourself. But leave it until the summer; it's not the best destination for a winter holiday. Not unless you're there for Up Helly Aa.'

'Ah yes, I read about that today; the Viking fire festival. That's what got my interest actually. It looks amazing.'

'It is. My husband always took part in it, and he would have been in the Jarl Squad for the next Up Helly Aa. He'd been looking forward to it for years.'

'The Jarl Squad? They're the ones that dress up in the Viking outfits?'

Julia nodded.

The following morning Julia borrowed the moped and took it for a tentative run down to the town. She negotiated her way to a grocery on the edge of the town and stopped to buy some fresh bread. She didn't feel confident enough to go exploring any further so she got back on the moped and rode back to the villa.

When she parked it on the driveway she got off, and stood beside it as she unfastened her helmet. The front door of Tony's villa opened and Tony came out.

'How did you get on?'

'It was great – I'm still alive!'

'Well that usually indicates a successful mission. Keep the keys and the helmet; take it out whenever you want.'

'That's brilliant thanks. I might try it again later; it was fun!'

Julia put the bread away in the cupboard and then got changed out of her jeans and jacket into a swimsuit and kaftan. She put on a wide brimmed hat and then selected the first of the series of books Tony had lent her and carried it out to the swimming pool and sat down on one of the loungers.

Julia read for a while, took a dip in the pool, dozed off in the sun and then woke up and picked up the book again. She carried on in this fashion for the rest of the day, stopping only to fetch a drink or a snack or to apply more sunblock. When the sun started to set she realised for the first time in ages she felt entirely relaxed. The book had been a welcome distraction and it was all the more interesting to read when she knew the author was just a few metres away in his villa, working on his next book. She thought it would be spooky reading about murders and violent crime and wondered if it would change the way she viewed Tony; but it was the brief scenes of romance and passion she found the most uncomfortable. She thought she might blush the next time she saw him.

Julia spent the next couple of days ploughing her way through Tony's novels. She didn't normally enjoy crime stories, but now she was hooked. The time spent in the sun meant she was gradually losing her luminous pale complexion in favour of a more flattering golden sheen. Breaking up the sunbathing and reading by vigorous bursts of energy in the swimming pool, stopped her from feeling totally sluggish and as the end of her first week in Sicily approached, she realised she had somehow turned a corner. She looked better, slept better and felt better than she had done in months.

On Saturday evening she borrowed the moped and took a trip into the town and walked along the promenade. She wore her new jeans, a black cashmere cardigan and her red boots and she rather hoped she looked as glamorous as the woman she had seen on the scooter earlier in the week.

Julia sat down on the sea wall and watched a young couple walking along the shore with their arms wrapped so tightly around each other she wondered how they managed to walk at all. They stopped to kiss and Julia turned away, although she doubted they cared about their privacy.

Her phone rang, from the depths of her handbag and she reached in to retrieve it. She frowned with surprise when she saw it was Cameron.

'Hello?'

'Aye Aye; how's Sicily?'

'It's lovely actually. I'm sitting on the beach – without a coat on!'

'Really, that good eh? You'd need a bloody survival suit on if you wanted to sit on the beach in Shetland tonight.'

Julia laughed. She watched the young couple walk away along the beach, and then turned her attention back to Cameron. 'So how are you getting on?'

'Fine; great actually, thanks to you!'

'Really, what have I done?'

'That German architect you met the other day, Jürgen Hoffmann, well he emailed me this week about some project he wanted some advice with. We spoke yesterday, and he's invited me over to Palermo to meet with him. I might end up with a great little project as a result of this.'

'Wow! I had forgotten all about that. I meant to text you to say he might email you, but I didn't know whether he was serious or not, or whether it was just dinner-party talk.'

'He was definitely serious. Anyway, I wanted to let you know I'm flying over to Sicily tomorrow, as I'm meeting Jürgen on Monday.'

'Tomorrow?' Julia replied, sitting up straight and fussing with her hair.'

'Yeah, you don't mind do you? I mean, we don't have to meet up if you don't want to, but I thought you might welcome a friendly face from Shetland.'

'Of course. It would great to see you. Where are you staying? How long are you going to be here?'

'I haven't booked anywhere yet. I've only just sorted out the flights and my knowledge of Sicily is pretty poor. I don't even know where you're staying.'

'I'm in Cefalu which is about an hour or so, by train, from Palermo. Or probably less if you're hiring a car. I haven't bothered with a car yet, but I'm getting about on a scooter.'

'A scooter? That's very brave of you.'

'Isn't it just!'

'Well, I have to meet Jürgen on Monday morning, and I think we will be busy for most of the day, but other than that I'll have some time to have a bit of a holiday. I'm flying back on Friday.'

Julia thought hard about what to say a hotel. She had a spare room which he could have. But did she want him so close to her? Oh what the hell, it would be stupid for him to book a hotel.

'I have a spare room in my villa. You could stay here. If you rent a car at the airport you could get back to Palermo easily for your meeting. Maybe I could even spend the day in the city and meet you later,' she said, thinking it might be nice to have company when she visited the busy capital city of Sicily.

'Really? Are you sure? That would be great.'

They made arrangements to meet at the airport the next day.

Julia woke early on Sunday morning. She hadn't slept well as she had fretted about Cameron's unexpected visit to Sicily. She put her swimsuit on and went for an early morning swim in the pool. She stretched out on her back in the water and stared up at the sky, listening to the birds singing in the olive trees. It was peaceful in this part of the garden. She could just see the top of Tony's villa protruding above the hedges that lent privacy to the pool area.

She had just started to enjoy her self-imposed exile and wasn't sure she was ready to see anyone connected to her normal life. She shivered, although the water was still warm. Julia climbed out of the pool and made her way indoors and headed straight for the shower.

She dithered about what to wear. She wanted to wear one of her new dresses, but wondered what signals it would send to Cameron. In the end she decided there was every possibility he wouldn't even notice what she wore. He was just a friend after all. They had been friends since they were teenagers. That drunken kiss of three weeks ago was ancient history; a mistake he wouldn't dare repeat.

Julia couldn't explain why, but she was keen to show she was coping well on her own. She put on a brightly coloured dress and her new gold sandals; did her hair, put on some make-up and perfume and stood and looked at herself in the mirror. She looked dramatically different to the frazzled, exhausted woman that had arrived in Sicily eight days earlier. She stood taller, her shoulders had lost some of their tension and the shadows that ringed her eyes had vanished, albeit with some cosmetic help. She smiled at herself and noticed her eyes sparkled back.

She didn't need to leave for the airport for hours so she made some breakfast then picked up her book and took it outside, intending to make the most of the remaining peace and quiet. She looked at her watch frequently, checked and rechecked the train timetable online, and then she realised she would either have to call a taxi to take her to the train-station, walk down to the town or ride the scooter. She decided to walk. She would wear a pair of plimsolls, and put her sandals on when she got to the train station.

Cameron strode through the door of the arrivals hall dragging his silver metal trolley bag behind him. He stopped when he spotted her, clearly surprised. He hurried forward, grinning at her, so obviously delighted to see her, Julia couldn't help but smile back.

'Julia, you look amazing. This holiday has obviously been good for you,' Cameron said, as he planted a suitably platonic kiss on her cheek.

'Thanks!'

'Well, let's go and find the car hire office and get back out into the sunshine, before the sun goes down.'

They walked over to the car hire desk and Julia waited patiently while Cameron negotiated over the car and a sat-nav. He handed over his platinum credit card and paid for it and picked up the keys and grinned at Julia.

Cameron had hired a two-seater SMART cabriolet, which raised an even bigger smile on his face when they reached the car, all shiny red and perfect. Julia opened the passenger door while Cameron put his suitcase in the miniscule boot. Julia hadn't been in such a small car before; the cabin space was uncomfortably intimate.

Cameron fiddled with the sat-nav with the seriousness of an airline pilot about to take off. He started the engine, checked the mirror and then drove out of the car park.

'Have you driven abroad much before?' Julia asked, envying his confidence on the road.

'At least once a year I suppose. We went to Portugal last year and Spain the year before. You get used to it after a while. What about you? Tell me about this scooter you've been running around on.'

Julia talked about some of her little trips into town on the scooter and about how nice and helpful her landlord was.

'You've certainly got yourself a dream holiday villa.'

'Definitely! Tony's really nice; you might get to meet him, although I noticed his car wasn't there this morning. I didn't get a chance to say you were coming to stay since you took me by surprise yesterday.'

'A nice surprise I hope,' Cameron said, turning briefly to look at her.

Julia grinned wickedly.

'We'll see. Just so long as you behave yourself.'

'Me? I'm always the perfect gentleman. Well apart from that one little whisky fuelled error of judgement.'

Julia turned and looked out of the window and stared at the cars driving past them. Cameron was driving quite sedately, which was a relief as the top was down on the car and Julia's hair fluttered around her face.

'Who knows you're here?' Julia asked, after a moment of silence.

'Um, nobody actually. My colleagues know I'm meeting with a German architect; but I let them assume I'm in Germany.'

'I'm glad. People would talk, and they would find this situation rather suspicious. I didn't even tell Marianne.'

'Really? So nobody knows?'

Julia laughed.

'No, and I prefer to keep it that way.'

When they reached Cefalu, Cameron insisted on taking Julia out to dinner before going back to the villa. He had left Shetland first thing that morning and had been travelling all day, and now he was hungry. They found a restaurant on the seafront and parked the car outside.

They ordered their dinner and while they ate they caught up with each other's news. Julia felt like she had been away from Shetland forever. As they talked she started to relax in Cameron's company. He was charming and entertaining, but he certainly wasn't trying to flirt with her, which was a relief.

Tony's car was not on the drive when they arrived home, but Julia still felt the need to be quiet as she led the way along the path to her villa while Cameron carried his case behind her.

'Nice solar lighting!'

'It's pretty isn't it? And very necessary, it would be pitch black without those lights. There's some around the pool too.'

'You've got a swimming pool?'

'Oh yes, not too shabby eh?'

'I quite fancy a swim actually.'

'I thought you were tired,' Julia said, as they reached the door to the villa. She reached into her bag to find the keys. Cameron stood behind her and admired the veranda.

'I'm knackered actually; but it feels wrong to pass up an opportunity to swim outside at this time of night, but maybe I should wait until tomorrow.'

Julia smiled in agreement and ushered him indoors. She switched on the lights in the villa and walked through to the spare bedroom.

'This is your room. It has a great view of the mountain in the morning. The bathroom is next door, and it's all yours. I have an ensuite in my room.'

Cameron set his case down with a broad grin on his face.

'Much nicer than a hotel. Thanks for letting me stay with you. This is just what I needed; a break from everything. I think you did the right thing getting away for a while.'

'It's been a bit up and down actually; but I do feel a bit better in myself.'

'You look good on it Jules.'

'Thanks!'

Julia turned on her heel and walked back to the kitchen. Cameron followed, his eyes taking in the décor and the furniture. Julia headed for the fridge and took out a bottle of wine.

'Fancy a drink now you don't have to drive anywhere?'

'I would love one, thanks!'

Julia poured two glasses of white wine and carried them outside to the veranda. It was a little cooler than it had been on the previous evening, but still warm enough to sit outside.

Cameron sat down on one of the loungers and put his feet up and shut his eyes for a moment, his head resting on the back of the cushioned head rest.

'I'm in heaven. Two days ago I was standing in a cold wet field with a client, discussing their plans to build a new house. I was freezing, and now I'm here, sitting outside with a glass of wine.'

Julia smiled and nodded.

'Tell me about this project Jürgen wants to talk to you about.'

'He's been commissioned to design a luxurious holiday resort on the coast not far from Palermo. But not just any old resort. His client specialises in upmarket eco-tourism holidays and the complex must be designed to be as eco-friendly as possible, using sustainable materials, renewable energy sources and recycled waste water to support the landscaping. And they want to design something that makes the best of the bonny views, with big windows and lots of light. Most of the local buildings tend to have small windows covered in shutters against the heat.'

'I didn't think you'd be interested in helping to design a holiday resort.'

'Ordinarily I wouldn't be; not my kind of thing at all. But this is a chance to try out some state of the art building techniques Scottish building regulations haven't approved yet. It's a really prestigious project and it would be great to do something different for a bit. I love designing individual houses, don't get me wrong; but there are so many things I would like to try out - new types of insulation, ventilation, renewable energy, different materials...'

Julia studied Cameron as he talked about the project. He was certainly fired up with enthusiasm. He seemed a completely different man to the one who had turned up at Marianne's birthday party. Despite the fact he was tired from a long day of travelling, he looked happy and excited. Julia was delighted she had somehow accidentally introduced him to Jürgen. And then she relaxed, safe in the knowledge Cameron had genuinely come to Sicily for a business meeting, and it wasn't some kind of underhand way of getting to see her again.

13

The next morning they set off to Palermo. The traffic was heavy as they approached the city, but thanks to the hired sat-nav they found their way through the maze of congested streets and complicated one-way systems. Julia spent the last part of the journey gripping her seat in fear, as pedestrians, scooters, buses and taxis hurled themselves in their path, horns tooting, people shouting and tempers flaring.

'I'm so glad I'm not driving,' Julia said, as they narrowly missed another scooter, ridden by a young man who was not wearing a helmet and was also holding a mobile phone to his ear as he shot out in front of them from a side street. 'That boy has a death-wish,' she added, as she watched him turn down another road and almost hit a pedestrian who was trying to cross on the green light.

Cameron found the car-park for Jürgen's company and parked the car. Julia opened the door and got out, looking around, trying to get her bearings. In the distance she could see the dome of the Teatro Massimo they had passed a few minutes earlier in the car. She decided to head in that direction.

'I'll ring you when I'm finished. No idea how long we'll be. I suppose it depends on whether we go out to visit the site or not.'

'Take your time; I'm sure there are plenty of things to keep me occupied in the city.'

'Would that involve shopping by any chance?' Cameron grinned at her.

'It just might; I haven't bought any presents for anyone yet.'

'Well, if it helps, I have plenty of room in my suitcase so I can take stuff back for you if you want.'

'Really? Well then, that's me sorted for the day. Have fun, and good luck with your meeting.'

Cameron walked around the car to Julia and touched her arm briefly, as they said goodbye. Then he headed towards the architect's office, swinging his briefcase. He stopped at the door and waved at her.

Julia strolled back towards the street where she had noticed a Prada store. Not that she imagined she would buy anything from this famous shop, but it seemed criminal not to go in and have a look, if only to brag to Marianne when she got home again.

Julia spent a hugely enjoyable morning browsing around the shops, most of which seemed to have end of season sales on. She bought trendy Italian shirts and jeans for her sons and a little handbag for Marianne. She ventured through a street market and was bullied into buying a fake designer belt, just because she had paused momentarily to look at it.

She stopped for a coffee and a slice of pizza at lunchtime, before walking down to the harbour. Palermo had a large and busy port, but it was easy to forget you were so close to the sea when you were walking around the city streets. From the city centre there were only occasionally glimpses of water to be had, although the surrounding mountains were a constant looming presence.

Julia found the faded grandeur of Palermo fascinating. She stared up at the ornate architectural details of the old buildings blackened by pollution and crumbling with age. Some attempt at modernising the city had been made and there were occasional new buildings; ugly apartments and soulless office blocks, designed for economy rather than aesthetics.

She watched the endless streams of traffic and wondered where everyone was going in such a hurry. She marvelled at the way people dressed, so effortlessly elegant, even if simply wearing jeans. There was something about the way the women walked that captivated her; they seemed so confident striding along the streets in high heels, chatting to their friends or flirting with boys on motorbikes. Julia lifted her chin a fraction, determined to try and emulate some of their style.

She checked her phone for messages but Cameron had not called. She put her phone back in her bag and headed back towards the Via Roma and decided to visit a big department store which had an intriguing window display of the new Autumn/Winter fashions.

Julia stood outside the shop and looked at the display of fur trimmed coats which looked more appropriate for the Shetland climate than here in Sicily. She wondered when it would ever get cold enough to wear something like the Alice Temperley Cossack-style fur hat, placed at a jaunty angle on the head of a mannequin.

She wandered into the store and took the escalator up to the first floor and perused the designer labels that hitherto she had only ever seen in magazines. Up close they didn't seem quite so attractive. In fact, the rack of cashmere sweaters selling for 500 euros didn't look half as nice as one she had bought in Marks and Spencer the previous year. She left the shop with the uplifting feeling she wasn't missing much in life by not being able to afford big-name fashion. She crossed the road deciding to wander back towards the Teatro Massimo, but instead she found herself staring in through the window of a lingerie shop.

The mannequins wore a selection of grey and navy silk and lace underwear, accessorised by scarves and legwarmers; a curious combination that would not have a place in the real world. She was tempted to go into the shop for a closer look but she changed her mind when she admitted to herself she had no need to invest in such gorgeous and expensive frippery. She sighed and turned away from the window and marched along the street and soon found herself in the square across the road from the Teatro Massimo. She sat down on a concrete bench and checked her phone for messages.

"Should be free soon. Where shall we meet?" Cameron had texted a few minutes earlier.

Julia replied: *"I'm sitting in the square in front of that big theatre we passed earlier. Shall I wait for you here?"*

There was no immediate reply so she decided to wait anyway. She watched two beggars approaching people who were sitting on the other side of the square. They were trying to sell something, and not taking no for an answer. She watched one young woman try to wave one of the men away. She was talking on her mobile phone, but still he persisted on trying to get her to part with her money. She got up and stomped away and Julia was horrified to see the man stalk after the woman, who subsequently increased her pace. The beggar finally gave up when she crossed the road. Julia grasped hold of her carrier bags, intending to move away if he came towards her, but he turned back towards a group of young women who were sitting on another bench.

Julia kept an eye on the two beggars, feeling increasingly nervous as she watched their rather aggressive pursuit of money. They were middle aged black men, and she wondered if they had families to support, which was why they were so persistent. She felt sorry for them, as well as a little afraid. The idea of having to beg for a living was an alien concept to her. There were never any beggars or visibly destitute people in Shetland. She checked her phone again, but there was still no response from Cameron.

She was still fiddling with the phone wondering whether to ring him when she felt someone grab her shoulders from behind. She leapt up from the bench and screamed, before turning around to confront her attacker.

'Cameron! For God's sake, you scared the life out of me!'

Cameron looked as shocked as Julia felt.

'Sorry, sorry. I didn't mean to frighten you.'

He put his arms around her and pulled her into a hug. Julia almost collapsed with relief into him, before she steadied herself and pulled away again.

'It's OK; no harm done. I was watching out for those beggars over there and getting kind of nervous. One of them practically chased after a young lass, when she wouldn't give him any money.'

'Yeah; there are some seriously poor people here. Anyway, I'm back now. Nobody is going to tell me what to do.'

Julia looked up at him and smiled. Cameron was at least 6'3, with the build of a lean and fit rugby player and she couldn't imagine anyone wanting to get on the wrong side of him.

'So, how did you get on with Jürgen?'

Cameron reached for her carrier bags and indicated they should walk towards the theatre.

'Brilliant. You should see the place where they're going to build the resort. It will be paradise.'

'Are you going to work with him then?'

'Yes; we agreed I would come over and act as a consultant on some parts of the project where they have less experience. I won't be designing the villas as such, but they would like some input on the scheme. Most of the consultancy will be done by email, but I should get at least another of trip out of it. Can't be bad eh?'

They stood at the side of a busy road, wide enough for three lanes of cars, and waited for a gap in the traffic. Cameron grasped Julia's hand and they sprinted across, laughing with relief when they got to the other side.

Cameron let go of her, but the warmth of his hand left an imprint on hers. She caught a waft of his light fresh aftershave as they stood close together on the pavement. His caring gesture reminded her of Duncan. He had never been one for public displays of affection, but he had been the perfect gentleman, and would have carried her bags and held her hand crossing a busy road.

'It sounds great. Lucky you, being paid to come over here,' she said, trying to shake off thoughts of Duncan.

'And I have you to thank. Let me take you out to dinner somewhere.'

'Perfect; but could we go back to Cefalu? It's a lot less manic there.'

They drove home in the rush hour traffic while Cameron told her more about his new project. She had watched his *Grand Designs* programme when it had been on the television, and she had visited his house many times. She knew he was committed to carbon-neutral architecture, but it was only now she realised how driven he was.

They drove back to the villa first, to drop off the shopping bags and to freshen up, by which time they realised their day had tired them out.

'That swimming pool is calling to me,' Cameron said, as he stepped out onto the veranda carrying a cup of coffee. The sun was setting and the birds were singing in the trees and there was a soft breeze cooling the air.

'We could just have something to eat here if you want to go for a swim. I could make some pasta. And there's plenty of wine.'

'Shall we? I know I promised to take you out for dinner, but we could always do that tomorrow. We could go exploring for the day. How about that?'

'Perfect!'

Julia wandered back to the kitchen, leaving Cameron outside. She bent down to inspect the contents of the fridge. Tomorrow would be her birthday and she didn't want to mention it to Cameron in case he started to make a fuss about it. But she conceded it would be nice to go somewhere on her birthday, even if she was celebrating it in secret.

Julia took out some vegetables and chicken from the fridge and then went out to the vegetable plot to find some garlic and tomatoes. Cameron came indoors and helped her peel and chop the vegetables and together they cobbled together something for their dinner.

They sat outside to eat. It was dark and the birds had hushed for the night, apart from one insistent tweeting from a bird perched on the roof of the villa.

'I know you should leave some time before going swimming but I will be asleep, or drunk, if I leave it any longer,' Cameron said, as he put his empty plate down on the table. 'I'm going in anyway; what about you?'

Julia did not relish the idea of wandering around in her swimsuit in front of Cameron, so she declined, saying she would come out and sit by the pool after she had tidied up the kitchen.

'I can help tidy up; I'm quite domesticated you know.'

'It's OK, I just feel like being lazy. You go and get changed; I'll come out in a few minutes.'

Cameron chose not to argue the point and headed off to his room. He came out a few minutes later wearing a pair of shorts. He walked out to the pool carrying a beach towel. Julia had already finished in the kitchen and had switched the dishwasher on, so she followed him outside. She took a seat at the edge of the pool and watched enviously as Cameron climbed into the water.

'It's really warm isn't it? I thought it would be colder.'

'It's solar heated apparently.'

Cameron nodded in approval.

He swam a few lengths up and down the pool. The twinkling solar lights enabled Julia to see him in the pool, but it was not too bright. She wished she could pluck up the courage to join him.

'It's lovely in here Jules, are you sure you won't change your mind? I have seen you in a swimsuit before. Don't be shy.'

'When?' Julia snapped, instantly revealing her real reason for not wanting to swim with him.

'Let me see? 1978 I would say; when we were at school.'

'That's different, we were kids.'

'I might have been, but you most certainly had the figure of a woman if I remember rightly.'

'Shut up! You're not helping.'

'Sorry. But I could keep my eyes shut.'

'Yeah, right.'

Julia could not be persuaded to change her mind about going for a swim even though Cameron teased her mercilessly about it. In the end she flounced back to the veranda, picked up her iPad and logged onto Facebook, listening to Cameron splashing about in the distance.

Marianne had sent her a message asking what her plans were for her birthday.

Julia sent a quick reply.

"Going out exploring tomorrow. I'm sure it will be sunny and warm and suitably pleasant for someone of my advanced years. I think I had better put another bottle of wine in the fridge. Might need whisky too. I canna believe I'm fifty tomorrow. Shit! Where did the time go?"

The next morning Julia woke up to the sound of Cameron moving around in the next room. She glanced at her watch to see what time it was. It was far too early to get up so she turned over for another little doze.

She opened her eyes again when she heard the outside door open and close and guessed Cameron had gone out for another swim in the pool. She put her dressing gown on and wandered out to the kitchen. The door to the veranda was closed and she opened it and stepped outside and looked around to see where Cameron was. He was nowhere to be seen. She shrugged and walked back indoors to make some coffee.

Next to the kettle was a handwritten note: *Had some urgent business to sort out – just nipped into town, back soon. Don't go anywhere.*

Julia took advantage of his absence to go for a quick swim, but she took the precaution of taking her kaftan to the poolside in case he returned. She swam lazily in the water, watching the wispy clouds drifting across the sky. She stretched out her legs and stared at her red painted toenails. Her legs were lean and toned from her love of walking along the beach in Shetland, and now they were pleasantly bronzed. Her tummy was held in by the Lycra of her "miracle" swimsuit, although there was much less of her to hold in, now she had lost so much weight. Marianne was right, she did look a little scrawny; but not bad for her age.

Moments after congratulating herself for arriving at the age of fifty in a reasonable state, she remembered it was six months to the day that Duncan had died, at the very same age.

She heard footsteps along the path and she raced to the steps, scrambled out of the pool and grabbed hold of the beach towel. She dried her face and then struggled into her kaftan, almost ripping it in her haste to get covered up.

'There you are!'

Julia looked up and saw Cameron standing at the gate, with his hand on the latch.

'I thought I may as well have a swim while I waited for you.'

'Don't let me stop you.'

'That's OK, we can have breakfast now. Unless you already had yours?'

'Not yet.'

He opened the gate for her and Julia followed him back to the villa. She stopped on the veranda for a moment and wrapped the towel around her wet hair. Cameron hovered in the doorway, with a curiously guilty look on his face.

Julia walked into the kitchen and the first thing she saw was a huge bouquet of flowers on the dining table. Giant red blooms of an unrecognisable flower along with white gerberas and blue irises.

'Oh wow, what's this?'

'Happy birthday!'

'How did you know?'

'It was on Facebook, you idiot.'

'Of course. I was going to keep it a secret so you didn't feel you had to make a fuss. But these are gorgeous; I love them.' Julia picked up the bouquet to smell the flowers. 'What are these red ones called?'

Cameron shrugged.

'No idea, I just pointed to them in the shop. They looked bonny enough. Do you like the red, white and blue theme? Very patriotic eh?'

Julia smiled; thinking patriotic was preferable to romantic.

'So where would you like to go today?'

'I don't know actually; you're driving, why don't you decide?'

Cameron wandered over to a large framed antique map of Sicily on the wall of the lounge. He reached into his pocket and pulled out some reading glasses and studied the map for a few minutes. Julia opened and shut all the doors in the kitchen units hunting for a vase. She finally found one at the top of the cupboard, just out of her reach.

She turned to look at Cameron as he took his glasses off and put them away.

'Right. I've found the perfect place to celebrate your birthday.'

'Where?'

'You'll have to wait and see. I expect we'll need the whole day so we'd better leave soon. I might go and put some stuff in a bag, just in case the weather changes.'

'Really? I've been here for ten days already; it hasn't changed at all.'

'Well anyway.'

'Could you just get this vase down for me first?'

Cameron walked over and took the vase down from the shelf and set it down on the worktop. He closed the cupboard door and turned around, bumping into Julia; he put his hand on her arm as he moved out of her way.

Julia felt the warmth of his touch, even after he had walked away. She picked up the vase and carried it to the sink to fill it with water. As the tap filled the heavy crystal vase Julia brushed her hand over the spot where Cameron had just touched her. She looked down and saw water was overflowing the vase already. She turned the tap off and emptied some of the surplus water from the vase and stood it on the draining board. She picked up the flowers, removed the cellophane and proceeded to arrange them. They were beautiful and she realised she hadn't even said thank you to Cameron.

She put the vase in the centre of the dining table then went to find Cameron. He was in his bedroom sitting on the bed fiddling with his phone. He looked up and smiled at her.

'Thank you! The flowers are lovely. It was really sweet of you to go out and buy them.'

'That's OK. I just wanted you to have a nice birthday. I bought some more Prosecco; it's in the fridge already, we can have it when we get back.'

Julia leaned against the doorframe and stared at Cameron for a moment. She realised she was still wearing her wet swimsuit under her kaftan. She shifted uncomfortably, but was inexplicably reluctant to leave. She needed to get dressed, have some breakfast, get ready to go out, but she remained anchored to the door frame.

'Everything alright Jules?'

'Um, yeah.' She turned to go, intending to get changed out of her wet costume.

Cameron stood up suddenly and walked towards her.

'I know what day it is today; six months to the day,' he said quietly. He put his hands on her shoulder; a sympathetic gesture. She shut her eyes.

'Hey, it's OK, I don't mind if you cry. Don't feel you have to hold it all in. I know how you feel.'

She felt him pull her into a tight embrace. She did not resist; but she did not cry. She wrapped her arms around him, her head against his chest. She could hear his heart thudding. She listened to its regular rhythm and savoured the warmth of his body against hers. She wanted to stand still and hold on to this warm and alive body.

Cameron broke the spell at last.

'You're all wet!'

Julia pulled away from him and laughed when she saw the dark wet imprint on his pale blue shirt.

'I'm so sorry. I really should go and get dressed.'

'I'll go and make breakfast then.'

Julia headed back to her room and shut the door behind her and leant against it, breathing deeply. She felt a little embarrassed at the unfamiliar intimacy with Cameron. She heard the radio switch on in the kitchen and heard Cameron began singing along with Ollie Murs. She had forgotten he could sing. She wondered if he realised she could hear him. He sounded cheerful and happy. It was a little infectious.

She decided to take a shower to wash the chlorine out of her hair. She dressed quickly, putting on a sleeveless floral dress and her new sandals. She put a pair of plimsolls into a bag, along with a cardigan and a lightweight jacket. She quickly put on makeup and spritzed on some perfume.

When she returned to the kitchen she found Cameron had set out a selection of Sicilian pastries, croissants and some freshly made coffee.

'Did you buy those today as well?'

'Yeah, I walked past this amazing bakery on the way back from the florist and I couldn't resist them.'

Cameron pulled out a chair for Julia.

'Come on birthday girl, we've got some exploring to do, after breakfast.'

Julia sat down and watched as Cameron poured her a cup of coffee.

'I really appreciate this. I wasn't looking forward to today, for obvious reasons. I mean who really wants to be turning fifty? And as for the other reason, well...'

'You don't look fifty that's for sure. You look great Jules.'

Julia took a bite out of an almond croissant, and then self-consciously checked to see if she had scattered crumbs all over herself.

'Aren't anniversaries strange? I mean, why should the fact he died exactly six months ago hurt more today than it did yesterday, or maybe will do tomorrow. It doesn't make sense, and yet...'

Cameron drank some of his coffee and then topped up his cup from the cafetiere.

'It's because as human beings we're obsessed with time. We've broken down every element of our lives into years, months, weeks, days and hours and we constantly monitor our lives against the clock, racing towards mad self-imposed deadlines, trying to hold back time, trying to celebrate time,' he paused, and gestured at the flowers, 'and finally, wishing we could turn back time.'

Julia put down her croissant and picked up her cup, but did not drink from it. She held it in her hands, thinking back to the last cup of coffee she had made for Duncan.

'Well yes, I guess I wish I could turn back the clock. I wish I could have stopped him from going to work that day. Maybe it was too soon. I don't know. I just wish…'

'I know. So do I. But it wasn't because he went back to work. It just happened. Nobody could have stopped it. I'm actually glad you weren't there when he died.'

'What do you mean?' Julia snapped.

'Let's face it Jules, you wouldn't have been able to live with yourself when you couldn't save him. You would have felt guilty for the rest of your life.'

Julia thought about the post mortem report. It was true; Duncan could not have been saved even if his heart attack had happened in the cardiac unit of a world class hospital. And yet she still felt guilty she hadn't been there to help him, to be there for him. She had witnessed so many deaths, held so many frail hands and stroked the hair on the heads of many elderly patients as they took their last breath. But she had not been there for Duncan. She had arrived at his side nearly two hours later. It was unforgivable. But would she have felt worse if she had been there when it happened? She had no idea.

Cameron walked over to the fridge and took out some juice and poured two glasses and brought them back to the table.

'Shall I tell you about my fiftieth birthday? That was a bundle of laughs too.'

Julia looked up and frowned. Her brain was completely scrambled and she couldn't remember when Cameron's birthday was. She had a feeling it coincided with a significant date.

'St Patrick's Day; we went over to Dublin remember?' Cameron said, as he reached for a pastry.

'Of course. I remember now. Duncan was really envious; he always wanted to go to Dublin for St Patrick's Day.'

Cameron took a bite out of the pastry and grinned with pleasure at the taste. He put it back on the plate and picked up a napkin to wipe a smudge of ricotta cheese from his finger.

'So, anyway, there we were at the Merrion Hotel in Dublin; five star luxury, not too shabby! And I had managed to get tickets for the Six Nations game as well – Ireland v Scotland. I couldn't have planned a better birthday if I tried. Amy was staying with John and Fiona, so we were all set to have a great time.'

He took another sip of coffee and then nibbled at the edge of the pastry. Julia drank her juice and waited for him to continue.

'Anyway, we arrived on the Friday night. We went out to dinner, and then for a drink in some raucous pub in Temple Bar. The next day we went sightseeing, did some shopping, went for another meal and drank more Guinness in yet more pubs. I was having a great time, but I could tell Laura didn't want to be there. She said it was because she hated being away from Amy. But that wasn't it. She'd been apart from Amy loads of times before; it was utter bollocks. And every time I went to the bathroom, or went to the bar she would be on her phone checking for messages or texting someone. I asked her about it and she said she was just seeing how Amy was. In fact she even showed me a message she got from my brother saying what Amy had been doing that day.'

Julia realised where this conversation was heading. She turned to give him her full attention, noticing his shirt was still slightly damp from where she had hugged him earlier.

'I woke up on my birthday on the Sunday morning, with a bit of a hangover, so I was a little grumpy and out of sorts. I decided to order breakfast in the room, but Laura started whinging about the extra cost of it. It was expensive, but since I was paying and it was my birthday I really didn't think she had the right to complain. We had a bit of an argument about it, and then I realised I was being a prat; so to try and calm things down I jokingly asked her where my present was. But she hadn't bought me one yet. She claimed she was going to take me shopping later. I know it's childish, but I was kind of upset about that. We had spent the whole of Saturday morning shopping in Grafton Street. Laura had spent a fortune on clothes for herself and Amy, and yet she hadn't even thought about me.'

Julia reached over and put her hand on his arm. He smiled and patted it.

'I asked her when she thought she would have time to go shopping that day since we had planned to go to the rugby. She replied she didn't really want to go to the match and that she would go shopping while I went to the game on my own. The fact the tickets had cost £120 each didn't seem to matter to her.'

'Jesus, what a bitch,' Julia said, and then looked embarrassed for voicing her criticism. 'Did she really not go with you then?'

Cameron shook his head. 'Oh, but it gets worse. Laura went to the bathroom and I noticed she had left her phone charging on the dresser. It was on silent, but it lit up when she received a text. I saw John's name flash up on the phone and immediately I thought something might have happened to Amy so I picked up the phone and read the text. It wasn't about Amy, and it didn't make any sense to me. But Laura has one of those Smart phones that mean you can scroll through all the messages to and from a person in one thread. And that's when I realised they were having an affair.'

'Oh crumbs. So what did you do?'

'I didn't say anything to her about it. I just set off to the Aviva stadium on my own. I sat and watched Scotland get hammered by Ireland, and everyone around me must have thought I was taking the game too much to heart. Some jolly Irish man slapped me on the back and said "cheer up Jock, it's only a game." I think he caught me wiping away tears.'

'Oh God, how awful. I didn't realise it had all happened on your birthday. I'm so sorry.'

'Well I didn't tell anyone at first; and then of course just a few weeks later, Duncan... Anyway, after the match I went back to the hotel and found Laura had gone. She'd left me a note saying she had gone to the airport. I hadn't told her I read her text messages, but she probably guessed since I had deleted every last one of them and then deleted John's mobile number from her phone and blocked it, just for good measure. I spent that night sitting in the hotel bar getting wasted. Not the best *day* of my life I can assure you, let alone birthday.'

Julia reached her hand out to stroke the velvet-soft petal of one of the white gerberas. She understood suddenly why Cameron had gone to so much trouble for her birthday. She turned to him and smiled sympathetically.

'She's a mad bitch to leave you. She'll regret it, that's for sure.'

'I think she already does. John's a moody bastard. And he's offshore for three weeks at a time, so she's on her own and bored out of her head while he's away. Let's face it Laura gets bored quicker than the average teenager. And when John comes home all he wants to do is sleep and do fuck-all. I think she's fed up with him.'

'Would you take her back; for Amy's sake?'

'No; not even for Amy. I don't think I could ever trust her again. Maybe if it had been anyone other than my own brother. But Jesus, that's sick. I lost my wife and my brother at the same time. Our whole family has been shattered by this; for what? Sex?'

'How's Amy getting along now?'

'Strangely enough she seems to be doing OK. I think she's too young to understand what's going on.'

'That's a relief at least.'

'Yes it is. Anyway, we can't sit around moping and being miserable all day. Let's go out and have some fun.'

Julia stood up, having finished her breakfast, and carried her plate over to the sink. She turned round to see Cameron was staring at her, deep in thought.

'Is that what you're wearing?'

'Um, well yes. Since I don't know where you're taking me I have no idea whether it's appropriate or not. Maybe you could give me a clue. Scuba diving? Pony trekking? Mountaineering? You tell me and I'll get changed.'

Cameron laughed, but Julia noticed his face had twitched when she had said mountaineering. They were, after all, surrounded by mountains.

Cameron scratched the back of his head and looked down at her feet.

'The dress is probably fine, but do you have any other shoes you could wear?'

'At the risk of sounding a bit lame, can I just point out a dress like this simply doesn't go with walking boots? Shall I put jeans on?'

He nodded his approval and Julia shook her head with mock exasperation. Cameron brought his plate and cup over to the sink. Julia was about to fill the sink to wash up.

'Leave that. I'll do the dishes; you get changed.'

Julia turned away from the sink and collided with Cameron who was standing behind her.

'Sorry,' she said, automatically and tried to scoot past him. Cameron stepped out of her way, but as he did he touched her arm. She looked up at him and hesitated. She had known Cameron for as many years as she had known Duncan, and yet she had never been alone with him like this. He grinned at her, his blue eyes twinkling in amusement at her.

'What?' Julia said.

'I feel like we're playing hooky from school. Nobody knows where we are.'

Julia laughed. 'God, I would give anything to go back to those days. What great times we used to have.'

'They'll be good times again. For all the bad luck we've both had, we still have lots of things to be grateful for. Our kids, our friends – our health.'

Julia smiled at him, acknowledging the truth in what he had said. She put her arms around him and hugged him. She had meant to pull away again and go off to get changed, but Cameron wrapped his arms around her and kissed the top of her head.

It was the second time that morning Cameron had held her in his arms. Julia inhaled the smell of coffee mingled with Prada eau de toilette. She had noticed the bottle in his room and had wondered what it had smelt like. And now she knew, she wanted to breathe it in and savour it. Cameron was taller than Duncan had been, broader too, so he felt alien to her, and yet he felt so alive and comforting. He also made her miss her husband more than ever. She craved the touch of another human; a man. The last six months had been the longest and loneliest of her life, despite the love and support she had received from friends and family. It was hard to admit to herself, what she really wanted would not be considered appropriate for a newly widowed woman.

She realised with a jolt she had been holding on to Cameron for an excessively long time, given the platonic nature of their friendship. She also realised Cameron seemed in no hurry to let go. In fact when she shifted a fraction she could feel something rather less than platonic pressed against her abdomen. Cameron pulled away from her but the devil in her pulled him back.

Cameron continued to cuddle her, but she could tell he was now rather nervous. His heartbeat had increased and his breathing was shallow. The muscles in his back and arms tensed.

Julia took a deep breath; what she was about to do might destroy their friendship forever. It was insane. If she walked away right this minute there would be no harm done. It would just have been a rather more extended version of a friendly hug, but nothing more. She could recover from this moment with her dignity intact if she let go of him.

She could not let go. She pulled him closer; making it obvious she knew he was turned on. She lifted her face and stared into his eyes. He held her gaze, not smiling, but staring intently back, as if he was trying to gauge what was going on in her head.

Julia reached up and touched his face. He still did not smile, but did not let go of her either. She ran her hand through his hair and then gently pulled his head towards her. Cameron finally gave himself permission to act on his instincts. His mouth met hers and they kissed. Julia shut her eyes, trying to control the adrenaline rush. Hands trembling, she held his face to hers and kissed him back, forgetting all about the last time he had drunkenly tried to kiss her before, which had resulted in sharp words.

They pulled apart from each other. Julia opened her eyes and looked into his, trying to read his reaction. He smiled and kissed her again, this time with more intent. Julia had lost all sense of reason by now and she reached her hand down towards his waist. She hesitated for a moment, considering this was really crossing all lines of friendship now. There would be no return now. She reached for his belt buckle and started to undo it.

Cameron pulled away sharply and frowned quizzically at her.

'Are you sure Jules?'

She nodded and then to underline this assertion she kissed him again. This time Cameron did not hold back. She felt the gentle tug of the zip of her dress inching its way down her back. Cameron pushed aside the shoulder of the dress and nuzzled against her bare skin. Julia decided she didn't want to continue this in the kitchen, and at the risk of killing the moment she pulled Cameron towards her bedroom. She held her dress around her shoulders until they were inside her room, then she shut the door and let the dress fall to the floor.

Cameron sat down on the edge of her bed and she walked towards him, inwardly stunned at her brazen behaviour. She kicked off her sandals and then sat astride him and kissed him, only half concentrating on the kiss, as she could now feel his hands undoing her bra. He seemed in no hurry though. She arched her back in pleasure as he stroked her bare skin. His hands were warm, travelling confidently around her body as if he had every right to do so.

Julia giggled suddenly; her nerves getting the better of her.

'You OK?' he said, holding her shoulders and leaning back to look her in the face.

'Is this mad, what we're doing?'

'Possibly; but we can stop now. It's OK; I won't take it the wrong way.'

'I don't want to stop. Do you?'

'Obviously not. But if you change your mind, at any moment, just tell me. You can trust me Jules.'

'I know I can. Maybe that's why I want to do this. I *need* to do this!'

'Need to do this? So you're just using me then?' Cameron grinned at her.

'Do you have a problem with that, boy?'

'No!'

'Good, so why have you still got all your clothes on? Come on, take them off; let's see what you've got.'

Cameron laughed out loud and pushed Julia off his lap. She lifted up the sheet on the bed and climbed in, and then watched Cameron undo his shirt and take it off.

'Not bad,' she said, nodding her head as she appraised his body. Although she was teasing him, in actual fact he did have a nice body. She had seen it before when he had been swimming, but this time when she looked at him, she saw him in a different light. She had never slept with anyone other than Duncan before. She was nervous, but at the same time she felt exhilarated; so much so she began to wonder what Cameron had put in her coffee.

Cameron sat on the edge of the bed and undid his shoelaces. He turned to look at her and she pulled the sheet up; an involuntary gesture of shyness. Cameron winked at her and then took his shoes and socks off and put them under a chair. He turned to face her and undid his belt and took off his jeans and draped them over the chair.

He was wearing navy cotton-jersey boxer shorts that clung to the curve of his hips and buttocks. Julia realised she was staring at his body, so she looked up at his face. He grinned at her, not arrogantly, but confident in himself. He really was rather fine to look at, Julia thought as he climbed into the bed beside her. He pulled her towards him and she cuddled up to him, feeling a complicated mix of nervousness, guilt and the anticipation of pleasure. She thought of Duncan, and her resolve wavered a little.

But then she felt Cameron half lifting, half guiding her to face him. She acquiesced and forgetting all about Duncan she found herself once more sitting astride Cameron. Within seconds he had removed her bra and before she had time to feel any further remorse he was fondling her breasts, teasing her nipples with his lips.

It was as if he had flipped some invisible switch; suddenly Julia wanted to speed things up. She kissed him urgently, desperately, clinging to him, trying to hold back the moans of pure pleasure that threatened to erupt every time he moved his mouth or his hands to another erogenous zone on her body.

The first time was unapologetically quick. Afterwards they lay in stunned silence, clinging to each other. Cameron stroked her back as she lay in his arms with her face half buried against his chest. Julia was scared to speak. She closed her eyes; dazed at how fast they had moved from friends to this. What was this anyway? Whatever it was, it felt good. It wasn't just the physical release of tension either; it was the connection with another human being. She felt alive again.

The second time, maybe half an hour later, they took their time. It was softer, gentler, sweeter, and in some ways more emotionally painful; at least for Julia. This time it was not just the crazy random act of hormones. It was deliberate, intentional and the deepening of a relationship. Julia lay in bed cuddled up to Cameron who appeared to have dozed off, and wondered whether she would live to regret this spontaneous seduction of her late husband's best friend.

She looked at her watch. It was now midday. So far it had been a memorable way to spend her birthday, and it wasn't over yet.

They were supposed to be going out somewhere for the day. Cameron opened his eyes and grinned at her. On the other hand, they could go out exploring Sicily tomorrow. Julia thought if she was going to end up beating herself up with guilt about this situation, then she may as well really do something to feel guilty about. She ran her hand down Cameron's thigh, and then up again, and let her fingers linger. Cameron responded by pushing her back against the pillows and seconds later he was inside her again, echoing their first time. Julia had no objections.

During her second shower of the day, Julia had a few moments alone to consider what she had done. She couldn't decide whether it was because nobody else knew about them, or because it was simply a perfectly acceptable thing to indulge in, that she hadn't felt any real sense of guilt; yet. She breathed a sigh of relief that she hadn't had her birth control coil removed yet and refused to scold herself for not even raising the issue of safe sex with Cameron.

Instead she thought about what it was like to kiss Cameron and was rewarded with the sensation of butterflies. She hadn't felt like this in years. It was like being a teenager again and she decided to give herself permission not to feel guilty about what had happened.

14

From the morning of Julia's birthday until Friday lunchtime, when Cameron flew back to Shetland, they spent the rest of their time together as if they were on honeymoon. They held hands when they finally ventured out to do some sightseeing. On Wednesday they drove to Mount Etna, where Cameron had planned to take her for her birthday. They made love on a picnic blanket on the lower slopes of the mountain, and watched the steam from the active volcano drifting over them. They talked endlessly about life and the universe, politics, religion, music, books and films. But they did not discuss how they felt about each other and they most certainly did not talk about the future.

Julia watched Cameron disappear through the departure gates at the airport and felt a heavy sense of loss, mixed with the giddy thrill of a secret affair. She knew she would see him again in a few weeks; but it would never be the same again. This time together had been perfect, but Julia did not anticipate any future for themselves as a couple. She knew her sons would be horrified if they found out about Cameron. She hadn't even risked telling Marianne yet; although she suspected she might give in to the impulse to talk about what had happened when she got back to Shetland.

She had fielded all the calls and texts she had received on her birthday quite well; insinuating she was enjoying her holiday all on her own. Marianne had commented she seemed positively upbeat and had jokingly asked her whether she had hooked up with an Italian waiter.

Julia had less than twenty four hours to go until Bryden and Anna would fly in. She walked out of the airport and crossed the forecourt to the car rental offices Cameron had hired his car from. She negotiated a two week rental on a Fiat 500 and when she was handed the keys she walked across to the car park and got into her new car with a confidence she could not have imagined a fortnight earlier. She hadn't even bothered to rent a sat-nav. She started the engine and pulled out into the busy traffic.

Julia parked the car on the driveway outside the villa and noticed Tony's car was there. She had not seen him for an entire week, so she ran up the steps to his front door and rang the bell. He opened it a moment later and invited her in.

'Sorry, I haven't been around this week. Is everything alright with the villa?'

'Yes of course. That's not why I stopped by though. I just came to say hello.'

'Oh well that's lovely. I see you finally got around to hiring a car; good for you.'

'Well, it's all thanks to you. I drove home like a native Sicilian today.'

Tony laughed. 'I do hope not!'

'Have you been anywhere exciting?' Julia asked, as she followed him in to the kitchen. He indicated for her to take a seat as he went to the fridge to get some wine.

'I had to dash up to Rome actually.' He sighed, and turned to look at Julia, as if he was sizing up whether he could confide in her or not. He opened the bottle of Italian Chardonnay and poured two glasses. He pushed a glass towards Julia and then sat down across the large farmhouse style table from her.

'My daughter's pregnant,' he said quietly. 'I will be a grandfather next year.'

'You sound like that's not good news.'

'Well since she has just split up with her boyfriend, I really don't think it is good news. Not that I'm being old fashioned. It's just…'

'It's not what you wanted for her,' Julia said, finishing his sentence as he gazed into the distance.

'Not really no. She may not even get a chance to finish her degree before the baby is born. She has nowhere to live, other than to come back here; which is great for me but maybe not so good for her. Sicily doesn't have much to offer the young; especially if they haven't finished their studies and don't have a trade.'

'That's a shame. Is she still in Rome now?'

'Yes. She's trying to complete her dissertation before the baby is due in March. But I wonder whether she will be able to. She's so distraught about her boyfriend; and she's missing her mother more than ever right now.'

'I don't blame her, poor lass. I remember when I was pregnant; the first person I wanted to share that with, other than Duncan obviously, was my mother.'

Tony took a sip of wine and then looked Julia up and down.

'There's something different about you; what have you been doing while I've been away?'

Julia felt her cheeks flush with embarrassment.

'Um well actually, one of my friends from Shetland came over for a few days. He came to meet Jürgen to talk about architecture.'

Tony looked puzzled for a moment and then appeared to remember.

'Ah yes, the holiday resort project; so did your friend enjoy Sicily?'

Julia giggled. 'What he saw of it; yes I think so.'

Tony raised an eyebrow.

'Have I missed some scandal?'

'Possibly.' Julia took a sip of wine, but found it hard to swallow, with the Cheshire cat grin on her face.

'Well good for you. I must say you do look a lot perkier than the last time I saw you.'

Tony stood up and went over to the fridge and took out a foil covered dish.

'Well, you really must stay for lunch and spill the beans.' He lifted the foil lid and smiled. 'Maria's lasagne; I'll just pop this in the oven.'

Learning to Dance Again

Julia surprised herself by telling Tony all about Cameron. She had imagined having this conversation with Marianne, but unsurprisingly Tony's own experiences of bereavement meant he understood Julia in a way that perhaps Marianne wouldn't. He certainly understood Julia's craving for affection and he also understood why she thought it would never develop into a proper relationship.

'Take my advice my dear, treasure the memory of what happened and use it to keep you warm at night. But you should be careful of falling in love with someone while you're still grieving. It's not fair on you or him.'

'You're right. There were moments when I felt so confused; I had to stop myself from calling him Duncan. It was lovely, but I know I'll feel guilty about it soon. I certainly don't want my sons to find out.'

'You mustn't feel guilty. You've done nothing wrong; and neither has he. But rebound relationships are tricky; and more so when you're rebounding from bereavement.'

Later that afternoon, after a lovely lunch with Tony, Julia walked back to her villa. She unlocked the door and the first thing she saw was the vase of flowers on the dining table. It was the only evidence Cameron had been there. She went to what had originally been his room and stripped the bed so she could get it ready for Bryden and Anna's arrival the next day.

She lazed around on the veranda for the rest of the day and evening, feeling listless and deflated by the she climbed into her bed that night. She stretched out and inhaled. She could still smell Cameron's presence. She decided she would need to change the bedding the next morning to remove all traces he was ever there. Her phone bleeped beside the bed.

"Home safe. Just picked up Amy for the weekend. Hope you have a great time with Bryden x"

Julia read the text and frowned. Apart from the little x there was nothing to suggest anything other than a platonic friendship existed between them. She decided Cameron must be as keen as she was to draw a line under what had happened. When she returned to Shetland it would be business as usual. She wasn't sure whether to feel hurt or relieved.

She tried to compose a text to Cameron but couldn't think what to say or how to say it. She couldn't make up her mind whether to be bright and cheerful, cool and distant, or to say what she actually felt. The bed felt lonely without him. But she couldn't bring herself to tell him that. It would make it too real.

Bryden sat down on one of the wooden loungers on the veranda. His shoulders were hunched over and he seemed to be staring at his feet, rather than at the very attractive view of the sea. He had not taken off the jacket he had been wearing on the plane, although he must surely be too warm in the late afternoon sun. Julia carried out a pitcher of iced lemonade and two glasses and set them down on the table between them. She went back to the kitchen and brought back some cakes. Bryden did not seem to notice.

'Have you tried calling Anna?'

'What's the point,' Bryden replied, more as a statement than a question. His shoulders tensed under the strain of making conversation. Julia was beginning to wish he had stayed at home. He clearly didn't want to be in Sicily.

'Darling, why don't you tell me what happened? Maybe I can help.'

Bryden sighed and unzipped his jacket. He struggled out of it and then dropped it on the floor, in a gesture that reminded Julia of Duncan. She picked up his jacket and set it down on a spare chair. She poured him a glass of lemonade and handed it to him. He took it, but did not say thank you.

Julia resisted the temptation to scold him for his bad manners; but he was miserable enough as it was.

Bryden took a sip of the drink and then put it down on the table. He shut his eyes, but it was not a relaxed pose. His fingers twitched on the arms of the lounger, and he crossed and uncrossed his legs.

'I asked her to marry me.'

'I see.'

Julia's heart sank in sympathy with her son, although she was secretly relieved Anna had obviously said no. They were both so young. It seemed such an unlikely thing for Bryden to do. He had only been going out with Anna for a few months, and she had not struck Julia as the settling down type. She was still at university, and would be for another year. Julia doubted the idea would have occurred to Bryden had it not been for Duncan's death.

'I'm such an idiot,' Bryden said, standing up suddenly and then pausing as if he forgotten where he was going.

Julia stood up and put her arms around him.

'You're not an idiot. Just because Anna isn't ready to get married and settle down, doesn't mean she didn't appreciate being asked. It doesn't have to be the end does it?'

'We had a huge row about it. She changed her mind about coming on holiday with me, so yes, I think it does mean the end. And now I'll have to find somewhere else to live.'

Julia let go of Bryden and motioned for him to sit down.

'Look, I was going to have this conversation with you and Jamie together. But maybe I should tell you now.'

Bryden looked at Julia, frowning slightly. He sat down and then picked up his glass and took a long drink. Julia sat down next to him and leaned forward and held his hand.

'I'm thinking of putting your granny's house up for sale. The tenants that are in there now are moving out soon. I don't really want the bother of renting it out again to anyone else, and I thought maybe it's time to sell the house, and then divide the money between you and Jamie. You might be able to buy somewhere in Edinburgh.'

'But I love that house!'

'I know; but we have no use for it now. An old house like that needs someone living in it and lots of care and attention. It really could do with being modernised, but it isn't worth the investment at the moment.'

'But what if me or Jamie want to move back to Shetland?'

'Is that likely to happen any time soon?'

Bryden shrugged, but he clearly didn't think so.

'With the money from the sale you would both have quite a nice deposit on a new place.'

'I suppose so,' he replied, without any enthusiasm.

'Anyway, it was just an idea. I'm not going to do anything about it until after the New Year. I expect I'll need to go in and get the place painted and tidied up first. We'll talk about it with Jamie when we're together again. I didn't want to mention it the other day when I was in Edinburgh as he seemed a bit stressed out.'

'So, what's this place like then? Have you seen much of Sicily yet?' Bryden said, as if he was keen to change the subject.

'I've been to Palermo, Agrigento and Mount Etna. They were nice. I was thinking we could drive over to Messina tomorrow and get on the ferry to the mainland. What do you think?'

'Drive to Italy? How far away is that?'

'It's just a thirty minute ferry crossing; a bit like going across to Whalsay, although I think the ferries are much bigger than we have in Shetland.'

Bryden seemed to brighten up at the idea of travelling to the mainland. He ate one of the cakes Julia had put out and then decided he would take a dip in the swimming pool while Julia made dinner.

Julia walked out to the swimming pool to find him. She found him sitting on the edge of the pool with his feet dangling in the water. He was looking down at the view of Cefalu.

'This is a fabulous place.'

'It is. Your father would have loved it here.'

'Yeah!'

Bryden pulled his legs out of the pool and stood up. He picked up a towel and dried his face, and then grinned at Julia.

'Feel better?'

'Much. Thanks Mam. It was a great idea coming over here. I nearly didn't, but then I thought you might be feeling a bit lonely out here on your own.'

'I'm glad you did.' Julia smiled to herself as they walked back to the villa.

Over the next few days, Bryden's mood zipped up and down like a yo-yo. One minute he was morose and miserable, and then he would become distracted by the sights and sounds of Sicily and he would resume his normal cheerful banter. Julia could tell he really needed a holiday. His first term of teaching had been exhausting, even if he was enjoying it.

Hearing him talk about his pupils and the school politics, brought back echoes of Duncan, and sometimes it was hard to look at Bryden without seeing glimpses of her late husband. Bryden took after his father in appearance too, and it was both comforting and unnerving to look at the same sea-green eyes and crooked smile.

Bryden's time in Sicily rushed by in a blur of archaeological ruins, pizza restaurants, swimming in the pool and shopping in Palermo. He had been impressed by Julia's confidence, driving around in the little car she had hired. He took a photo of her leaning against the car while it was parked at the side of a winding mountain road. He sent the picture message to Jamie with the words – *mam taking a break from driving*.

Jamie replied a while later.

"Cool, I'm impressed. Wish I could have come over too."

Bryden showed the text to Julia.

'I wish he could have come too. Mind you, he's getting more than his fair share of adventure and travel.'

'True. Jammy git. Although I don't think I would like to do that job. I know I get tired sometimes, but he's like a zombie when he's been on nights.'

'I used to hate nights too. But it will be worth it when he qualifies.'

Bryden bounced back from his sudden breakup with Anna. Over dinner in a restaurant, on his last evening in Sicily, he opened up to Julia about his feelings for Anna and finally concluded he had been too hasty. He acknowledged that if his father had not died he probably wouldn't have moved in with Anna.

Julia hadn't had a conversation with Bryden like this in a long time. She wondered how much her sons had been holding back on discussing their worries, first because of Duncan's illness and then because he had died.

'You do know you and Jamie can tell me anything. I may be a little sad and miserable at the moment, but I would still do anything for you two. Please don't feel you have to only share the good stuff with me.'

Bryden smiled and shrugged his shoulders.

'You had enough on your plate.'

'I guess I did; but we're going to get through this together. You, me and Jamie; we will find a way to be happy again. It's what your father would want for you both.'

'And you!' Bryden leaned across the restaurant table and reached for her hand.

'And me.'

Julia went to bed that night feeling uplifted by her conversation with Bryden. She felt closer to him than she had done in a while. As she lay in bed trying to get to sleep, she started making plans for when she returned to Shetland. She was going to do something positive for her sons, and find something worthwhile to do with her life that would make them proud of her.

On Friday morning Julia drove Bryden back to the airport. She was almost tempted to book a flight back home with him. She had just over a week left to go of her holiday and she was missing Shetland now. But Bryden persuaded her to stay a little longer.

'I think this holiday is doing you good. How can you be in a hurry to leave this sunshine?'

'I suppose so. Marianne sent me a text to say it was trying to snow yesterday.'

'Exactly; and yet here we are, not even needing to put on a jacket. I will definitely come back to Sicily again at this time of year.'

'Next time with Jamie.'

'Definitely; next October we'll all come back.'

Bryden hugged Julia at the departure gate.

'Enjoy the rest of your holiday.'

Julia nodded, and reached up and ruffled his hair.

She drove back to the villa feeling despondent. In tandem with her mood the sky started to cloud over and a few miles further on it started to rain. It was the first time since she had arrived in Sicily it had rained during the day. She had heard rain during the night a couple of times, but never seen it. She glanced at the sea to her left as she drove along the motorway to Cefalu; it was a dull grey colour and it reminded her of home. She regretted not getting on the plane with Bryden as she wasn't sure what else she wanted to do on her holiday.

She parked her car on the drive next to Tony's and she got out and hurried through the rain to her villa. By the time she reached the front door she was drenched. She hunted through her handbag for the key, cursing the weather. She eventually found it and was about to open the door when a loud rumble of thunder made her jump. She turned and looked back at the sea just in time to see a white fork of lightening light up the dark sky.

Julia hurried indoors and shut the door behind her. She stood at the kitchen window for a moment waiting to see if there was more lightning. Thunderstorms were quite rare in Shetland and she was fascinated by them, as well as a little nervous.

The thunder rumbled again, followed swiftly by another jagged flash. The storm was immediately overhead. She watched out the window for a few minutes and then decided to get changed out of her wet clothes into something dry, and warmer. She shivered, feeling cold for the first time in weeks.

It was gloomy inside the villa without the sunshine to brighten up the rooms. Julia put on a pair of jeans, a tee shirt and her Fair Isle cardigan. She still felt cold so she fetched a blanket from the bedroom and wrapped it around her shoulders. She picked up her iPad and logged onto Facebook.

There was no interesting news, so she checked her emails. There was nothing of any importance there either. She realised with a jolt she had not heard from Cameron. It had been a week since she had seen him, and she felt like she had imagined their affair.

Julia prodded her feelings and decided it was probably for the best. She had no desire to pick up the relationship again when she returned home, and she doubted Cameron would either. It had been a moment of madness.

The thunderstorm stopped, and Julia stood up and went outside to the veranda. The loungers were soaked so she could not sit down. She leaned against the railings that surrounded the veranda and inhaled the scent of dark, damp earth and watched as a glimpse of blue sky started to reappear in the distance. Birds sang in the trees and the sun came out again. It was hard not to feel cheerful.

The last few weeks in Sicily had made a dramatic difference to Julia. She had turned a corner. The alien landscape and the break away from her normal life had shaken her out of her depression.

She thought about what she had achieved during the last few weeks. She had tackled the terrors of driving in a foreign land, not just a car, but also a scooter; and she had survived without so much as a scratch. She had brightened up her wardrobe with some out of character purchases and treated herself to some new cosmetics. Her suntanned skin made her feel less washed out; and the hours spent walking around tourist attractions had toned up muscles that had suffered from weeks of lying around at home doing nothing.

She had made new friends and had proved to herself she could, if she really wanted, embark upon a new relationship. She could survive on her own. She realised the holiday had been a success, even if some of what had happened would have to remain a secret.

But she still hadn't worked out wanted she wanted to do with her life. She had absolutely no idea how to spend her remaining working life. She pictured herself at her old desk, managing the staff rota, balancing the budget, and dealing with the usual mundane problems. It didn't make her heart sing. It was too far removed from the people she liked to work with.

She thought of Marianne giving up her job to look after her new grandchild, who was due any day now. She was jealous. She would love to sit at home with a new baby, but that was unlikely to happen for a good few years.

She was still thinking about Marianne when her phone rang. It was Marianne. Julia smiled at the coincidence as she answered it.

'Hello, I was just thinking about you and wondering what you were up to.'

'It's a boy!' Marianne said, shrieking with excitement. '7lbs 5oz, Charlie Alexander Johnson.'

'Oh wow, congratulations. How's Rachel?'

'She's fine now. Poor lamb; it all happened in a bit of a rush. She went along to an ante-natal appointment at the hospital, mentioned to the midwife she had a bit of a back ache, and promptly discovered she was in labour. An hour later, out he popped. Luckily Ivan had driven her to the appointment otherwise he might have missed it. I was at work, but I managed to sneak off to the hospital to see them and have a quick cuddle. Oh Julia, he's gorgeous.'

'I bet he his; excellent genetic pedigree!' Julia said, laughing as she realised Marianne was in tears. She felt her own eyes well up, and for once it was nice to be crying with happiness. 'I can't wait to see him. I dropped Bryden off at the airport this morning, and I nearly came home with him. I wish I had done now.'

'Don't worry; I'll post up some pictures on Facebook. You'll be home soon. It will fly by. How are you doing anyway?'

'Pretty good really. I feel like I'm on the mend at last.'

'That's great. You needed that holiday. And now you can get yourself back home and in a few months you'll be working again. I've decided I'm going to leave work before Easter.'

'Really? That soon?'

'Oh yes. Rachel won't need me until much later in the summer, but I decided I'm going to take some time off for myself. I feel like I need a break too.'

'You should come to Sicily. This place is lovely. I'm definitely coming back again.'

'I might just do that.'

Julia realised she was getting warm and she started to shrug off her Fair Isle cardigan.

'Oh, by the way, I ran into Cameron yesterday. He seemed remarkably cheerful,' Marianne said.

'Really?' Julia replied, trying not to sound too interested.

'Yes, it was very strange. He told me Laura has just split up with his brother, which is probably why he was so happy. I wonder if they're going to get back together again. I didn't get a chance to ask him. His mobile rang and he had to rush off to meet Laura and Amy.'

'Right, well that's good news I suppose.' Julia said, as she stood up and walked into her bedroom. She stared at the bed she had shared with Cameron, albeit for just a few nights. It really hadn't happened. She had imagined it.

'Anyway, must dash, I have to go out and buy something for Charlie and Rachel.'

Julia put her phone down on the bedside table and lay down on the bed. She felt overwhelmed by the news. On the one hand, it was great news about Marianne's new grandson. And it was probably good news about Cameron getting back together with his wife, if only for Amy's sake. She presumed they would get back together; despite his protestations to her he would never consider it. Didn't Marianne say he looked cheerful? That must be the reason. She had to fight off the feeling of disappointment; hadn't she only just told herself there was no prospect of a relationship between them.

'Oh God, I'm a dreadful person,' she said out loud. She sat up suddenly and got off the bed. 'This won't do!'

She glanced in the mirror and then picked up her hairbrush and brushed her hair. She reapplied some lip-gloss and then she marched out of the villa, not pausing even to lock the door behind her.

Without consciously thinking about where she was going, she marched up to Tony's house and rang the bell. He answered it a moment later, wearing jeans and a cotton rugby shirt and holding a pair of reading glasses in his hand.

'Hello, everything OK?' Tony said, opening the door wider to let her in.

'You're busy writing, aren't you?'

'I am; but I was just thinking about stopping for lunch. Care to join me? Maria made some pasta earlier, and her famous homemade bread.'

'Um, well if you're sure.'

'Certainly my dear; you look like you need company.'

'Is it that obvious?'

'It's written all over your face.' Tony smiled, and led her into the kitchen, where Maria was sitting reading a newspaper and drinking a cup of coffee. She looked up at Julia and smiled.

'Buongiorno!' Maria said, as she folded her newspaper and stood up.

'Buongiorno', Julia replied, wishing she could think of something else she could say in Italian, like "please don't get up on my account."

'You like coffee?' Maria said, walking over to the coffee pot on the stove.

'Actually Maria, I was thinking Julia and I might open a bottle of wine and enjoy the last of the sunshine on the terrace. It might be the last chance to eat lunch outside. I think winter is on its way now.'

Maria stared at him, and Julia realised she was translating what he had said. They conversed in Italian normally.

'OK! Lunch, it is outside?' Maria replied.

'Yes, but we'll manage. You may as well get back home if you like. I'll clear up afterwards.'

Maria smiled again, and picked up her handbag and newspaper and said goodbye.

After she had gone Tony excused himself to go and switch off his computer. Julia sat down at the kitchen table, feeling a little guilty. She had clearly interrupted his day, and she wondered what Maria thought about being sent home early. Would she wonder what they were up to? Julia realised she was becoming paranoid. She took a deep breath, and noticed the kitchen was full of the most heavenly smell of food. In her anxiety she hadn't seen the rosemary focaccia bread cooling on a rack beside the sink.

She stood up and walked over to the bread and held her hand over it, feeling the heat rising up. She turned at the sound of footsteps on the marble floor behind her.

'Maria does make the best bread in the world.'

'It smells heavenly.'

'You should get her to teach you how to make it, before you go home.'

Tony walked over to the French doors that opened out onto the terrace. The sun had come out again, and steam rose from the lawn, but it was definitely cooler than it had been. Julia shivered.

'You know, I don't think it is warm enough to sit outside is it?' Tony said, pulling the doors closed again. 'Let's just sit at the kitchen table shall we?'

Julia nodded and looked at the date on her watch. It was 21st October and it was finally too cool to sit outside. Back home it was cold and wintry and she would soon miss the sunshine she had started to take for granted.

Julia helped Tony lay the table, smiling at how familiar she felt with his kitchen. She opened the fridge, knowing full well what wine she would find inside. She took out a bottle of Prosecco and held it up for Tony's approval.

'My thoughts exactly!'

'I've lost count of how many bottles of this stuff I've drunk on this holiday. I must be a borderline alcoholic.'

'I don't think alcoholics drink Prosecco,' Tony said, laughing as he set a large terracotta dish of pasta onto an ornately decorated tile in the centre of the table.

They sat down to lunch and Tony opened the wine and poured a glass each.

'Now, tell me, what's troubling you today?'

'I don't really know where to start actually.'

'Does this have anything to do with your architect friend?'

'Partly; mostly. My friend Marianne said his wife has just split up with his brother, and so they might be getting back together.'

Tony put down his knife and fork and leaned back in his chair grinning at Julia.

'My God, you couldn't write this, could you? Oh, but I'm sorry; I suppose this must be a bit disappointing for you.'

Julia smiled back; acknowledging the soap opera nature of the situation.

'Well, I'm not sure what to feel really. I mean, for his daughter's sake I hope they do get back together. And it's not as if I expected anything more to happen between us, but…'

'I know. But it probably feels as if what happened between you was totally insignificant to him. You feel slighted.'

'Exactly!'

Julia sighed with relief. It was good to feel understood, especially when she didn't quite understand herself entirely.

'Well, if I may say so, it's probably for the best. It solves the problem of how to tackle the situation when you go home again. You can both pretend it never happened.'

'That's true. This morning I wanted to go home with Bryden, but now I wish I could stay here forever.'

'It is the perfect place to hide away from the world.'

Julia turned her head and looked out of the window at the garden. She nodded her head in agreement.

'Have you had any more ideas about what you're going to do when you get back? I seem to remember you were going to spend some time thinking about your future,' Tony said.

'I still have no idea. I need some inspiration.'

Tony stood up and walked to the fridge and took out a bottle of sparkling mineral water and brought it back to the table. He poured two glasses and handed one to Julia.

'I've been giving some thought to how you might come up with a solution.'

Julia looked puzzled. She took a sip of water and waited for him to continue; flattered he had spent any time at all mulling over her problems.

'When I'm starting a new novel I have to spend a lot of time creating new characters. And because I have such a bad memory I tend to write down all the details about these people so I can look at my notes while I'm writing. I have come up with a funny kind of interview questionnaire for my characters I fill in, after asking them a series of questions.'

Julia snorted with laughter.

'Hold on; let me get this straight. Are you telling me you're inventing people and then asking these imaginary folk to tell you about themselves?'

'I suspect you think I'm losing my marbles.'

'No, but it does seem a little strange; but what would I know, I'm not a writer.'

'I can show you how it works if you like. We'll make up a character right now. Male or female?'

'Female,' Julia replied, nodding her head emphatically.

'What's her name?'

'Rebecca?'

'Good name; timeless, solid Biblical roots. Surname?'

Julia looked around the kitchen for inspiration and a bottle of sherry beside the stove caught her attention.

'Sherry; her name is Rebecca Sherry.'

'I like that. So what does this Rebecca look like? Is she young, old, blonde, brunette?'

'Well she's younger than me, maybe forty? And she's definitely a brunette.'

'What does she do?'

Julia bit her bottom lip and frowned in concentration.

'She works for the mountain rescue service in the Cairngorms.'

Tony laughed.

'She does, doesn't she? See how a person can start to come alive after just a few thoughts about their name?'

Julia nodded in understanding and then she frowned again.

'But what does this have to do with my situation? How is that going to help me decide what I want to do with my life? I already know who I am.'

'Precisely. You do know who you are. But perhaps you haven't spent enough time working out what makes you tick. This is where my questionnaire comes in. But we need to write stuff down on paper, so we'll finish this after lunch. But I might keep Becky Sherry for one of my books. I like the sound of her; mountain rescue, hmm...'

They finished their lunch whilst talking about Tony's latest novel. When they had finished, Julia helped him clear away the table and stack the dishwasher. Tony made some coffee and then he disappeared off to his office and came back with a large pad of drawing paper and some pens. He set them down on the kitchen table and sat down.

After he had served the coffee, he picked up a pen and drew a little stick figure in the middle of a sheet of paper.

'This is you in the middle,' he said, pushing the pad towards Julia and handing her the pen.

'OK?' Julia replied, doubtfully.

'Right; what you have to do now is surround yourself with all the things that are precious to you. Family, friends, hobbies etc. Just write them all down.'

Julia instantly drew two more stick figures and wrote Jamie and Bryden beside them. Then she drew a little circle and wrote Marianne and family. She drew some more circles and wrote down some other names of friends, which included Cameron. She drew a childish sketch of her house and included a figurative map showing how close to the sea it was. Then she paused, not sure what else to include.

'What about hobbies?' Tony prompted.

'I don't really have any. Isn't that an awful admission?'

'What do you do in your spare time then?'

'Up until Duncan died, I never really had much spare time. We used to do lots of things together; walking, going out. I can't think of anything specific. We use to join in with whatever was going on in the community; you know, dances, quizzes, craft sales…We also used to go to the theatre and the cinema and out to dinner. But nothing you could really class as a hobby.'

'So you're quite a sociable person then. Write that down.'

Julia wrote "sociable" next to her little stick figure.

'Do you consider yourself to be creative or artistic?'

Julia shook her head sadly.

'Musical?'

'Not really. I like music, but I don't really spend much time listening to it.'

'Gardening, cooking?'

'Gardening is a bit tough in Shetland. I keep on top of the weeds, but that's the extent of my gardening. I love cooking, but I'm not exactly brilliant at it.'

Tony shook his head slowly.

'I'm a hopeless case aren't I?' Julia said, staring down at the paper with its sparse detail about her life. 'I wouldn't make a very interesting heroine in one of your novels. I bet you would kill me off in chapter one.'

'Not at all. This simply says to me your character – Julia Robertson – is a family and community minded person. She's sociable and a bit of a homebody. Nothing wrong with that. You haven't written down anything about your work. Is that significant?'

Julia wrote "nurse" and "care home manager" in the top left corner of the page.

'Well, that speaks volumes in itself. You've listed your profession as far away as you could from your icon.'

Julia looked down at the paper and nodded.

'I just don't want to do that again. I don't want to work with people who are in the later stages of their lives. I don't want to spend my time with old people. I used to love my job, but I need a change now and I would rather be with younger people, children even. I envy my friend Marianne. She became a grandmother today.'

'So children and grandchildren are important to you.'

'Well yes, of course my children are important, but I don't expect to be a grandmother for years yet.'

'But you would rather work with children?' Tony said, tentatively.

Julia snapped her head up suddenly.

'Yes, I would actually.'

'Well there you have your answer.'

'It's not quite so simple though is it? I don't have the qualifications for teaching, or even for working in a nursery; and I don't think I would like to work with large numbers of children.'

Tony leaned forward and pulled the paper towards him and then tapped the sketch of Julia's house.

'Didn't you say the other day you have a five bedroomed house, and now there's just you living in it?'

Julia nodded.

'Plenty of room for a child or two.'

'I don't get it; are you saying I should do an Angeline Jolie and adopt some orphans?'

'No, but I bet you would make a brilliant foster mother.'

Julia put the pen down and folded her arms and leaned on the table. She dipped her head in thought. She spoke without looking up.

'About a year after Bryden went away to university, and before Duncan was ill, I actually thought about fostering. But we kind of dismissed the idea, as Duncan felt it would be difficult, what with him being a teacher. He would have felt awkward if he had to foster someone who he might be teaching. But that doesn't apply now does it?'

Tony shook his head and smiled sadly at her.

'It's definitely worth a thought isn't it?'

Julia looked down at the paper, looking for more inspiration.

'Julia Robertson, a petite attractive blonde widow starts to rebuild her life when she becomes a foster mother to a series of children in need of love, affection and a safe home environment,' Tony said, as if he was narrating a story.

'It sounds a bit like a sickly sweet Christmas movie plot,' Julia replied.

'Actually it sounds like lots of hard work, but I imagine you're not afraid of that.'

That evening Julia was sitting in her bedroom reading one of Tony's novels. It was chilly in the room and she was too sleepy to continue the book, so she put it down and turned out the light. She pulled the blanket up around her shoulders and stared through the window at the starry night. She had not stopped thinking about the idea of becoming a foster mother. She couldn't decide whether it was a brilliant idea and the perfect career change, or whether it would be madness. Choosing to take children into her home when she would effectively be a single mother might be too much. It would be exhausting, emotionally draining and even heartbreaking. She knew quite a few social workers and she had heard numerous horror stories about the reasons why some children were taken into care.

Fostering was not an easy thing to do; but she didn't necessarily want an easy job. After losing Duncan, she realised she wasn't afraid of the emotional rollercoaster fostering might present; but she wondered what Bryden and Jamie would think. After all, it was their home too; at least when they were in Shetland. She wondered whether they would try and talk her out of the idea.

She realised she had stopped stressing out about Cameron and sighed with relief. Yes indeed, fostering would keep her far too busy to worry about new and unsuitable entanglements with men. It was perfect. She shut her eyes and drifted off to sleep, dreaming about her house ringing with the sound of children's laughter.

15

Julia battled her way down the rickety steps of the aircraft; her raincoat flapped around her legs and her hair whipped across her face in the strong winds that raced unchecked across the runway at Sumburgh Airport. Welcome to Shetland, Julia thought, as she hurried across the tarmac to the arrivals lounge.

While she was waiting for her suitcase to appear on the carousel, she stood by the window and looked out at the weather. The rain lashed down from lead grey skies, and an empty crisp packet flew past the window on a non-stop flight to Norway.

Julia heard the carousel start up and she turned to retrieve her suitcase, for which she had had to pay excess baggage charges on, the result of spending the remainder of her holiday indulging in some retail therapy. She heaved it off the conveyor belt and pulled up the handle and started to drag it out towards the exit.

By the time she reached her house she was exhausted. She had left the warmth of Sicily three days ago, having stopped off briefly in Edinburgh to see Jamie and Bryden again. It was late afternoon and it was dark by the time she parked her car on the drive. She sat and looked at the house for a moment. The last time she had driven home from the airport was when she had come home with Duncan from the hospital in Aberdeen. She normally loved returning to her home. Today she wasn't quite so sure she wanted to go inside.

She took a deep breath and steeled herself to get out of the car into the hideous weather. When she opened the kitchen door she was met by a not particularly pleasant smell of dusty, musty air.

She was tempted to open a window to let in some fresh air, but it was too cold for that. The heating in the house had been switched to a bare minimum in her absence, and she shivered as she walked into the kitchen. The heat may have been enough to make sure the pipes didn't freeze in a cold snap; but it was not enough to make her feel comfortable taking off her coat. She walked over to the thermostat and cranked up the heating.

She leaned the suitcase against the kitchen wall and then went back to the front door to retrieve the post. She sifted through the large collection, depositing a large bundle of junk mail and leaflets straight into the recycling bin. There were a couple of letters for Duncan, which made her feel sick. She dumped all the letters, unread, onto the table and walked over to the kettle, before realising there wasn't any milk in the house so she couldn't make herself a cup of tea or coffee.

'Fuck, fuck, fuck!' Julia muttered out loud to herself, regretting she hadn't stopped off at the supermarket on her way home from the airport. Her words echoed in the cold kitchen. She felt bad tempered and not in the least bit glad to be home. It was like Sicily had never happened. Standing there in her coat, she simply couldn't conjure up the memory of what it had been like to feel the warm sun on her skin.

The kitchen phone rang, making her jump. She considered not answering it, but thought it might be Jamie or Bryden.

'Hello?' she said, hesitantly.

'At last, you're home; I wasn't sure if it was today or tomorrow.' Marianne said, excitedly.

'I still have my coat on; I just walked in the door,' Julia replied. 'Mind you, it's so cold here I can't take my coat off.'

'You know, I did wonder about coming round and switching your heating on and buying some milk and bread in case you got in late, but I didn't get time today.'

'Don't be daft. I might go back out to the shop in a while and get some things; it will give the house a chance to warm up.'

'Look, why don't you come over here instead. I'm just about to start cooking tea. We can catch up.'

Julia looked around the kitchen, wondering whether she really ought to spend her first night at home unpacking and putting things away. She barely hesitated before replying.

'Actually, I think I'll take you up on that offer, thanks. I have some presents in my suitcase for you, so I may as well just put it back in the car and drive over now. Bugger the unpacking and the post. It can wait until tomorrow.'

'Well, if you're bringing your suitcase, you can just stay over. Then your house really will be warmed up again.'

'Perfect!'

Julia put the phone down and walked over to her suitcase and wheeled it back out to her car and drove round to Marianne's house with a huge sense of relief. She was guaranteed a much warmer welcome there.

When she got to Marianne's house she found Ivan and Rachel had just arrived for an unexpected visit with their baby. Marianne was sitting at the kitchen table cuddling Charlie.

'Look, at my lovely new grandson,' Marianne said, as Julia walked in.

'Oh my goodness, he's gorgeous,' Julia said. She parked her suitcase in the hallway and took her coat off and hung it up before hurrying back to the kitchen.

Julia sat down at the table and leaned in to get a closer look at Charlie, who was fast asleep in Marianne's arms and oblivious to the fuss being made over him. Isobel came into the kitchen and squealed with delight when she saw Julia; earning a hush from her mother.

'Hello Auntie Jules, did you have a good time?'

'Yes thanks. I have some presents for everyone. I'll get them out of my bag in a moment. But first I must see your little nephew.'

'Izzy, you could put the kettle on for us; there's an angel. I expect Julia's desperate for a good old fashioned cup of British tea. Unless you'd rather have a glass of wine?'

'Tea would be perfect thanks.'

While Isobel put the kettle on and made a pot of tea, Julia talked to Rachel about Charlie. Marianne passed the sleeping baby to Julia and she held him up close to her face, breathing in the soft sweet scent of a new-born. It brought back delicious memories of when Jamie and Bryden were babies.

They heard the front door open and close and a moment later Brian appeared in the kitchen. His face lit up when he saw Julia and he hurried over and kissed her cheek then he went around the table kissing Marianne, Rachel and Isobel.

'This is a nice surprise, all these lovely women in my house. Although I can't smell anything like dinner cooking.' Brian said, laughing at Marianne, who pulled a face at him. 'How's my little Charlie boy today?' Brian added, sitting down next to Julia and taking a peek at the baby.

'He's been asleep since he got here,' Marianne said.

'Despite your best efforts to wake him up no doubt,' Brian replied, winking at Rachel.

Rachel smiled and then yawned, before apologising.

'Don't be silly, my lamb, why don't you go upstairs and have a little snooze, we can look after Charlie. You must be exhausted.' Marianne said to Rachel.

Rachel nodded gratefully and left the kitchen.

'Poor girl looks shattered,' Brian said, as he stood up again and went to look in the fridge. 'What's for tea?'

'I was going to cook pasta and salad, but then Rachel and Ivan brought Charlie round. Ivan's upstairs helping Sophie with her maths homework. Anyway, I haven't started cooking yet.'

Brian looked at his watch and then grinned wickedly at Marianne.

'Why don't you ring an order through to the Chinese, I'll get changed and go and collect it in a few minutes.'

'Brilliant idea!'

An hour later, they were finishing their takeaway meal in the kitchen. Rachel was still sleeping upstairs and Ivan was holding his son, who had woken briefly and was now dozing again. Isobel and Sophie had wandered off to the lounge to watch television, and Julia was telling them about Sicily. She told them all about Tony Hugo, the famous author and his lovely villa, and she told them about Bryden's visit and all the places they had visited. She talked about the scenery, the weather, the beaches, the food and her day trip to Mount Etna; but she did not say a word about Cameron.

Charlie opened his eyes and started to pucker up his face as if he was going to cry.

'I think he's hungry. I'll take him up to Rachel,' Ivan said, as he stood up with the baby.

'Tell her we've saved some Chinese food for her,' Marianne said.

'So, anyway, what gossip have I missed while I was away?' Julia said, as Ivan left the kitchen. Brian stood up to leave the room shaking his head in amusement at Julia and Marianne.

'Nothing much, only what you know already, about Laura and John splitting up. That's the only big news. Laura's apparently really pissed off with John, as he sent her an email while he was offshore, saying he wasn't coming back.'

'That's a bit cowardly,' Julia said. 'What's Cameron said about it?'

'I don't know. I haven't seen him since. He did seem really happy when I bumped into him a couple of weeks ago. The happiest I have seen him in months, so perhaps they are getting back together again. Although I think he would be a fool to trust her.'

Brian came back to the kitchen and walked over to the cupboard and took out some glasses.

'Anyone want to try some of this Limoncello Julia brought me?'

'I will. Can I have lots of ice in mine please?' Marianne said.

'I know what I meant to tell you,' Brian said, as he dispensed ice-cubes into the glasses. 'I met Cameron's secretary at the Chinese. I mentioned Julia was back from Sicily and we were just about to celebrate with a takeaway, and she said, what a coincidence, Cameron went over to Sicily a few weeks ago. He's got some new project over there.'

Marianne smiled quizzically at Julia.

'Sicily's a big place. It's about the same size as Wales. You would have to be really lucky to bump into someone you knew there,' Brian continued, with his back to the kitchen table.

Julia felt herself blushing. She stared down at the table, noticing a few stray grains of rice on the table cloth. She picked them up and deposited them on her side plate.

'Julia! You saw him, didn't you?' Marianne said, leaning forward and staring hard at Julia.

Brian turned round from the fridge and looked at them.

'Whoops! Have I said something wrong?'

Julia looked up at him and despite her embarrassment, couldn't help but smile.

'Oh my God. What happened? Something happened! Oh Lord, get me a drink,' Marianne said, flapping her hand urgently in Brian's direction.

Julia covered her face with her hands.

'You're such a witch,' she said to Marianne.

'No I'm not; I have just learned to read your face.' Marianne replied, drawing circles in the air around her own face. 'Every emotion, is written as clear as day. I knew you'd been hiding something. I just didn't know what. I thought you may have hooked up with that writer fellow.'

Brian handed Marianne her drink and took a seat back at the table. Marianne tried to wave him away.

'No, I'm staying to hear this!' Brian said, grinning at Julia, who groaned in despair.

Julia walked over to the kitchen door and closed it and then sat down again. She picked up her glass of wine, brought it to her lips but put it down untouched, with an air of resignation.

'OK, I'll tell you, but you have to promise not to tell a single soul.'

'Cross my heart!' Marianne said, miming drawing a cross over her chest and looking pointedly at Brian, who nodded seriously.

'You remember I told you I had dinner with Tony and some of his friends on my first night in Sicily?'

Marianne nodded.

'Well, one of them was an architect; he's German, but he works in Sicily, and we got to talking about architecture in Shetland and he mentioned he would love to speak to Cameron about his famous eco-home, as he'd read about it in a magazine. When I said I knew Cameron he asked for his email address which I gave him.'

Julia took a sip of wine, remembering the conversation with Jürgen and wondering if she now regretted joining Tony and his friends for dinner.

'Anyway, I thought nothing of it, but a week later Cameron rang me and said he had spoken to Jürgen and had been invited over to Sicily. He had just booked his flight and wanted to know where I was staying and whether I could recommend a hotel.'

Brian suppressed a smile, his eyes twinkling with amusement.

'Anyway, I said he may as well stay with me since I had a spare room. So he turned up the next day. And it was fine. It was actually nice to see him, as I had spent quite a few days on my own, so it was great to have company. I went to Palermo with him the next day while he had his meeting and did some shopping. Then afterwards we went back and cooked dinner and sat around talking.'

'He's such a crafty bastard!' Brian said, interrupting Julia.

Julia shook her head, trying to stop Brian from jumping to the wrong conclusion.

'Shut up; let her talk!' Marianne said, glaring at her husband.

'Anyway, to say thanks for helping him get this new contract Cameron wanted to take me out for the day. And it was the day of my birthday, although I hadn't reminded him. I didn't want to make a big deal of it, but I heard him go out early in the morning and when I got up I saw he had left me a note saying he had to pop into town. I just assumed he needed to go to the bank or something. But he bought me a huge bouquet of flowers and some lovely pastries for breakfast.'

'How sweet of him,' Marianne said, smiling meaningfully at Brian.

'He'd seen on Facebook it was my birthday.' Julia closed her eyes for a moment. She could still see the flowers in her mind. She smiled at the memory.

'So where did he take you for your day out?' Marianne said. She stood up to help herself to more Limoncello.

'We didn't go anywhere...'

'Why not?'

'I don't really want to say any more.'

'Why? What happened?' Marianne demanded.

'What do you think?' Julia said, holding her head and looking even more embarrassed.

'I really ought to start buying more flowers,' Brian said, grinning at Julia and Marianne.

'No!' Marianne shouted, rushing back to the table. 'You didn't!'

'We did.'

'Oh my God. I can't believe he tried it on with you,' Brian said.

'It wasn't Cameron's fault. But in my defence, I was feeling lonely. It was exactly six months after Duncan died, and I was kind of demented. I just launched myself at him; poor man.'

'Poor man; don't give me that rubbish. I bet he didn't try to resist.' Marianne said sternly.

'He did actually. He was really sweet.'

Marianne made another attempt to get Brian to leave the kitchen. She wanted to hear all the juicy details, but Brian refused to leave, and Julia felt her shame was so great it didn't matter if one more person heard. It would save Marianne repeating it to him later. She knew they didn't keep any secrets from each other.

Julia told them about the few days she had spent with Cameron but then finished by saying she had barely heard from him since.

'How do you feel now?' Marianne said.

'I just feel guilty, and so stupid. And now he's getting back together with Laura, I feel a bit shabby. Suppose he tells her?'

'You've done nothing to feel guilty about,' Brian said. 'Do you really think Duncan would have wanted you to be on your own forever?'

'No; but I don't think he would have expected me to have a fling with someone in less than a year. Especially one of our friends. How would you feel Brian?'

Brian grinned at Marianne. He reached over and squeezed his wife's hand.

'Marianne would be checking out all the single men at my funeral.'

'I would not! That's a horrible thing to say,' Marianne replied seriously, but winking at Julia.

Brian laughed at her.

Julia reached for her handbag and took her phone out. She found a text message Cameron had sent her over two weeks ago and showed it to Marianne, who frowned with disappointment. Brian leaned in to look at it. He shrugged.

'It doesn't mean anything at all. Why do you women get so hung up on the small stuff?'

'I don't know; it just seems so formal. It's like there was nothing between us.'

Marianne nodded sympathetically.

'So do you want anything to happen?'

'I don't think so; no. It's too soon. I don't know what I was thinking.' Julia put her phone back in her bag and then covered her face with her hands and groaned out loud. 'Oh God, I just don't want to see him again for a while. I want to forget it ever happened.'

The kitchen door opened and Ivan popped his head in and looked at everyone.

'Can we come in?'

'Yes of course love. Is Rachel ready for something to eat now?'

Ivan opened the door wider and Rachel appeared behind him, carrying Charlie who was awake again.

Marianne jumped up from her chair and gestured for Rachel to sit down. Then she went over to the oven and took out a plate of food that had been kept warm, and set it down in front of Rachel and then fetched a glass of water with ice.

Julia watched Marianne fussing around her daughter-in-law and smiled to herself. She was glad she had come over to see Marianne, even if it had led to her confessing her secret. The kitchen was warm and cosy and filled with the happy sounds of family life. Marianne had Charlie in her arms again and was cooing happily at him. Rachel was eating her dinner and Ivan and Brian had started talking about football. Sophie and Isobel wandered back to the kitchen and went to the freezer to find ice-creams and then stopped to look at their new nephew, teasing their brother about how the baby was too good looking to be his.

This normal, noisy, busy kitchen, filled with people, was what Julia missed. She had missed her boys when they had gone off to university, and that hole in her life had opened up to the size of a crater now Duncan had gone. She thought about her conversation with Tony, about what she was going to do next and she realised with a renewed sense of clarity it was the right choice for her.

'I forgot to tell you my other news,' Julia said to Marianne, who looked up in surprise. 'I've decided to apply to be a foster carer. I don't want to go back to the care home after all. I want to look after children instead.'

'Good for you; you'd be a great foster mum,' Brian said.

'Really? Are you sure? It can be quite tough sometimes. You could get some really difficult children to look after. It can be very stressful,' Marianne said.

'I know; but it can't be more stressful than sitting with somebody's granny or grandpa while they're really poorly.'

Marianne shook her head doubtfully.

'Well, anyway, I'm going to apply. It takes months to go through the process, and who knows, I might not be accepted. And I have plenty of time to change my mind.'

'Of course they'll accept you. You would be perfect. A nurse, professional carer, great mother, big family home, a secure environment and you're definitely not doing it just for the money.'

Julia smiled an acknowledgement. When Marianne put it like that, she realised she probably would be a suitable applicant. She looked at the people sitting around the large kitchen table and wondered whether she would soon have this again in her own home.

16

Over the next few weeks Julia kept herself busy. She made an appointment with a social worker in the fostering and adoption team. She had never met the social worker before, as Miranda had only just moved up to Shetland from Manchester. However, Miranda was very helpful and positive about Julia's application. Her only reservation was connected to Julia's recent bereavement. Miranda wondered whether it was too soon to make such a decision, but conceded the point the process would take a few months in any case.

Julia put a lot of energy into avoiding Cameron. She was hardly ever at home as she had decided to do up Alice's old croft house, now the tenants had moved out. It needed a thorough clean, and redecoration. She had given in to pressure from her sons not to sell the house, so she decided she would rent it out again and use the money to put towards helping the boys buy property in Edinburgh.

She employed two young men, who had just finished their training at Shetland College, to help refit the kitchen and a new bathroom. They helped her paint the whole house inside and out. They sanded the floors and re-varnished them, and Julia bought new curtains, rugs and light fittings. Within a few weeks the house looked bright, fresh and welcoming.

Julia decided to wait until after Christmas before advertising it for rent. She wanted to show Jamie and Bryden what she had done to the house before anyone moved in. Christmas was just a couple of weeks away, and she wasn't sure whether to look forward to it or to dread its arrival. She couldn't wait to see the boys, who would be arriving home on the 22nd December; but she knew this would be a difficult first Christmas without their dad.

The day before they were due home, she went to the supermarket late in the evening to avoid the crush of shoppers. She took a large trolley with the intention of stocking up for the holidays. The turkey and meat had been ordered from the butcher already, so she just needed fresh fruit and vegetables and other bits and pieces to spoil her sons.

She was pushing the trolley past the drinks aisle when she decided to buy some tins of beer for the boys. She had plenty of wine and spirits in the house, but they tended not to drink that. She was studying the packs of beer trying to remember what brand they drank, when she felt someone standing close to her. She looked round and saw Cameron.

'Hello,' he said quietly, smiling at her.

'Hi. How are you?'

'Great. I see you're getting the Christmas shopping in. Are Jamie and Bryden home yet?'

'Tomorrow.'

'That's good. I bet you can't wait.'

Julia smiled and nodded. 'It will be a bit strange this year,' she replied.

'Yes it will. But at least you'll all be together.'

'What about you? I heard you and Laura are back together.'

Cameron shook his head and frowned.

'No, wherever did you hear that?'

'Um, well, Marianne said Laura and John had split up, and that …'

Julia stopped, realising Marianne had never actually said anything conclusive about them getting back together. It was just an assumption.

'No, we're not back together. That's definitely not going to happen,' Cameron said.

A couple with an overfilled trolley tried to squeeze past them in the aisle and Cameron stepped closer to Julia to get out of their way. He pushed Julia's trolley to the side and held on to the edge, effectively trapping her, against the shelves.

'You look great,' he said, after a fraction of time that was just beginning to feel like an awkward silence.

'I've been busy doing up Alice's old house,' Julia said, not knowing how to respond to his compliment. She looked at Cameron. Under his bulky winter jacket, he was wearing a navy Aran jumper and dark jeans. His hair was freshly cut, shorter than normal, which made him look quite youthful.

'Is everything alright?' Cameron looked directly into Julia's eyes. 'I haven't heard much from you since…'

'Yes of course. I just didn't know what to say to you, especially when I heard about Laura. I mean, we never…'

Cameron leaned in closer.

'This isn't the best place to talk.'

'No, it's not,' Julia agreed.

Cameron looked at his watch and frowned.

'It's a bit late now, otherwise I would suggest going for a drink, but you probably want to get home.'

Julia nodded and looked down at her full trolley.

'I'm driving down to the airport tomorrow afternoon. I could drop by on my way.'

'Yes; do that,' Cameron said, his eyes lighting up with pleasure. 'Come along in the morning if you like. I'll make us some lunch, and I can tell you all the news about the Sicilian project. I'm still at my mum's old house.'

Julia smiled and nodded.

'See you tomorrow then.'

Julia watched him walk away in the direction of the checkouts. She turned her attention back to the beer and put two slabs of lager into the trolley.

Later that evening she poured herself a glass of red wine, carried it into the lounge and switched on the Christmas tree lights. The solid fuel burner in the corner of the room was still glowing, but the warmth had diminished so she opened the door and threw in some lumps of dried peat and shut the door. The house was cosy and smelt of Christmas, thanks to the real tree, and the mulled wine scented candles she had bought a few days ago.

She sat down on the sofa without switching the television on. The fire crackled and a large old-fashioned carriage clock ticked on the bookcase. Rain lashed against the window and the wind was picking up.

Julia thought about Cameron. It had been less awkward seeing him than she had imagined. She felt rather foolish for avoiding him for so long, and realised she had built the whole episode into a much bigger drama than perhaps it warranted.

She thought back to the crazy conversation she had had with Tony when she had tried mapping out her future as if she was the heroine of a novel. She tried to imagine Tony narrating the story of what had happened to her since she had left Sicily, but gave up when she realised it was too dull to be included in a book. He really would have killed her off a few chapters ago, and even the detective trying to solve the murder mystery would have had trouble remembering her name. She remembered the female character they had invented, Rebecca Sherry, the mountain rescue worker. She sounded much more glamorous and exciting. She wouldn't have wasted a moment worrying about what people thought of her, dithering about what to do with the rest of her life, and full of self-pity. She would have been too busy rescuing people, and was probably a bit of an eco-warrior in her spare time, campaigning for the reintroduction of wolves into Scotland. Julia imagined a beautiful young woman sitting in a mountain lodge, wearing jeans, walking boots and a chunky fleece, having a pint with some of her rescue team after a successful mission. The men in Rebecca's team were young and hunky and they all adored her; although Rebecca was happily married to a helicopter pilot. Julia wanted to be Rebecca Sherry.

She finished her glass of wine, and decided against having another, since she was clearing losing the plot. Imagining she was a fictional heroine was ridiculous. Then again, maybe she could learn something from this. She still had time to change the direction of her life. She might not be able to take up mountain rescue, not least because there were no mountains in Shetland, but she could start to become more of a star in her own life story.

She would start by making this a brilliant Christmas for her sons. They would rise above the sadness and have a great time. It was what Duncan would have wanted. It had always been his favourite time of year.

Julia went to bed thinking about what she could do to spoil her sons. She had already bought them presents, which were sitting under the tree, but she planned to do something else too; maybe organise a party so they could invite their friends round. She was so busy thinking about that, she didn't give any more thought to seeing Cameron again.

The next morning Julia woke up with a great sense of excitement, the way she always did when her boys were coming home. She leapt out of bed and headed for the bathroom, pausing only to touch the photograph of Duncan she had hung on the wall above her chest of drawers.

'Good morning,' she said, smiling at the photograph. 'Big day ahead of us today.'

Julia put on a new dress she had bought in Lerwick. It was made of wool jersey with a dark paisley print and it was perfect for getting into the festive spirit. It looked fabulous with her new long black boots.

When she arrived at Cameron's house she got out of the car, and felt the first ripple of nervous anticipation. She opened the front door to the vestibule and hesitated before knocking on the inner door. She heard footsteps running down the stairs, child-sized footsteps, accompanied by a girlish shriek of excitement.

The door was opened by Amy who seemed disappointed to see Julia; she was clearly expecting someone else. Amy ran back inside the house calling for her dad, who appeared from the kitchen and smiled a welcome to her.

'Come in, I'm just making some lunch. Amy is expecting one of her cousins to come round to play in a while.'

'Oh that explains why she looked so disappointed to see me.'

'Hah! Well I'm pleased to see you.'

Julia took off her coat and hung it over the bannister and followed Cameron into the kitchen. The floor had been dusted with flour and Amy's cat, Jessie J, stalked through the flour and left paw-prints trailing into the hallway.

'As you can see, I've had some help with the cooking today. We made pizzas.'

'They smell nice.'

'They're nearly done, so I'd better clear up the kitchen before Lucy comes round, or the whole house will be covered in flour before too long.'

'Let me give you a hand. Where's the mop?'

Cameron looked at the floor, then back at Julia; he scratched his head and sighed.

'If you wouldn't mind? The mop's in the pantry,' he replied.

Julia made quick work of the kitchen floor while Cameron finished putting together the salad and took the pizzas out of the oven and set them in the middle of the table. He fetched plates, cutlery and glasses and he was just putting out some juice when they heard Amy running out to the front door, and judging by the shrieks coming from hall Julia could tell her cousin had finally arrived.

Julia put the mop away, and picked up the dishcloth to clean a corner of the table that still had a trace of flour spilt on it. She took the cloth back to the sink to wash it out and turned when she heard someone come in and say hello. It was Cameron's sister Heather, who nodded at Julia, but did not smile. She seemed distracted and stressed out.

'I'll pick Lucy up about six if that's OK?'

'If you're busy I could bring her home; I have to take Amy back to Laura's later.'

'No, best not; John's coming over.'

Cameron shrugged, his face clouding over with annoyance.

When Heather had gone Cameron went to find the girls and there were a chaotic few moments of serving up pizza, imploring them to try some salad and pouring out juice. The girls sat at the kitchen table, talking at each other non-stop. Jessie J jumped up onto the window sill and meowed to go out which made Lucy jump up to try to catch the cat. It evaded her grasp much to Lucy's disgust and to Amy's loud amusement.

'Why don't we go in the lounge and wait until they have finished eating. I'll put our pizza in the oven when it's safe to go back to the kitchen,' Cameron suggested.

'Good idea!'

Cameron led the way and took a seat on the sofa. The floor of the lounge was covered in colouring books, crayons and the contents from an ornate doll's house that stood under the window.

'I see Amy's been busy this morning.'

'Yeah, Laura dropped her off early; she was going off to do her Christmas shopping.'

'What are you doing over Christmas? Will Amy be coming to stay?'

'I'm not sure yet. Laura's being a bit funny at the moment. She seems to think I had a hand in her splitting up with John; so now I only get to see Amy when it suits her.'

'Well, that's not very good. Can't you talk to your lawyer?'

'We haven't been to see a lawyer yet. I really don't want things to escalate. At the moment she has the house and enough money to keep her going. If we start to formalise everything, it might get ugly. If she doesn't get all her own way I can see her leaving Shetland and taking Amy with her. It's not like she has a job here to make her want to stay.'

'That would be awful.'

'Yeah, it really would. I couldn't stay here without Amy.'

'She wouldn't really leave Shetland though would she? I mean, her family's here, and she would have to get a job then wouldn't she?'

'Maybe not, but I wouldn't want to take the chance. She's been acting so strangely since John dumped her.'

There was a loud clatter from the kitchen and Cameron jumped up to investigate. Julia followed him and saw the girls had allowed the cat to jump up onto the table and it had knocked over one of the plastic beakers of juice; and a plate of half eaten pizza was lying on the floor.

'Have you two finished eating?' Cameron said, as the girls got up to leave the room.

There was no reply, just the sound of footsteps charging upstairs.

'I'll take that as a yes then.'

Julia helped Cameron clear the mess from the table while he put their pizza in the oven.

'Would you like a glass of wine? I haven't even offered you a drink yet?'

'Tea would be better. I have to drive down to the airport soon.'

'Of course. I don't suppose your house will look like it's had a wrecking ball hit it just an hour after the boys get home,' Cameron said, as he swept up pizza and pieces of cucumber from the floor.

'Don't you believe it!'

Cameron put the kettle on and made two mugs of tea. He carried it over to the table where Julia was sitting.

'I would invite you round for Christmas Day, but it might be a bit tense this year,' Julia said quietly.

'Don't be silly. I'll be fine. If John is at Heather's I might go over to Dawn's house instead. I shan't be on my own. I'm hoping Laura will let me come over in the morning to see Amy open her presents. She might even be civilised enough to let me stay for dinner. Who knows?'

'Why don't you come over on Boxing Day then? We don't have anything planned, although I expect the boys will want to go and catch up with their friends at some stage. We might even have a bit of an open-house that night.'

'I might do that, thanks!'

When the pizza was ready Cameron took it out of the oven and put it on a plate in the middle of the table. Julia helped herself to a slice and some salad.

'Yum, this is nice.'

'Thanks; I bought myself a new Italian cookbook. This is a Sicilian recipe.'

Julia smiled at him. He reached across the table for the pepper. For a split second she thought he was reaching for her hand. She realised she had flinched, and she put down her fork and picked up her glass as if that had been her intention. Cameron did not seem to notice.

While he was occupied with the pepper mill she watched him. She had never been alone with him in his house before. He seemed different; quieter but more relaxed. She looked around the kitchen and observed he kept it spotlessly clean, at least when Amy was not around to untidy it. In this respect he was different to Duncan who simply did not notice untidiness. She wondered whether Cameron looked after the house on his own. She couldn't resist asking.

'Do you employ a cleaner?'

Cameron looked around the kitchen guiltily.

'Um no, why? Do you think I should get one?'

'No, of course not. It's just that apart from the obvious Amy related mess this house is immaculate, and what with you being so busy at work, I wondered how you managed.'

'Well, I do get someone to do the ironing. But only because I hate ironing. But other than that I do everything myself. I always have been rather domesticated. It surprises people.'

Julia nodded and laughed.

'Yes, I suppose it doesn't go with your playboy image.'

'Oh please; I hope I've shaken off that idea by now. I'm not that kind of man at all. Especially not now.'

He pointed upstairs to where Amy could be heard singing along to a Jessie J song with Lucy. They listened for a moment to the strains of the two five year old girls singing "it's not about the money, money, money…"

'Point taken.' Julia said.

'So anyway; did you enjoy the rest of your holiday? I haven't seen you since to ask.'

Julia detected a hint of hurt in his voice, but his face looked untroubled as he bit into another piece of the potato and rosemary pizza.

'Yeah, it was great thanks. Although, Bryden split up with his girlfriend the day before he arrived, so that was a bit sad for him. But he perked up a bit by the end of his week. Then I had a week or so on my own again, and I managed to make some decisions about my future. So yeah, the holiday was a success.'

Cameron reached for his glass of water and looked enquiringly at her.

'What kind of decision?'

'About work; what I'm going to do with my life; how I'm going to move on.'

'That's good; what did you decide?'

Julia was busy chewing pizza so she didn't answer for a moment. Cameron watched her; a serious expression on his face.

'I've applied to become a foster carer. It takes a few months to get approved, but if I am, then I shall be looking after children at my home.'

'Wow, fostering; that's brave.'

Julia shook her head. It didn't feel like a brave thing to do. It felt a little bit like hiding away from the world, but perhaps she was being naive.

'I don't really have any other skills to offer, so I don't have that many options.'

Cameron nodded thoughtfully, but before he could reply they were interrupted by the sound of vigorous bouncing on a bed above their heads.

Cameron stood up and walked to the foot of the stairs and shouted up to the girls.

'Amy! What have I told you about jumping on the bed?'

The bouncing stopped instantly, to be replaced by giggling, which morphed into cackling as the girls realised there wouldn't be any further repercussions.

Cameron sat down at the table again.

'Seriously? Fostering? You want to do all this again with young kids?'

'Yeah! Can't wait. I would much rather be chasing after a couple of hooligans like those two than sitting around on my own. What's the point of having such a lovely big home when I have nobody to share it with? Jamie and Bryden don't come back very often now. They have their own lives.'

'When you put it like that.'

'Speaking of which. I really ought to be going soon. I have to pick them up.'

Cameron looked at his watch in surprise.

'Where did the time go? We never really got a chance to talk. Maybe when I don't have Amy?'

Julia stood up and picked up her handbag.

'Thanks for lunch; it was great. Have a lovely Christmas won't you!'

'And you!'

Cameron followed her out to her car. As she fiddled in her pocket for the keys he put his arm around her shoulder and kissed her cheek. It felt like old times when they were just friends. Julia put her arm around him and hugged him back.

'We'll always be friends,' Cameron said. 'I don't expect anything from you. You don't need to worry about what happened.'

'Thanks. I'm sorry I haven't been in touch. I wasn't sure how things would be once we got home again.'

'Well, if I can paraphrase Humphrey Bogart in Casablanca – we will always have Palermo.'

Julia laughed. She got into her car and drove away, feeling a huge sense of relief, and then a moment later, a rush of excitement at the idea of picking up her boys. Christmas would start in less than an hour.

17

Julia leaned against the window sill and watched the plane taxi back to the terminal. A couple of minutes later the ground crew had put the steps in place and were busy unloading baggage from the hold. She watched the first passengers descend onto the tarmac and make their way across to the building. It was only just after three in the afternoon but the sky was darkening quickly. It wasn't raining, but it was cold and breezy. Julia recognised Bryden in the gloom but saw he was on his own. He walked quickly away from the plane to get out of the cold and Julia stared at the steps of the aircraft wondering what had happened to Jamie.

Bryden stopped and looked back at the plane, and Julia realised he too was waiting for Jamie. She sighed with relief, and then saw the man himself walking slowly towards her. He carried a duty free bag and a book, and his head was lowered as if he was not interested in any of his surroundings. He did not look happy to be home.

Julia headed towards the door where the passengers would appear just as Bryden walked through. He grinned at Julia and held his arms out to her. He hugged her and then picked her up and swung her around.

'I'm back!'

'Yeah, I can see that. Did you have a good flight?' Julia said, as he put her down again.

'Yes, but word to the wise, our boy Jamie's in a foul mood. Approach with caution!'

At that moment Jamie appeared and Julia smiled at him. She went to hug him, but he moved out of her grasp. He headed straight towards the luggage carousel, even though there were no cases on it yet.

Bryden pulled a face at Julia, and then wrapped his arms around her again. He let go abruptly when he noticed one of his friends and went over to speak to them. Julia was left standing on her own for a moment. She watched Jamie who was standing with his back to her. She looked at the duty-free carrier bag containing a bottle of Russian vodka. It was a strange thing for Jamie to buy; she imagined it must be a present for someone.

The carousel started up and Bryden came back to retrieve his bag. Jamie's was the last bag to appear, which did nothing to shake off the dark cloud of annoyance surrounding him.

Julia and Bryden led the way out to her car. Jamie lagged behind, making no attempt to catch up or to join in with their conversation. Bryden jumped into the front passenger seat, earning a scowl from Jamie who climbed into the back seat and then leaned back and shut his eyes as if to cover his mood behind a shield of exhaustion.

Julia drove home trying to fight off the urge to tackle Jamie on his rudeness and sullen manner, but she knew it would inflame the situation. It could not be connected to anything she had said or done, so she shouldn't take it personally. But it was hard not to be hurt, particularly as she had been looking forward to their arrival for weeks.

When they arrived home, Jamie and Bryden took their bags up to their rooms. Bryden came downstairs straight away and headed for the fridge. He opened the door and peered in at the contents and grinned appreciatively. He then inspected the contents of the slow cooker, which was bubbling away contentedly in the corner. Next he lifted the cover from the cakes Julia had made early that morning and smiled.

'Someone's been busy!'

'Thought you two might need feeding up over the holiday.'

Bryden opened a drawer and took out a packet of crisps and stood by the sink munching them cheerfully. Julia was relieved at least one of her sons seemed happy.

'What's happening tonight?'

'Nothing really. I made dinner already as you can see. I was hoping we could all catch up this evening. But I'm not sure now…' Julia tilted her head in the direction of Jamie's bedroom.

Bryden pulled a face and shook his head. He screwed up the empty crisp packet and chucked it into the bin and walked back to the sink to wash his hands.

'I was hoping we could go round to Granny Alice's house. You can show me what you've been doing to it.'

'It's dark now.' Julia said, surprised at his interest.

'So? It still has electricity and light bulbs doesn't it?'

'Of course.'

'Come on then; let's go out for a drive. There's something I wanted to tell you and I can do without Mr Happy butting in.'

'OK, but we'd better tell him we're going out.'

Just as Julia spoke, they heard footsteps above them and a moment later Jamie came downstairs. He scowled at Bryden who ignored him and reached for a glass and went to the fridge to get some juice.

'Can I borrow your car please?' Jamie said.

'Um, well we were just about to go out actually. We won't be long though.'

'That figures!' Jamie replied, glaring at Bryden.

'Where were you going anyway?' Julia said, looking from one son to the other, wondering what was going on between them.

'I was going to meet Liam in town for a drink. I'll probably stay over at his tonight.'

'Oh, well in that case you definitely can't take the car. I need to go out first thing in the morning. I have to go and collect the turkey from the butchers. But I'm sure we could drop you off.'

'It's OK.' Jamie strode off towards the lounge and seconds later they heard him talking to someone on his mobile.

Julia was impatient to find out what was going on so she picked up her handbag and keys and unhooked her coat from the rack in the hall.

'Come on then,' she said to Bryden, who instantly put down his glass and followed her out to the car, not bothering to put a coat on.

Bryden fastened the seat belt and then sighed dramatically.

Julia started the car and set off up the hill back towards the main road. 'So tell me; what is going on with you two?'

'It's kind of complicated. Can I tell you when we get to the house?'

Julia drove on in silence; Alice's house was less than two miles away and a few minutes later they pulled up outside.

She opened the front door and turned the lights on and Bryden followed her inside.

'What a difference! I can't believe it's the same house. The new kitchen is brilliant,' Bryden said, as he walked around the downstairs of the property. He seemed genuinely impressed and Julia smiled gratefully. Nobody else had visited the house yet, so this was the first reaction from someone who knew what it had been like when Alice lived in it. They went upstairs and Bryden admired the new bathroom and the paint colours in the two bedrooms.

They went downstairs again and Bryden went back to the kitchen. He leaned against one of the cupboards and looked at Julia.

'I have some news; at least I might have some news. It isn't certain yet.'

'Good news I hope,' Julia replied.

'That depends; Jamie doesn't think so.' Bryden took a deep breath before continuing. 'I've just applied for Dad's old job. It was re-advertised a few weeks ago as they didn't manage to fill it earlier in the year. I found out yesterday they want to interview me.'

'Oh, wow,' Julia said, 'I wasn't expecting that.'

She stared at Bryden who seemed to be expecting disappointment. He chewed his thumb, a gesture that reminded Julia of when he was a child.

'Do you mind?'

'What? Why would I mind? You would be coming back to Shetland. I would be delighted.'

'I just thought you might think it was a bit strange. Jamie was horrified. It's one of the reasons why he's so pissed off with me.'

'Well I suppose it is a little unexpected. I thought you would stay in Edinburgh for a few more years. I never expected either of you to come back so soon, if ever. But are you sure? You're not just doing this because of me, are you?'

'Because of you? No; I miss Shetland, and I thought about applying for the job the first time it was advertised but I was only half way through my probation, so I didn't think I would stand a chance. But when they re-advertised I rang the Head and asked whether she thought she would consider an application from me. She said yes. She seemed really pleased actually. I mean, I know I might not get it, but I feel like I have a good chance.'

Julia smiled and put her arms around him and hugged him.

'Your dad would have been so proud of you. He said you'd be after his job one day.'

Julia let go of him and stood back and thought for a second.

'So what's wrong with Jamie?'

'Where do I start?' Bryden stuffed his hands into his jeans pocket and looked down at the floor. 'He has been a bit off since I went over to Sicily. He made some comment about me sponging off you and getting a free holiday. Which was stupid, because he was invited too, wasn't he?'

Julia nodded.

'He's still fed up because I've got Dad's car, and his golf clubs. And now I've applied for Dad's old job he's really mad at me. He said I won't stop until I've got everything. I think he's jealous for some reason.'

'Jealous? I would have thought his career prospects would have meant you would have envied him.'

Bryden shrugged, as if to acknowledge this might have been the case at one time.

'The thing is I don't think he's enjoying his work. I met him a few weeks ago after he had been working in A&E. He'd been dealing with a horrible car accident. Some little kid died and Jamie just couldn't cope with it.'

Julia nodded; she understood exactly how Jamie would have felt. She had experienced similar incidences when she had been a nurse. She felt sick for her son and wished he had shared this with her. She might have been able to help him.

'It takes a lot of getting used to,' she said.

'Anyway, the reason he's not speaking to me now is because when we were waiting at Edinburgh airport I mentioned to him I was going to ask you if I could move into this house if I got the job in Shetland.'

'Oh! So that's why you were in such a hurry to see it.'

'Well that, and I wanted to talk to you about everything without Jamie being around.'

'OK, well in theory, yes you could live here. It makes sense; after all you're an adult now and you don't need me ironing your shirts and cooking your dinner anymore.'

'Hey, steady on, I never said you couldn't cook my dinner!' Bryden said, lightening the mood a little.

'But I don't want to upset Jamie. He's having a tough time at the moment and I can see how everything looks from his point of view. We need to make sure he feels you're both being treated equally.'

'I could give him Dad's car.'

'No, I don't think that would work. He won't be impressed with getting it back just because you don't want it anymore.'

'But I do want it.'

Julia shook her head.

'It's going to take more than a car. Let me think about this. Anyway, it's cold in here, let's go back to the house and have dinner. Don't say anything to Jamie about what we talked about.'

When they got back home Liam's car was parked outside. They found him talking to Jamie in the kitchen. Jamie had his coat on and they looked like they were just leaving.

'Hello Liam, I haven't seen you for ages. How are you?' Julia asked, giving him a little hug as she entered the kitchen.

'I'm great, thanks. I'm working most of Christmas, so we're going out tonight. Hope you don't mind me taking Jamie out when he's only just got home.'

'Don't be silly. We've got plenty of time to catch up later, haven't we?' Julia replied, looking pointedly at Jamie, who had the grace to smile at her. 'Aren't your parents going away for Christmas this year?' Julia said to Liam.

'They've gone to Tenerife for two weeks. I couldn't get the time off to go with them.'

'Oh that's a shame. Where are you going to have your Christmas dinner then?'

'It'll be a turkey sandwich in the station if I'm lucky,' Liam replied, smiling grimly.

'What time will you finish that day?'

'Not until six. But it's no big deal; I don't mind.'

'Nonsense. Come round here after work. We'll have our dinner in the evening this year.'

'Really?' Liam said, looking at Jamie to see his reaction.

'Of course. I never like eating a big meal in the middle of the day anyway; you just want to fall asleep in the afternoon. And it will be great to see you,' Julia said.

'Well if you're sure.'

'Yeah, and you should stay over; then you can have a dram.'

After Jamie and Liam had left, Bryden talked some more about why he wanted to move back to Shetland and about how much he was enjoying teaching. He also divulged more information about Jamie's experiences of working in the hospital, which did not fill Julia with ease.

Bryden was tired and wanted to have an early night. After he said goodnight, Julia decided she would go upstairs and read in bed. She walked past Jamie's room and noticed there was a light flashing on the bed. She switched on his bedroom light and saw he had left his laptop plugged in. She switched it off at the wall, as she hated to leave electrical devices on unnecessarily. She noticed Jamie had not unpacked his bag; it looked like all he had done in his room was lie down on the bed, as the duvet was crumpled in the middle. She turned to leave and then noticed the duty free bag was in the bin and the box holding the vodka had been opened. She picked it up and saw the box had been ripped open in such a way it would not make much of a present. She took out the bottle and was shocked to see it had been opened and quite a lot of vodka had been drunk already.

Julia sat down heavily on Jamie's bed, still holding the bottle in her hand. She tried to calculate how much he had drunk and quickly came to the conclusion it was too much; particularly as he had been heading out to the pubs where he was bound to drink more. She looked around the room noticing there was no sign of a glass. He must have drunk it neat from the bottle.

'Bloody hell!'

She put the bottle back in its box then went to her room and picked up her phone to ring Marianne, but there was no reply. She wondered about discussing the situation with Bryden but decided against it. The boys were already at war with each other.

She wondered who else she could ring. She looked up at the picture of Duncan, wishing she could talk to him. She felt very scared for Jamie. It was so out of character for him to be both uncommunicative and to drink excessively.

She rang Cameron.

'Hi, it's me; are you busy?' Julia said.

'Er no, what's up? You sound a bit stressed.'

'I'm a lot stressed.'

Julia told him about Jamie's behaviour and finding the vodka bottle.

'That doesn't sound good,' Cameron said, 'do you know where they're going tonight?'

'Liam picked him up; I think they were just going to a pub in Lerwick. I don't know which one. I know he'll be alright if Liam is with him; but I just don't know what to say to him when he comes home.'

'Well, I haven't had much experience of dealing with young men, other than when I used to be one. It sounds like he's deeply unhappy about something and I suppose it's no surprise really.'

'No I guess not. But Bryden told me he doesn't appear to be enjoying his job either. I can't bear the thought of him messing that up after all that studying.'

'My advice is to keep calm and see if you can get him alone. Maybe he'll open up to you over the holiday.'

'I hope so. I'm so worried about him. I was really looking forward to seeing them both. I know it's going to be a tough time with it being the first Christmas without their dad; but I didn't expect this.'

'I would say "don't worry" but that's pointless. Just wait until he comes home. Maybe a night out catching up with his friends will sort him out. Liam's a good man; he'll look after Jamie.'

Cameron put the phone down and sat for a moment with the television still on mute. He had been Jamie's unofficial Godfather, unofficial inasmuch as there hadn't been a church christening, but there had been a big party to celebrate his birth. Jamie had always been the golden boy. He was clever, sporty, good looking, confident and had always looked like he was on the fast track to success. Cameron wondered how much pressure Jamie had put on himself over the years. Medical school was tough and as a junior doctor in his first year in a hospital setting he imagined Jamie would now be working up to eighty hours a week in a demanding and stressful job. He would not have had much time to himself to grieve for his father.

Cameron stood up, picked up his keys and wallet and went out to his car. He drove into the town centre and parked on the pier. He could see a number of pubs from where he stood beside the car and he wasn't sure where to start. He watched a gaggle of young women tripping along the street in short skirts and high heels. They fell into one of the pubs Cameron never went to because of the loud music in the bar. He decided to start there.

He pushed his way through the throng of young people and looked all around the pub but couldn't find Jamie or Liam. He saw someone he recognised and asked if he had seen them, and was told they might be in the Queen's Hotel.

Cameron hurried in that direction and as he walked past the window of the hotel bar he saw Liam and some other young men standing at the bar. He couldn't see Jamie but he went inside. He went up to Liam and just before he spoke to him he saw Jamie slumped in a corner, with his head against the wall as if he was sleeping.

'Hi Liam, I just had call from Julia. She was a bit worried about Jamie. I came along to see if he was OK.'

'Well as you can see, he's a bit tired and emotional,' Liam said, as he glanced over in Jamie's direction. 'It's not even ten, and he's minced already.'

'I think he had quite a bit to drink before he came out.'

'Oh, that explains it. We were just wondering how to get him out of here. None of us can drive now, and I doubt any taxi driver's going to want to risk him spewing in the back of their car. The barman wants him to leave as well. I think it's only because some of my colleagues are here he hasn't thrown us all out. But if Jamie wakes up and starts shouting again, then we'll all be out.'

'Shouting?'

'Yeah, just before he passed out he was getting a bit out of hand. God knows what's wrong with him. I've never seen him like this before.'

'I've got my car on the pier, do you think we can frogmarch him out of here and I'll take him home.'

'Yeah, good idea.'

Jamie barely opened his eyes when Liam pulled his arm to help him stand up. He was as pliable as a ragdoll, but significantly heavier. Liam called over one of his off-duty colleagues to help, and between the three of them they managed to manoeuvre Jamie out of the bar and down the hill to the pier. They levered him into the backseat of Cameron's car and managed to get the seat belt around him.

'Tell him I'll see him on Christmas Day for dinner. And tell Julia I'm sorry. I didn't realise he'd already been drinking when we came out.'

'It's not your fault. I think he's a bit down on himself at the moment.'

Cameron started the engine and drove off; he hadn't got very far when Jamie woke up. He started to heave as if he was going to vomit. Cameron stopped the car and sprinted round to the back and opened the door just in time for Jamie to lean out and vomit copious amounts of foul liquid onto the pavement.

'Shit!' Cameron said, leaping out of the way.

Jamie looked up at him, without seeming to know where he was or who he was with. He leaned out of the car again, trapped by the seat belt he was struggling to undo. He spewed again, and as he did he let out a sob of despair.

'It's OK son; get it out of your system,' Cameron said.

Jamie finally managed to undo the seatbelt and he staggered out of the car ending up on his hands and knees on the pavement, retching unproductively. Cameron fetched a packet of baby wipes he kept in his car for sticky mishaps with Amy. He grabbed a couple and passed them to Jamie who sat back on his heels and wiped his face and hands.

Cameron stood next to Jamie, waiting patiently for him to recover.

'Are you feeling any better? Do you think you can get back in the car?'

Jamie nodded and Cameron helped him to his feet. He returned to the back seat of the car and Cameron made sure he fastened his seat belt before getting into the driver's seat. He started the engine and turned around to check on Jamie. He was leaning against the door with his eyes shut. Cameron set off again and a moment later Jamie started to cough.

'I need a drink. Got any water?'

'We'll stop at my house. You can get a drink there and sort yourself out before I take you home.'

Jamie sat slumped over the kitchen table with his head in his hands. He had drunk two glasses of water, but they seemed destined not to settle in his stomach. Cameron had fetched an old plastic washing up bowl and had set in on the table in case Jamie was sick again. He was. Cameron turned the radio on and pottered about making himself a coffee and fetching more water for Jamie. He sent Julia a text.

"Don't worry; Jamie is at my house, pissed as a fart, but safe. Will bring him home in the morning. You can go to sleep now."

Julia replied almost immediately.

"Thank you. You sure you don't want me to pick him up now?"

"No it's OK, probably best if he stays put." Cameron replied

"Thanks again x."

Cameron put the phone down and sipped his coffee. He watched Jamie for a moment, thinking of his own misspent youth. He knew exactly how it felt to have had one too many. He opened up cupboard and found a packet of aspirin and offered them to Jamie.

'Not yet, I'll wait until I stop spewing.' Jamie said, looking up at Cameron gratefully.

'Good idea. Would it help if you ate something? Toast?'

Jamie shook his head; the idea of food repelled him.

'Who called you to come and get me?'

Cameron stared at him for a moment, unsure whether to tell the truth or not.

'Your mother rang me. She was a bit worried about you. She said you'd been drinking vodka before you went out and you didn't seem very happy.'

'Why did she ring *you*?'

'Because we're friends; because I was one of your dad's best mates.' Cameron replied, reaching for a tin of biscuits he kept for Amy. He opened the tin and sat down opposite Jamie and took out a biscuit. 'Tell me, Jamie; man to man, what's going on with your life that you feel the need to get so pissed you can't even stand up? This isn't like you.'

'You wouldn't understand.'

'Really? You don't think after being married and divorced, married again and having my wife run off with my brother, I don't understand human suffering?'

Jamie sat up a little and reached for the glass of water. He sipped at it tentatively, expecting his stomach to revolt against the liquid. He sipped again and feeling a little more confident he reached for the aspirin and took a couple with some more water. He didn't reply so Cameron tried another tack.

'How about if I try and guess what's wrong? You tell me if I get it right.'

Jamie frowned at him and shrugged non-committedly.

'First of all, you miss your father; that's obvious and to be expected. It was a dreadful shock to all of us who loved him.'

Jamie turned his face away, but not before Cameron noticed the pain in his eyes.

'You also miss your mother too. You're worried about her and feel guilty for not being in Shetland. You feel like you need to look out for her; and your brother too. But at the same time you're working like a dog, with no sleep, no money, stressed out, exhausted, still having to study and pass exams and you can't take your eye off the ball for a second to even look after yourself, let alone anyone else. Am I right?'

Jamie didn't reply, but Cameron could see tears in his eyes. Jamie bowed his head and covered his face with his hands.

'Meanwhile Bryden has started work, earning money, enjoying the long school holidays, driving around in your Dad's car, playing golf, thinking about settling down. He has it easy doesn't he?'

This last comment struck gold. Jamie sat up straight and glared at Cameron.

'He thinks he's just going to walk into Dad's job and then he's going to live in Dad's old house, rent free as well. He gets everything he wants. He moans when some of the kids in school give him cheek. Well at least he hasn't had one dying on a trolley in front of him with his guts hanging after being hit by a car, and his mother screaming hysterically outside the door, having to be held back by her husband. If I try and talk to him about how tough it is training to be a doctor, he just says I won't be saying that in a few years when I'm earning four times what he does. Because *that's* why I'm doing it – just for the money; the stupid ignorant bastard!'

Cameron took another biscuit and pushed the tin towards Jamie who shook his head and pushed it back.

'The way I see it, you have both chosen difficult careers. Each job has its own stresses and rewards; but maybe neither of you is sure about whether you chose the right option. Medicine is the toughest job there is, and yes the money will be good, so maybe Bryden is a bit jealous of you. In the long run you will have the best financial rewards, but it may well be the Bryden has the easier life. Is this why you're pissed off with him? And then you have your dad. You both miss him. You both want to keep a part of him with you. Your mum gave Bryden the car for purely practical reasons, but that's got to hurt a bit eh? You know you don't really need a car yet, but why the hell should Bryden get it? And as for the house?' Cameron paused for a moment. Jamie's hands were trembling, and a trickle of sweat meandered down the side of his face, despite the fact it wasn't particularly warm in the kitchen.

'I'll tell you something,' Cameron continued, 'I could easily have beaten my brother John to a pulp when he moved into my house with Laura and Amy. The house I designed and built for myself and my family; so maybe I do understand a little of how you feel. Why should Bryden get handed a car, a house and your dad's old job without much effort on his part?'

Jamie stared at Cameron for a moment, trying to work out whether he was genuinely sympathetic or just being provocative.

'You don't want to fall out with Bryden over this. He's your brother, and up until now you've been close. Believe me; you don't want to lose your brother over a stupid thing like this. I will probably never speak to John again, and that's one of the worst things about what has happened; that and not having my daughter living with me.'

Jamie rested his head on his arms and for a moment Cameron thought he had fallen asleep. He got up and made himself another coffee. He looked at the clock on the wall; the clock he had bought his mother for her birthday to replace the one he had broken when he had been bouncing a football around in the kitchen. He smiled at the memory. His parents had both passed away, but this little house where he had been born still felt alive with their presence. He didn't know how long he would stay living here, perhaps until after the divorce, but he was in no hurry to leave. It was comforting to sit in the old kitchen, drinking coffee out of the same mugs he had used when he was a teenager.

Cameron sat down again and reached for another biscuit. He was tired, but he didn't want to leave Jamie on his own yet.

'You can sleep on the sofa if you want. I'll fetch a blanket for you.'

Jamie sat up and looked at him.

'I don't want to let Mam down.'

'How are you letting her down?'

'I don't think I can be a doctor.'

Cameron put down the half-eaten jammy dodger and gave Jamie his full attention.

'Well first of all, what you choose to do for a career is entirely your business. You won't be letting your mother down if you decide you want to do something else.'

Jamie shook his head, as if Cameron was talking nonsense.

'But even so, are you really sure it's wrong for you? Can't you just change your specialism?'

Jamie stood up; stumbling a little as he nearly knocked the chair over.

'Can I use the bathroom please?'

Cameron pointed the way and watched Jamie lurch off, still clearly suffering the effects of alcohol. Cameron finished his coffee and thought about Julia. This was not going to be the Christmas she had envisaged. He remembered how happy she had been when she left him that afternoon to go and pick her sons up from the airport. She had commented on the fact this first Christmas without Duncan would be tough, but he was sure Jamie was far more miserable than Julia could have imagined. Cameron got the impression Jamie was on the edge of a breakdown and was defiantly trying to man-up and hide it from his mother; disguising his pain behind anger and self-righteousness.

He wondered whether he should call Julia to warn her, particularly with regard to Bryden's decision to move back to Shetland. He could imagine her being happy to have him home, and probably would suggest he moved in to his Granny's old house. She needed to know how Jamie felt. It was too late to call her now; and in any case this needed to be handled with great care. Once Jamie had sobered up he would probably feel embarrassed at what had happened. He would not be happy if he thought Cameron had gone running to his mother to discuss his feelings.

He heard the toilet flush and then the taps running for a while. Jamie returned a moment later, the fringe of his hair wet from where he had washed his face. He seemed a little brighter and steadier. He sat down at the table again and drank some more water.

'Are you ready for something to eat now?' Cameron said.

'Yeah, maybe.'

'Toast; a bacon sandwich; there's some pizza Amy made today.'

'Pizza sounds good,' Jamie smiled for the first time as Cameron stood up and went to the fridge and took out a plate of pizza slices. He walked over to the oven and switched it on.

'I like cold pizza actually.' Jamie said.

'So did your dad. I remember him eating cold pizza for breakfast the night after you found out you'd got into medical school. It was the same day Amy was born, so we both had lots to celebrate. Your mum and dad stayed over at my house that night. It was some party.' Cameron smiled at the memory. 'Happy days.'

'That's why I can't give up. Dad was so proud of me. But I just can't cope with it.'

'You need to speak to your mother about it. Maybe she can help. She knows what it's like to work in a hospital. It was hard for her at first. I can remember my twenty first birthday party in Aberdeen. She was late as she had been working in A&E that day.

She had dealt with a young man who had been knocked off his motorbike in the city centre. He died unfortunately, and your mother was in pieces. She was only twenty and she had already seen a lot more trauma in her life than any of us could imagine; but this young man seemed to get to her. He had been holding her hand when he died, asking for his mother.'

'Is that why she started working in the care homes?'

'I don't know to be honest. But she's had enough of that too, hasn't she?'

Jamie looked puzzled. He put down the slice of pizza he was eating and frowned at Cameron.

'What do you mean?'

Cameron bit his lip and swore inside his head.

'Well the last time I saw her she was talking about maybe becoming a foster carer. I don't suppose she's had a chance to tell you herself yet.'

'Oh right. She talked about it a few years ago, before Dad was ill. That makes sense I guess.'

Cameron sighed with relief.

'What else can you do with a medical degree?' Cameron said, trying to change the subject.

Jamie took a bite of pizza and shrugged, although clearly he had been giving it some thought.

'Medical research, medical journalism.'

'Do either of those interest you?'

'Well I like the idea of going into research. I'm really interested in the area of immunology, but I would need to do more studying.'

'What's wrong with that?'

'That depends on whether I can get a bursary or not. My degree has already cost a fortune, I can't ask mum for more money.'

'Why not? If she has it, she would give it to you wouldn't she?'

'Yeah, but...'

'Yeah, but... talk to her! She wants you to be happy. She wouldn't want you to spend the next forty odd years at work doing something you don't enjoy.'

The next morning Cameron crept downstairs to the lounge and found Jamie fast asleep on the sofa. He tiptoed into the kitchen and put the kettle on then opened the curtains and looked out at the bright sunshine. There wasn't a breath of wind outside and the grass was white with frost. Cameron walked over to the thermostat and turned up the heat a little. He picked up a Fair Isle jumper he had left on a chair and pulled it on over his shirt. His mobile phone bleeped and he saw there was a text from Julia.

"How's Jamie this morning? Do you want me to come and pick him up?"

"He's sleeping. I will deliver him back to you when he wakes up." Cameron wrote; to which Julia replied, *"Bless you, thanks."*

Cameron walked over to a large portfolio case that was leaning against the wall under the window. He unzipped it and flicked through the sheets of paper until he found what he was looking for and pulled out a couple of large architectural drawings and laid them out on the table.

He made himself a cup of coffee and grabbed a croissant from a packet in the bread bin and sat down at the table and studied the drawings. He chewed the croissant without bothering to put butter or jam on it. He was deep in thought when Jamie walked into the kitchen looking pale and bedraggled.

'Got any more painkillers?' Jamie said.

Cameron nodded and pointed to a cupboard. Jamie opened the door and took out a packet of paracetamol and gulped back two tablets with a glass of water. He sat down at the table and peered at the drawings Cameron was still looking at.

'Are you working this morning?' Jamie asked.

'No, I was just thinking about something after our conversation last night.'

'Oh?' Jamie said, with a hint of embarrassment in his voice.

'You want to stay in Edinburgh right?'

Jamie nodded.

'Well, I've been involved in a private investment project in Edinburgh to build an apartment block. It was part of a consortium and I did the drawings in my spare time, put some money into the project to buy the land and get through the planning process. And when it's finished I will own two of the apartments on the top floor.'

'Cool!' Jamie said. He leaned forward to get a better look at the drawings, and then looked at Cameron for further explanation.

'I had thought this would be a brilliant investment for the future; for Amy. I had visions of her living in one of the apartments when she goes off to uni. It's a long way off I know; but until then I was going to rent one of them out and sell the other. The project has been a bit of a nightmare really, what with the recession and the tram works. It won't make as much money as we thought it would in the beginning.'

Jamie nodded in sympathy.

'Anyway, my other problem with regard to the properties is the fact I will be getting divorced at some stage in the future; which means everything I own is going to be fought over in the courts and I will lose half.'

'Yeah, but if you have two apartments, you can still keep one for Amy.' Jamie said.

'In theory, yes. But I'm already going to lose my house and will spend the next fifteen years or so supporting Amy, so I'm really pissed off at the idea that all the work I put in to this project is going to waste. I'm perfectly happy to support Amy and always will be, but I resent the fact that Laura will get to keep the house and half the money I make from the apartments. It's not like Amy will get the benefit from it. Laura will just piss it all away on clothes and shoes.'

Jamie narrowed his eyes; shocked at the bitterness, but realising he would possibly feel the same way. 'OK, but what does this have to do with what we talked about last night?'

'At the moment Laura doesn't know about the project. She's never taken an interest in my work; well at least not until the *Grand Designs* project, when suddenly she became quite the expert in architecture. So in theory I can offload the properties without her knowing.'

'If you don't mind me saying, that seems a little underhand.'

'So was sleeping with my brother.'

'Fair point! Do you mind if I get a cup of coffee?' Jamie stood up and went to the kettle and switched it on. Cameron passed him his mug and gestured for him to make him one too.

'Anyway, I was thinking about a conversation I had with your dad a year or so ago. I was telling him about this project and he said he would love to buy one of the apartments for you and Bryden. But he didn't think he'd be able to afford it at the time, and in any case you probably wouldn't want to share a place for very long.'

Jamie shook his head in agreement.

'So what I'm thinking about now, is whether or not you would want to buy one of the apartments. They're not finished yet, but they will be next year.'

'I can't afford to buy a shoebox!' Jamie said. He had the kettle in his hand and he put it back in its place a little clumsily. He turned to Cameron and lifted his hands questioningly.

'I think you could, with a little help from your brother. Take a look at this.' Cameron pointed to the floor-plan of one of the apartments. 'It has two bedrooms and a box-room, which could be a third bedroom at a push. If you lived here you could rent out two of the rooms to other students or junior doctors, which would cover your mortgage and maybe even some of your living expenses. If Bryden moves into your Gran's old house, you could suggest he re-mortgages it to let you have a deposit towards buying your place. That way you both get to own a property from your family's inheritance. Whether you carry on with your medical training or even change direction, you still want to stay in Edinburgh, and if for some reason you want to move somewhere else you'd be able to sell it.'

Jamie picked up the drawings and studied them. He turned his attention to the site plan and its close proximity to the new tram line that was being installed.

'From the top floor you will be able to see across to Murrayfield stadium.'

'Great, but I still don't think I would be able to afford it. These apartments look expensive; more than can be raised from re-mortgaging an ancient croft house,' Jamie said, tapping the drawing.

'You can have it for a little over cost price.'

'What? Seriously? Why?'

'I would feel much happier if you ended up living there. If it would make you feel any better we could agree that if you decided to sell up, then you would sell it back to me for an agreed percentage under the market price. And if I'm able to keep hold of the next door apartment then you could manage it for me.'

'Sounds fair to me.'

'Anyway, you've got to talk to your mother and Bryden about this. Please don't ruin your Christmas by falling out with each other; and on that note I'd better get you home soon, Julia has already sent me a text to find out how you are.'

Jamie gulped back his coffee and stood up.

'Yeah, I guess I have some apologising to do for yesterday.'

'We can stop off at the shops and buy flowers if you like.'

'What, for Bryden?' Jamie said, laughing.

Half an hour later Cameron pulled up outside Julia's house. He saw her at the kitchen window and lifted his hand in greeting. Jamie opened the passenger door and got out, then he turned and leaned back into the car.

'Are you coming in?'

'No, it's OK; I don't need to hear a lecture on the perils of vodka from your mother.'

Jamie laughed, knowing exactly what was in store for him.

'What are you doing for Christmas day?' Jamie asked.

Cameron shrugged. 'Probably going to my sister's. Not sure yet.'

'Mum's invited Liam round for dinner that night; I wondered if you wanted to come too.'

Cameron smiled at him.

'Yeah, thanks mate. That would be nice.'

'Thanks for last night.' Jamie said.

'Don't mention it.'

Cameron waved again at Julia who had just come to the door. She smiled and waved back and then put her arm around Jamie and led him indoors. Cameron saw Jamie hug his mother and he sighed with relief as he drove off home.

18

Christmas Day dawned; a bleak and miserable day that had followed a wild night. Julia looked at her clock and saw it was already after nine. She went to leap out of bed, shocked at how late it was; then she relaxed and pulled the duvet back around her shoulders. She didn't need to rush around this morning as she wouldn't have to start cooking the turkey until much later in the day.

She listened for a moment to see if there was any noise coming from Bryden or Jamie's rooms. Silence. How unlike this Christmas was compared to when they were little, when by now all of the presents would have been opened and the boys would have been high on chocolate and fizzy pop. Instead they were sleeping off the excesses of the night before; they had all gone over to Marianne's for the traditional Christmas Eve drink, which had gone on for a lot longer than normal.

Julia had enjoyed the evening much more than she thought she would; perhaps because the atmosphere between Bryden and Jamie seemed much better, almost back to normal in fact. Perhaps, because there was a large crowd of young people in the house, with their infectious high spirits and readiness to laugh and joke. Julia had loved sitting in the kitchen with Marianne and her sisters and daughters, drinking Champagne and talking about everything and nothing. She couldn't really remember what they had talked about, but it had been lightsome. They hadn't mentioned Duncan much, but Julia knew they were all thinking of him, and that was enough.

She was thinking of him now. He was always the first person to get up on Christmas morning. He'd been worse than any child. She stretched out in the warm bed and pulled his old sweatshirt from under his pillow. It no longer smelled of Duncan, in fact it probably smelled more of her perfume than his. She had worn it so much and had finally had to wash it, but she kept it in the bed with her, tucked under the pillow and occasionally she would wear it when it was cold.

She held the sleeve of the sweatshirt to her face. 'Merry Christmas darling, wherever you are.'

She heard the toilet flush in the bathroom along the hall and knew at least one of her sons was awake. She got out of bed and put her dressing gown on and went to the window and opened the curtains.

She couldn't see the beach through the low cloud and rain. It was a disgusting day so they might not be able to go out for their Christmas walk along the beach. She wondered what else they would do today. Nothing would be the same as in previous years. It was time to start some new traditions.

Julia went downstairs and found Jamie slumped on the sofa, wearing his dad's old dressing gown. She smiled at him and ruffled his hair as she walked past on the way to the kitchen.

'Merry Christmas. How are you this morning?'

'Tired.'

'Why did you get up then?' Julia replied.

'It's Christmas,' Jamie said, grinning a like a school boy and sitting up expectantly. 'Where's my present?'

'You know the rules; everyone has to be up, dressed and have had their breakfast first.'

Jamie flung himself down on the sofa again, in the manner of a toddler beginning a tantrum.

'That's not fair!'

Julia laughed at him.

'Want some coffee, or would you rather have Ribena?'

Jamie stood up and followed her into the kitchen.

'Coffee please.'

He hugged her and she wrapped her arms around him and stood for a moment enjoying the fact her old Jamie was back.

'So what's the plan for today?' Jamie asked.

'Well since we're not eating our dinner until this evening, I thought I might cook up a nice big breakfast, and then we won't need to bother with lunch. What do you think?'

'Great. Tell you what, I'll just go up and have a shower and get dressed and then I'll cook breakfast. I'm getting quite good in the kitchen now.'

Julia grinned at him.

'Really? Well this will be interesting. I think I'll go and have a shower too. Then we'll get Bryden up. There's something I want to do when we're all dressed.'

Julia made a cup of coffee and took it upstairs to her bedroom. After her shower she put on a pair of jeans and a scarlet cashmere jumper. This was a break from her tradition of wearing a dress on Christmas day. She didn't think the boys would notice, but she wanted to make some subtle changes to the day.

She went downstairs and found Jamie and Bryden in the kitchen. They were laughing about something and looked round guiltily at her.

'What's going on?'

'Jamie's just burnt your frying pan.' Bryden said, ducking out of the way of Jamie who tried to flick a tea towel at him.

'Never mind, there's another one in the cupboard in the utility room.' Julia said, walking out to fetch the frying pan. She handed the new one to Jamie and then picked up the burnt pan and took it over to the sink. She scrubbed the bottom of the pan and quickly saw it was a lost cause. She carried it over to the bin and dropped it in. 'What was that about getting quite good in the kitchen?'

Jamie laughed and turned back to chopping up mushrooms and tomatoes. He had beaten up some eggs in a Pyrex jug and had sausages and bacon on under the grill. Bryden was making a stack of toast and they had already laid the table with juice, cutlery and pots of marmalade and butter. They had a CD of Christmas songs playing on the stereo, which made a cheerful contrast to the gloom outside the window.

Julia left the boys to their cooking and went back to the lounge and switched on the Christmas tree lights. She noticed there was a new stack of presents under the tree and she felt the first thrill of anticipation.

She sat down on the sofa for a moment and shut her eyes. She heard the boys talking about a band they had been to see in Edinburgh and realised with relief the storm had passed. Whatever it was they had fallen out about, it seemed to have been resolved. Jamie certainly seemed to have cheered up after his night out. He hadn't said much about spending the night at Cameron's but he had been markedly happier since then, although they had all been so busy with Christmas related shopping, cooking and socialising they still hadn't spent much time together.

'Breakfast is ready,' Bryden called.

Julia stood up and walked back to the kitchen and sat down as Jamie handed out the plates.

'This looks lovely,' she said, appreciatively.

Bryden patted Jamie on the back.

'Well if medicine doesn't work out, you could always get a job as a chef.'

'Very funny,' Jamie said.

After breakfast Bryden sat down in the chair nearest the Christmas tree. He reached down to pick up one of the presents.

'Before we get to the presents I thought we would do something for your dad first.' Julia said, as she opened the cupboard under the stairs. She reached inside and took out a box and set it down on the coffee table. Inside was a large fat candle which she put on a metal dish and carried over to the window sill. She picked up a box of matches and turned to Bryden and Jamie.

'We're going to light a candle for your father; and we will do this every Christmas from now on. We will miss him every single day for the rest of our lives, but I think you'll agree Duncan always made Christmas really special, and I will really miss him today.'

Jamie stood up and walked across the room to his mother and put his arm around her. He looked back at Bryden and beckoned him over. Bryden stood up, reluctantly. He walked slowly over and stood next to them.

'There are three wicks in the candle, so we will light one each and it should burn all day long.' She handed the box to Jamie who struck a match and lit one of the wicks, then handed the box to

Bryden who took a deep breath. He paused for a moment and looked as if he was gritting his teeth in pain. He lit a wick and then handed the matches back to Julia. Bryden stepped back and turned away as Julia lit the candle; he sat down heavily on the sofa with his head in his hands.

Julia sat down next to him and put her arm around him.

'It's OK to get upset.'

Bryden nodded without replying.

'Have you got any more candles?' Jamie said. 'We should light one for Grandma Alice too.'

Julia nodded and pointed to the cupboard. Jamie found a smaller pillar candle in a glass holder. He took it over to the window sill and after lighting it he set it down next to the other candle.

Julia smiled her thanks at him and then patted Bryden's arm.

'Now then, shall we open our presents?'

Bryden nodded, but with a sombre expression.

'Isn't it about now Dad would have been opening a bottle of Champagne?' Jamie said.

'Shall we?' Julia said to Bryden.

Bryden shrugged.

'We don't have to, if you don't feel like it. We can do whatever we want to this Christmas. We don't have to celebrate if we don't want to.' Julia said to Bryden. 'On the other hand, you know if there is a heaven and your father is up there watching us, he would be shouting for us to crack open the Champagne.'

'Or whisky,' Bryden said, his face twitching with the start of a smile.

'Sounds good to me,' Jamie said, walking over to the wooden cabinet that housed the drinks and glasses.

Jamie poured out three little nips of whisky and handed them round. They stood in the centre of the lounge and raised their glasses.

'To dad; to Duncan,' they said, before taking a sip each.

Bryden appeared to shake himself out of the gloom and he walked over to the tree and sat on the chair nearest the hoard of presents.

'Who's first?' he said, bending down to pick up a gaudily wrapped present. 'This one's for you, Mam.'

They spent the next half an hour opening their presents. The boys were delighted with their new iPads, and their traditional assortment of socks and underwear Julia had bought them. Julia had also bought a large wooden scrabble board to share, as the last hardboard one had disintegrated through wear and tear over the last twenty years.

They sat in the lounge surrounded by the shreds of wrapping paper and packaging, sipping whisky and playing scrabble. Julia felt something close to happiness.

A couple of hours later, the weather brightened up a little and they decided to walk down to the beach. They huddled into warm coats, hats and scarves and set off across the field and over the stile. Jamie and Bryden raced each other to the bench and collapsed onto it, pushing at each other in a way that reminded Julia of when they were teenagers, rather than the twenty-something men they had turned into, seemingly overnight. Julia caught up with them and squeezed in between them on the bench. They stared out to sea for a moment, and then the old ritual of daring each other to swim to the island started up.

'Not in this weather, and certainly not when you've been drinking,' Julia said sternly, hoping this wouldn't be the year they finally decided to attempt it, just when she didn't have Duncan to hold them back.

They were all talk though; and they quickly switched their banter to how much turkey they would consume later.

'Don't forget Liam will be here too,' Julia said, checking her watch and wondering whether it would soon be time to put the turkey in the oven.

'And Cameron,' Jamie said, 'did I forget to tell you, I invited him over too?'

Julia felt herself flush.

'What? Yes, you did forget. What time is he coming? He knows it's going to be this evening doesn't he?'

'Yes of course. You don't mind do you? It's just he's on his own tonight, and after all he was pretty good about dragging me out of the pub and me spewing all over his shoes the other night.'

'Oh for God's sake; you didn't did you?' Julia said. She covered her face with her hands, mortified at Jamie's behaviour.

'Just a splash,' Jamie replied, pulling a face at Bryden, who giggled.

'Jamie! Honestly,' Julia said, slapping him on the leg in disgust and then slapping Bryden for laughing.

'He was OK about it, and he was pleased to be invited over.'

Julia looked at her watch again and stood up.

'Well, since we have two guests coming for dinner, perhaps it's time to get back and start the dinner. We haven't even washed up after breakfast yet.'

Liam arrived just after seven, looking slightly worn out after a shift that involved two domestic disputes and a minor traffic accident. Julia hugged him and led him into the lounge where Bryden and Jamie were sitting watching the television. They turned the television off and put on some music and fetched Liam a beer. Within minutes Liam had taken his shoes off and had his feet up on the sofa looking visibly more relaxed.

A few minutes later Cameron turned up, with Amy, which was a pleasant surprise for everyone.

'You don't mind do you? Laura said she was going to a party later. I thought it was best if she came with me. She'll probably fall asleep soon; she's been up since five.'

'Of course I don't mind. There's plenty of food, and I'm sure she could have a little sleep in the downstairs bedroom, if she's tired.'

Cameron smiled his thanks and took Amy into the lounge where Bryden immediately engaged in conversation with her about what Santy had brought her for Christmas. Amy had brought along her new doll and she proceeded to show Bryden all of Barbie's new outfits, much to the amusement of Jamie and Liam.

'Santy bought me this new iPad. You can watch films on it. Do you want to have a look?' Bryden said to Amy, deftly trying to change the subject from dolls.

He downloaded a Jessie J video and Amy sat entranced with the iPad on her lap.

Cameron followed Julia back to the kitchen as she was almost ready to start serving up.

'I've got you a present,' he said quietly, not wishing to be overheard.

'Oh?' Julia said, thinking quickly about what she could give him in return and failing to come up with anything. 'I feel bad now, I didn't get you anything.'

'This is enough, just having me over for dinner,' Cameron said, walking back to the hallway where he bent down to pick up a large flat box wrapped in gold paper. He handed it to Julia who wiped her hands on her apron before taking it. She looked up at him quizzically, wondering what it could be. Then she peeled away the sellotape and opened the box. Inside was a bubble-wrapped picture. She ripped off the bubble wrap and revealed a large framed photograph of Duncan, who looked like he was doing some woodwork in a workshop.

'Where was this taken?'

'It was the last time Duncan came along to the bunker. He designed the shields for the Jarl Squad and he helped carve some of the axe shafts.'

'Really? I didn't know he designed the shield.'

'Well it's top secret until Up Helly Aa isn't it? You weren't supposed to know anything about it. I shouldn't really be giving you this picture yet.'

'It's a great picture,' Julia said, glued to the image of Duncan, who had clearly been enjoying himself at the time. On the worktop beside him was a bottle of beer and Duncan was holding a piece of wood that was obviously about to be turned into an axe shaft. On an open laptop next to the beer was a picture of an ornate Celtic pattern, and a diagram of an axe.

'You can't show this to anyone yet.' Cameron said, pointing to the laptop in the picture.

'Rubbish!' Julia said, walking straight into the lounge. Cameron sighed dramatically and followed her.

'Look at this lovely picture of your dad. It was taken at the Up Helly Aa bunker this year.'

Cameron and Bryden jumped up to see it. They took it in turns to hold it and both nodded in approval.

'I told your mother it was supposed to be a secret until January, but she wouldn't listen.'

'Typical woman!' Bryden said, grinning wickedly at Julia.

'This is great, Cameron, thanks,' Jamie said. 'Are there any more pictures of Dad at the bunker?'

'Yeah, one of the squad has been taking photos and videos of all the work that has gone on during the last year. You can have copies after Up Helly Aa is over.'

'Cool!' Bryden said, slapping Cameron on the back.

Julia took the photograph and placed it on the window sill beside the candle.

'I'll take it upstairs later and put it in my room so nobody else sees it,' she said to Cameron. She stood and admired the photograph for a moment and then turned on her heels and headed back to the kitchen, with a noticeable bounce in her walk.

'Dinner will be on the table in a few minutes,' she said, as she passed the sofa, pausing to ruffle Bryden's hair.

'Oh goodie,' Amy said, leaping up from the sofa, almost knocking the iPad onto the floor. Bryden caught it and put it away in a wicker basket under the coffee table.

When Julia brought the plates of food into the dining room, she found everyone sitting there expectantly. Jamie was sitting at the head of the table, Julia noticed with a smile. Julia sat down and then jumped up again immediately to fetch juice for Amy and the bottle of white wine that was still in the fridge.

'I didn't bother with starters,' she said apologetically, as she took the only vacant seat between Jamie and Cameron

Jamie reached for the gravy and laughed at her.

'So you're not counting the pringles, nuts and chocolates you ate earlier as a starter.'

'Of course not!' Julia said, prodding him in the ribs. 'Come on everyone, help yourself to gravy, cranberry sauce; don't be shy.' She nodded at Liam, who was sitting back waiting for everyone else to start.

'This looks great; thanks for inviting me,' he said.

'Thanks for coming along, and you too, Amy and Cameron; this is a lovely having so many people for dinner.'

As everyone start to tuck in to their food, Julia thought back to the previous Christmas. It had been a strange day. Duncan had been so tired he had slept for most of the afternoon, and had not been able to eat much of his dinner. A few days before the holiday he had been along to the hospital for tests, to see how successful his treatment had been and they were told they would not know the outcome until the New Year. It had felt like a lifetime to wait. The doctors had been fairly optimistic, but because Duncan was still feeling lethargic and had not bounced back to his normal self, it had been hard for them to share the optimism at the time.

Bryden and Jamie had come home, worn out from studying and the stress of worrying about their father. They had been quiet and anxious over the holiday last year. Now they were sitting around the table loudly sparring with each other and Liam, and teasing Amy about her taste in pop music.

It was lovely, Julia thought, to sit here with family and friends, even if the weight of grief and sadness was still visible in the faces of her sons. They had aged a little over the last year, and she most certainly had too.

She reached for her glass of water just as Cameron put his hand out to pass Amy the dish of cranberry sauce. His hand brushed against hers and she flinched. She dropped her hand onto her lap, surprised at the tingling sensation she still felt where they had touched.

'So what have you been doing today?' Cameron asked the table as a whole.

'Scrabble marathon and drinking whisky for the most part,' Jamie replied.

'Picking up the pieces of some people's overindulgence in alcohol,' Liam said, raising his glass of wine like a toast, and taking a sip. 'Cheers!'

'I got roller-skates,' Amy said, 'and I fell over and banged my knee. Mummy got cross with me.' Amy picked up a roast potato with her fingers and took a bite out of it. Julia saw Cameron frown at his daughter and silently gesture to her to use her fork. Amy grinned and picked up her cutlery again, and carried on eating. Cameron turned and raised his eyebrows at Julia, suggesting he was a little anxious about his daughter.

Julia watched Amy picking at her food. She clearly wasn't very hungry but she seemed to relish the attention. She constantly looked at her dad for reassurance, and Julia noticed him wink at Amy and pull a funny face that made her laugh.

'Why haven't you got any crackers?' Amy said to Julia. 'We had crackers, and a hat.'

'Do you know something, Amy, I completely forgot about crackers.'

'Waste of money anyway,' Bryden said.

'I like your flowers. They have an architectural quality to them,' Amy said, making Julia choke with surprise.

Jamie burst out laughing and Amy looked around at the adults, not understanding what was so amusing.

'What's funny, Daddy? You said that to the lady in the flower shop and she didn't laugh.'

'Nothing's funny, we just thought you were being very clever, sweetie,' Cameron said.'

Julia wondered who Cameron had been buying flowers for and hated herself for feeling jealous. She had no right.

They finished their dinner. Amy started to wilt and said no to pudding, so Bryden took her to the lounge and put on a cartoon for her. Julia brought out a tray with a large homemade Black Forest Gateau and set it in the middle of the table. Bryden and Jamie looked perplexed.

'Didn't you make Christmas pudding this year?' Jamie said, almost sulkily.

'Not this year. I decided to make your dad's favourite cake instead. We had this on our very first date.'

'Very retro,' Cameron said. 'I think all first dates involved Black Forest Gateau back in the day.'

Julia rewarded him with a warm smile of gratitude. They lingered over coffee and cake, talking about Duncan. Cameron recounted stories about their school days, for the benefit of Bryden and Jamie. Then he excused himself to check on Amy and came back to report she was fast asleep.

'Perhaps I had better call a taxi and take her home.'

'Oh no, it's way too early.' Bryden said. 'Why don't you put Amy in the spare room; I expect she's out for the count now.'

Cameron looked at Julia, who nodded.

'Please stay, this has been so nice. Come on; you carry Amy and I'll show you to the room.'

Cameron followed her to the lounge, stopping to pick Amy up who remained zonked out as he carried her through to the bedroom. Julia pulled back the duvet and held it while he laid Amy down on the bed. He bent down to take off her shoes, and a plastic bracelet she had on her wrist. Julia covered up the sleeping child, and wondered how long it would be before she would be doing this again for a foster child. She felt a rush of excitement that having children staying in her house might be part of her future. She looked at Cameron and smiled at him and then switched on a dim lamp in the corner of the room in case Amy woke up.

As they stood by the bedroom door, Cameron put his arm around Julia's shoulder and pulled her towards him in a brief hug. He kissed her cheek.

'Thanks again,' he said, before standing back to let her out of the room.

Julia hurried out, flummoxed by the sudden affection that threatened to open the floodgates on her memories of Sicily. She felt the tumble of butterflies as an image of him naked in her bed entered her thoughts. She waved her hand in the air, subconsciously batting away the idea as she walked back to the dining room, where her sons and Liam were still sitting amid the detritus of the meal.

'Anyone want some more wine or coffee?' Julia said, picking up her glass and draining it, as she stood waiting for a response.

'Nah, I'm good. Shall we go and sit in the lounge?' Jamie said to Liam and Bryden.

'What about clearing the table?' Liam said, standing and picking up his plate.

'No, no; leave it to me. You go on, all of you; it won't take me five minutes to load the dishwasher,' Julia said.

Without any protest, the young men left the room, and Julia sat down heavily on her chair and reached for the bottle of wine and refilled her glass. She took a sip and shut her eyes for a moment. She had boxed up the memories of Sicily and packed them away in her head, marked "never to be opened." Cameron's, relatively innocent kiss had undone the box in such a way the memories might not fit back in.

She couldn't understand why she felt so confused. In theory at least, she was a single woman, free to love whoever she wanted to; and in a way, Cameron was single again too, albeit with an estranged wife and a young child. But in reality she didn't think the people closest to her would consider her ready to move on from Duncan. She imagined her sons would be horrified if they knew what had happened in Sicily.

It had been less than a year since Duncan died; a little over eight months in fact. She didn't know how long she would need to wait before it would be acceptable to take up with another man, but it most certainly wouldn't be before the first anniversary.

'You OK?' Cameron asked, startling her.

He sat down in the chair Jamie had vacated. He crossed his arms, signalling he didn't intend to touch her, but he smiled warmly at her.

Julia felt her eyes water.

'I don't know. Really, I just don't know how I feel.' She brushed the tears away with the back of her wrist and stared down at the table cloth. 'One minute my heart is breaking for Duncan; the next I'm making plans for the future. I feel angry, then I'm sad, then like today I felt something close to happiness again. And now I'm back to sad. Why did he have to die?'

'I don't know. I wish he hadn't. I wish lots of things, but most of all I wish he was still here.'

'I'm sorry.'

'What for?'

'You know what for?' Julia said, looking up at him, but finding it hard to maintain eye contact.

'Don't be! You did nothing wrong; neither of us did.'

'So why do I feel guilty?'

'Because you loved him. I think I would feel more concerned if you didn't feel any kind of guilt. I feel it too. He was one of my closest friends remember.'

'I can't bear the fact that we're moving into a new year soon. It's like every day that passes takes me further away from him. It doesn't get any easier, despite what people say about time being a great healer.'

'I think when they say that, they generally mean a few years, not a few months.'

Jamie walked back to the dining table and looked at Julia and Cameron.

'What's up?' he said, reaching for a box of chocolate mints.

'Your mother is missing your Dad.'

Jamie put down the chocolates and walked around to Julia.

'We all miss him Mam,' he said, standing behind her and leaning down to hug her. 'This Christmas will always be the hardest, and we've had a good time despite everything. Dad would be pleased with us, wouldn't he?'

'Yes, he would,' Julia replied, reaching for Jamie's hand. As Jamie straightened up, Julia saw that Cameron had left the room as silently as he had arrived.

'Come on Mam, leave the dishes until later, or even tomorrow. Come and sit down with us.'

Julia picked up her glass and followed Jamie into the lounge where she found Cameron chatting to Liam about houses. Cameron looked up and winked at her. She smiled back and sat down next to Jamie.

'Who's up for a game of poker? The loser has to tidy up the kitchen,' Jamie said, picking up a pack of cards and a turntable full of poker chips.

Bryden and Liam doled out the poker chips, while Jamie cleared some space on the coffee table for the game.

Before the first hand had been dealt the phone rang. Jamie was the closest to the handset so he leaned over and answered it.

'Robertson household; merry Christmas,' he said. Julia looked at her watch and noticed it was after nine. She wondered who would be calling as she had spoken to most of her closest friends already.

'It's for you, Mam. Some guy called Tony,' Jamie said, passing the phone to her.

Julia stood up and carried the phone into the kitchen.

'Hello Tony; this *is* a lovely surprise. How are you?' She looked back into the lounge as she spoke. She noticed that everyone was watching her and she turned her back on them, fiddling with an ornament on the window sill.

'I hope you don't mind me ringing you on Christmas Day, but I had some news and I also wanted to ask you something.'

'Of course I don't mind. We were just sitting around playing cards. What's your news?'

'I've just booked a holiday to Scotland; and I'm going to visit Shetland for Up Helly Aa, just like you suggested.'

'Really? That's brilliant; oh, but you must stay here. You'll never find a hotel room at this short notice.'

'I know; that's why I rang. I booked the flights online, and then discovered I couldn't find anywhere to stay. You don't mind do you?'

'Of course not; it will be lovely. It will give me a good excuse to go to.'

Julia spoke to Tony for a while longer, exchanging their news, and discussing the details of the holiday. Then they agreed to speak in a couple of weeks to finalise arrangements.

Julia went back to the lounge, feeling cheerful. She took her seat on the sofa next to Jamie and only then realised that they had been waiting for her.

'Was that the Tony who owned the villa in Sicily?' Bryden asked.

'Yes it was. He's coming over to Shetland for Up Helly Aa. Isn't that great?'

'Why?' Jamie asked.

Julia heard the tension in his voice, but because she had a clear conscious with regard to Tony she wasn't too concerned.

'It's very funny really. We had this silly conversation about how I could make my mind up about what I want to do with my life. It involved a discussion about how he creates characters and the motivations for their actions. We came up with this new character, Rebecca, who I decided worked for the mountain rescue service in the Cairngorms. Anyway, it was all very silly really, but after I left Sicily Tony got an idea for a new novel. The detective in his latest series needs a holiday and he's decided to send him to the Cairngorms and have a bit of an adventure in the mountains, and maybe even some romance with Rebecca. Isn't that amazing; a character I helped to create is going to be in his next book?'

'I must read his books sometime,' Cameron said, nodding in approval.'

'Yeah, but why is he coming to Shetland?' Jamie demanded. He had dropped the pack of cards he had been holding onto the coffee table. A few of them had fallen on the floor, but he appeared not to notice.

'Because I told him all about Up Helly Aa and he wanted to see it for himself. I didn't think he would come over so soon, but it will be nice to have company. He's going to stay here.'

Jamie jumped up as if he had been stung.

'Here? He can't stay here. Why can't he stay in a hotel?'

Julia glared at him.

'Because all the hotels are fully booked already, and in any case he's a friend. Why on earth are you upset about it? What do you imagine is going to happen?'

'Bryden told me about him. He's widowed isn't he? I just want to know why he's so interested in coming to stay with you.'

Julia stood up and walked out of the room without replying. She went upstairs to her bedroom and sat down on the bed. She could hear the rumble of disgruntled male voices downstairs. She thought about Amy asleep in the spare room and realised that Jamie's belligerence was likely to wake her up. She sighed and hurried downstairs to confront him.

She passed the door to Amy's room and saw Cameron standing just inside. He came out and smiled sympathetically at Julia.

'Maybe it's best if I call a taxi.'

'I'm so sorry; I don't know what's got into him.'

'He's just looking out for you. It's only natural he's going to worry about you.'

'But I'm a grown up, and more than capable of looking after myself. Honestly, he is so patronising sometimes.'

'He means well.'

'I wasn't looking forward to Up Helly Aa this year, for obvious reasons, but now I feel like I have something nice to look forward to. At least until Jamie threw his dolly out of the pram.'

'If it helps, I wanted to throw my dolly out of the pram too.' Cameron leaned against the door frame, hiding out of view of the lounge that was just along the passage. 'But I don't have the right either.'

'Oh for goodness sake; Tony and I are just friends.'

'And so were we.' Cameron said, smirking just a little.

'We still are, you fool.' Julia took his arm and walked out to the lounge with him.

Julia stood in front of Bryden and Jamie with her hands on her hips.

'Let's just get a few things straight; there is nothing going on between myself and Tony, OK? So I would appreciate it if you didn't insult me by treating me like I'm your teenage daughter, instead of your mother, with twice as much life experience as the pair of you.'

'It wasn't me that said anything,' Bryden said, leaning over and prodding Jamie, who scowled at him.

'I don't expect an apology, but I would appreciate it if you didn't behave like idiots when we have guests. Cameron was just about to call a taxi and go home. I was going to suggest that he stays over instead and we carry on and play poker. Is that OK?'

'Actually Jules, I think I had better get Amy back home. But thanks anyway, it was a lovely night.'

When the taxi arrived Cameron carried Amy out to the car, while Julia picked up the toys and shoes that had been discarded around the house, and followed him out with them.

'Are you going to Marianne's Hogmanay party?' Cameron asked, as he got in the taxi.

'I don't think so. I don't think New Year's Eve is going to be a good night for me.'

'Me neither!'

Julia hurried back inside the house to get out of the cold and found Jamie, Liam and Bryden bickering over the game of poker they had started. She shook her head in mock despair at them.

'I think I might go to bed now. Goodnight.'

Jamie stood up and hugged her.

'I'm sorry. I just can't get my head around the idea that one day you'll meet someone else.'

'What do you think I'm going to do? Go to grab a granny night at the British Legion?'

'Well no; but...'

'But nothing. Goodnight everyone. Don't drink too much. And Liam; you're in charge.'

Julia couldn't sleep. She listened to the low murmur of voices in the lounge. A while later she heard someone switch on the television. The volume was turned down low but occasionally she would hear gunfire and shouting. She wondered what film they were watching downstairs. She considered getting out of bed and going to join them again, but she changed her mind and snuggled down under the duvet.

Jamie's reaction to Tony's visit didn't really surprise her. But she had seen a glimpse of how he would react if he found out about Cameron. She didn't think she would like to put it to the test.

19

Julia sat reading in bed on Boxing Day morning. It was one of Tony's novels that she had downloaded onto her iPad. She loved reading his books. They took her out of her ordinary world of sadness to the seedy underworld of criminal gangs, drug warlords, shady Mafioso and the gentle, good humour of Tony's detective, Arthur King. Now that Julia knew Tony, she could recognise aspects of his character in Arthur.

Later, she tiptoed down the stairs, believing that everyone else in the house would still be asleep. She was surprised to find Liam in the kitchen, standing at the sink doing the washing up.

'Oh there was no need for you to do that; but thanks, you're a star.'

'I thought I might as well. I have to get off to work soon.'

'Let me make you some breakfast first,' Julia looked at her watch and laughed, 'or maybe some lunch. Turkey sandwich?'

'That would be great thanks.'

Julia took the turkey out of the fridge and carved off some slices. She made a large platter of turkey, stuffing, bacon and cranberry sauce sandwiches.

'I expect the other two will want food soon.' Julia said as she gestured for Liam to help himself. As Liam sat down at the table, Julia brought over a pot of tea and then sat down with him. She picked up a sandwich and took a bite.

'This was Duncan's favourite meal, the post-Christmas dinner sandwich; although he would have had it last night with a glass of Port.'

'I never get tired of turkey leftovers either. I think my parents are mad going away over Christmas. No amount of sunshine makes up for missing a traditional Christmas.'

'Oh, I don't know; I discovered there is something quite magical about being in the warm sun when you know everyone back home is shivering.'

'Sicily sounds great. I should go over there myself one day,' Liam replied. He put down his sandwich and took a gulp of tea.

'It was lovely. I shall definitely go back again. Maybe we can all go over there. I would really love to take Jamie this time. He needs a holiday doesn't he?'

'Yeah; he's not himself at all.'

'I think I need to sit down with those two and have a serious talk. I want to start the New Year in a better place.'

'I hate New Year's Eve,' Liam said, frowning and shaking his head.

'Really? You're far too young to be so cynical and weary.' Julia looked at him in surprise.

'I think being a policeman ages you a bit; even here in Shetland, where not a lot of serious crime happens.'

'I suppose it does; but that's a shame. I know I'm not really looking forward to the New Year, but I hate to think I'll never find any reason to celebrate ever again.'

'I'm sure you will. There'll be weddings and christenings; lots of good things.'

Julia nodded thoughtfully, although it occurred to her that Liam only expected these things for her sons. It was another reminder that people expected her to live a quiet and celibate life now.

'I'd better go. I need to go home and get my uniform on. Thanks for inviting me over for dinner. It was great.'

Julia went to the front door with Liam and hugged him goodbye.

'You take care now,' she said.

When she came back to the kitchen she found Jamie standing in his boxer shorts peering out the window.

'Liam's just gone.' Julia said, 'I've made some turkey sandwiches, so why don't you go up and get dressed and drag your brother out of his pit. I want to sit down and have a talk with you two this afternoon.'

'Oh dear; are we in trouble?' Jamie said, teasing her.

'Not at all; I just think it's time we discussed how we all move forward.'

Jamie stopped smiling and looked serious for a moment. He turned and ran upstairs and a moment later Julia heard him thumping across the landing above her head.

Half an hour later her sons were sitting down at the table, freshly showered and dressed. Julia had made some more tea and she sat down opposite them. She shuffled through a pile of papers she had brought to the table, trying to find something.

'Ah, here it is,' she said, pulling out a printed document. 'Your father's unofficial will.'

'I thought he made a proper will. Wasn't that sorted out ages ago?' Jamie said.

'Oh yes; all the pensions, life assurance and property have been sorted out. But when your dad was ill we sat down and discussed how we would use the money to help you two out. He made me promise that I would leave it a few months, so that you had a bit of time to get used to the situation. So I decided to wait until after Christmas. Is that OK?'

'Sure,' mumbled Bryden.

'Good. Well, first of all we discussed whether or not to use some of the money to settle your student loans, but we decided that wasn't the best use of it. Instead we wanted to give you the chance to buy somewhere to live. Now you're both earning money, albeit not huge salaries just yet, you can probably get mortgages.' Julia paused for a moment, looking at her sons, who were half-heartedly eating their sandwiches while they listened.

'I was thinking of selling your grandmother's cottage and splitting the proceeds, but now Bryden has said he would like to live there if he gets a job in Shetland; so that changes things a little.'

'Actually, I have some news that changes things too.' Jamie said nervously.

'Really?'

'Um, yeah. I didn't tell you before because I didn't want to ruin your Christmas, but I've decided I don't want to be a doctor anymore.'

Jamie explained about how unhappy he was working in the hospital and how he had changed his mind about working directly with patients, preferring instead to move into medical research.

'So where will you do this?' Julia asked, partially reassured that he wasn't throwing away his promising career entirely.

'Probably Edinburgh still. I'm considering whether to finish my medical foundation programme so that I'm still a fully qualified doctor and then go into research, or just jumping ship now and starting a PhD next year.'

'How much does that cost?' Bryden said.

'If I'm lucky, it won't cost anything. I should get paid, if I can get onto a research programme that comes with a bursary. I should get about 25k a year for three years.'

'So you still might be able to get a mortgage?' Bryden said. 'That's about the same as my salary.'

'That's the other news actually. I think I might be able to buy a flat in Edinburgh soon. I was talking to Cameron the other day and he told me he's building an apartment block in the city, near Murrayfield, and he said I can buy an apartment at just a little over the cost price.'

'Really?' Julia said. She bit her lip, wondering why Cameron hadn't said anything to her about this plan. Was this because of Sicily? She felt a flush of pleasure that he thought so much of her that he wanted to help Jamie; but then again, surely this would mean she owed him something. The pleasure turned quickly to anxiety.

'Yeah. But only if I can buy it before he gets divorced. He wanted to keep the apartments as an investment for Amy, but he doesn't think Amy will ever benefit from it, if Laura gets hold of the money.'

Julia's ego crashed and burned. So it had nothing to do with her after all. He just wanted to hide his assets from his wife. Typical bloody man, she thought angrily.

'That's awful. He can't do that; it's not ethical,' she said.

'Neither's sleeping with your husband's brother,' Jamie said cynically, echoing what Cameron had said to him.

'Maybe not, but she's still Amy's mother; he can't just bury his assets to get out of supporting her, no matter what he thinks of Laura.'

'Laura's going to end up with their house. He just didn't want her to benefit from the apartments as well. And I don't see why she should either.'

Julia stood up and walked over to the sink and got a glass of water. She stood looking out of the kitchen window for a moment, listening to Bryden and Jamie discussing the apartment.

'He reckons I could rent out the spare rooms to help pay the mortgage while I'm still studying.'

'Cool. Hope there'll be room for me when I come to stay.'

Julia walked back to the table and sat down again.

'I don't know what your father would have said about this.' Julia said, looking from Jamie to Bryden, who didn't seem in the least bit concerned about her anxiety.

'Dad would say I should go with my gut feeling and I think this could be a good investment. As a research scientist, I will never earn as much as I would have done as a doctor, so this will help me get set up in a way that I probably wouldn't be able to do otherwise.'

Bryden nodded in agreement.

'I need to think about this. Perhaps I should talk to Cameron,' Julia said. 'But in the meantime, we need to discuss Bryden's idea to move to Shetland.'

Bryden shrugged, as if to say, what needs to be said.

'Are you really sure this is what you want to do? You're not just moving back because you think I'm lonely on my own.'

'I'm very sure. I miss being here, and I would rather teach Shetland bairns than work in some huge inner-city school. It was always my plan to move back one day, although admittedly I didn't think it would be this soon. But after I split up with Anna I realised I had nothing to keep me in Edinburgh once I'd finished my probation year. I would rather come back now and get my career established here. But after living away from home for so long, no offence Mam, but I would like to get my own place.'

Julia smiled at him. She reached across the table and touched his arm.

'I hope you get the job then. And if you do, you can have the cottage.'

She noticed Jamie sit up straight, his eyes narrowing slightly at her.

'But!' Julia said, cutting Jamie off before he protested. 'In order to be fair to the both of you, we will ensure that you both have somewhere to live, and you both have an identical sized mortgage, especially if, as you say Jamie, you will only have the same income as Bryden. Therefore, if there is any shortfall in money, then Bryden will have to re-mortgage the cottage and help put a deposit down on the property in Edinburgh.'

Bryden and Jamie looked at each other and grinned.

'Yeah, of course,' they said in unison.

'But I'm still not convinced about Cameron's offer. However, the other thing I wanted to tell you was I have applied to become a foster carer. Sometime soon both of you will be contacted by social workers to talk about my aptitude for this, so I would be grateful if you don't make jokes about how I beat you up or locked you in your rooms.'

They both laughed at her.

'That's a great idea. You'll be a great foster mother,' Jamie said, nodding his approval.

'Yeah really; that's awesome,' Bryden said, inexplicably speaking in an American accent.

'Well good,' Julia said, relieved not to have met any kind of opposition to the idea. She was rather surprised they hadn't raised the possibility that she might end up looking after difficult and emotionally damaged children. Perhaps they gave her some credit after all.

After they had discussed their various plans for the future, Julia handed them both letters that Duncan had written to them, and explained that he had written them at the time he thought he wasn't going to survive the cancer. They each took their letter away to read in private.

Julia went to the downstairs spare room to strip the bed that Amy had slept in the previous evening. As she pulled the duvet off the bed she found a Barbie doll. She picked it up and put it on the bedside table while she finished remaking the bed. She imagined

Amy would be missing her toy. She decided to drive over to see Cameron to return the doll and to discuss the idea of Jamie buying one of his apartments. She was still a little annoyed that he had spoken to Jamie before her. If she had known it was simply to stop his wife getting hold of the money she would have told him not to make such a generous offer to Jamie.

She went upstairs to find her sons. They were both sitting in Jamie's room reading each other's letters and they seemed surprisingly upbeat. The letter that Duncan had written to her had reduced her to tears. She had read it the day after the funeral, which was why she had waited so long to give her sons their letters.

'You two OK?'

'Yeah, sure. Have you read these?' Jamie said.

'No darling.'

'Do you want to?'

Julia shook her head. 'Maybe later; I found it difficult to read my own.'

Bryden was still reading and he burst out laughing. Jamie turned and grinned at him.

'Dad was so funny.' Jamie said.

'Yeah, he was,' Julia replied, grateful that whatever Duncan had written had amused them.

'I'm just going to drive over and see Cameron. Amy left one of her dolls behind.'

'OK, see you later.'

Julia pulled up outside Cameron's house and got out of her car. He came to the front door and opened it, looking a little sad and she wondered what was wrong. She held up the doll and smiled.

'I found this and thought Amy might miss it.'

'She's at home now. I'll take it over later.'

Julia handed him the doll and stood waiting for him to invite her in. He seemed distracted, so she turned to leave.

'Aren't you going to come in and have a coffee?' Cameron said, as Julia reached the bottom step.

'Sure!' Julia followed him inside and took a seat at the kitchen table. 'What's up? You don't seem very happy this afternoon?'

'There was a bit of a row with Laura when I took Amy home this morning.'

'I see.'

'She's thinking of moving to Aberdeen.'

'What? Why? What about Amy?'

'My thoughts exactly,' Cameron replied, his face tense with anger.

'Is she serious? She's not just saying it to upset you?'

'I've no idea. She just said she has nothing to stay in Shetland for. She's fed up with not having anything to do.'

'She should get a bloody job then.'

'I don't think that's the kind of activity she had in mind. She wants a better social life.'

'But she can't do much with a small child? She doesn't have any family in Aberdeen, does she?'

'No.'

'Oh Christ. That is bad news; I'm so sorry.' Julia watched him moving slowly around the kitchen. He had his back to her while he made the coffee, his shoulders hunched over in misery.

'Do you think you'll end up moving there too?' Julia said, working through the consequences and realising she would be devastated if he moved away.

Cameron shrugged.

'I don't know. I could work in any city, but…' He turned and set a mug of coffee in front of Julia then sat opposite her. He held his mug with two hands, as if he needed to warm his fingers. 'I don't want to move away,' he said quietly. 'But if Amy goes, I think I'll have to. I know it sounds a bit melodramatic, but I just don't trust Laura to look after her.'

'What do you mean?'

'Do you remember what Amy said yesterday about Laura shouting at her?'

Julia nodded.

'Well it seems like she does that a lot. She has no patience with Amy, and she's also smacked her a few times. Now, I'm of the generation that doesn't get too upset at the idea of smacking kids, within reason of course, but I've hardly ever raised my voice with Amy, let alone considered smacking her. She's a really well behaved child, so I'm a bit concerned about Laura.'

'That doesn't sound good. Have you spoken to Laura?'

'She told me to mind my own fucking business.'

'Right. Well, have you thought about trying to get custody yourself?'

'I could try, but it would be quite a battle. All things being equal, Laura's likely to win, since I'm working all the time, and she's *allegedly* the homemaker.'

'But you might be able to stop her moving to Aberdeen.'

'I don't see how.'

'I don't know much about the law myself, but if you were awarded joint-custody this might make it difficult for Laura to take her away.'

Cameron was silent for a moment. Julia thought about the other reason she had stopped by to see Cameron.

'Jamie told me about your offer of a cut-price apartment in Edinburgh. I was going to ask you about that; but maybe now is not the right time.'

Cameron looked at her blankly as if he had no idea what she was talking about. Then the fog lifted and he went to fetch his portfolio.

He showed Julia the plans for the building and showed her on a map where the apartment would be. He explained again his reasons for offering it to Jamie and told her how Duncan had wanted to buy the apartment for Bryden and Jamie. He told her how much money he wanted for it.

'But that's so cheap compared with what you'd make on an open market.'

'So what; who cares about money? I'm doing it for Duncan anyway. It was his dream to see his sons settled.'

'That's really good of you. We'll sort something out, just as soon as Bryden finds out whether or not he gets Duncan's old job.'

Cameron put his elbows on the table and rested his chin on his hands. 'How did we end up here?'

'What do you mean?'

'You widowed; me getting divorced *again*; Bryden getting Duncan's job; Laura taking Amy away.'

'I know. I never expected any of this.'

'I feel sick. I really do. I have never hit anyone in my life, let alone a woman, but honestly I could kill the bitch; I really could.'

Julia recoiled a little at the venom in his voice. Cameron noticed and his face softened a little.

'I'm sorry. You must think I'm a monster.'

Julia put down her coffee and stood up. She walked around the table until she stood beside Cameron. She put her arms around him, and to her horror he started to cry, although within seconds he had composed himself again. He rubbed his eyes with the heel of his palms and smiled grimly at Julia.

'It's OK; I understand. I could kill the stupid bitch too. I don't want you to leave Shetland. I would hate that.'

'Would you?'

'Of course I would! We'll sort this out. Aberdeen isn't so far away. If you have to sell your house in Shetland, you could buy a little place in Aberdeen. Maybe I could come and visit sometimes.'

Cameron smiled at her.

'Thanks! Now you're almost making me look forward to it.'

Julia grinned. She bent forward and kissed his cheek and then went to move away. He pulled her back towards him, but she resisted.

'No Cameron; I can't do this yet.'

'Yet?'

'You saw how Jamie reacted to the idea of me having a new man in my life.'

'We could keep this a secret. Nobody needs to know.'

'Don't be daft. This is Shetland. We cannot possibly get away with seeing each other in secret. All your neighbours know my car is parked on your drive today. If this happened a little more frequently it would be all over town. And you really wouldn't want Laura to find out. She would find a way to make you pay; you know she would.'

'You're right; I'm sorry. It's just that every time I see you now, I think of Sicily.'

'So do I.'

Julia reached for her handbag and turned to go.

'Come over again before the boys go back to Edinburgh,' she said. She stood by the door and looked back at him, tempted to go back and kiss him properly. But she knew where that would lead, so she hurried out to her car, got in and slammed the door shut.

When Julia got home found the house was empty. She called for the boys but there was no reply. She looked around to see if they had left a note, but there was nothing. She was a bit put out, but then decided to check the garage. She found them inside playing snooker.

'Here you are. I thought you'd both gone out.'

'How? We don't have a car.'

'Good point.'

'What are you doing?'

'Well duh Ma, we're playing snooker. Have you been drinking or something?' Bryden said.

'Very funny? What I meant to say is what are we doing tonight? Do you want to stay in or shall we go visiting?'

Bryden and Jamie looked at each other questioningly.

'Stay in?' Jamie said. 'Come and play snooker with us.'

'Really?' Julia said, flattered that they wanted her company. 'Alright then, let me go and sort out some food and I will be back in a moment.

'Turkey sandwiches!' Bryden roared, lifting his snooker cue in triumph.

Julia grinned. 'Is there enough beer in the fridge in here?'

Jamie opened the fridge door with a flourish; the fridge was completely full.

'But you'd better get yourself a sweet sherry Mam.'

'Cheeky bastard!'

Julia hurried back to the kitchen and put together a tray of sandwiches and snacks. She went upstairs and changed out of her high heeled boots and put on a pair of trainers and grabbed her quilted body-warmer. She carried the food out to the garage feeling elated to be included in their game. She hadn't played snooker with them for years. This was where they came to get away from her; she knew that. The garage had been a kind of youth club during their teenage years; full of young people hanging out and playing loud music, safe in the knowledge there were no neighbours to disturb. They had probably tried their first alcohol in this garage, not that Julia was proud of that fact; but she had always maintained it was probably better that her sons drank in her presence rather than somewhere else, where she couldn't look after them.

Julia walked over to the ancient stereo and picked out a CD from the rack. It was Duncan's favourite band; Runrig. She put the music on and the garage filled with the cheerful sound of fiddles, guitars and drums.

'Right, who am I going to thrash first?' Julia said, standing with her hands on her hips.

'Very funny Mam; unless you have been practicing while we've been away, I think it's you that's going to get thrashed.'

Julia picked up a cue and chalked the end of it. This is going to be a great evening she thought.

Julia put up a brave fight, but she was indeed thrashed by Jamie and Bryden. She gave up and took over as the party's DJ, putting on the music and talking about Duncan. She drank beer, ate turkey sandwiches and too many crisps and laughed at their tales of life in Edinburgh. It was close to being a perfect night.

After a while she excused herself and went back indoors. It had been a very strange Boxing Day she thought, as she switched on the Christmas tree lights for the first time that day. She walked over to the candle she had lit for Duncan and re-lit the wicks. She looked out of the window and watched the moonlight bouncing on the sea. Then she looked down at the picture of Duncan that Cameron had given her that she had left on the window sill. Duncan looked so happy. If she shut her eyes she could imagine he was just outside in the garage with their sons. She could imagine him standing with a snooker cue in one hand and a bottle of beer in the other, trading banter with the boys. It was an image that both warmed her and cut to the quick.

She carried the photograph upstairs to her bedroom, mindful of the fact that all things to do with Up Helly Aa were supposed to be a closely guarded secret until the day. She put the photograph on her chest of drawers and stood and admired it for a moment. It was such a lovely present; but then she thought of Cameron. She remembered how close she had come to kissing him again. This would not do, she thought. She could not get involved with him again. At least not until Jamie and Bryden were ready for her to move on; and for that matter, when she was ready to move on. The love of her life was the man in the photograph, and that would probably never change, despite the craziness that had happened in Sicily.

She went back downstairs to the lounge and turned on the television, needing to distract herself from thoughts of Cameron. As she sat on the sofa she noticed that Jamie and Bryden had left their letters from Duncan on the coffee table. She picked one up.

Dear Jamie

The day you were born was one of the happiest days of my life, right up there with marrying your mother and the birth of your brother. If this cancer gets the better of me, I will still have been the luckiest man on earth. To some people it might seem like such a humdrum kind of life. Grow up, go to university, study maths, become a teacher, get married, build a house, have two boys. Nothing to set the world alight eh? But I didn't need to set the world on fire. I love my world exactly as it is.

I remember being so proud of you when you started school. You took it all so seriously, so determined to be the best at everything. I was never very competitive myself, so you surprised me.

Do you remember when you first talked about becoming a doctor? You decided at such a young age. We didn't take you seriously, even though we both knew you had the brains to do whatever you wanted. But you stuck by your goal from the beginning and now here you are, as I write, just about to finish your medical degree. I could cry with joy.

Your future is assured. You will have a great career. You will do well so I don't need to worry about you. But it still hurts to leave. I want to share in your success. I want to stand by your mother's side at your graduation and when you get married and start your own family. I want to be there, but there is a chance that I might not get to see all of that.

But I will still be with you. I'm in your DNA. I'm a part of you and always will be. You will see me in the mirror when you shave each morning. You will see me in your brother too. You will find yourself saying things that I said to you. The kind of things that made you lift your eyes to heaven in despair, yes indeed, you will say them too to your kids. You will become your old dad, and I hope you don't mind. I hope I'm a part of your life for many more years. But if not, know this, I love you and always will do.

Whatever happens in your life, take your mother and brother with you. Don't let my departure be a reason to fall out or grow apart.

There may be tough times ahead. I don't want you and Bryden to be miserable on my account. I want you to be happy, to live life to the full, to take advantage of the good things you have going on.

I also want your mother to be happy. She will need your support though. She is one tough independent cookie, but she is not the kind of person who should spend her life alone. I really don't want her to end up like my mother, who was widowed when she was still young, but whose life seemed to end when my father's did.

So even though it might hurt, I would appreciate it if you could encourage her to forge a new life for herself, and if that involves a new man, then you and Bryden will need to man-up and accept that.

Julia set the letter down for a moment, there was still a couple of pages left, and a cursory scan showed they contained some amusing anecdotes of Jamie's childhood. She couldn't read any more though. She slumped on the sofa and shut her eyes, trying to think when Duncan had written the letters. She hadn't been aware of him doing this, although he had told her during one of his later hospital appointments that he had. He had laughed and said it was just an insurance policy against the treatment not working. He said he had every intention of ripping them up as soon as he was cured.

Luckily he seemed to have forgotten the letters. They had obviously cheered up her sons a great deal, although she didn't feel quite so cheerful herself.

20

Jamie and Bryden flew back to Edinburgh on 5th January. Julia drove them down to the airport and stayed to watch their plane taking off; soaring into the cold grey winter sky, containing everything she held dear to her. She drove home again, emotionally drained, and wishing she could keep them at home with her forever.

Bryden's job interview had taken place they day before, and a few days later Bryden rang her to say that he had got the job. He would be starting after the Easter holidays. Julia could not contain her happiness.

Over the next couple of weeks she had more meetings with social workers as part of the fostering assessment process. References had been sought from various friends and colleagues and she had been told that the Panel would meet at the end of March to discuss her application, but without making a commitment, the social worker had hinted that it was pretty certain she would be accepted.

Julia set about the process of making her house child-friendly again. She redecorated two of the spare bedrooms, creating a warm, friendly and gender-neutral environment. After asking permission from Bryden, she also removed his remaining possessions from his old bedroom and moved them into his new house. She then bought new bedding and curtains for the room, ensuring it would be suitable for an older child or teenager. In the meantime it would also be the room that Tony would have when he came to stay.

These activities kept her so busy that she had not seen Cameron since the Christmas holiday, but then he had also been busy with preparations for Up Helly Aa.

On the Saturday evening before Up Helly Aa, he rang Julia, asking for a favour. He needed someone to look after Amy while the official squad photographs were taken on Sunday morning. Amy wanted to come and watch, but Laura had refused to take her.

'Of course I will. I would love to; shall I come over to your place tomorrow morning?' Julia said.

'Yes please. We're setting off early to get to the beach, so we have to be on the coach about 8.30. The weather forecast is not looking brilliant for later on tomorrow so we're hoping we can get all the photographs taken before the storm.'

'Ah yes; I had better dress for the occasion then.'

'Hmm, that's what I said to Amy too, but she has a Viking "princess" dress that she wants to wear. I don't suppose I'll be able to get her to put a coat over the top of it.'

'She'll be fine. I'll make she doesn't freeze.'

'Thanks Jules. Are you sure you don't mind?'

'Don't be silly. I would have been there to watch if Duncan…'

'I know; that's what I meant.'

'I'll be fine. I'm looking forward to it.'

Julia put the phone down and hurried upstairs to put out some clothes ready for the early morning start. At the risk of looking like the Michelin man she decided on leggings to wear under her jeans, walking boots, a thermal vest, a long sleeve tee-shirt and her favourite Fair Isle jumper, gloves, hat and scarf. She knew that most of the other WAGs would be dressed up in their finest, as they would be posing for photographs with their men. However, Julia was not a wife or girlfriend of a squad member. She wouldn't be appearing in any of the photographs.

The next morning was as cold and windy as anticipated, but at least it was dry for the time being. Julia got dressed, without bothering to put on any make-up and had a quick cup of tea before setting off to pick up Amy.

Cameron opened the door wearing jeans and a thick sweater. He had not shaved since Julia had seen him last and he had a thick red beard, flecked with grey, which made Julia smile; but she did not comment. It was funny seeing him looking so hairy and unkempt. He was always so neat and tidy.

'We're meeting at the bunker to get changed. But come in; Amy's all ready to go.'

Amy ran out into the hallway, dressed in a long green velvet tunic, trimmed with gold braid and fake fur, with black Ugg boots, black leggings, and a medieval style tiara on her head.

'Look at me; I'm a princess,' she shouted, jigging around in the manner of a child who has consumed too many E numbers.

'Calm down Amy; you need to save your energy for later,' Cameron said soothingly.

Julia laughed. 'Calm down? Yeah, like that's going to happen?'

'That's why I needed you to come too. One of the other mothers could probably look after her, but their own kids are likely to be just as over-excited.'

'Good point. So; will we go in one car, or shall we meet you somewhere?'

'It's best if you come and meet us in a little while. We'll need to get suited and booted which will take a while. If you drive along to the bunker in about an hour, we'll be ready to get on the coach then.'

'OK then; off you go. We'll see you soon.'

Cameron touched Julia's arm as he headed for the front door.

'Thanks, I really appreciate this. Amy! You be good for Julia won't you?'

Amy nodded vigorously, sending the tiara tumbling across the floor.

Julia picked it up.

'Let's get this fixed into place,' she said, as Cameron smiled at them and closed the front door.

Julia took Amy up to her bedroom and found a hairbrush and grips. She sat the little girl down at the dressing table and brushed her long brown hair. It was soft and silky from having just been washed, so it would be a struggle to keep the tiara in place.

'I don't suppose you have any hairspray,' Julia asked, doubtfully.

'No, my mummy does, but she doesn't live here,' Amy replied.

'Alrighty, let's see what we can do with your hair to make your tiara stay still. I'm not very good at doing girls' hair because I had two boys. But we'll give it a try eh?'

Amy nodded confidently back at Julia through the mirror.

Julia decided to create two plaits around the crown of Amy's head and then joined them together at the back with an elastic band. Then she anchored the ends of the tiara into the plaits at the side, and secured them with grips for added resilience against the wind. She spotted some fresh roses in a vase on Amy's window sill and pulled out a tight pink rosebud. She snapped off the end and de-thorned it and then tucked it into the elastic band that held the plaits together.

'There; how's that for a princess hairdo?' Julia said, pleased with the effect.

'That's magic. I will be the best princess today.' Amy said, without a trace of humility.

Julia smiled, wishing she had some of Amy's confidence.

'Right then, maybe you should use the bathroom before we go,' Julia said, standing up and walking towards the door.

'My daddy likes you,' Amy said, as she stood up and turned to admire her hair once again.

'Oh?' Julia said, turning to look at the child.

'But my mummy doesn't. They had an argument about you. Isn't that funny, because I like you too, so I don't know why mummy doesn't. Did you have an argument with her?'

'Er, no, I've never had an argument with your mummy.'

Julia headed downstairs quickly, not wanting to prolong the conversation about Laura's opinion of her, although she was curious as to what had been said and why.

Julia waited for Amy to come downstairs from the bathroom. She heard the little girl singing and talking to her cat that had snuck into the bathroom with her. She heard the toilet flush and then the taps running.

Amy emerged from the bathroom and came downstairs looking rather dishevelled. Her tunic was caught up in her leggings at the back.

'Come here darling, let me sort out your dress,' Julia said, turning Amy around.

Julia crouched down and tugged the end of the tunic away from where it was caught up in Amy's leggings. As she did so she caught a glimpse of skin and a rather ugly bruise just above the waistband. Julia instinctively lifted the tunic to get a closer look and was alarmed at the extent of the purple bruising with its yellow core. It looked painful.

'That looks like a nasty bruise you have on your back.'

'It was a bit ouchy; I was playing trampolines on my bed.'

'Oh dear, did you fall off?'

'Yes, and then Mummy said I had to go to bed for being naughty.' Amy sighed, as if the indignity of being sent to bed was still troubling her.

Julia pulled down the tunic and straightened it, removing some stray cat hairs from the velvet.

'There, now you look gorgeous again,' Julia said. She picked up Amy's floral anorak, which earned a disapproving shake of her head.

'I can't wear that today; it's not very princessy.' Amy stood with her arms folded defiantly, looking every inch a bossy princess.

Julia looked around the room for inspiration. She could hardly take the child out in this weather, wearing just a velvet dress. She spotted a green tartan rug on the back of the sofa. She picked it up and showed Amy.

'Did you know that Viking princesses used to wrap blankets around themselves when it was cold, because they didn't have anoraks in those days?'

'Really?' Amy said doubtfully.

'Yes, they called them cloaks and they used to fasten them with a brooch, a bit like the one I have on my jumper.' Julia pointed to the silver Celtic style brooch that Duncan had given her a few years ago.

'That's pretty. Can I wear it please?'

'Yes you can; if you promise not to lose it.'

'I won't. I'm very good at not losing things. Um, though, I did lose one of mummy's rings the other day. It fell off my finger and went down the plughole. She got a bit cross with me.'

'Oh dear, did she manage to find it again?'

'Yes, she got the plumbing man to get it out. It was very smelly; but it was still OK. I'm not allowed to play with her jewellery box anymore.'

'Never mind. One day when you're big you will have your own jewellery box to play with.'

'That's just what daddy said.'

'Anyway, we had better go and find your daddy now. They'll be ready soon.'

'I don't like daddy's new beard do you?'

'Um, well, not really. I don't like beards much, but it's just for Up Helly Aa. I expect he will shave it off soon.'

'It's all scratchy when he kisses me. Yuck!' Amy said, pulling a face and rubbing her cheek with her hands, as if her father had only just kissed her.

Julia laughed. 'Well I'll have to make sure I don't kiss your daddy then.'

'No, it's yucky!'

Julia drove Amy into Lerwick and they parked a short distance from the bunker. The coaches were waiting and there were quite a few people milling around outside waiting for the Jarl Squad to come out of the bunker.

'Shall we go and watch or shall we wait in the car?'

'I want to go and watch,' Amy said, immediately undoing her seat belt in the back seat of the car. Julia grabbed the tartan rug and draped it around Amy's shoulders, although she could tell that Amy would probably discard it in order to show off her outfit.

They hurried along the street towards the bunker; the building that successive Jarl Squads used to build the galley ship, make the shields, torches, axes and costumes each year, in secret.

A ripple of applause from the waiting family members indicated that the squad were about to leave the building. The men emerged from the doorway and hurried to the waiting coach. Julia got there just as Cameron was about to board it. He grinned and waved at her and Amy.

Julia took Amy to the other coach. She found a seat near the back with Amy and sat down.

'Hi Julia; it's a surprise to see you here.'

Julia looked around and saw Paula sitting behind her. Her heart sank; she had forgotten Paula would be there today. She hadn't seen her since she had stolen her taxi at Marianne's birthday party.

'I'm just bringing Amy along to watch her dad.'

'I can see that. Hi Amy!'

Amy turned to look at Paula and smiled.

'I'm a princess! Julia made me a princess hairstyle. Do you like it?'

'Yes, it's lovely,' Paula said, giving Julia a knowing look.

The coach started up, and the woman Paula was sitting next to starting speaking and Julia was relieved when Paula lost interest in her and Amy.

Julia had no idea where the coach was going; it was all part of the secret ritual. Nobody was to know the venue for the photographs, although it was normally one of the picturesque beaches; which didn't exactly narrow down the options, since most of Shetland's beaches were beauty spots.

The coaches left Lerwick and then headed down the road towards Scalloway, before turning off towards Trondra and Burra. Julia wondered whether they were heading for Meal Beach, the sheltered sandy bay which was a popular place to visit; although rather less so on a bitterly cold January morning, when it had only been light for a couple of hours.

Julia had guessed correctly. The coaches parked next to each other in the small car park and the occupants all hurried out and picked their way down the path to the beach.

Julia held Amy's hand and occasionally picked her up to lift her over puddles. They climbed over the stile at the bottom of the path and then scampered down the slope of rocks and grass onto the shore. The photographer was assembling his tripod and erecting an A-frame ladder on the beach.

The squad of latter-day Vikings assembled on the beach with their backs to the sea. For the next hour the photographer took photographs of the squad, the Jarl, the wives and girlfriends, the children, and numerous combinations. The rain held off, although it was still cold and breezy, particularly down on the sand, away from the shelter of the rocks.

Julia sat on a rock, with Amy on her lap wrapped in the tartan rug, which she was now wearing without protest. They both watched as Cameron raise his axe above his head and roar at the photographer, in unison with his Viking brothers.

Julia studied the shield that Duncan had designed. It was an intricate geometric, Celtic inspired pattern of silver metal on an emerald enamelled background. The men wore green tunics, fringed with rabbit fur and intricate black and silver embroidery, over black felted wool leggings and black sheepskin boots decorated with silver braid and buckles. On their heads they wore black and silver helmets, with an emerald enamelled design on the front, echoing that on the shields, and again on the axe shafts. They all wore long black cloaks that almost grazed the ground. Every year Julia marvelled at the work that had gone into creating the unique costumes that each squad designed, but this year she truly believed it was the most beautiful she had ever seen.

Her eyes watered, as much as a result of the salt laden wind, as the fact that she wished Duncan was standing on the beach wearing the outfit he had helped to design. She turned away and saw Kim, the photographer's wife, walking towards her.

'Are you not coming to get your photograph taken too?'

'Ah, no; I'm only here to look after Amy.'

'Don't be silly. Wasn't it your Duncan that did the design for the shields? You have to get a photo taken, even if it's just for your boys.'

Julia looked down at her jeans and parka and lifted her arms in protest.

'I'm not dressed for it; I didn't even bother with make-up this morning.'

'Dunna you worry about that; you look gorgeous Julia. All windswept and beautiful. Come and get your photo taken with Amy. The squad are all asking for you.'

Julia stood up reluctantly, although Amy, realising she had another photo opportunity instantly discarded her rug and ran down the beach to find her dad. Kim slipped her hand through Julia's arm.

'It's good to see you here. You should be here; you were a part of all this too.'

Julia nodded, not trusting herself to speak.

'We all miss him you know,' Kim said, squeezing Julia's arm.

As they reached the gathering of men on the beach, there was a spontaneous roar of welcome from the squad, led by the Jarl, distinguishable by his rather more ornate headgear and a bushy grey beard he had cultivated for at least two years. Julia felt herself blushing.

'Now go and find yourself a nice hunky Viking to stand next to,' Kim said, gently pushing Julia towards the men.

Amy gestured for Julia to stand next to her, which was pretty much in the centre of the group. Julia had the Jarl on one side of her and Cameron on the other; with Amy holding on to her hand and posing coquettishly for the photo. Julia could not help smile at Amy's exuberance.

The photographer clicked away; the flashes from the camera bouncing off the shiny shields and axes. Kim gave Julia a double thumbs-up as she stood behind her husband. Julia saw her lean in and speak to him and a moment later he asked Julia to pose for a photo with Cameron and Amy. Julia was too polite to refuse, although she wanted to. She felt the eyes of all the other women on the beach watching her; judging her.

Cameron whispered, 'once in a lifetime Jules! I asked them to take this photo. Once in a lifetime!'

Julia sighed, and put on her best smile for the camera. Out of the corner of her eye she saw Paula nudging one of her friends and whispering to her.

After the photographs were taken, Julia led Amy back to pick up the blanket and to make their way back to the coach. This time she made sure she sat further away from Paula. She didn't want to hear what she had to say about getting a photograph taken with Cameron.

When they got back to Cameron's house Julia made Amy a drink and a sandwich and they sat down to watch the television while they waited for Cameron to return.

An hour later Cameron arrived home, carrying a huge bouquet of roses which he handed to Julia.

'Just a little thank you.'

'Don't be silly. It was nothing.'

'They're not just from me; they're from the squad. We were all so pleased to see you there. It meant a lot to us.'

'Oh, really. That's lovely. Say thank you to everyone, won't you.'

Julia picked her coat up and her car keys.

'Can't you stay for lunch?'

'I'm sorry, I need to get home and get ready for Tony. He's flying in from Inverness tomorrow morning. I have a few things still to do.'

'Well, in that case I guess I'll see you on Tuesday then. Which hall are you taking him to at night?'

'Marianne managed to get us tickets for the Town Hall. She's one of the hostesses there, so it should be a great night.'

'I think that's the third hall we'll be visiting, so I will see you quite early on.'

'Great. I'll keep my fingers crossed for good weather.'

Cameron shrugged, as if he didn't particularly care what the weather gods threw at him.

Julia said goodbye to Amy who looked rather sleepy on the sofa now. She wondered if she should mention the bruise to Cameron, but she was too embarrassed. He might think she was accusing him.

'Dance with me, won't you?' Cameron said, as she put her parka on.

'Of course I will,' she replied. 'Nobody says no to a Viking.'

Cameron smirked, but didn't say anything else.

21

Tony's flight landed just as the rain started. Julia watched the first passengers emerge from the aircraft and hurry down the steps. Two young women, who Julia vaguely recognised raced each other to the building and barged through the door, giggling. They hurried towards their waiting parents, still laughing. Julia watched as Tony walked slowly towards her, his head up, looking around at the view, unconcerned by the rain. She felt a sense of relief when she saw he was appropriately dressed for the weather. The last time she had seen him he had been wearing a linen shirt and chinos. Now he looked like he had just returned from climbing the Cairngorms, with his bulky North Face parka, a fleece hat, and gloves.

She hurried over to meet him and was rewarded with a hug and three kisses on her cheeks. Julia blushed with pleasure and surprise.

'Hello my dear! Isn't this delightful? I can't wait to see more of Shetland. It looked superb from the air.'

'Really? I was just thinking it was such a horrible day to arrive.'

'Dreich!' Tony said, tentatively trying out a new Scottish word. Julia grinned.

'Dreich definitely; or as I like to say, a day of shite.'

'Well it was worse in Inverness.'

The luggage carousel started up and Tony picked up his brown leather holdall and then they walked out to Julia's car.

'Do you like my outfit?' Tony said, with an air of campness.

'I do. It's just the thing for this weather.'

'I know. I had to go to a shop in Inverness to buy some more suitable clothing. I knew it would be colder here, but I still wasn't quite prepared enough.'

'Yeah, you Sicilian softie; you'll see some proper weather now.'

They drove out of the airport along the road that separated the runway from the sea. The rain shower had passed over but the clouds were still gloomy; although that did not dampen Tony's enthusiasm for the view.

'What's up there?' Tony asked, pointing to a steep hill, less than a mile from the airport.

'That's Sumburgh Head, where the lighthouse is. It's a great place to see the puffins in the summer.'

'Can we go and have a look?'

Julia turned her car in the direction of the lighthouse road.

'There won't be much to see today.'

'You should know I tend to see things in a different way to most people. I love the drama of bad weather. It feeds my writer's imagination.' Tony said, pulling a face and mocking his own pretentiousness.

Julia parked the car close to the lighthouse. She could feel it being buffeted by the wind, and had no real desire to get out. But she knew Tony would. As he undid his seatbelt she put her hand on his arm.

'Whatever you do, don't let go of the car door as you get out.'

Tony nodded, and then carefully opened and closed the door and hurried over to the wall to look over. He turned and grinned at Julia, who felt obliged to join him.

'This is glorious!' Tony yelled, above the wind.

They leaned over the solid stone wall and looked down at the sea, many metres below them. Julia pointed to a rabbit huddling in a hollow a few feet away.

'The puffins live in those burrows down there,' Julia explained. 'With rabbits for neighbours; but the puffins are only here for a few weeks in the summer.'

Tony nodded, and then pointed down at the sea.

'There's a seal.'

'One of the thousands that live here,' Julia replied, as Tony grinned with pleasure.

They arrived back at Julia's house in the late afternoon as Tony had insisted on stopping off at various sites to take a closer look. He didn't seem to care about missing lunch, and Julia was happy to show him around while it was still light.

'What a great day it's been already,' Tony said, as he sat down in the lounge.

Julia handed him a mug of coffee and took a seat on the sofa and slumped back in a pose of exaggerated exhaustion.

'What a shame it isn't summer though.'

'You keep saying that; stop it. I really don't mind the wind and the rain; it's a bit of a novelty for me.'

'So, what do you fancy for dinner later? Steak, chicken, fish?'

'What's a typical Shetland dinner for a cold Monday night in January?'

'Mince and tatties!'

'Sounds good to me.'

'Really? It's not very exotic.'

'I'm not very exotic.'

Julia smiled at him, as if she didn't agree. 'OK then, mince and tatties it is.' She put down her mug and sighed. 'Nobody will believe me when I say that the first time I ever cooked for a celebrity, I made them mince and tatties.'

Tony roared with laughter.

'Did you see anyone recognise me today? I'm not much of a celebrity. Nobody knows me these days; and that's the way I like it.'

Julia stood up and went out to the kitchen and Tony followed her. He took a seat at the kitchen table and watched as she set about making dinner. He offered to chop onions, but she refused his help. He walked over to his bag and pulled out two bottles of bubble wrapped Prosecco and put them in her fridge. He grinned when he saw that there were already two bottles of Prosecco in the door rack. He lifted one out and showed her.

'Thought you'd feel more at home,' Julia said, nodding towards the cupboard where the glasses were stored. She was peeling potatoes at the sink and her hands were wet from rinsing them. 'I think it's time to celebrate your safe arrival in Shetland.'

Julia put the potatoes in a saucepan to boil and then washed her hands and dried them, in time to take a glass of sparkling wine from Tony. She clinked her glass with his and took a sip, just as the phone rang.

'Excuse me!' Julia put her glass down and picked up the handset, expecting it to be either Bryden or Jamie. It was Cameron.

'Hi, what's up?' Julia said, having picked up on the anxiety in his voice.

'Laura has accused me of hurting Amy. She says she's going to get a court order to stop me seeing her.'

'What do you mean, hurting her?'

'She says that Amy was covered in bruises when I took her back home yesterday, and that I must have been responsible. She said a social worker has been to see her already, and that they want to see me too.'

Julia instantly forgot about her guest. She walked into the lounge and sat down heavily on the sofa.

'I meant to say something to you yesterday actually. I noticed a bruise on Amy's back when she was getting ready. But it was an old bruise; there was no way that happened over the weekend. I asked Amy about it and she said she fell off her bed when she was playing trampolines.'

'You saw it? Why didn't you say?'

'I didn't know what to say. Kids are always falling and hurting themselves. Amy didn't seem distressed or anything. She was perfectly happy. I only noticed it because she went to the bathroom before we left and her dress got caught up in her leggings. I was helping to straighten it out.'

'I see. You're sure it was an old bruise.'

'Definitely; it was all yellow in the centre. I'm sure Amy will tell the social worker what really happened. Don't worry.'

'Don't worry? How can I not worry? And tonight of all nights; I really need to get a good night's sleep.'

'Don't you see? She's doing this deliberately to ruin your day; just like she tried to ruin your Christmas with all that nonsense about moving to Aberdeen. That didn't amount to anything did it? Take no notice. I bet she never even spoke to a social worker.'

'Maybe you're right. Thanks!'

'That's OK, but I had better go now; I'm cooking dinner for Tony.'

'Of course! Well, I'll see you tomorrow; if I haven't been arrested for child abuse that is.'

'Don't be silly. Goodnight.'

Julia went back to the kitchen and put the phone down on its cradle.

'Sorry about that, a bit of a domestic drama for my friend Cameron; you remember, the man who came over to Sicily to see Jürgen.'

'Ah yes, Jürgen mentioned him when I saw him at Christmas. He was very impressed with him. I gather they're collaborating on a project now. Has anything happened with him since your little fling?'

'No, not really. It's far too complicated. He still has a wife in the background, even if they have separated; and I feel it's too soon for me to be moving on.'

'Is this a too soon for you, or too soon, what will the neighbours think, kind of thing?'

'Not so much my neighbours as my sons.'

'That could take a very long time.' Tony said, nodding his head.

Julia shrugged. 'I don't think I'm ready yet either.'

She sat down at the table opposite Tony and picked up her glass and held it in both hands, staring at the delicate bubbles that rose up from the bottom of the glass in continually evolving patterns. She twisted the glass, watching how the bubbles sparkled in the light.

'My daughter thinks I'm ready now. Fancy that; I thought my children would resent me ever meeting someone else. But she told me on New Year's Eve that I ought to start looking for a new wife. She wants her child to have a grandmother when it's born.'

'That is surprising!' Julia said, looking at Tony, who shrugged in response.

'I know. I thought she would miss her mother even more now.'

'She probably does. Perhaps she's realised you must be missing her too, and that you must be lonely.'

'Maybe. Or maybe she doesn't think I would make much of a babysitter without a woman around. She'd probably be delighted if I just married Maria. That way she would have an excellent babysitter, housekeeper and cook all in one.' Tony took a sip of his wine and nodded thoughtfully. 'Actually, that's not a bad idea.'

Julia laughed. 'Are you sure you're not on the lookout for someone half your age, like most men seem to be?'

'Oh heavens no! What young woman could bear to be with a wrinkled old wreck like me? No, they would only want me for my money, and how depressing would that be?'

'You're not an old wreck. But Cameron married someone much younger than himself and that didn't end well. His wife still wanted to go out partying all the time and was not satisfied with their life, despite the fact they have a lovely daughter and an award winning house.'

'The youth of today! It's wasted on them. I would give anything to turn the clock back a few years and appreciate what I had, when I had it.'

'Me too.'

Julia heard the saucepan lid start to rattle away on the stove, so she got up to turn down the heat. She turned her attention back to the cooking and thought about Cameron's phone call and wondered what trouble Laura was stirring up for him. She wished she had spoken to him about Amy's bruises. He might have been able to pre-empt her accusation.

'How's your plan to become a foster mother going?' Tony said, interrupting the silence and reminding Julia that she had a guest to entertain.

'Really well thanks. I haven't been officially approved yet, but the social worker thinks it will be a pretty smooth process. It's a very longwinded procedure; loads of forms, interviews, training, references, and then all the evidence of my "worthiness" gets submitted to a panel that basically gets to say yes or no. And of course I have to get my house in order, fire certificates, first aid boxes, etc etc.'

'That's progress for you. My mother was sent away during the war to live on a farm in Wales. She was put on the train in London by her mother, with a whole crowd of other children, who were also being distributed to strange families. My mother had a great time. The family she went to had two other little girls, so she felt like she had new sisters. They kept in touch for years after the war. But there was no social workers interviewing the families in those days.'

Julia smiled at him, as she stood stirring the pan of mince on the stove.

'But I bet not all of those children were treated well by their new families during the war.'

'I suppose not. Better to be safe than sorry. So when do you think you will get your first child to look after?'

'I said I wanted to wait until after the first anniversary, of Duncan - I don't know why, but it seemed like a sensible thing to do, and the social worker agreed with me. My son Bryden has just got Duncan's old job; did I tell you that? He's moving back to Shetland soon.'

'Good news? You sound a bit doubtful.'

'I was at first. He's young; he should see a bit more of the world before settling down here. But actually, he won't be living with me; he's going to live in Duncan's old family home. It's a couple of miles away; I'll show you it sometime.'

'Isn't that funny; we both have children who are moving back home. Eleni is going to take over the villa you stayed in. So I won't have any more tourists coming to stay. I'll just have to rely on my books to make a living.'

'I'm sure you'll do OK.'

'Yes, I probably will; thanks to you.'

Julia turned round quickly, dropping the wooden spoon on the floor. She stooped to pick it up and then reached for some paper towel to clean up the mess.

'What do you mean, thanks to me?'

'You've shaken me up a bit. Made me realise that I need to get out more and start living again.'

Julia leaned back against the kitchen unit and frowned at him. She was a little uncertain where this conversation was heading.

'How did I manage to do that?'

'When you came over to Sicily to help you come to terms with your loss it made me see that grieving is an active process, not passive. You can't simply sit around and wait for the pain to pass. You have to force yourself to do things that you might find difficult; like travelling somewhere new and meeting new people. When I first met you, I thought you were a little mad to be going on holiday on your own so soon. But then I started to realise that I should have done the same thing, because this is really the first time I have been away in five years, and I do feel different. I still miss my wife obviously, but the change of location has somehow dialled down the pain a little.'

'I see what you mean. But when I came to Sicily I didn't think of it as doing something positive. I was really just running away from it all.'

'I know. But I think it had the same affect; don't you?'

'I'll tell you in five years.'

Tony smiled an acknowledgement that she still had a long journey ahead of her.

'It wasn't just the fact that you went on holiday on your own,' he continued, 'you've been making changes to your career, and you still get out and about and see your friends. You're not a recluse, like I was.'

'I suppose not; although I don't go out as much as I used to. If you weren't here, I wouldn't be going to Up Helly Aa tomorrow.'

'Oh; is that a problem? Don't you want to go?'

'No, don't be silly. I'm very happy to take you. But if I'd been on my own, I really wouldn't have had the appetite for it. I'm glad you're here. I need to do this tomorrow, even if it will be hard to see the Jarl Squad without Duncan. I know if I didn't go I would regret it.'

Later that evening when they had finished their dinner, they sat in the lounge, although Tony couldn't seem to sit still. He got up and wandered around, studying the photographs of Duncan and the boys.

'He was a good looking man, wasn't he? I see your sons really take after him.' Tony picked up a large gilt framed wedding photograph and examined it closely. 'You look so happy in this picture.'

'I was happy. That was a great day; although I do wish I could go back and change that hideous veil and headdress, and as for the mad hair...'

'Early 80s?'

'Ha, yes it was.'

'You should see our wedding photos. I look like I'm about to be executed. I was terrified.'

Julia looked at him quizzically, demanding more details.

'At that time I didn't speak much Italian. We got married in this big old church in Palermo, surrounded by Eleonora's huge family, none of whom were pleased she was marrying me. The few friends and family of mine that came over were convinced I was marrying some mafia man's daughter, and thought my days were numbered. Eleonora spent most of the day crying, because we would be moving to England straight after the wedding and she was going to miss her family.'

Julia smiled, partly out of sympathy, but also with amusement at the way Tony was telling the story. She imagined he had recited it many times before.

'But you were happy together. It all worked out.'

'Yes it did. I decided we should stay in Sicily instead of going back to London and when I told Eleonora that, the rest of the wedding was great. We all got drunk, laughed, sang and danced. My mother even danced with Eleonora's father. They couldn't communicate with each other in any language, but they seemed to have a great time. We had a ball. It was the best decision I ever made.'

'Did you miss England?'

'Sometimes. We came over for holidays; and when my writing took off, I had to travel back quite a lot to meet with publishers and do book tours and that kind of thing.'

'Would you ever move back?'

'No, not now. My parents have passed away. I have nothing to come back for. I love Sicily, and the rest of Italy, and it's where my first grandchild will be born. I could never leave now.'

On Tuesday morning Julia woke with the same feeling of anticipation that she normally had on Christmas Day. She got out of bed and wandered over to the window and peered out at the darkness. She listened for wind or rain. Silence; she smiled and headed for the shower.

When she got downstairs she found Tony in the kitchen cooking bacon and eggs.

'Hey, you're a guest. I should be doing that.'

'I'm still on Italian time. I wake up so early in the morning, so I thought I'd better do something useful.'

'Ooh, that coffee smells good,' Julia said. 'This is going to be a long day, I can tell you.'

Julia poured herself some coffee and topped up Tony's mug. She sat down on a chair and watched him making himself at home in her kitchen. He had already set the table.

'Tell me, why do you have a housekeeper, when you're perfectly capable of looking after yourself?'

Tony turned around, holding a spatula in his hand and grinned.

'My dear girl, I can definitely look after myself, but if I got rid of Maria, she would lose her much needed income, and I would spend weeks never speaking to another human being.'

'And I suppose you wouldn't get much writing done either.'

'Probably not.'

They sat down to eat their hearty breakfast. Tony told Julia about his travels around Scotland and his plans for his new novel, incorporating the character they had dreamed up together in Sicily. Julia protested when he told her that Rebecca Sherry was going to become the love interest in the story.

'But she can't. She's happily married to a helicopter pilot.'

'Is she now?' Tony replied, laughing.

'Well yes. I've given her some more thought; as you do to imaginary people that don't exist. God, I'm going nuts!'

'Welcome to my world. My head is full of people that don't exist.'

Julia looked at her watch. 'If we want to see the street parade this morning we'd better get our skates on. Parking will be a nightmare in town today.'

Tony stood up and took his plate and cutlery to the kitchen sink.

'We'll clean up later. I was thinking we should come back this afternoon for a bit of a siesta,' Julia said, as she stood up and walked over to the coffee maker and switched it off.

The traffic was busy as they drove into Lerwick, but Julia managed to find the last parking space at the Toll Clock shopping centre.

'It's a bit of a walk, but this is as close to the centre as we'll get this morning. The roads will be closed soon for the procession.'

They got out of their car and followed a group of people who were also making their way to the centre. They stopped when they reached the road leading up to the 16th Century Fort that overlooked the harbour.

'Here's a good place to watch. We'll be looking down at them on the street below.'

Julia unzipped her jacket, feeling a little warm after their brisk walk. She looked up at the sky which was an unnatural shade of blue for the end of January. It was sunny and bright today; a perfect day for Up Helly Aa. Duncan would have been delighted.

They looked around at the assembled mix of locals and tourists who stood around chatting to each other, smiling and laughing at the weather and the occasion. Julia checked her watch.

'They'll be here soon,' she said, as Tony unzipped his camera case and took out an expensive looking Nikon camera.

Tony fiddled around with his camera and then took a few shots of the scenery. He pointed the camera up at the fort and snapped away. He turned back and took a sneaky picture of Julia. He was too quick for her to protest.

He showed her the picture in the viewport and she pulled a face.

'It's a lovely photo,' he said. He showed her some of the other pictures he had just taken. Julia was still standing close to him, leaning in to look at the camera, shielding the screen from the sun with her hand, when she heard the first faint notes of the bagpipes.

'They're coming,' she said, craning her neck to see around the bend in the road. There was a rustle of excitement in the crowd who had also heard the music.

Julia strained to listen, and a moment later she recognised the tune. Within seconds she was transported back to the day of Duncan's funeral. She was walking down the aisle to take her place at the front of the kirk between Jamie and Bryden. The piper was standing in the doorway of the kirk, playing *The Gael* a song chosen by Duncan. Her eyes had fixed on the pale wooden coffin with its colourful display of spring flowers and heavily scented lilies on top. Julia had noticed one of the red tulips had lost a petal which had floated down to the floor, and lay like spilled blood. She had bent down to pick it up and held it throughout the funeral, as she sat rigid with fear that she might break down uncontrollably. She had avoided eye contact with anyone inside the kirk, including Marianne who had sat behind her.

'Isn't this the theme to *The Last of the Mohicans*?' Tony said, bringing her back to the present moment. 'Julia? Are you alright?'

Julia grabbed hold of the railings that ran alongside the pavement. She felt unsteady on her feet for a moment.

'This tune,' she said, not able to find the words to explain, although none seemed necessary, as Tony quickly grasped the situation. He put his arm around her and pulled her close.

'Don't worry. It happens all the time. You get blindsided when you least expect it. A song here, a waft of perfume there; the strangest thing can ambush you. Take a deep breath and think of something happy. Think of your sons.'

Julia stood up straight; she closed her eyes for a second and took a few deep breaths. She cleared her mind of images of the funeral and then opened her eyes. The first thing she saw was Cameron marching past. He caught her eye and grinned. He lifted his axe and roared. Julia smiled, despite herself.

They watched the squad of Vikings march down the street, accompanied by the Kirkwall pipe band. The tune had changed to *The Road to the Isles*, which was far less emotive and Julia was able to breathe a little easier.

When the spectacle had passed, they wandered down look at the Galley ship that was displayed on a trailer on the pier.

'What a shame it's going to be burned later; it's a work of art,' Tony said, as he walked around the boat, examining the handiwork and taking photographs.

'Aye, it is a shame isn't it. But this time next year, there'll be another one just like it. It's all part of the tradition.'

They spent the rest of the morning walking around Lerwick. Tony bought a tiny Fair Isle jumper for his unborn grandchild, as well as two pairs of Fair Isle gloves for Enzo and Eleni. He also bought Maria a joke present of some Shetland tea-towels, although Julia noticed he also bought her an expensive silver brooch.

They went to the museum and wandered around looking at the exhibits before heading upstairs to the café for lunch, after which Julia drove them home, intending to have a rest before the evening's entertainment, which was scheduled to go on until eight, the following morning.

'Really, it all finishes tomorrow morning?' Tony said, as he helped Julia stack the dishwasher with their breakfast dishes.

'Yes, but you aren't forced to stay till it finishes.'

'Have you ever made it to the bitter end?'

'Lots of times!' Julia said, grinning.

'Is that a challenge?'

'Not really, I don't think I'll be up for staying out the whole night.'

Tony wandered upstairs to his room. Julia took her shoes off and sat down on the sofa for a moment. She didn't think she would be able to get to sleep. Her mind was a whirl of thoughts. She shut her eyes and thought of Duncan. It made her feel sick to think he had missed this day. He had looked forward to his turn in the Jarl Squad for over ten years, ever since he had first got involved with Up Helly Aa, at Cameron's invitation.

Julia fell asleep on the sofa and only woke up when Tony came downstairs and turned on the light.

'Oh sorry. I thought you were in your bedroom,' he said, as Julia sat up and looked at him in surprise.

'I didn't feel sleepy at the time.' She laughed and looked at her watch. 'Oh dear; I had better go up and get ready.'

'You do that. I'll make us something to eat before we go. Pasta?'

'Perfect!' Julia hurried upstairs to her bedroom wondering what she could wear that would take her from watching the torchlight procession, the galley burning and fireworks, to the town hall for a night of dancing. She wanted to put on jeans, boots and a cosy sweater, but that wouldn't do for dancing. She shivered as she got undressed. It may have been a sunny day but it was now dark and freezing cold outside.

She settled for a pair of smart black trousers, a silver sequinned floaty top, and silver strappy sandals which she would put in her handbag and change into when they got to the Town Hall. For the procession she would wear her walking boots and parka.

The taxi dropped them off as close to the centre as possible. Many of the roads were now closed and the streetlights had been turned off in readiness. Thousands of people lined the route, and they jostled along the pavement in the moonlight. Julia took Tony's arm and led him to her favourite viewing spot. She knew she would find Marianne there too.

'Hello,' she said, finally spotting Marianne in the crowd, 'where are the girls?'

'Off with some boys,' Marianne said, shaking her head in despair, and then kissing Julia on the cheek. 'You must be Tony,' she added, turning to shake hands.

'Lovely to meet you,' he said, 'what a great time to come and visit Shetland.'

'It is indeed. Julia's got us all reading your books now. I'm really enjoying them, although some of them are a little scary. I even locked my front door the other day, and I never usually think about doing that.'

'Sorry!' Tony said, grinning at her.

They chatted for a while, talking about Shetland, Sicily and Tony's novels until they were startled by the loud boom of the maroon sounding out, accompanied by a red flare that rocketed up into the night sky above the Town Hall.

The crowd hushed for a moment, turning to look towards the Town Hall where the Up Helly Aa flag fluttered in the light of the paraffin torches. The ghostly shadow of the Jarl's winged helmet could be seen against the building as he took his place on board the galley that would soon be dragged through the streets.

Tony got his camera ready, grinning like a child on Christmas Eve.

He was still grinning an hour later, when it was all over. The last firework had fizzled out and the crowds were starting to disperse. The galley ship was still alight but the Vikings and the other squads of guizers were leaving to get ready for the next phase of the night.

'Wow. That's all I have to say to that; wow!'

Julia and Marianne laughed.

'But I don't understand why the Pope was there, or why some of the men were dressed up as women, or the cast of Star Trek for that matter. I expected them all to be dressed as Vikings.'

'Ah yes, it's a bit strange for outsiders to comprehend. I'll let Julia explain that to you. I need to get back to the hall to get ready for the party. I'll see you two later,' Marianne said.

Marianne left them watching the remains of the fire and Julia took advantage of the relative quiet to explain the history of Up Helly Aa and some of the more bizarre traditions which had precious little to do with the remnants of Viking culture after all.

'So in reality this is just one big excuse to dress up, drink all night and go crazy once a year?'

'Pretty much. It's kind of like celebrating that the worst of the winter is over. The days are getting noticeably longer now.'

'Well, I loved it, even if there is only a tenuous link to authentic culture.'

Julia nodded and smiled.

'I love it too. I wish my boys had been able to come back for it. But they're both working today and couldn't get away. So I'm glad you came for a visit.'

'I shall come back again one day. I love it here. I can see why you wouldn't think about leaving Shetland. Even in the bitter cold of winter, it's still delightful.'

Julia took his arm and they headed up the hill towards the Town Hall. The streets were almost deserted again, as people had left to get ready for the next stage of the Up Helly Aa celebrations.

They were too early for the party, but Julia persuaded the doorman to let them in, promising that they would go and do something useful in the kitchen while they waited. Julia found Marianne in the kitchen wearing her long white pinny, buttering bread for sandwiches.

'Ah great, more helpers,' she said.

Julia put down her rucksack that contained bottles of wine and whisky. There was no bar, so guests had to bring their own drinks, but there would be plenty of food available to keep everyone going all night.

Julia went over to the large cauldrons of soup that were simmering on the hob. She stirred them, as she introduced Tony to the other hostesses, who seemed star struck and quiet in the presence of a celebrity. However, Tony soon put them at ease, making them laugh with his interpretation of Up Helly Aa.

Marianne sidled up to Julia. 'He's quite a catch; aren't you tempted?'

'Don't be daft; we're just friends.'

'Well he seems like a very nice friend to have.'

'He is, isn't he.'

They left the kitchen to go upstairs to the hall just before the doors were opened to the rest of the guests. Julia grabbed two seats in the centre and while Tony guarded them Julia took the drinks bag out to one of the ante-rooms and handed it over to a steward in return for a cloakroom ticket. She returned to her chair carrying two glasses of wine and handed one to Tony.

The room filled up quickly and there was a rush for the best seats close to the dance floor. The band had taken their places on the stage and were tuning up. Tony was quiet as he watched the scene. Julia could see he was taking it all in, probably storing it all away for future use in a book; the laughter and the snippets of conversation in dialect or English. A party of young people occupied the seats immediately behind Julia and Tony. They spoke with a variety of accents, mostly Australian or New Zealand. Two young women were speaking in Italian and Tony turned round instantly and introduced himself.

Julia watched with amusement as he turned on the charm with the young women who were surprised to meet someone who spoke their language.

'They're all on a coach trip – haggis tours, or something like that. Sounds like a blast. They visited a whisky distillery in Orkney yesterday. They have Up Helly Aa today and then on Thursday they're flying over to Edinburgh to tour the castle and go drinking in the city,' Tony explained to Julia when he turned back to speak to her.

'Sounds exhausting!'

Their conversation was interrupted by the arrival of the first squad. They watched in bemusement when the cast of Star Trek marched into the room and did battle with an evil alien, which turned out to be the Chief Executive of the council.

Tony laughed along with the audience, but seemed mystified all the same.

'What was that about?'

Julia shook her head, smiling with amusement at him.

'The council always comes in for a lot of ribbing at these occasions. I can only guess that someone saw the latest Star Trek film and took their inspiration from that.'

The band started to play and the cast of Star Trek, who on closer inspection looked a little less glamorous than the Hollywood originals, circulated around the room looking for dance partners. Lieutenant Uhura, in real life a butcher with a bit of a paunch, approached Julia and asked her to dance.

Julia grinned at Tony and then stood up to dance with the man.

'I've never danced with a man who had bigger boobs than me.' Julia said, tapping the man's plastic décolleté.

'I'm not sure I should wear such a short skirt with my legs,' he replied in a camp voice, 'but I do like the wig.'

Julia danced a Boston Two-Step with the man and then made her excuses after the dance and returned to Tony.

'That's made my day already,' he said, as Julia sat down beside him, 'a short fat white man, dressed up as a black woman in a Star Trek uniform. Madness!'

Julia managed to avoid being asked to dance again and instead talked Tony through the etiquette of Up Helly Aa and the dancing. He said he would watch a few more dances before he gave it a try.

They watched a few more squads come and go. They watched a sketch about the Pope's resignation, with a comedy Prince Charles trying to persuade his mother to abdicate too, only for him to die of old age, immediately after. One act produced some fine juggling skills, the humour provided by the fact that the men were dressed as old women.

'You'll have noticed that dressing up as women is a bit of a recurring theme,' Julia said, 'which is why today is sometimes referred to as Transvestite Tuesday.'

Tony nodded and then turned round to the two Italian girls and translated that for them. They both roared with laughter. Julia turned and smiled at them. They had only just sat down after being dragged around the dance floor by two young men who were dressed as women. The women looked flushed and happy and Julia was delighted they were enjoying themselves. She turned and looked at an older couple of tourists who sat watching in stone faced silence, clearly bemused by the whole event, but possibly not really enjoying it.

Julia noticed one of the ushers open the door to the hall and glance out. He shut the door again and motioned to the band leader. The Jarl Squad had arrived. When the dance finished, the music stopped and the floor cleared. There was a ripple of excitement around the room, even from the tourists who weren't really sure what was happening, but had gleaned that something special was imminent.

The doors opened again and this time the Jarl strode triumphantly into the hall, followed by the rest of the squad. The audience all rose to their feet and clapped, as if Royalty had just arrived.

Julia pursed her lips together as she watched the Jarl Squad do their customary march around the room as they sang their anthem. She scanned the faces looking for Cameron, but in truth, what she really wanted to see was her husband. She brushed aside the rising panic that accompanied her feelings of grief and concentrated on finding a friendly face. She was rewarded a moment later by the wide grin on Cameron's face as he marched past.

'Is that the man?' Tony said, nudging her.

'Yes.'

'He has the look of a protagonist.'

'A what?' Julia replied, turning to look at Tony.

'The main character of a novel; the hero.'

Julia laughed and pushed him gently.

'Don't be silly.'

When the singing and grandstanding by the Jarl Squad had finished, the Vikings began to mingle with the crowd. Julia watched as Cameron was ambushed by a group of tourists who wanted his photograph. He gamely posed with the young women, and then he made his way through the crowd to Julia. She hugged him before introducing him to Tony, who in turn introduced Cameron to the two Italian women who had pushed forward in order to get a closer look at his amazing outfit.

Julia smiled at Cameron as he passed his axe and shield to the women who exclaimed excitedly over it, and giggled as they posed for photos with the weapons. Julia noticed that Tony had sat down and looked a little tired; either that or he wanted to give Julia some space with Cameron.

The music started up for the St Bernard's Waltz and Cameron took off his helmet and set it down next to Tony, then took Julia's hand for a dance. As they headed for the centre of the dance floor Julia noticed that one of the Italian women had asked Tony to dance. He smiled and stood up hesitantly; as if he wasn't sure he wanted to try out his Scottish dancing skills with someone who probably didn't know the steps either.

Julia soon forgot about Tony as she was whisked into the arms of Cameron who expertly steered her around the crowded dance floor.

'Did you know that you're the first woman I ever danced with?'

'Tonight?'

'No, I meant ever.'

'Really?' Julia caught her breath as they whirled around at the edge of the floor, conscious of Cameron's hand firmly on her back, holding her close.

'Don't you remember those awful dancing classes at school, where we were forced to dance with each other? We would have been about thirteen. I was the one with the hideous acne.'

Julia laughed. 'Oh God, I remember now. All the boys tried to get out of the classes, using any excuse possible.'

'I didn't. I quite liked learning to dance. I knew it would come in handy one day.'

The music stopped and they stood for a moment, still holding hands as they waited for the band to play a different tune. Julia looked over to where she had been sitting and saw that Tony had sat down again. He looked out of breath and she grinned at him when he looked up, although she realised he hadn't seen her. He seemed lost in thought.

The music started and they began dancing again.

'How's your day been?' Cameron asked; his voice heavy with meaning.

'Oh, so so. I'm glad Tony has been here. He's kept me so busy I haven't really had time to mope around. There was a moment earlier in the day when the pipe band was playing the same tune that was played at the funeral...'

They circuited the room one more time, almost like bumper cars, trying to avoid other couples. There was a sudden pile up of people in the centre of the room, and Julia heard a shriek of fear above the noisy chatter and music. The dancing stopped and people stood watching something that was going on at the side of the dance-floor. The music stopped in the middle of the tune, and a panicked call for help made Julia's heart skip a beat. She couldn't see what was happening so she pushed through the crowd expecting to see someone had fallen over.

She found Tony lying on the floor, with one of the Italian women kneeling down beside him, tapping the side of his face, trying to wake him.

'Let me see. I'm a nurse,' Julia said, indicating for the woman to give her some space.

Julia fell to her knees beside Tony, quickly feeling for his pulse in his neck, and not finding one.

'Call an ambulance. He's not breathing!' Julia yelled, as she bent down to see if she could feel any breath. She opened Tony's mouth to check for obstruction and then started chest compressions.

She heard someone calling for an ambulance and was vaguely conscious that members of the Jarl Squad were guiding people downstairs to give them some space. Julia had snapped into her professional nurse mode and was trying to block out everything else. A young man came over and knelt down on the other side of Tony.

'I'm a first aider. Can I help?'

Julia nodded breathlessly and let the man take over, seamlessly carrying on the rhythm of compressions and breaths.

'Come on Tony. Don't do this to me. Stay with us, please,' she implored. She looked up and saw that the two Italian women were still sat in their seats, holding hands and praying. Julia smiled in sympathy.

'The ambulance is on its way.'

Julia felt a hand on her shoulder and looked up and saw Cameron standing beside her. She held his hand briefly and then took over the CPR from the other first aider.

A couple of minutes later the paramedics entered the room and as they took over she explained what had happened. She sat down on a chair and let one of the Italian women hug her wordlessly. They watched the paramedics using a defibrillator on Tony and on the second attempt, they got a pulse.

'Will you be alright?' Cameron said. 'Do you want me to come to the hospital with you?'

'No, I'll be fine. You carry on. I know this has ruined your night. But please, carry on. I have my phone on me. I'll text you.'

Julia stood up and hugged Cameron, then grabbed her handbag and followed the paramedics out to the waiting ambulance.

At the hospital, Tony was rushed straight into the resuscitation room and Julia was left in the waiting room feeling shell shocked. She knew so little about Tony she was unable to answer most of the questions the triage nurse asked. She had no idea how to contact Tony's son or daughter. The nurse managed to retrieve a mobile phone that Tony had in his pocket. To Julia's relief she found that it was not protected by a passcode and she scrolled through the numbers and found his son. She checked her watch, realising it was well after midnight in Italy. As she dialled the number she realised that she wasn't entirely sure whether Enzo would even speak English.

'Ciao Papa.'

'Hello, is that Enzo?' Julia said, hesitantly.

'Si, yes. Who is this?'

'My name is Julia Robertson. I'm a friend of your father's. He's in Shetland with me.'

'Ah yes, he told me. Is something wrong?'

'Yes, I'm sorry to have to tell you this, but your father is in hospital. We think he may have had a heart attack.'

'Another one? Oh shit.'

'He's already had one before? Can I pass you onto the nurse so that you can tell her about your father? We don't know anything about any medication he might be on.'

Julia handed the phone over to the nurse and slumped down in the chair again, feeling even less confident about Tony's situation. The nurse took the phone away so she could relay the information to the doctors. Julia sat with her head in her hands and only looked up when she heard her name. Marianne hurried over and sat down next to her and grabbed hold of her hand.

'What's happening? I heard some tourist had been taken ill. I didn't know it was Tony until Cameron came to find me.'

'It's probably a heart attack. The paramedics managed to get a pulse, but it was weak. We managed to get hold of his son; apparently this isn't his first.'

'Oh Lord; poor thing.'

They sat in silence for a moment, before Marianne got up and fetched two cups of coffee from a vending machine. She passed a cup to Julia who took it gratefully.

'I can't believe this,' Julia whispered.

'Me neither. Let's hope they can save him.'

Julia leaned forward and set her coffee down on a table. She covered her face in her hands and rocked silently in the chair. Marianne put her arm around her shoulders, but didn't speak.

Nearly an hour later a doctor came to find them in the waiting room. He didn't smile but there was something about his body language that made them think he wasn't bearing bad news.

'We've managed to stabilise him, but he's not conscious yet. We're keeping him sedated as we need to fly him down to Aberdeen for surgery. I understand you're not related to him, but will you want to accompany him to the hospital? I spoke to his son Enzo. He's going to fly over from Rome, but that could take a while.

'Of course I'll go with him. We're friends; he was over here on holiday and staying at my house.'

'That's good. We're just waiting to hear back from the air ambulance but we should be good to go in a few minutes if that's alright? Have you got any photo ID on you, for getting back home again?'

Julia opened her handbag and checked inside her purse and found her driving licence. She nodded with relief.

The doctor hurried off and Julia sat back in her chair and sighed.

'Oh thank God.'

Marianne stood up suddenly and walked over to the waste bin and threw her coffee cup in it, with a touch of exasperation.

'It's not fair though. How did they manage to save him, but not Duncan?'

'Don't go there, please.'

'I'm sorry. It's just...'

'I'm glad I was there to help him,' Julia said firmly.

'Oh so am I, but...'

'I need to use the loo. Make sure they don't go without me.'

Julia hurried off to the relative privacy of the ladies toilet. She could not admit to feeling the same feelings of frustration that Tony seemed to have survived something that her husband couldn't. She knew that comparisons should not be made as Duncan's heart attack was not something that anyone could have survived; but even so, it hurt.

She walked back to the waiting room to find that they were waiting for her. She hurried out to the ambulance after hugging Marianne goodbye and promising to ring her with any news.

It did not take long to make the transfer into the waiting helicopter and within minutes they were airborne and on their way to Aberdeen. Julia sat buckled into her seat, feeling ridiculous in her sequinned top. She hadn't even stopped to get her coat and now she was shivering with cold. One of the crew members noticed her discomfort and handed her a blanket. It was too noisy in the cabin to speak so she simply mouthed her thanks. She looked back at Tony who was lying on a stretcher, with a paramedic sitting beside him, monitoring his vital signs. The paramedic nodded comfortably at her and gave her the thumbs up.

At Aberdeen Royal Infirmary Tony was whisked away to the operating theatre, and once Julia had answered the bare minimum of questions about what she knew about his health, she was left to wait while he underwent surgery. It was still the middle of the night and Tony's family would not arrive for hours.

Julia took a taxi to a 24-hour supermarket in the hope that she might be able to buy something more suitable to wear. She was freezing and she knew Tony's surgery would take a few hours.

He was still in surgery an hour later when she returned wearing a new, rather hideous but warm, quilted jacket, carrying a bag of emergency toiletries and clean underwear.

She was exhausted and looked around the waiting room for somewhere to lie down. There was a battered looking cushioned bench in the corner so she settled down to rest; although sleep was out of the question.

Two hours later a nurse came to find her.

'Mr Hugo has come out of surgery now. He's in the recovery room.'

'Oh, can I go and see him?'

'Ah no; he's not conscious yet. We'll let you know when you can see him.'

'Oh please, could I not just see him for a minute? I'm a nurse. I used to work here.'

The young woman looked blankly at Julia, clearly unimpressed with this news.

'No, I'm sorry. We'll let you know when you can see him.'

Julia sighed, feeling even more shattered now. It was nearly five thirty and she was thirsty. She got up and went in search of the vending machines. The hospital had expanded beyond her recognition now. She doubted there was a single person still working here that would remember her from nearly thirty years ago when she had worked in the operating theatres. She bought a cup of coffee and a bar of chocolate and went back to her seat.

She picked up a magazine from a coffee table and then put it back in disgust when she realised she didn't have her reading glasses with her, and couldn't see clearly enough to read.

Julia sat and stared at the dull green walls of the waiting room and watched people coming in and out, all oblivious to her presence.

Just as she was about to drift off to sleep, an alarm sounded down the corridor, and a pager went off on the waistband of a passing doctor. Julia watched him glance at the pager and set off quickly towards the sound of the alarm. She sat up straight. She knew from experience that somewhere, just a few feet away from her, somebody's life was hanging in the balance.

She stood up and walked over to the window. It was still dark outside, but street lights burned over the car-park. She watched a heavily pregnant woman creep slowly towards the reception holding the arm of a man who carried a small suitcase. They stopped at the edge of the car-park and waited for an ambulance to pass before they crossed over the road, and as they were half way across, the woman paused, bending over in pain.

The nurse that Julia had spoken to earlier walked back to the waiting room and looked at Julia without smiling.

'Your friend is asking for you.'

With that she turned, clearly expecting Julia to follow her. Julia picked up her carrier bag and hurried along after the nurse who opened the door of a side room and waited, somewhat impatiently for Julia to catch up.

'Long shift?' Julia said, trying to empathise with the nurse.

'It always is.'

The nurse hurried away and left Julia to go inside, where she found Tony lying on a trolley with the guard rails up. His eyes were shut, and his hands were lying motionless at his sides.

Julia walked over to him and dumped her bag on the floor beside the trolley. She took Tony's hand in hers, noticing that he seemed cool to the touch. She pulled the blanket up around him. His eyes flickered open, blinking at the glare from the overhead light.

'Hey there,' Julia said, leaning closer to him, knowing that the after effects of a general anaesthetic would mean he would have trouble focussing.

'Julia?'

'Yes, I'm here. How are you feeling now?'

'What happened? Where are we?'

'We're in Aberdeen hospital. You had a heart attack, and you've just come out of surgery.'

'Surgery?'

Before Julia could reply she sensed that Tony had drifted off in a morphine induced sleep. Julia let go of his hand and picked up his notes from the foot of the bed, reading them quickly before realising she probably shouldn't be so nosy. She replaced the clipboard and pulled a chair over to sit beside him. He looked pale under the fluorescent lights, and there were dark shadows under his eyes that she had never noticed before.

She reached for her handbag and took out her phone and sent texts to Marianne and Cameron. The Up Helly Aa celebrations would continue for another hour, so she didn't expect a reply from either of them.

'Julia?'

She put her phone back in her bag and reached for Tony's hand again.

'I'm still here. I called your son; he's flying over later.'

But Tony did not hear, as he slipped back to sleep.

The nurse came back and told Julia they were taking him up to a ward shortly. She suggested that Julia went home to get some sleep.

'I can't; I live in Shetland. We flew down in the air ambulance last night.'

'Ah yes, sorry. Why don't you see if there's any room at the Shetland hostel. You can ask at patients' services.'

Julia stood up and then bent to kiss Tony's cheek.

'I will come and see you later.'

Julia left the hospital. She did not want to stay at the hostel, which was used to provide accommodation for islanders waiting for treatment or accompanying sick relatives. She wanted somewhere anonymous and quiet.

She rang Bryden who had just got up for work and explained what had happened.

'Oh Christ, is he going to be alright now?'

'I've no idea, but I can't go home and leave him here on his own, at least not until his family arrive. I was hoping you might be able to go online quickly and find me a hotel. I really need to sleep for a few hours.'

'Yeah, of course. I'll do it right now and ring you back. Any preferences?'

'No, it will be hard enough to find a room anywhere in Aberdeen at such short notice.'

'OK, I'll do my best.'

Bryden rang her back ten minutes later with the news that there was a room at the Jury's Inn hotel at a price of £120 per night. Julia walked over to the taxi rank and went straight there; only to find the room wasn't available until mid-day, but there was a room free immediately for £150. She sighed with frustration, but took it anyway. Within ten minutes of entering the room she was fast asleep.

She woke four hours later, momentarily unsure where she was. Daylight peeped through the edges of the blackout curtains, and she sat up wondering what time it was. She grabbed her phone and rang the hospital to see how Tony was, and then she slumped back in the bed and read the texts that were waiting on her phone.

Marianne had written: *thank God, been worried sick about you all night. Ring me later xx.*

Cameron had written: *glad to hear the good news. See you soon, take care x.*

Julia was too tired to respond to the messages, but she made herself get up and take a shower, in preparation for a return trip to the hospital. She put on some clean clothes and brushed her teeth, and used the hotel's complementary hand cream in lieu of moisturiser for her face. She stared at her reflection in the mirror. She looked ghastly, but she had nothing other than a lipstick in her handbag to brighten her features.

She was stopped by a nurse before she got to the ward and interrogated as to who she was. Julia was puzzled for a moment, but the nurse explained there had been a journalist hanging around wanting to speak to anyone connected with Tony.

'A journalist?' Julia replied.

'Yes. He's a famous writer isn't he,' the nurse said, looking at Julia as if she was stupid.

'I suppose he is.'

Julia stepped into the relative quiet of the ward and found Tony. He opened his eyes as she approached him.

'Julia! I'm so glad you came back. I thought you must have gone back to Shetland.'

'Don't be daft. I just went and booked into a hotel and had a bit of a sleep. It was quite a tiring night, more than usual for an Up Helly Aa, I can tell you.'

'Sorry about that. I can't think what I was playing at.' Tony smiled, as she sat down next to the bed after greeting him with a kiss on his cheek.

'How are you feeling now? You were a bit groggy earlier.'

'I think I'm OK, thanks to you?'

'Thanks to me? I don't think so; more like thanks to the surgeons who patched you up.'

'I understand that there probably wouldn't have been much left to patch up if you hadn't been so quick with your first aid.'

'That was nothing. Someone else helped me too.'

'Well anyway, I'm truly grateful, and I'm very sorry I spoilt your night.'

'Don't be silly.'

'No really; I was just watching you dancing with your friend Cameron and feeling just a little bit jealous, and then it was lights out. That will teach me.'

Julia didn't reply for a moment, as she wasn't sure whether Tony was being serious, or just flirting again.

'Have you heard when your son and daughter might arrive?'

'Enzo rang a little while ago; he couldn't get here until tomorrow, and Eleni is too pregnant to travel, so I told them not to bother. It was so expensive, and I'll be flying home again soon enough. There's nothing for them to worry about now.'

'Really? I would have thought Enzo at least would still want to come and see you.'

'Oh, he did, but he has exams coming up; I would hate him to miss anything important on my account.'

Julia shook her head in disbelief.

'Has the doctor said how long you might be in hospital for?'

'He said it depends on how I get on over the next forty eight hours. They want to make sure I don't get any infection or any complications. But he doesn't want me to fly back to Italy just yet. I won't be fit to travel that far for another week or so.'

'As long as that? Will you be able to come back to Shetland though?'

Tony shrugged, looking a little embarrassed.

'You can stay as long as you like; it's no bother.'

He smiled. 'Thanks; I appreciate it. I might be let out of here by the weekend, if I'm very lucky.'

22

Tony was allowed to fly back to Shetland on Friday evening. The hospital booked both them onto the evening flight, and the patient transport ambulance delivered them to the airport. As they sat together in the departure lounge, Julia observed that Tony seemed to have shrunk; not so much in stature, but in his demeanour. He seemed nervous about flying, checking and rechecking his boarding card, and fiddling with his Italian driving licence, the only piece of photo ID he had on him when he was admitted to hospital.

'Won't be long now. I expect you'll feel much better sleeping in a real bed tonight.'

Tony appeared not to be listening to her. He was staring at an advert for Highland Park whisky. Julia gave up trying to make conversation with him.

'I should just fly back to Sicily. This is nonsense. I don't see why I can't fly home now.'

'Don't be silly; Shetland is less than an hour away. It would take three different planes to get you back to Sicily. You need to be a bit more rested before you take that on.'

'But I'm going to be a nuisance for you.'

'No you're not. Of all the people to be staying with after having surgery, a trained nurse has to be the best. What kind of nuisance do you intend to be? I doubt you're going to be running around drinking and partying.'

Tony smiled for the first time since they had left the hospital.

'You're a good friend,' he said, touching her arm.

'Exactly; and you were a good friend to me when I came to Sicily. So don't go making a fuss about staying with me. It really is no bother at all.'

'Thank you.'

They boarded their flight and less than an hour later they arrived at Sumburgh. This time Julia's car was not waiting for them in the car park so they had planned to get a taxi back, but waiting for them at the airport was Marianne.

Julia hugged her gratefully.

'Oh, you didn't have to do this, but thank you,' Julia said to her friend as they walked out to her car.

They walked slowly, on either side of Tony. Marianne put her arm through his.

'Well, I never really got a chance to speak to Tony, so at least this way I get to see him. You did give us a fright; and something to gossip about too. I should warn you it's in the *Shetland Times* this week. Famous author is airlifted to hospital after Up Helly Aa gives him a heart attack.'

'Really?' Julia said, alarmed at the thought.

'Well not quite as dramatically as that. But you could tell the editor thought it was more of an interesting story than the usual goings on. There is a little bit of an insinuation that you two are an item though. So you may need to warn Bryden and Jamie. They're bound to hear some ridiculous gossip.'

'Ah, well, it was in the *Press and Journal* too, so they already know. Some horrid young reporter ambushed me in the hospital café and then wrote some stupid piece about me. His angle seemed to be that I was a lonely unemployed widow that had latched onto Tony, hoping to add a bit of glamour and excitement to my life.'

Tony chuckled and winked at Marianne.

'Glamour and excitement, playing nursemaid to an old man like me. That would take some imagination.'

Marianne filled them in on the rest of the news, which wasn't really much at all. She drove them back to Julia's house, and then left them alone, after extracting a promise that they would come round for Sunday lunch.

Marianne had been into the house earlier and left a casserole in the fridge, and some fresh bread and milk.

'You have lovely friends,' Tony said, as Julia took the lid off the casserole dish.

'I do, don't I? Now, why don't you go and have a rest, and I will make us something to eat.'

'I'm not really hungry actually. But I could do with an early night. I've been looking forward to sleeping without a light on, and some nurse coming in to check my vital signs every couple of hours.'

Julia laughed. 'Well you can certainly turn the light off, but don't count on me not creeping in to see if you're OK.'

Tony looked at her in alarm and then realised she was joking. He smiled and then made his way slowly up to the bedroom.

Julia made herself a cup of tea, relieved to be back in her own home. The hotel had been very nice, but there was nothing like coming home. She sat down on the sofa and switched on her iPad, curious to know what she had missed on Facebook over the last few days.

It seemed that all she had missed were a series of photographs of Up Helly Aa and some strange comments alluding to her new "relationship." She didn't bother to respond, but switched off the iPad and lay back on the sofa feeling exhausted.

She rang Jamie, only to find he was working and couldn't speak. She rang Bryden who assured her that although they had heard some of the crazy rumours about her, they knew they were not founded on anything sensible.

She put the phone down and then sat in blissful silence for a while. She wasn't hungry either and couldn't be bothered to make anything to eat. She shut her eyes and was almost falling asleep when her mobile phone bleeped. It was a text from Marianne.

"I meant to say that Cameron seems to be a bit miffed about you and Tony. Do you think he's jealous?"

Julia sighed and shook her head in disbelief. She didn't know how to reply to that snippet of news so she got up and went to bed, even though it was only just after nine.

The next morning she woke up late, despite the fact there was a gale blowing outside. Wind and rain battered the window, which made her reluctant to get up. She would have been tempted to turn over and go back to sleep, but for the fact she had a guest to look after. She put her dressing gown on and tip-toed along the landing to see if she could determine whether Tony was awake yet.

She tapped on his door. There was no reply, so she turned and walked away, presuming he was still asleep. Then she stopped and listened, and then walked back to the door and leaned in with her ear up to the door. Silence. Julia knocked on the door sharply.

'Tony?'

When he failed to reply she opened the door, holding her breath with anxiety.

His bed was made; the room was tidy and he clearly wasn't in it. Julia sighed with relief and went downstairs to see where he had gone.

He wasn't in the lounge or the kitchen. She walked over to the kettle; it was hot, so clearly Tony had been downstairs recently. She could not believe she hadn't heard him get up. She switched the kettle on again and decided to make herself a cup of tea. She couldn't imagine where he had gone, since the weather did not invite anyone to go out walking, but she decided she didn't need to go looking for him; he was obviously feeling well again.

She took her cup of tea over to the kitchen table and sat down. Rain drizzled down the kitchen window and the clock ticked. It was peaceful. Julia sipped her tea and thought about ringing the boys later. She heard a noise outside and looked up to see a man walking past the window. She dropped her mug in shock, and barely noticed the tea cascading over the table and onto her feet.

'Duncan!'

Julia stood up suddenly, and then sat down just as quickly, when she realised how stupid she had been.

She was still sitting with hands covering her face when Tony opened the door and stepped into the kitchen.

'Are you alright, Julia?' Tony said, as he unzipped the khaki parka he had been wearing, and took off a multi-coloured Fair Isle hat.

Julia withdrew her hands from her face and stared at Tony. He watched him take off Duncan's coat; still reeling from the shock of thinking she had seen her husband. Her fingers were trembling and she couldn't speak.

Tony laid the coat over the back of another chair. He noticed the spilt tea and reached for the kitchen roll. He pulled off a few sheets of paper and started to mop up the liquid.

'Julia? Are you alright? You're as white as a sheet,' he said, picking up the mug and taking it over to the sink.

All Julia could feel was crushing despair. That fraction of a second when she thought she had seen Duncan had undone months of recovery.

Tony crouched down beside her and took her hand.

'What's happened; tell me.'

'I saw you walk past the window; I thought you were my husband.'

Tony looked back at the coat he had borrowed and swore under his breath.

'Oh Julia, I'm so sorry. I didn't think. I seem to have lost my coat and I wanted to go outside to see what the weather was like.'

'It's OK; don't worry. It was just a shock, that's all.'

Tony stood up and patted her on her shoulder.

'Let me make you another cup of tea.'

'No, please; I think I'll just go up and get dressed. I need a few minutes to get my head together.'

Julia went upstairs and when she got to her bedroom she slipped under the duvet and pulled it over her head. Her eyes were hot with unshed tears, but she couldn't cry. Too exhausted with the process of grief, she curled up into the foetal position and prayed for peace.

Two hours later she awoke to the sound of someone knocking on the door. She pushed back the duvet, unsure of how long she had been asleep. The door opened hesitantly, and she was surprised to see Marianne standing there carrying two steaming mugs.

'I made you some tea,' Marianne said. She sat down on the edge of the bed facing Julia. 'Tony told me what happened. Are you OK now?'

'Oh God, I feel so stupid,' Julia replied, looking at her bedside clock and realising how long she had left Tony downstairs on his own. 'Poor man; it wasn't his fault. He must feel awful.'

'Don't be silly. He was telling me how he would often think he saw his wife around the town, long after she had passed away. He knows how it feels.'

'I suppose. But look at the time, I really should get up and start looking after my guest.'

'He's fine. He's downstairs talking to Brian and the girls; telling them all about Sicily. I bought your coats and your drinks bag back from the Town Hall. You left them there when the ambulance came.'

'Oh thank you. At least he won't need to borrow Duncan's coat again.'

Julia came downstairs twenty minutes later to find that Marianne had made everyone drinks and had set out some homemade cakes she had brought along. Julia hurried over to Tony and gave him a hug, to show that she was OK. He smiled, and kissed her cheek in reply.

'So, what are everyone's plans for today?' Julia asked, as she helped herself to more tea and a piece of fruit cake. She glanced out of the window and noticed that the storm had moved on.

'I think I might just take it easy today,' Tony said, 'I've got some writing I need to catch up on.'

'We're going round to see baby Charlie soon. We're babysitting tonight,' Marianne said, looking smug with pleasure.

'I see; well I think I might just have a quiet day too.'

Marianne and her family left half an hour later and Julia was left alone with Tony. He went upstairs to retrieve his laptop and then made himself comfortable at the kitchen table. Julia fetched her iPad and did likewise, after making some more tea. They sat there in companionable silence for most of the afternoon.

Later on, Julia left Tony to carry on writing while she made something for their dinner. While they ate, they talked about his new book, and then moved on to the subject of their children. The atmosphere had lifted, and Julia felt a sense of calm and optimism by the time the evening came along.

Tony had put his laptop away and they settled down to watch television. The weather had become a little coarser, but with the curtains drawn and the solid fuel fire burning peats in the corner, the lounge was warm and cosy.

As they sat on the same sofa together, with a tartan blanket over their legs, Julia realised they must look like some old married couple. She had often sat in a similar position with Duncan over the years. She smiled at the memory and turned to look at Tony who had nodded off.

She leaned over to wake him up.

'Maybe you should go up to bed now; you need to rest after your surgery.'

Tony smiled, and yawned. 'Maybe I should. I've enjoyed this evening, thanks. It's a long time since I did anything so ordinary; and I mean that in a good way. I either seem to spend my evenings alone, or "entertaining." Neither of which is as much fun as simply hanging out with a friend. I could get used to this.'

'So could I,' Julia replied smiling, before realising there could be a double meaning to this.

She stood up quickly and folded up the tartan blanket and draped it over the back of the sofa. She walked over to the fire and made sure the door was secured firmly. Then she walked out to the back door to lock it, not that there was any need to, but she suddenly felt anxious.

What had he just implied? "I could get used to this." When she walked back to the lounge he had already gone upstairs to bed. She hurried up to her own room and called out goodnight to him. He replied in Italian, with a hint of amusement in his voice.

Julia got into bed, but sat up, leaning against the headboard, thinking about Tony. He was a lovely man. He was kind, thoughtful, funny, clever, and rather good looking for his age. He was fifty eight; she knew that now from seeing his hospital notes, although he did not seem that much older than her. He had aged well considering how much time he spent in the sun. She liked talking to him and she knew that Tony seemed to enjoy her company just as much. She had thought he had only come over to Shetland for Up Helly Aa, but now she wondered whether it was also because of her. Julia didn't know how to process that idea.

She fell asleep dreaming about Sicily.

Over the next few days Julia and Tony either lazed around her house or they went out for a drive under the pretence of sightseeing, but quite often just to go somewhere to have lunch or dinner. Tony was still tired after his operation although he was clearly on the mend. But a week after he had been discharged from hospital he decided that he really needed to get back to Sicily and so he booked his flights and got ready to leave.

Julia drove him down to the airport and after he had checked his bag in they sat in the waiting area.

'I'm going to miss you,' Tony said seriously.

Julia didn't reply for a moment. She watched a couple walking past, hand in hand, on their way to a quieter part of the airport.

'I'll see you again; I've decided I should come over again this October. It's a great time to take a holiday; the last chance for sunshine before the winter.'

'Well you must stay with me. I insist. There's plenty of room in my villa, for you and your family. It would be great to see you. This has been a momentous holiday in more ways than one. I'm going to make some changes to my life. I'm going to get out more; live a little, and if I have less time for writing, well so what, life's too short to spend it at a desk.'

Julia nodded enthusiastically. She rested her hand on his arm for a moment.

'That's very true. But you must finish your new book. I want to see how our character turns out.'

'Ha, well, yes. I will finish that one. But I'm going to take a break after that, and maybe spend some quality time with my new grandchild. This will be a new phase of my life.'

Tony started to pat down his pockets, nervously checking for his tickets and passport, and then he switched off his mobile phone. He looked up at the departures board and then relaxed again.

'I think it's time to move on,' he said, turning to Julia. 'It's time to stop thinking of myself as this tragic widower, and start to think about sharing my life with someone else. I've spent far too much time on my own.'

'I don't think of you as a tragic figure at all; but then again, I never knew you as a married man.'

Tony nodded. 'That's why it has been great getting to know you. I've been able to be myself with you; there's no baggage.'

'Baggage?' Julia repeated. 'I don't think of Duncan as baggage as such, but I suppose he is in a way. I'm weighed down by my emotions, and maybe always will be. It is a kind of baggage, isn't it?'

'Indeed, and unfortunately there are no restrictions on the weight we allow ourselves to carry around. Unlike the airlines,' Tony said, waving his hand in the direction of the check-in desk. 'We should treat our emotional baggage much like a cut-price airline and restrict what we carry around with us. We don't do ourselves any favours by holding on to grief. It's very heavy.'

'Do we have any choice?' Julia replied. She had never thought about whether she had any option but to spend the next few months and years in sorrow.

'I think we have more choice than we imagine. It may not feel that way in the beginning, but we can decide how to process grief.'

Julia wasn't sure she agreed with him, but she decided to give his idea some thought later on.

23

Julia felt rather low as she drove home from the airport. She had enjoyed Tony's company, and she had no wish to go home to an empty house. She looked at her watch and contemplated going to see Marianne, but remembered that Marianne had mentioned that she would be busy with her family that night. Instead she decided to stop off to see Cameron under the pretext of discussing the purchase of the apartment for Jamie. Not that she really needed an excuse to go and visit him. She had been so busy with Tony that she hadn't seen Cameron for ages. It had been over two weeks since Up Helly Aa.

Julia opened the front door and stepped into the vestibule and knocked on the inner door. It was opened almost instantly by Cameron who smiled hesitantly at her and then looked over her shoulder as if he expected her to be with someone else.

'I just dropped Tony off at the airport. He's well enough to travel home now,' she said.

'That's good.' Cameron replied; turning and walking towards the kitchen.

Julia followed him and watched as he picked up the kettle, the automatic response to a visitor, and yet, somehow Julia sensed she was not particularly welcome.

'I just thought I would come round and see how we're fixed for buying your apartment for Jamie. He's definitely keen on it, and has been to see the bank about getting a mortgage, which won't be a problem at all.'

'Oh yeah, sure,' Cameron said vaguely, as he pottered around the kitchen making coffee. He had yet to make eye contact with her, which Julia found disconcerting, but she couldn't think what was wrong.

'Did I tell you that Bryden is definitely moving back to Shetland, so he's going to be living in Alice's old house? I'm going to try and get it ready for him over the next few weeks. That will keep me busy I guess.'

Julia stopped speaking; she had been rambling on about things he already knew. She was standing beside the fridge and in Cameron's way when he wanted to get the milk. She stepped aside, feeling the sudden chill as the fridge door opened, which seemed equal to the frosty vibes that Cameron was giving off.

'Is everything alright?'

'Er, yeah, just a busy week at work; glad it's Friday,' Cameron said, unconvincingly.

'I'm sorry; I should have rung you before I came round. I was just passing and I haven't seen you in ages. I was wondering how things were going with Laura now.'

'Haven't you heard? She was arrested for drunk-driving the other day. She had Amy in the car with her.'

'Oh my God. Is Amy OK? She didn't have an accident did she?'

'No, thankfully. Someone grassed up her up and the police stopped her before anything could happen.'

'Silly bitch,' Julia said, feeling some relief that Cameron's bad mood was not directed at her. Cameron did not offer any further comment about Laura and after a moment of awkward silence Julia changed the subject back to the apartment.

Cameron handed her a mug of coffee and then he coolly discussed the progress of the apartment and when he thought Jamie would be able to move in. He seemed a little more comfortable talking about business, but once that was finished, Julia decided to leave.

'Well thanks for that, and the coffee. I had better get home now. I'll see you soon.'

Cameron walked to the front door and stood watching as she got into her car, but he had gone inside before she turned the key.

She drove off feeling very uncomfortable; and not convinced that his bad mood was solely down to Laura's arrest.

The next few weeks Julia kept herself busy making Alice's cottage even more comfortable for Bryden. She bought new kitchen utensils and crockery. She visited the furniture shops in Lerwick and looked at sofas and other furniture, but stopped short of buying anything when she realised that her taste was probably not the same as her son's, and that she really ought to stop interfering.

She spent her evenings reading, or chatting to Tony via Facebook. He had been to visit his doctor back in Italy and was feeling much better. His son and daughter had been delighted to see him again and he was now busy getting his little holiday villa ready for his daughter to move into later that year. Julia was amused at the symmetry of their lives; until one night when he dropped a bombshell.

I have got a date! A lovely woman named Rosaria; she's divorced with two teenage boys. A friend of Maria's – wish me luck. Tony wrote in a private message on Facebook.

Julia gasped with surprise when she read this. She wrote back, *good for you. I hope you have a lovely time x*. But even as she typed she couldn't help think she had been reading the situation wrong. Hadn't Tony been hinting at the possibility of a relationship with her? All his talk of missing her and implying that she had changed his life for the better. What had that been about?

Tony replied immediately: *It's all thanks to you. You've given me the confidence to make a fresh start. Thanks x.*

Julia logged off her iPad and went to bed feeling confused, and a little jealous. Not that she had any romantic feelings towards Tony, but she had a feeling that their special friendship would be altered if Rosaria became a permanent fixture.

Julia lay in bed contemplating the men in her life. Whilst Tony might have been open about his new relationship, Cameron had maintained complete silence on any matter since she had been to see him a few weeks ago. She hadn't had so much as a text from him. It was very strange. She started to feel the tentacles of loneliness grappling at her heart again. It really didn't take much to bring her down these days. But she remembered what Tony had said to her at the airport before he left and started to wonder if she could choose to react differently.

She decided to try and take a more positive attitude and to get on with her life without relying on these two men; neither of whom could adequately replace Duncan in her affections.

The next morning Julia rang the Social Work office to chase up her application to become a foster carer. She was told that she would find out by mid-April, but she had been recommended to the panel, so it was almost a formality.

Whilst Julia was delighted with this news, there was one dark shadow on the horizon. She turned over the page on the calendar and ignored the photograph of the cute otter cubs playing on the beach. Her attention was drawn instantly to Tuesday 11th April, the first anniversary of Duncan's death. Bryden would be starting work in Duncan's old job on the Monday. There was a curious symmetry to these events, but not one that gave her any comfort.

She thought back to her last morning with Duncan and recalled how he wished their sons would come home to Shetland one day. Well, his own death had facilitated Bryden's return. He had also expressed concern over Jamie's long hours as a newly qualified doctor. That would all change too, when Jamie took up his studies for his PhD in immunology. Duncan had got his wishes, but he was not here to appreciate it.

Julia wondered what they could do to mark this date. Bryden would be in Shetland already, so she wondered about asking Jamie if he could come home that week as well. It was time to hold some kind of memorial service. Her residual memories of the funeral were full of tension and fear, and not the fitting tribute to Duncan she had wanted.

She sent Jamie and Bryden text messages to ask for their opinions on what would be the best way to celebrate their father's life. They had less than two weeks to organise something. Bryden would be busy packing up his flat in Edinburgh and saying goodbye to his friends and colleagues. He was due to come home in a few days.

Julia decided to go and see if Marianne had any ideas. She hadn't seen Marianne for ages, as she was always either busy at work, or with her grandson Charlie. Julia got in her car and drove to the care home.

Marianne was on the phone when she arrived so Julia went to the day- room to see some of the elderly residents who had been living at the care home for a few years. They were delighted to see her again and she spent a few minutes catching up on everyone's news. Marianne came to find her and they returned to her office and closed the door.

'I don't suppose you came here looking for a job did you?' Marianne asked optimistically. 'I was just trying to get some cover for the night shift. Morag has the flu and Beth's on holiday and Jack's wife just had a baby so we're short for the next few days.'

'Actually, I probably could help out, but I don't think you'll get Personnel to agree; I would need to have a criminal records check done again.'

'But you must have had that done again for your fostering application. I might ask if that is acceptable.'

Julia shrugged. She knew how bureaucratic and unbendable the rules were; she doubted they would allow this, despite her thirty years nursing experience and not so much as a speeding ticket on her criminal record.

Marianne sighed in despair, realising it was pointless to pursue this option.

'Anyway, what brings you here?'

'I wanted to pick your brains about doing something to celebrate Duncan's life. It's nearly a year now. I don't know how to mark the occasion, but I feel I should.'

'That's a great idea. It's a Tuesday though, not sure what we could do on a weekday and at quite short notice. Could we make it the Saturday or Sunday?'

'I guess so, but I still have no idea.'

'Leave it with me; I'll give it some thought once I've sorted out the night shift. In the meantime, what's the news with Tony? Is he still pursuing you?'

'Pursuing me? No, whatever gave you that idea? The last I heard from him he was dating some Italian divorcee.'

'Oh; I kind of imagined you too might get it together. He's really nice,' Marianne replied, looking disappointed.

'Well, we did become good friends, but that's about it. I still hear from him which is nice, particularly as my other good "friend" has dropped me like a hot potato.'

'What do you mean?' Marianne said, fiddling with the pot of paperclips on her desk.

'I haven't heard from him at all. The last time I saw him was the day Tony went home, and he was a bit cold and distant then. I thought it was something to do with Laura and Amy, but he hasn't been in touch since. Something's changed in him; and I wish I knew why.'

Marianne jumped up quickly and walked over to the little kitchen area of her office. She switched the kettle on and then peered out the window as if there was something interesting outside. She turned back to Julia and held up her hands in surrender.

'I think that Cameron's moodiness might be my fault actually.'

'How could it be your fault?'

'He came round to see Brian while Tony was staying at yours, and I might have mentioned how "well" you and Tony seemed to be getting on. He seemed a bit pissed off.'

'Why would you do that?'

'Well, I thought it was the truth, that's why. I thought Tony would be good for you, and far less complicated than Cameron. I'm sorry!'

Julia smiled, and then started to laugh.

'So he's just jealous then?'

'It would seem so.' Marianne smiled with relief at Julia's reaction to her interference.

Julia started to shake with suppressed giggles.

'For heaven's sake, look at me. I'm a washed up old woman and suddenly you think there are two men fighting for my attention. That's hilarious.'

'Yeah, but one of them really is keen on you isn't he; otherwise why would he be giving you the cold shoulder when he thought you were going off with the dashing English man?'

Marianne's phone rang and she turned to answer it.

'I'll ring you later!' Marianne said, just before she picked up the handset.

When Julia got home Jamie rang to say he was going to come home with Bryden and stay for a couple of weeks. He sounded cheerful at the prospect of returning to Shetland for a little holiday. He sounded very much like the old Jamie; relaxed and happy.

'So Mam, do I still have a bedroom or are you booked up with waifs and strays now?'

'Don't be daft. I won't be starting to foster until May at the earliest, and even then there'll always be a room for you my darling.'

'Just kidding Mam. Anything you want brought home from the big smoke? I could do a knicker raid on Marks and Spencer's if you like.'

'I don't think that will be necessary. I have heard of internet shopping you know.'

Jamie laughed.

'So, what are you planning for Dad's memorial? It's not going to be in the kirk is it?'

'No, but I can't think of anywhere appropriate at the moment. We could just have a party here I suppose,' Julia replied, doubtfully.

'Why don't you let me and Bryden organise it? I have some ideas, and I know who Dad would want to come along. The funeral was a bit formal; I think he would have wanted something much more fun, don't you?'

'I have never yet been to a fun funeral.'

'You know what I mean. And it's time to remember the good things about Dad isn't it?'

'You're right. That's settled; you and Bryden can organise it and I promise I won't interfere.'

'That will be a first!'

24

Bryden and Jamie came home on the ferry together, with the boot and the back seat of Duncan's old Ford Focus full to the brim of Bryden's possessions. They spent the first couple of days at his new cottage making sure Bryden had everything he needed to settle in, prior to starting his new job the following week.

It was strange sitting in Alice's old kitchen drinking coffee with her sons. It was stranger still leaving Bryden there and driving home without him; but he was keen to take over the new house on his own, although Jamie stayed over the first couple of nights with him. Julia guessed they were busy planning Duncan's memorial, although she still didn't know what they were up to. They simply asked her to keep the whole weekend free.

On Saturday morning Julia got up early. It was a rare morning of warm spring sunshine. Her daffodils looked particularly pretty in the kitchen window box. She was alone in the house as Jamie had stayed over at Bryden's on Friday night. She had tried not to feel excluded from their "boys club," but that hadn't really been successful. She felt lonelier when they were just a couple of miles down the road from her, than she normally did when they were both in Edinburgh.

The phone rang and she took it into the lounge and sat down to speak to Jamie.

'Mam, I've a favour to ask you. I need you to come to Cameron's to discuss the apartment. Would you be able to come over in about two hours? Bryden and I want to take you out to lunch after, is that OK?'

'Yeah, sure,' Julia replied, pulling a face at the thought of seeing Cameron again. But as Jamie would be with her, she realised they wouldn't be able to talk about anything personal, so it wouldn't be too embarrassing.

'Good; see you at eleven then. Don't be late! Cameron is busy later.'

Julia hurried off to get ready. This was the first time her sons had offered to take her out to lunch, so she decided to wear something nice. She put on a dress and her high heeled black boots. She took time to blow dry her hair, put on some make-up and perfume and then grabbed her handbag. She checked to make sure she had her purse on her; just because Jamie had said they were taking her out to lunch, this didn't mean she might not need to pay.

She drove over to Cameron's house and as she got closer she felt a little nervous. She hadn't seen him for so long and she hoped it wouldn't be awkward. As she turned into the road where Cameron lived she noticed a coach parked close to his house. She pulled up behind it without giving it any more thought. Julia got out of the car and walked up the drive and then stopped.

Standing outside Cameron's house were some members of the Jarl Squad, all dressed up as if it was Up Helly Aa. Julia wondered why they were there, and then decided there must be some kind of event going on. Throughout the year it was traditional for the Jarl Squad to appear at carnivals and charity events in Shetland. They sometimes travelled as far away as New York for a parade. The sight of Vikings stalking the streets was always a popular spectacle.

Julia walked up the drive, smiling and saying hello to the men. Julia hurried into Cameron's house thinking that he must have something planned that morning. She assumed Jamie had forgotten to check with Cameron to see if he was free.

In the kitchen she was met by Cameron, Bryden and Jamie all dressed up as Vikings. They were laughing like naughty school boys.

'Surprise!' Jamie approached his mother and hugged her. 'Do you like my outfit? I borrowed it for the day.'

'I see. What's happening today then? I thought you were taking me out to lunch,' Julia said, smiling indulgently at her sons. 'Not that I mind; I'm sure I can find something else to do.'

'No need; lunch is still happening later. But there'll be quite a crowd there.'

Julia pulled out one of Cameron's kitchen chairs and sat down.

'I think it's time you explained what's going on here.'

'We had an idea about how to pay our respects to Dad, so we asked Cameron to help us,' Bryden explained. 'Dad didn't get to have his Up Helly Aa, so we decided to bring Up Helly Aa to Dad. We're all going to visit his grave together and then we're going to have lunch at the Town Hall. So; are you up for that Mam?'

Julia shook her head, not with the intention of being negative, but more because she was flabbergasted.

A few minutes later Julia was invited to join the rest of the Jarl Squad on board the coach and then they set off to the cemetery. She had never admitted to anyone that she had not been back to the cemetery since the funeral; not even when the headstone had been erected. She imagined her friends and family would be shocked to hear this. But she struggled to cope with the idea that Duncan was buried in the ground; and now she was a little anxious at the thought of standing beside his grave again.

The atmosphere on the coach was rather jovial given the circumstances. Clearly they had been briefed by Jamie and Bryden that this was an opportunity to celebrate, and they were all doing it in true Shetland style, with whisky and beer, and plenty of banter.

When the coach stopped, Julia noticed that Marianne's car was parked close by and she breathed a sigh of relief. Up until that point there had been no other women in the party.

As she got off the coach Marianne appeared, all dressed up for a party, and surrounded by her family. She hugged Julia and took her arm.

'Don't worry, I've got tissues; this could get messy!'

Before Julia could respond, she heard the unmistakeable sound of a bagpipe stirring into action. She turned round and saw a piper in full Highland gear standing next to the coach.

'Oh heavens,' Julia exclaimed, knowing full well that the sound of bagpipes could reduce her to tears even when it wasn't an emotional occasion.

'Chin up; have a sip of this,' Marianne whispered, passing Julia her silver hipflask. 'It's apricot brandy; delicious.'

Julia took a sip and giggled nervously.

'What on earth is going on here? I had no idea they'd planned this. I thought I was just going out to lunch with the boys. Thank God I wore something decent.'

'Yeah, I should have warned you, but they swore me to secrecy, and for once I managed it.'

'Yes, it was probably best I didn't know.'

Once the squad had emerged from the coach they gathered in a huddle, as if they were having a final team briefing. Then they got into formation of two rows, led by the Jarl who raised his axe and roared theatrically as the signal to move.

The piper walked ahead of the Jarl and began playing and the procession set off into the cemetery to the spot where Duncan had been buried nearly a year ago.

Julia, Marianne and some other friends who were not dressed in Viking costume followed the procession in silence.

It was fortunate that Duncan's grave was in a spacious corner of the cemetery as the Jarl Squad took up a lot of room. When Julia and Marianne arrived at the grave they found that someone had set out a bench nearby, so they sat down gratefully, as the men converged around the grave.

The piper stopped at the end of the tune and there was a moment of quiet shuffling into position. Jamie and Bryden stood either side of the Jarl, looking resplendent in their borrowed costumes. Julia's eyes were drawn to the shields that their father had designed.

The Jarl lifted an ancient looking cow horn and blew into it; one long mournful note, before he spoke.

'My friends; we are here to pay our respects to Duncan Robertson, who was a fine member of our squad and we have missed his presence throughout the year, and particularly at Up Helly Aa. He was a great man, a great teacher and a great friend to many of us. He was also a wonderful father to Jamie and Bryden and husband to Julia. He was a friend to hundreds of people; far too many to bring to his graveside today; however, we will see many of them later at the hall.'

Julia turned to look at Marianne at this point and raised her eyebrows in question.

'I will now ask Jamie and Bryden to lay our wreath,' the Jarl continued.

Julia watched as someone passed a large wreath of dark foliage, at the centre of which was a wooden disk painted in the same design as the shield.

As Jamie and Bryden carried the wreath to the grave and propped it against the headstone the piper started to play *Amazing Grace*. Julia gritted her teeth against the swell of emotion that threatened to erupt from deep within her. She felt Marianne's hand tighten around hers and sensed she was feeling the same way.

She concentrated on watching her sons, as they stepped back from the grave with their heads bowed. The other members of the squad looked equally sombre.

When the piper finished, the Jarl lifted his horn and blew it, clearing the air of the melancholy bagpipes, then they all launched into the Up Helly Aa anthem, which visibly lifted their spirits, judging by the energetic way they waved their axes around.

They finished with a loud hailing of three cheers for Duncan Robertson, after which the men started making their way back to the coach, leaving Julia and Marianne behind; sitting on the bench still holding hands.

'That was rather nice wasn't it? What do you think Duncan would have made of that?' Marianne said.

'I think he would have enjoyed it. I don't know what other people must have thought,' Julia replied, pointing at an elderly couple walking through the cemetery who had stopped to watch.

'Well, it's a little unexpected for a quiet Saturday morning; but this is Shetland after all.'

'I guess we'd better go and see what's happening next.'

'Oh, you'll love this bit, and look, we didn't need these tissues after all,' Marianne said, stuffing the packet back into her handbag.

'Keep a hold of that hip flask though!'

Julia stood up and took Marianne's arm and with one final glance at the beautiful wreath they made their way back to the car-park where everyone was waiting for them.

Julia got back onto the coach after going up to the Jarl and kissing him on the cheek in gratitude. Jamie and Bryden were seated next to each other so Julia took a seat across the aisle from them.

'Was that OK, Mam? Did you like our surprise?' Bryden said, grinning at her.

'Yes; but I can't believe you managed to organise this so quickly.'

'Well, we had a little help from Cameron. A lot of help actually. In fact, we didn't really do much at all other than ring him,' Jamie confessed.

Julia turned to see where Cameron was. He was at the back of the coach, deep in conversation with someone. She decided to thank him later.

The coach set off again and a few minutes later it stopped outside the Town Hall. Julia could see quite a few people she recognised walking into the building, including Duncan's colleagues and a few teenagers, looking smarter than they normally would on a weekend.

They all went inside the Town Hall and made their way upstairs to the great hall, where Julia found tables and chairs set out for lunch. It was quite an informal layout with white paper tablecloths on the tables, but there were real flowers in the vases on each table. Julia noticed that most people were walking towards one end of the room where a set of display stands was erected. There were too many people gathered around to see exactly what was on display but she caught a glimpse of some photos and guessed they were of Duncan.

She went over to get a better look and discovered there were lots of photographs from the Up Helly Aa bunker and quite a few taken at school, showing Duncan throughout the years.

Duncan's friends and colleagues greeted her warmly, and pointed to different pictures, sometimes laughing at a memory and sharing it with her.

Julia was so busy enjoying the display she didn't realise people were starting to take their seats at the tables. She looked up to see Jamie beckoning her over to a table in the middle of the room. She hurried over and sat down, just before the Jarl climbed up onto the stage to make a speech.

'For those of you who have just joined us, we have come back from laying a wreath on the grave of our dear friend Duncan Robertson. I would like to thank everyone for coming along to this impromptu memorial lunch. Last year when we said goodbye to Duncan it was a very sad and solemn occasion. Today we want you to be happy. We want to celebrate his life and to remember the good times; of which there were plenty. So please enjoy the lunch that Jamie, Bryden and Cameron have organised for you. We will have the pleasure of listening to some talented fiddlers while we eat, all of whom are pupils that Duncan taught at the High School. So let's put our hands together and give them a warm welcome.'

Julia watched the group of teenagers join the Jarl on the stage. As they started to play their fiddles, the doors opened from the kitchen area and some women started to bring out plates of food. Cameron had sat down at the table opposite Julia, although she had barely noticed his presence in all the goings on. He leaned over and opened a bottle of red wine and started pouring it out for everyone.

'I hear you had a great deal to do with organising this little party,' Julia said as Cameron passed her a glass.

'A little; we didn't have much time to do anything very sophisticated, but the Town Hall was free, and so were a few of the Jarl Squad; it seemed an appropriate gesture.'

'It's perfect, thank you. I had no idea what to do to mark the occasion; I would never have thought of this, but it's entirely appropriate. And I love the photos.'

'You'll be able to take them home later, Mam.' Bryden said, joining in with their conversation. There's a DVD too, but we won't play that here. But it's really good. Dad's singing on it; it's dreadful!'

Jamie sniggered and nodded in agreement.

'Well, that wasn't really one of his talents,' Julia replied, smiling at Jamie.

Someone put a tray of sandwiches on the table, and set a soup tureen in the middle.

'Shall I be mother?' Bryden said, lifting the lid of the tureen, and ladling some into a bowl. He passed it to Julia. 'Leek and tattie soup; Dad's favourite.'

'Really? I thought he liked my carrot and coriander soup best.'

Jamie shook his head. 'No Mam, he told us he preferred his mam's leek and tattie soup; sorry!'

Julia laughed. 'The lying little devil,' she said.

They tucked into their food, with the volume of chatter almost drowning out the musicians. The atmosphere was lively, and not exactly in keeping with Julia's idea of what a memorial lunch should be; it felt more like a wedding reception, but she was delighted all the same.

The soup and sandwiches were cleared away and in turn replaced by plates of homemade cakes and cups of tea. Julia poured herself another glass of wine. She was starting to relax now. It was lovely to see Duncan's friends and colleagues in such a nice setting. She could hear snippets of conversation about him.

She got up and went to sit at another table to chat to people she hadn't seen for a while. It made her realise she had been keeping to herself too much. After a while she went over and sat next to Marianne, who was talking to mutual friends.

Julia went back to her table just as Cameron stood up and walked over to the stage. He waited until the fiddle players had finished and then he called for silence.

'I just wanted to say a few words, and I know Jamie and Bryden also want to come up here and say something. You might want to top up your glasses while I speak,' he began. He looked over at Julia and smiled and paused for a moment.

'Last year when Duncan died, we were all stunned and saddened. We still are; but Jamie and Bryden decided we should have some kind of memorial event for Duncan. They didn't want a kirk service or anything terribly formal, so we came up with this. For those of you who aren't involved in Up Helly Aa, you may not realise Duncan contributed so much to this year's costume. This shield I'm holding; this was Duncan's design. Beautiful isn't it?

'Duncan was one of my closest friends. I was best man at his wedding and I cannot remember the time before I knew Duncan. We were friends before we went to primary school, so it has been hard to see him go; harder still for his family.

'But we're not here to be sad and miserable. Today is about celebrating his life and his achievements. And with this in mind we have been circulating this book.' Cameron lifted up a large leather bound book and held it above his head for a moment. 'If you have not already done so, we would like you to share something about Duncan in the book. You can write anything you want, but we would prefer it to be something funny.

'Here is a perfect example. Written by Sarah Anderson: My best memory of Mr Robertson is when we went on a school trip to Inverness. We were sitting in a restaurant and Miss Phipps was complaining to the waiter about the soup being cold, and she was being really grumpy with him. Mr Robertson pulled a face behind her back, but she saw him in the mirror and got really cross with him. I literally wet myself, it was so funny.'

Cameron paused while people laughed; the laughter increasing in volume when Miss Phipps stood up and took a bow. Julia almost cried with laughter. She had heard many stories about Miss Phipps over the years, and she couldn't believe she was taking that story so well.

'I'm sorry Agnes, I didn't see you there,' Cameron said, bowing to Miss Phipps. 'Anyway, this is the kind of thing we want to hear. These are the stories Jamie and Bryden will be able to share with their own children one day, when they ask about their grandfather. Duncan was a real character, and we want to be able to remember the good times. Now, I can see that Bryden has something to say.'

Bryden climbed up onto the stage and shook hands with Cameron.

'I would also like to thank everyone for coming today. As I'm sure you know, I'm going to be taking over my Dad's old job as a Maths teacher on Monday morning. These are big shoes to fill and I have to say I'm a little nervous.' Bryden paused, as a ripple of supportive applause rang out.

'Anyway, it's great to be back in Shetland. Dad wanted us to get out and see the world, and maybe I haven't done as much of that as he wanted, but to be honest, I have seen enough of the world to know where I want to be. I would be very happy to have the kind of life Dad had. He enjoyed his work, he loved Shetland and he loved us. I can't imagine a better life. I'm proud to follow in his footsteps and I hope I will do him proud in my new job.'

Bryden stepped down off the stage and passed the microphone to Jamie, who had to wait a minute while the applause died down before he could speak.

'First of all, I would like to thank Cameron for helping us to organise today. Dad would have loved it. He was a great inspiration to us when we were growing up, although he seemed to think he was a boring old fart, just because he was a Maths teacher. But he was a great teacher, and I don't think Bryden and I would be starting out on such good career paths without his help. And Mam's of course! The funny thing is I have just decided to change my career. I'm going into medical research, and that will involve a lot more of the maths Dad taught us. So maybe I have more in common with him than I ever thought.

'This year has been hard on everyone. We thought Dad was on the mend, so it was doubly cruel to lose him like that. But as he said in a letter he wrote to me while he had cancer - he will never leave us; he is in our DNA. He didn't want us to be miserable if he died, and it has been very hard not to be, but a year later we know we have to make more effort to live the life he wanted for us. It starts today. So thank you all for coming along to celebrate his life, and adding to the happy memories we have of him.'

As Jamie stepped off the stage, there was a loud and enthusiastic round of applause. Cameron slapped him on his back and shook hands with him again. Julia smiled at the sight of her two sons standing next to the stage with Duncan's best friend. The late afternoon sun pierced the stained glass windows of the hall and threw a heavenly spotlight on them, catching on their armoured breast plates. They turned and marched across the room towards her, their black cloaks sweeping the ground as they walked. Julia wished she could have a photograph of them like that.

Jamie and Bryden sat down at the table again, while Cameron walked over to speak to some other friends.

'Well done. I'm so proud of you both,' Julia said.

When they got a taxi home that evening, both Bryden and Jamie were a little bit tipsy. They sat in the lounge still wearing their Viking costumes, which they seemed reluctant to change out of, giggling and being silly.

'You know something Mam, I think Cameron likes you,' Jamie said, learning forward to help himself to a sandwich that Julia had put down on the coffee table. She hoped some more food might sober them up a little.

'Of course, he likes me, we've been friends for decades,' Julia said, as she picked up her mug of tea. She held it in her hands without drinking, squinting at her son, and waiting for him to explain himself.

'I meant he kind of fancies you.'

'Don't be silly. This isn't the day to talk about things like that anyway,' she replied, gulping back her tea and nearly choking.

'I know, but Dad did say we had to encourage you to "get back out there," didn't he Bryden?'

'Yeah; Cameron's OK Mam. You should go for it one day. You scrub up well.'

'You two are cheeky bastards when you've had a drink! I think I might go to bed now. But thanks for today, it was fabulous.'

25

Julia made breakfast for Bryden before he went to school. He had stayed over the night before the dreaded anniversary. She made him coffee, and a bacon sandwich, and she had put together some chicken and salad in a lunch box for him. She watched him drink his coffee and remembered.

Bryden left the house and got into his father's old car. He waved at Julia who stood at the kitchen window watching him. She lifted her hand and smiled at him. She turned and bumped into Jamie who had wandered barefoot into the kitchen without her hearing.

'Oh, you made me jump,' she said, stepping back.

'He left early; I was going to get a lift into town.'

'Your father always used to leave at this time…I can drive you into town later if you want. I have a meeting with the social worker about my application. I should hear their decision today.'

'Cool. I'd better go and get dressed then.' Jamie turned as if to go upstairs and then he stopped. 'Are you alright Mam? Are you thinking about Dad?'

'I'm always thinking of him. But yeah, I was just remembering how I watched your father drive away in the same car this time last year. He was so excited to be back at school, but kind of nervous too; just like Bryden is at the moment.'

'I'm glad Bryden has come home, aren't you?' Jamie said, as he wrapped his arms around his mother. He kissed the top of her head, and held her for a moment.

'I am actually. I think he'll get on well here. And I'm glad you're happier now too.'

'I am. I really am, and I hope you will be too one day.'

Julia shrugged, as Jamie let go of her.

'I have you two in my life; what's not to be happy about?'

Jamie laughed, as she had intended him to do and then he turned and sprinted upstairs like a teenager.

Julia met Miranda, her social worker from the fostering and adoption team, in reception. Miranda smiled and shook hands with Julia and led the way to a private meeting room. Julia had not been anxious about the decision before now, but as she followed Miranda she got the distinct feeling something was not quite right. Miranda was not her normal chatty and friendly self.

They sat down at the table and Miranda put down a manila folder and offered Julia a cup of tea. Julia declined; she could sense Miranda was stalling for time.

'They've turned me down, haven't they?' Julia said.

Miranda looked up from the folder, startled at Julia's forthrightness.

'Um, well yes, actually. I'm really sorry. Personally, I thought you would be perfect, and Lord knows we need all the foster carers we can get.'

'So why then?' Julia demanded, even though she was on the point of just getting up and walking out. Her hands clenched around the strap of her handbag.

'There were a couple of things actually. First of all, the panel decided it might be too soon for you to take on this responsibility after losing your husband.'

'It's been a whole year! And yes, I may still be sad, but frankly, I'm not an emotional wreck am I?' Julia said, holding her head up defiantly.

'Well, the thing is, one of the panel members knows you, and she said that in her opinion you hadn't been coping very well. She believed your alcohol consumption was far higher than you had declared on your application, and you had a habit of picking up men at parties and taking them home.'

'Huh? What? Are you sure they were looking at the right file?' Julia sat back in her chair with her mouth open in surprise.

'She also said you told her that all you wanted to do was to jet off around the world and have fun with your husband's life insurance money, and just a week after you said that you flew off to Italy for a whole month.'

'Oh my God, don't tell me Paula Adams is on the panel? Well that explains everything. That two-faced bitch would say anything to stab me in the back.' Julia stood up, knocking her chair over in her haste. She turned to pick it up, brushing a tear away from her face.

'Julia, wait! I can see you're upset about this. Sit down; maybe we can sort this out.'

Julia did not reply, she opened the door and rushed out of the building. She got in her car and drove off, but didn't get very far before she had to pull over to wipe angry tears from her face. She calmed down a little and then set off again, before realising she was just about to drive past the cemetery. She stopped the car and got out and hurried through the gates, almost breaking in a run towards Duncan's grave. She sat down on the bench and burst into tears, ignoring the sympathetic smile from an elderly woman who was putting flowers on a grave nearby.

A few minutes later the woman came over and joined Julia on the bench. Wordlessly the old woman put her arm around Julia's shoulder and sat with her as Julia continued to sob. When Julia started to rummage in her pockets and handbag for tissues, the woman reached into her coat pocket and pulled out a freshly laundered handkerchief and handed it to Julia.

'Thanks!' Julia said, taking it to wipe her eyes and then to loudly blow her nose.

'I used to know your husband,' the woman said, 'we worked at the same school.'

Julia turned to look at her properly and then recognised her.

'Oh yes, Martha Plummer, I remember you. You taught History didn't you? And your husband was an English teacher.'

'That's right. Richard died three years ago, but I come along to see him every week. I know how you feel my dear. It's a heavy cross to bear.'

Julia took a deep breath. She felt a little guilty that her tears weren't really for Duncan, but her own self-pity. She didn't feel like explaining this to Martha.

'What a lovely wreath,' Martha said, pointing to Duncan's grave, 'I heard about the memorial lunch; what a lovely thing to do for him.'

Julia smiled and nodded. She looked down at the grave properly and noticed there was a pot of daffodils next to the wreath. She wondered if they had been there on Saturday. She had barely looked at the grave when the Jarl Squad had performed their ceremony. She took a deep breath and studied the grey marble headstone. Seeing her husband's name etched in gold lettering did nothing to add to the reality of the situation.

'When does it sink in that they're never coming back?' Julia said.

'I still make Richard a cup of tea sometimes. When I'm tired and about to go up to bed, I find myself putting out two cups and saucers, and then I remember. I found it very hard at first to come and visit him. I couldn't bear it; but I felt so guilty.'

Julia turned to Martha and nodded slowly.

'This is only the second time for me. The first time was on Saturday when my sons dragged me here for the ceremony. I've never told anyone that before.'

'Your secret's safe with me. I quite like coming here now, especially on a day like today when it's quite sunny and quiet. I sit and tell Richard all the gossip,' Martha said, smiling at Julia. 'And now he can't get up and walk out of the room when he's fed up with me.'

Julia laughed, and then blew her nose again.

'The truth is though; I was upset today about something entirely different. I had applied to be a foster carer and I've just found out I got turned down. It's a year to the day that Duncan died, and here I'm crying because I got rejected. I feel so stupid.'

Martha nodded and looked away into the distance before she turned her attention back to Julia.

'Forgive me for interfering, but that might be a blessing in disguise.'

'How do you mean? I was looking forward to having a house full of children again,' Julia replied.

'Hmm, I can see why you would think that might be good for you, but actually, I think it might be better if you did something that took you out into the world, not kept you at home without any adults to talk to. One of the loneliest things about being widowed is the lack of adult company. I have a dog and a cat at home, and that's it. My children and grandchildren visit at least once a week and that's great, but it's not enough to stop me from feeling alone.'

Julia didn't reply. She had never really considered the situation in that light before.

'Anyway,' Martha continued, 'about a year after Richard died I decided I needed to get out more, so I started doing voluntary work. I work in a charity shop on Mondays; I help with the pensioner's lunch club on Wednesdays; I go to a knitting group on Thursdays and on Friday I play bridge. And during the winter I teach a night class in local history. I'm always busy now, and that helps. I think if I didn't have any reason to leave the house I would be in a very sorry state by now.'

'I never thought about it like that. I think you could be right.'

Martha looked at her watch and sighed.

'Anyway, I really must be off, I'm babysitting my grandson in a little while. It was lovely to chat to you, and remember, don't be so hard on yourself. It takes time!'

Julia watched Martha walk away. She remained on the bench for a little while longer, staring at the wreath on Duncan's grave. She thought about what Martha had said and wondered if somehow Paula had done her a favour. She smiled at the idea that Paula would be truly pissed off if that was the case.

She stood up and walked over to the grave and crouched down and put her hand on the gravestone, touching Duncan's name.

'What should I do now, Duncan? Give me a clue why don't you?' She stood up again and turned to look down at the sea. Seagulls circled overhead and she could hear waves crashing on the rocks on the other side of the cemetery wall.

Julia gave Jamie a lift down to the airport that afternoon. They talked about her disappointment about being turned down as a foster carer. Jamie was angry on her behalf, but when she told him about her conversation with Martha, he concluded Martha might be right.

'But now what should I do?'

'If in doubt, do nothing.' Jamie replied as they sat in the airport lounge, having a last cup of coffee together before his flight back to Edinburgh.

'How's that going to help?' Julia relied.

'What I mean is, it's early days, so don't rush into doing anything. Maybe you should just go back to work part-time while you think about it. That way you get contact with other people, but still have some time to yourself. I know you think fifty is ancient, but it really isn't. Fifty is the new forty, and isn't that when life begins again.'

Julia smiled. 'I suppose you're right. I'm not really too old. If Martha can run around doing all sorts of part-time jobs, and she's in her seventies, perhaps I shouldn't write myself off yet.'

'Exactly!'

Jamie's flight was called and he stood and lifted his bag onto his shoulder. They walked over to the security gate and kissed goodbye.

'Love you Mam; you're the best. I'll see you in a few weeks, unless you want to nip down to Edinburgh for a visit before then. Maybe you should come down and see the apartment I'm buying. Bring Cameron!'

Julia drove away from the airport, her head spinning with ideas. She still felt crushed by Paula's meanness and at a loss of what to do next, and now the weight of the anniversary was starting to make an impact. She did not want to be alone so she drove to Marianne's house.

Brian was at home, but Marianne had gone to the supermarket. He invited Julia in and made her a cup of tea. They sat in the kitchen, as Isobel and Sophie were in the lounge watching the television.

'Marianne was going to call you later. Didn't Jamie go back today?' Brian said, as he opened up a tin of biscuits and set it down on the table.

'I just dropped him off at the airport. I was going to have dinner with Bryden later, but he's been invited to play football tonight. I said he should go. He needs to get his old social life back now he's is living here again.'

'That's true, but I don't think it will take him long to fit back in. Why don't you stay over tonight? I'll ring Marianne and tell her to add one more for dinner. Or we could go out if you like.'

Julia smiled with gratitude, and then unexpectedly, she started to cry. Silent tears streamed down her face, much to Brian's consternation. He pulled his chair next to hers and put his arm around her shoulder. He didn't speak, but simply let her cry.

When Marianne walked in a few minutes later, Julia had stopped crying and was laughing with embarrassment at her emotional outburst. She explained what had happened earlier in the day.

Marianne was apoplectic with rage. She paused in the middle of putting her shopping away, and stood with her hands on her hips as Julia told her what Paula had said about her.

'That evil minded bitch! I'm never speaking to her again. How dare she? Where's my phone? I'm going to give her a piece of my mind.'

Brian took the mobile phone out of his wife's hand. 'What happened to never speaking to her again?' he said, as he winked at Julia. 'Anyway, don't be too hard on Paula; she has enough troubles of her own right now?'

'Huh, what kind of trouble gives her the right to be such a cow?' Marianne protested.

'Her perfect husband has been caught shagging someone else, and you'll never guess who?'

Marianne looked crestfallen for a moment, and turned to look at Julia who was equally surprised by this news.

'Who?'

'Laura Moncrieff. Apparently Dave has said he's leaving Paula and moving to Aberdeen with Laura.'

'What? No! They can't!' Julia shrieked.

Marianne was startled by Julia's outburst. 'Why not; good riddance to bad rubbish.'

'But she'll take Amy with her and then Cameron will have to leave Shetland too.'

'Oh Christ, I forgot about Amy.' Marianne said. She abandoned her groceries and sat down at the table opposite Julia. 'What a fucking mess!'

'It might not be as bad as you think,' Brian said. 'I saw Cameron today. He was just coming out of the solicitor's office. He has started divorce proceedings and has applied for custody of Amy. The solicitor is fairly confident that with Laura's recent arrest for drunk driving with Amy in the car, and her numerous affairs with different men, drinking, drug taking and making false accusations of child abuse, Cameron is likely to be successful.'

Julia didn't know how to react to this news. She was delighted Cameron might get to keep Amy, but she was disappointed he hadn't talked to her about it. She felt a little hurt to be left out of the loop.

Brian looked at Julia and smiled enigmatically.

'He told me something else too.'

'What?' Marianne snapped, before Julia could reply. Both women stared at him, impatient for him to continue.

'I'm not sure I should tell you,' he said. He picked up a newspaper and opened it as if he intended to read it. Marianne snatched it away from him.

'Tell us!'

Brian laughed and took the paper back, although he put it down on the table again.

Julia was impatient for him to spill the beans too, so she didn't join in with the laughter.

'OK, OK!' Brian said, raising his hands in surrender. 'Cameron said he was going to sort out the custody issue, and then once that was secure he was going to ask Julia out. That's if she was ready to move on.' Brian turned to face Julia, 'and if you're not ready, then he will wait until you are.'

'Oh!' Julia said, looking from Brian to Marianne. 'Oh, crumbs. He told you that.'

'He did indeed.' Julia sat and talked to Brian and Marianne for a little while longer, but she decided she didn't want to stay over after all. She needed to be alone to process the events of the day, so she drove home. She went upstairs to her room and sat on the bed and stared at the photo of Duncan, Cameron had given her.

The late evening sun lit up the bedroom and a blackbird was singing outside. She got up from the bed and walked over to the window and looked down at the garden. There wasn't a breath of wind outside. She looked out to sea and there were no boats in view, just the lonely, empty island.

There were no signs of any other human as far as she could see, and as beautiful as the view was, she knew she didn't want to keep this to herself for the rest of her life. But that wasn't a good enough reason to get together with Cameron, or indeed, anyone else.

She wanted to fall in love again. She wanted the real thing, and if that was being greedy, then so be it. She wasn't prepared to settle for a relationship based on convenience or companionship, or even just sex.

26

On Saturday morning Julia woke to the sound of someone moving around downstairs. She went down to the kitchen to find Bryden with his head in the fridge looking for something to eat.

'What's up; haven't you heard of supermarkets?' Julia said, grinning at her son, as he shut the fridge door.

'I'm not very organised yet. I was going to go into town but I thought I would drop in to see you, but you were still in bed, and I was hungry.'

Julia looked at the kitchen clock.

'Is that the time; I'm getting lazy in my old age?'

'Are you alright Mam, you seem a bit fed up at the moment?'

Julia shrugged and walked over to the kettle.

'You're not still upset about that fostering stuff are you?'

'Not really, no.'

'Is it about Dad?'

'Kind of; anyway, how was your first week at the Anderson? I've hardly seen you.'

'Great; really great, I love it.'

'I'm glad to hear it,' Julia replied. She put some bread into the toaster and started to make some tea. Bryden helped himself to a bowl of cereal and sat down at the kitchen table.

'I had a date last night; with Katrina Wilson. Do you remember her? She was in my year at school. She teaches PE now.'

'Wasn't she the one who swam for Scotland a few years ago?'

'Yeah, and she represented Shetland in the Island Games last year. She got a gold medal.'

'Did you go anywhere nice?'

Bryden looked a little sheepish.

'Actually we just got a take away and had it at my place.'

Julia shook her head in disgust, 'how very romantic!'

'It was actually,' Bryden replied, 'although Katrina couldn't have anything to drink as she's doing a triathlon this morning.'

'So, are you going to see her again?'

'She's coming over tonight, and this time I'm going to cook.'

Bryden picked up his empty cereal bowl and spoon and carried them over to the dishwasher. Julia detected an energetic bounce in his walk as he came back to the table and sat down again. He grinned cheerfully at her.

Julia smiled, 'I'm happy for you. I hope it works out.'

'I think it will actually. I'll bring her round to meet you sometime, if you like.'

'Really? Isn't it too soon for her to meet me?'

Bryden shrugged.

'I don't see why not? It's no big deal is it?'

'No, I suppose not.'

Julia sipped her tea and looked at her son. He was embarking on a new relationship without a care in the world. She envied him.

Bryden stood up again and walked over to the bookshelf where Julia kept her cookery books. He picked up *Jamie Oliver's Italy* and brought it back to the table and flicked through the pages looking for inspiration.

Julia ate her toast and wondered what she would do for the rest of the weekend.

'What are you up to tonight?' Bryden asked.

'I don't know; I was going to ask if you wanted to come over to watch a film later or maybe go to the cinema; but you're busy now.'

'Why don't you go with someone else? You could ask Cameron. He's on his own too, isn't he?'

Julia put down her toast and looked at Bryden in surprise. He was still studying the cookbook. 'What about this pizza recipe? Do you think this would be easy to make?' Bryden continued.

Julia glanced at the book. 'Yes I think so. You could borrow the bread-maker if you want. It's good for making pizza dough.'

'Really? I might do that; thanks. Can I borrow this book too?'

'Keep it. I've got loads of cook books.'

Bryden closed the book and stood up to go.

'So, are you going to ask Cameron out then? Go on Mam, I dare you.'

Julia choked on her toast, and took a swig of tea.

Bryden grinned at her. 'You know he likes you, don't you? You should go for it.'

Julia motioned for Bryden to sit down again.

'Are you serious? You really wouldn't mind if I went out with someone else?'

Bryden stopped smiling and looked thoughtful for a moment.

'Like Dad said, he didn't want you to be on your own like Grandma Alice. And neither do Jamie or I. We like Cameron, and we know he likes you, so why not? It's not like you need our permission is it? But even so I wouldn't mind.'

'Well then, I might just do that.'

'Good for you. Anyway, I'm off to the supermarket. See you later.'

Julia washed up the breakfast dishes and thought about what Bryden had said. Despite what he had said about her not needing permission to move on, it was exactly what she had needed. She dried her hands on the tea towel, picked up the phone and dialled Cameron's home number, before she had time to lose her nerve.

'Hi, it's me,' she said, when he answered.

'Hello you,' Cameron replied. She detected a smile in his voice. 'What can I do for you today?'

'Well, actually, I was ringing to see if you were free this evening.'

'Hmm, that depends,' Cameron replied, sounding cautious, which deflated Julia's confidence immediately.

'Oh, well, if you're busy, it doesn't matter,' she replied, back-tracking a little.

'No; but I have Amy this weekend, so I'm a bit limited as to where I can go.'

'Oh, but you could come over for dinner then?'

'Yes actually, we could. We would love to.'

'You can stay over if you like.'

Cameron didn't reply for a moment. She could hear Amy in the distance talking to Jessie J. Julia wanted to know what was going through Cameron's mind. Perhaps inviting him to stay the night was a step too far.

'That's a good idea. Amy goes to bed early, so I wouldn't be able to stay out long otherwise.'

'Great, well that's settled then. Come over early. We can take Amy for a walk on the beach if it's still nice out.'

Julia and Cameron sat on the bench watching Amy as she collected shells from the beach. Amy was singing to herself as she explored the tiny patch of sandy shore, close to Julia's house. Julia was glad of the distraction, as she had no idea what to say to Cameron now he was here.

Almost immediately after she had invited him to dinner she had regretted her hasty decision. She had fretted all day about what to cook, what to wear, what to say and, more importantly, what to expect. Frankly, she was exhausted already.

Cameron seemed equally ill at ease. He sat at the other end of the bench, leaving an unsociable gap between himself and Julia.

'DR loves JR,' he said, looking down at the carved initials on the back of the bench.

Julia reached out and traced her fingers over them. She smiled to herself.

'Did you know Duncan and I fell out over you; many years ago?'

Julia shook her head and frowned.

'He was so happy when you got together. But I told him he shouldn't settle down so quickly. I thought he should play the field a bit more; have some fun.'

'Well thanks; we did have fun actually,' Julia replied, indignantly. She turned her attention away from Cameron and watched Amy.

'I know you did. But I was jealous. I never seemed to find anyone I could be happy with.'

'Did you even try? It seemed to us you were happy going out and "playing the field" as you put it.'

'No; I was always looking for what Duncan had with you. I never found it.'

'I see.'

'Do you?'

Julia looked at him and chewed her bottom lip as she considered her response.

'Not really, no.'

Cameron shifted along the bench towards her and took her hand. Julia instinctively looked to see where Amy was, but the little girl was still stockpiling shells in an untidy heap on the beach. The knees of Amy's jeans were damp where she had knelt in the sand, but she seemed not to notice.

'After Sicily, I began to wonder if I might finally end up with the perfect woman…'

'I'm far from perfect,' Julia interrupted, not least because she was uncomfortable with the direction of the conversation.

Cameron shrugged, as if that wasn't the issue.

'Since you rang this morning, I've been thinking about whether we might have a future or not,' he continued. He paused and looked for Amy who had wandered a little further away. He half stood as if he was about to call after her, but sat down again when Amy turned around on her own accord and started walking back towards them.

'Duncan was my best friend. It occurred to me today, that if you and I got together, then at some stage in the future, I might have reason to be grateful he died. I'm not sure I want to be in that position.'

Julia snatched her hand away from his. She felt the urge to get up and walk back to the house. She wished Cameron would just go home without saying another word on the subject. She couldn't understand how they had suddenly arrived at this situation. It sounded as if he wanted to break up, before they had even got together.

'Daddy, I need a bag to put all my treasures in.'

'I don't have one sweetie. Why don't you just pick a few of the best shells and put them in your pocket. Leave the rest for the mermaids.'

Amy spun around in the direction of the sea and scanned the water as if she was looking for mermaids. She giggled and turned back to Cameron.

'Daddy, that's silly. There's no such thing; it was only a cartoon.'

Julia stood up and smiled at Amy.

'We had better go and have our dinner now. You must be starving.'

Amy nodded as she bent down to choose some shells to take home. Cameron went over to help her; then he picked her up and swung her onto his shoulders and followed Julia back to the house.

While Cameron took Amy to the bathroom to wash the sand from her hands, Julia stood in the kitchen and stared out of the window. She had made a fish pie and it was still in the oven. Julia was tempted to ask Cameron to leave, but because Amy was expecting to have her dinner in a few minutes she was too embarrassed to say anything.

She sighed and reached for the oven gloves and opened the oven door.

'That smells nice,' Cameron said, as he walked back into the kitchen.

Julia put the hot dish down on the marble worktop and turned to face him.

'This isn't how I imagined it.'

Cameron frowned and looked at the pie and then back at Julia as it dawned on him she wasn't talking about the food.

'Do you want me to go?'

'I don't know; maybe.'

Cameron stood and stared down at the floor, with his arms crossed. Amy was in the lounge and had put the television on and was flicking through the channels with the volume uncomfortably high.

Cameron walked into the lounge and took the remote control from Amy and turned down the volume. He came back to the kitchen and looked at Julia as if he was waiting for her instructions.

'Brian said you were going to wait for me. And yet here we are, less than a week later, and you've changed your mind. I don't get it.'

'It's not that simple.'

'I feel so stupid. For the last six months I have been trying to put everything that happened out of my mind, because I wasn't ready to deal with it. And now, when I finally decide that maybe I do deserve another chance, you shoot me down.'

Cameron pulled out a chair from the kitchen table and sat down. He rested his elbows on the table and sat with his head in his hands as if he was in pain.

Julia took a bowl from the cupboard and dished up a small helping of fish pie. She put it on a tray with a spoon and a glass of water and carried it into the lounge for Amy, then came back to the kitchen. She covered the remaining pie with tin foil; then took a seat at the table opposite Cameron.

'After everything that happened with Laura, I never expected to fall in love again. Especially not with you; not even when we were in Sicily. It was all so crazy and so sudden. And then it was all over and we were back home and pretending it had never happened. I stayed away from you. I knew you needed time, and Lord knows I had my own problems to sort out.'

Cameron stood suddenly and peered into the lounge to check on Amy. He sat down again and looked at Julia.

'The other day I went to see a solicitor to sort out the divorce. He was hopeful things might work out better for me than I had expected. He thinks I could get custody of Amy. I might even be able to keep my house too, although I expect I'll have to pay Laura off somehow. I can't count my chickens yet, but it did allow me to think the future could be bright. And then I hoped, one day when the time was right, you and I…'

Julia leaned back in her chair with her hands braced against the edge of the table as if she was about to get up.

'But now you've changed your mind, because suddenly you've remembered Duncan was your best friend? That didn't seem to be uppermost in your mind when we were in Sicily.'

Julia stood up suddenly and walked to the front door and opened it. She stood outside on the step, breathless. If Amy had not been in the house she felt sure she would have lost her temper with Cameron. She felt so foolish.

'I'm sorry. I'm not explaining this very well am I?'

Julia turned to find Cameron standing behind her in the doorway. She pushed him away and hurried down the steps to the garden. She stopped in the middle of the lawn and stood still, staring into the distance, not knowing where to go or what to say.

She tried to put herself in Cameron's shoes. She tried to understand what he meant by not wanting to be grateful Duncan had died, but she couldn't.

She strode back to the house to find Cameron. He was sitting on the step outside the front door.

'I will never be grateful that my husband died. Ever!' Julia said, as Cameron stood up. 'But does that mean I have to spend the rest of my life being miserable? On my own? Because, God forbid I should ever be happy again with anyone else. That is not what Duncan wanted for me, or for our sons, or for anyone else I imagine.' Julia realised she was yelling loud enough for Amy to hear. She folded her arms and glared at Cameron, who looked at her in bewilderment.

They stared at each other without speaking for a few moments. The front door opened and Amy appeared, looking anxious.

'There you are Daddy? I thought you'd gone home without me.'

'Don't be silly; why would I do that?' Cameron replied, as Amy climbed onto his lap and grinned cheekily at Julia, oblivious to the unfolding drama.

'Aren't you going to eat your dinner now? It was yummy scrummy, in my tummy.'

'I'm not really hungry at the moment. But I think we ought to go home and feed Jessie J; don't you?'

Amy jumped off his lap and ran indoors to get her shoes and coat.

'We should talk about this when Amy's not around,' Cameron said, as he stood up.

Julia didn't reply. She followed him indoors, picked up a plastic hair slide that Amy had dropped and handed it to Cameron. He put it in his pocket, pulling out his car keys a second later.

As Julia watched them drive away, she felt like she had been flattened by a bus. She put the remains of the still-warm fish pie into the fridge then she went upstairs to her bedroom and lay down on her bed. It was still early and the sun was shining in through the window. Her resident blackbird was singing sweetly from the roof, but it was not enough to cheer her up. She shut her eyes and replayed the conversation with Cameron in her head.

A part of her had expected something like this to happen. It had all been too convenient. They hadn't sought each other out. It had simply happened. She had never looked at Cameron in all the years she had known him with anything more than simple platonic affection. He was funny, charming, generous and cheerful. He had been Duncan's closest friend for forty five years. He had supported Duncan when his brother Martin was killed, and a few years later when his father passed away. They had shared a flat together in Aberdeen when they went to university. They had liked the same books and the same films; they had shared a similar sense of humour. And yet in many ways they were quite different. Where Duncan had been steadfast and dependable, Cameron was known to be fickle. Duncan had been thoughtful and cautious while Cameron took risks.

Cameron had cried at Duncan's funeral; one of the few men to openly do so. It had touched Julia then. She knew how much he felt the loss of his friend.

She thought about Marianne; trying to imagine how she would feel if her closest friend died. It would break her heart, and she most certainly couldn't imagine starting a relationship with Brian, no matter how fond she was of him. It would feel like incest.

Julia sat up on the bed and reached for her phone and dialled Marianne's number.

'Hi, what's up,' Marianne said. Julia could hear the television on in the background.

'Something strange just happened with Cameron. We've kind of fallen out.'

'Oh?'

Julia heard Marianne walking into her kitchen where it was quieter.

'I didn't tell you this, but I invited him around for dinner tonight, and he came along with Amy. I guess it would have been our first "date" but he didn't even stay long enough for dinner.'

'Why not?'

Julia carried the phone over to the window and looked down at the beach where she had been sitting with Cameron earlier.

'I'm not entirely sure what happened, but it seems as if Cameron got cold feet. He went on about how he would feel guilty if he was happy with me because then he would have to be grateful that Duncan died.'

'Hmm, well I guess there is a curious kind of logic there. So what did you say?'

'I shouted at him and got mad; so he went home.'

Marianne laughed, 'Oh dear.'

'So, now what do I do? I feel so stupid inviting him over. I spent all day in a panic wondering whether anything might happen tonight. And for what; just so he can say he's changed his mind. If he felt so guilty, why didn't he think of this before?'

'To be fair, Julia, he has been in a bit of a state since Laura left. It's been one mad thing after another with those two. Are you really sure you even want to be with him?'

Julia thought for moment.

'I don't know what I want, to be honest.'

'Well then, until you do, you shouldn't waste any more time worrying about what is going on in Cameron's head.'

'I guess not.'

Julia hung up and went downstairs to the kitchen. Marianne hadn't been the comfort she needed. She took out the fish pie from the fridge and microwaved it. She stood in the kitchen as she ate, staring at the clock. It was nearly nine and the sun had set. She had imagined she would have been sat on the sofa sharing a bottle of wine with Cameron by now.

What would have happened? Would he have kissed her? Would she have kissed him first? That triggered a memory of Sicily. Julia felt her stomach churn with butterflies. She put down her plate; her dinner unfinished. She poured herself a glass of water and drank it, trying to force Cameron out of her mind. It was impossible.

She yearned to feel his arms around her. She wanted to reach up and stroke his face as he bent forward to kiss her. She wanted to wake up and find him next to her in her bed. She wanted to talk to him as they walked along the beach. She wanted to laugh with him in the company of their friends. She really did want him. He wasn't just a poor substitute for Duncan. It was an entirely different feeling altogether. But it was still love.

'Oh, for fuck's sake!'

Learning to Dance Again

She glanced at the clock and then hurried upstairs to the bathroom. She brushed her teeth, combed her hair, spritzed on some more perfume and applied some lip-gloss. Then she ran downstairs and grabbed her coat and car keys.

She opened the front door and was stunned to see Cameron walking towards her. She looked over at his car expecting to see Amy in the back seat of the car, but she wasn't there.

'I dropped Amy off at my sister's. She's going to stay for a sleepover with her cousins,' Cameron said, as he stopped before he reached the steps leading up to the house.

'Oh, right!'

'Were you just going out?' Cameron said, as Julia fiddled with her car keys, and dropped her coat on the step.

'Actually, I was just about to come and see you. I wanted to …' Julia didn't finish the sentence. She bent down to pick up her coat.

'I wanted to apologise for earlier. I don't think I explained myself very well. It was difficult with Amy around,' Cameron said.

'I think I understand how you feel; now I've had time to think about it.'

'Do you? Because I don't.'

'Yes, but I think you're mad. You have nothing to feel guilty about. Admittedly we wouldn't be having this conversation if Duncan hadn't died, but that doesn't mean we should stop right now and never see each other again. Does it?'

Cameron stuffed his hands deep into his jacket pockets, his shoulders hunched against the evening chill.

Julia walked down the steps towards him and stood on the bottom step. She still had to look up at him, but his face was closer to hers. The light from the porch lit up his eyes. He didn't smile, but his expression softened when she made eye contact.

'Can't we just start this evening over again?' Julia said.

'I would like that.'

'Come inside then; it's cold out here.'

Julia took his arm and led him indoors. She hung her coat up and put her keys back on the hook by the door. She had so many things she wanted to say, but now he was here she had lost her nerve.

'Look Jules, I'm sorry I said all that stuff earlier. It's just… well you know me; I have a tendency to screw things up, especially when it looks like it's all going too well.'

'Yes, I do know you.'

They stood in the vestibule as if they were both reluctant to enter the house. Cameron had not taken off his jacket, as if he hadn't committed himself to staying.

'Do you think it might be better if we try not to overthink this? Perhaps we shouldn't even talk about it. Maybe we should just go and watch a film or something,' Julia said.

Cameron grinned. He unzipped his jacket and hung it up and followed Julia followed into the kitchen.

On autopilot Julia walked over towards the kettle, then stopped and tilted her head to one side, silently questioning Cameron.

Cameron didn't respond. He stared at Julia, a smile playing on his lips.

'What did you mean by *or something*?'

'Huh?' Julia replied. She leaned against the kitchen unit and looked at Cameron who grinned cheekily at her.

'You suggested watching a film, or something. I was hoping *something* might be a euphemism – as in *something* happened in Sicily.'

'Something really did happen in Sicily. But that was a long time ago. Perhaps you could remind me.'

'I'd be happy to. I think it all started when you launched yourself at me in the kitchen. It was quite a surprise, but I rather liked it.'

Julia looked around the room and smiled.

'Well, we are in a kitchen. But there wouldn't be any element of surprise now, would there?'

Cameron pulled Julia into his arms and kissed her. Julia flung her arms around his neck fusing all of her hopes and dreams into the kiss as she returned it.

'I think you will always have the power to surprise me,' Cameron said.

The End

ABOUT THE AUTHOR

Frankie Valente is the author of Dancing with the Ferryman and Chasing an Irish Dream. She has a Masters in Professional Writing from University College Falmouth and a BA (Hons) in Cultural Studies from University of the Highland & Islands. She writes a regular column for the Shetland Times. She is currently writing a novel called Dreaming in Norwegian which will be published in 2014. She lives in Shetland, but has previously lived in Ireland, England and Wales.

www.frankie-valente.co.uk
Twitter @frankievalente

Printed in Great Britain
by Amazon.co.uk, Ltd.,
Marston Gate.